Jātaka Tales of the Buddha
An Anthology
Volume II

Retold by

Ken and Visakha Kawasaki

Illustrations by

N.A.P.G. Dharmawardena

PARIYATTI PRESS
an imprint of
Pariyatti Publishing
www.pariyatti.org

ISBN: 978-1-68172-311-2 (Print)
ISBN: 978-1-68172-110-1 (PDF)
ISBN: 978-1-68172-371-6 (ePub)
ISBN: 978-1-68172-109-5 (Mobi)
Library of Congress Control Number: 2017956359

First Pariyatti Edition, 2018

Table of Contents

Volume II

Contents

97

For a Handful of Seeds
Tilamutthi Jātaka

It was while staying at Jetavana that the Buddha told this story about a bad-tempered bhikkhu.

There was a bhikkhu who was full of rancor and quick to flare up. Even the slightest correction could provoke his rage. When he was angry, he spoke roughly and fiercely. One day, in the Hall of Truth, other bhikkhus were discussing his behavior. "Friends," one of them said, "our brother is often angry and bitter. He snaps at everyone like salt in the fire. You would think that, having ordained as a bhikkhu, he would try to control his anger."

The Buddha heard this and sent another bhikkhu to fetch him. "Are you really as bad-tempered as they say?"the Buddha asked. The bhikkhu admitted that he was. "This is not the first time you have been bad-tempered," the Buddha told him. "You were like this before." Then the Buddha told this story of the past.

Long, long ago, when Brahmadatta was reigning in Bārānasi, he had a son who was also named Brahmadatta. In those days, many kings sent their sons to study in Takkasilā, even though there were famous teachers in their own capitals. The experience, they reasoned, was broadening. The princes

1

underwent hardship in travel, were exposed to the ways of the world, and learned to quell their pride. Thus, when Prince Brahmadatta was sixteen, the king gave him sandals, a palm-leaf umbrella, and one thousand coins and sent him to Takkasilā to finish his education.

The boy bade his parents farewell and set out on his long journey. When he arrived in Takkasilā, he asked where the teacher lived and found the house very easily. The teacher had just finished his lecture and was walking up and down in front of the house. The prince removed his sandals, closed his sunshade, and respectfully greeted him.

Seeing that the boy was weary, the teacher offered him a meal and let him rest a little before he asked, "Where have you come from?"

"From Bārānasi, sir."

"Whose son are you?"

"I am the son of Brahmadatta, king of Kāsi."

"What brings you here?"

"I have come to learn."

"Have you brought your payment?"[1]

"Yes, sir. Here it is, sir," the prince replied, laying the one thousand coins at the teacher's feet.

One day, after the prince had been studying for some time, he went with the teacher to bathe. On the way, they passed some sesame seeds that an old woman had spread out to dry in the sun. Thinking that she wouldn't notice, the prince picked up a handful and ate them.

"That fellow must be hungry," the old woman thought, and she said nothing.

The next day, he took another handful, and, again, the old woman was silent. The third day, when he took a handful of seeds, the old woman raised her arms over her head and cried, "The great teacher is letting his student rob me!"

The teacher turned back and asked, "What is wrong, Mother?"

"Master, I have been drying these seeds for three days. Everyday, as you passed by, your student has taken a handful and eaten them! He did it today, he did it yesterday, and he did it the day before! Surely, he will eat me out of house and home!"

"Don't cry, Mother. I will repay you," the teacher replied.

"Oh, Master, I don't want payment," she declared. "Just teach your student not to do it again."

"Very well, Mother," the teacher said. "Please watch."

---

1 Students who paid for their lessons were treated with considerable respect and studied during the day. Those who could not afford to pay worked as servants and studied at night

The teacher told two other students to hold the prince's arms. While they held him, the teacher struck him sharply on the back with his bamboo cane three times, one stroke for each day, warning him never to do such a thing again.

The prince was furious. With hatred burning in his eyes, he glared fiercely at the teacher, but he did not say anything. Nor did the teacher say anything more, though he could easily see how angry the prince was.

Although the prince applied himself diligently to his studies and finished his course with distinction, he never forgot this grievance. He hid his anger and hatred in his heart and nursed an implacable grudge, which grew into a determination to murder his teacher.

When he had mastered all his subjects, he said, "Teacher, when I inherit the kingdom of Kāsi, I will send for you. Please come and visit me then." His teacher promised that he would surely do so and bade an affectionate farewell to his student.

In Bārānasi, the king was delighted when the prince displayed all that he had learned. "I have lived to see my son well educated!" he exclaimed. "Now I want to see the magnificence of his reign." The king stepped down and declared his son king.

The young King Brahmadatta enjoyed his new position. He reveled in the splendor and pomp of royalty, but, whenever he recalled the grudge against his teacher, his anger flared up as though the incident were yesterday. "I cannot forgive that villain!" he swore. "Now I will have him killed!" He sent a messenger to Takkasilā to invite his teacher to Bārānasi.

When the teacher received the message, he thought, "As long as King Brahmadatta is young, I will not be able to appease him." Accordingly, he did not go to Bārānasi.

After some years had passed, the teacher felt that he might be able to pacify the king. He traveled to Bārānasi and, when he arrived at the palace, asked the porter to inform the king that his teacher from Takkasilā had arrived.

The king was pleased that his teacher had come, and he told the porter to show him in. Suddenly, however, he remembered his grudge, his anger reawakened, and his face turned red. He beckoned to his courtiers and said, "Years ago, my teacher struck me very hard with his bamboo cane, and that place on my back still hurts! Now he has come to see me, and I will repay him. He has death written on his forehead!"

When the teacher came in, the king greeted him by saying, "Sir, for a few measly seeds, you had me seized and held, while you beat me with a stick! Did you come here thinking that I had forgotten? What brought you here? Aren't you afraid of death?"

The teacher calmly replied, "One who is gently born uses violence only to tame ungentleness. I applied the correct discipline without anger. Your Majesty, you must understand yourself and recognize your own character. You have no just cause to hate me. If I had not taught you that lesson, you would have gone on stealing cakes, sweets, fruit, and anything else that caught your fancy. Those petty acts of thievery would have lured you on, by degrees, to bigger things, such as burglary and highway robbery. If anyone had stood in your way, you might have even attempted murder! In the end, you would have been caught and punished, and you never would have become king. If you are honest with yourself, Sire, you will realize that you could not have attained all this prosperity and glory except through me."

The courtiers, who knew the king's character very well, recognized the truth of the teacher's words. "Sire," they said, "please listen to your teacher. Truly, all your magnificence is due to his wise discipline. We can respect you today because he corrected you at that time when you were still very young."

The king understood his own fault and recognized the virtue of his teacher. "Dear teacher," he replied humbly, "I am extremely sorry for the animosity I have long felt toward you. You are much worthier than I, and you are better suited than I to be king. I grant you all my authority. Take my kingdom!"

"No, Sire," the teacher protested. "I have no desire for the kingdom. Please continue to rule, but rule wisely."

Feeling rightly admonished and truly grateful, the king appointed the teacher as his chief advisor, brought his family from Takkasilā, and established them comfortably in Bārānasi. For the rest of his life, the king treated his teacher like a father and followed his wise advice. Under his guidance, the king gave alms generously and performed many good deeds. When he died, he was reborn in heaven.

Having concluded his story, the Buddha taught the Dhamma. The bad-tempered bhikkhu attained the third path, and others attained the first, second, and third paths. Then the Buddha identified the birth: "At that time, this bad-tempered bhikkhu was the king, and I was the wise teacher."

98
Humble Fare
Kundaka-Kucchi-Sindhava Jātaka

It was while staying at Jetavana that the Buddha told this story about Venerable Sāriputta.

One year, after spending the rainy season at Jetavana, the Buddha went traveling with the bhikkhus. When the devotees in Sāvatthī heard that the Sangha was returning, they organized a great alms-giving ceremony. Bhikkhus were assigned to the various houses according to the number that each host requested.

One poor old woman could afford to prepare only one portion, so, at sunrise, she announced to the clerk that she would like to serve one bhikkhu.

The clerk replied, "All the returning bhikkhus have already been assigned, but Venerable Sāriputta is still in the monastery. You may give your food to him."

The woman was overjoyed and waited by the gate of Jetavana for Venerable Sāriputta to come out. As soon as she saw him, she greeted him, took his bowl, and led him to her house, where she offered him a seat.

When King Pasenadi learned that Sāriputta was taking his meal in that woman's house, he sent a sari, a purse of one thousand coins, and several dishes of food. There was a note attached which said, "Please wear this sari, use the money to entertain the Venerable Sāriputta, and let these dishes supplement your meal offering."

Many other devotees, including Anāthapindika and Visākhā, also sent money to the old woman. That day, she received more than one hundred thousand coins.

Venerable Sāriputta drank the simple broth the woman had prepared and ate the curry and rice she offered. After the meal, he taught the Dhamma, and the woman attained the first path.

Later that day, the bhikkhus gathered in the Hall of Truth and were talking about this incident. They praised Venerable Sāriputta for not disdaining the woman's humble food, for rescuing her from poverty, and for establishing her in the first path. When the Buddha heard what they were discussing, he said, "This is not the first time, Bhikkhus, that Sāriputta has been the refuge of this woman. Nor is it the first time for him not to disdain the food she offered. He did the same before." Then he told this story of the past.

Long, long ago, when Brahmadatta was reigning in Bārānasi, there was, in a town not far from the capital, a great mansion that had once belonged to a rich merchant. The merchant had died, and the family had dwindled to the point that only one elderly woman was left in the old house.

One day, a horse trader with a herd of five hundred horses took a room in the mansion and kept his horses in the stables. That night, one of his thoroughbred mares foaled, so he had to stay for an extra few days, until the mare was strong enough to continue the journey to the capital. When the trader asked how much he owed for the room, the old woman requested that he give her the colt as part of the payment. The trader agreed and went on his way. The woman loved the colt like a child, feeding him parched rice gruel, leftovers from her own simple meals, and grass.

Some time later, a horse trader from the northern part of the kingdom took a room there. When his five hundred horses caught the scent of the well-bred colt, they refused to enter the stables.

The trader remarked to the woman, "There seems to be another horse here, Mother."

"Yes, my son," she said, "but it is only a young colt which I love as tenderly as my own child!"

"Where is he now, Mother?"

"He's gone out to graze, but I expect he'll be back shortly."

The trader kept his horses outside and waited for the foal to return. As soon as the trader saw the colt, he thought, "This is a priceless thoroughbred!"

After the colt had gone into his own stall, the other horses were willing to enter the stables.

The trader stayed there for a few days, and, as he was preparing to leave, he said to the woman, "Mother, let me buy this colt from you."

"What are you saying, sir? One does not sell a foster child!"

"What do you give him to eat, mother?"

"Parched rice gruel, leftovers from my own meals, and grass."

"Well, Mother, if you let me have him, I'll feed him on the best hay, oats, barley and molasses. In his stable, he will stand on a carpet, and there will be a cloth awning above him."

"My goodness, young man, will you really take care of him like that?" she asked.

"I give you my word," the trader assured her.

"In that case, how could I deny my son such luxury?" she exclaimed. "Take this child of mine! May he be happy!"

The trader gave the woman one thousand coins for each of the colt's feet, one thousand for his tail, and another one thousand for his head. He also gave her a fine silk sari and expensive jewelry. As she started to say farewell to her child, the colt opened his eyes, looked at her fondly, and shed tears. She stroked his neck and said, "Go, my son! I have received adequate recompense for what I have done for you."

The next day, the trader prepared rice gruel and offered it to the colt, but he refused to touch it.

"Why don't you eat?" the trader asked. "This is exactly the same food as you had yesterday. I have prepared it just as your mother told me."

"From one who does not know another's birth and breeding," the colt told him, "rice-gruel is an acceptable offering, but you know that I am the best of thoroughbred steeds. I will not accept that from you!"

"Do not be offended," the trader replied. "This was simply a test. I wondered whether you really knew your true worth. From now on, you will receive only the finest clover hay, grain, and molasses!"

The trader took his horses to the palace and herded them on one side of the courtyard. On the other side, he hung an awning and laid a carpet for the colt.

When the king came out to inspect the horses, he asked why that one animal was kept apart.

"Sire," the trader replied, "if this horse were not kept separate, all the others would run away out of shame."

"Is he such a treasure?" the king asked.

"Yes, indeed, Sire."

"Then let me see his paces."

The trader saddled the colt, mounted him, and raced around the courtyard. To the king's eyes, there appeared an unbroken line of horses.

The trader stopped in front of the king and said, "That, Sire, was his medium speed!"

"Let him have his head!" the king urged.

Before taking off, the trader attached a red leaf to the colt's mane. As the colt raced at his fastest speed, the king could see only one red line encircling the courtyard. Both horse and rider disappeared.

The trader rode the colt across the surface of a pond without wetting his hooves. Next, he galloped over lotus leaves, without pushing a single one of them under the water.

The trader dismounted and stood before the king. He clapped his hands and held out an open palm. The colt leaped onto the trader's hand and stood with his four hooves close together. "Sire!" the trader exclaimed. "The whole world does not offer sufficient scope for this horse to display his skill." Then the trader proceeded to instruct the king in generosity and righteousness.

The king was so pleased that he gave the trader half of his wealth for the colt, which he sprinkled with lustral water and installed as his horse of state.

Great honor was shown to the colt as he grew to become a magnificent stallion. His stable was as beautiful as the king's own chamber. The floor was sprinkled with perfume, and the walls were decorated with flowers. On the ceiling was hung a cloth awning spangled with golden stars. He was fed the finest grains with molasses.

After acquiring this great horse, the king became the ruler of all of Jambudīpa. Following the teaching given by the trader, the king did good deeds and gave alms. When he passed away, he was reborn in heaven.

Having concluded his story, the Buddha taught the Dhamma and many attained the first, second, and third paths. Then he identified the birth: "At that time, the old woman was the same, Sāriputta was the thoroughbred, Ānanda was the king, and I was the horse-trader from the North."

99
The King's Officer
Gāmani-Canda Jātaka

It was while staying at Jetavana that the Buddha told this story in praise of wisdom.

Once, in the Hall of Truth, some bhikkhus were talking about the Buddha's sharp and penetrating wisdom. When the Buddha heard what they were discussing, he said, "This is not the first time, Bhikkhus, that the Tathāgata has been wise." Then he told this story of the past.

Long, long ago, when Janasandha was reigning in Bārānasi, the Bodhisatta was born to his chief queen. The infant had a golden complexion, and his face shone like a well-polished mirror, so he was named Ādāsamukha.

The king died when Prince Ādāsamukha was only seven years old, but, by then, he had already completed his education. On the seventh day after the king's death, the ministers gathered to discuss the succession. Some felt that the prince was too young to become king, but others pointed out that he was an unusually mature child. It was agreed that, before they could decide, they had to test the prince.

The next day, they sat the prince down in the court and brought in a trained monkey, cleverly disguised as a courtier. As he'd been trained to do, the monkey walked in on two feet, and sat properly on a couch.

"My Lord," the ministers said, "in your father's time, we depended on this man to design the most important buildings in the kingdom. He personally designed this palace for your father. Please give him a post in your court."

"This is not a man," the prince replied. "It's no more than a monkey with a wrinkled face. I doubt that he could build anything, for monkeys only destroy what others make."

"It must be as you have said, My Lord!" said the ministers, and they led the monkey out. In this way, they tested him three times, but, each time, he saw through their ruse. At last, they concluded, "This is a wise prince; he will be able to rule!" In a grand ceremony, Prince Ādāsamukha was proclaimed king.

One of the former king's servants, an old man named Gāmani-Canda, thought, "The new king is young. His advisors and servants should be those closer to his own age. It is time for me to retire." He left Bārāṇasi, moved to the countryside, and took up farming.

Gāmani-Canda had no oxen of his own, so, as soon as the rains began and the ground was ready to be worked, he borrowed two strong oxen from a neighbor. After working all day long, he fed the oxen ample grass and took them back to the neighbor's house. When he arrived there, he saw that the man and his wife were eating supper. Since they did not invite him to share their meal, he led the oxen to their stalls and returned home, without bothering the couple and without formally returning the oxen.

When the owner went to the shed early the next morning, the oxen were not there. He could see the tell-tale marks, and he was sure that the oxen had been stolen by a gang of thieves, but he decided to accuse his neighbor. "I'll make Gāmani pay me for my oxen!" he muttered as he went to find his hapless neighbor.

"Where are my oxen?" he shouted as soon as he saw Gāmani-Canda.

"Aren't they in their stalls? I put them there last night."

"No, they are not in their stalls. Did you formally return them to me?"

"No, I didn't. You were eating, so I didn't want to bother you."

"I don't believe you!" retorted the neighbor. "Here's the king's officer! Come along!" he shouted. It was the custom at that time for a person to make a citizen's arrest by holding a small stone or a shard of pottery and announcing, "Here's the king's officer!" A person who refused such an arrest would be punished, whether he were innocent or guilty of any other crime. Intimidated by those words, Gāmani-Canda meekly submitted.

On their way to Bārānasi, the pair passed through a village where a friend of Gāmani-Canda lived. "I'm very hungry," Gāmani-Canda said to his captor. "Please wait while I get something to eat!" and he went into his friend's house.

His friend was not at home, but the wife greeted him and said, "There is nothing left from breakfast, but, if you can wait a moment, I will fix you something." She climbed to the top of the granary to fetch some rice, but her foot slipped, and she fell off the ladder. Servants immediately carried her to her bed, but she was seven months pregnant, and the fall caused her to have a miscarriage.

The husband returned a few minutes later and, seeing her condition, shouted, "Gāmani, you hit my wife and caused her to lose her baby! Here's the king's officer!" This man dragged poor Gāmani-Canda out and found the neighbor waiting for him. Now two captors held poor Gāmani-Canda between them as they headed toward Bārānasi.

As they approached the village gate, a horse came galloping toward them. "Uncle Gāmani!" a man shouted. "That's my horse! Throw something at him. Send him back this way!" Gāmani quickly picked up a stone and threw it at the horse. The stone struck the horse's hoof, causing the beast to fall and to break its leg.

"Gāmani!" the man cried. "Why did you do that? You broke my horse's leg! Here's the king's officer!"

Poor Gāmani-Canda was now the prisoner of three men! "These three will denounce me to the king," he moaned to himself as they continued toward Bārānasi. "I can't pay for the oxen. I can't pay the fine for causing the miscarriage. I have no money for a horse. I'd be better off dead!"

Near the road, he spied a clump of trees on a slope. The other side of the hill fell away in a steep precipice. "Excuse me," Gāmani-Canda said to his captors, "but I need to answer the call of nature. Please wait here a moment while I go into the woods." He quickly ran to the top of the hill and threw himself over the precipice, intending to end it all. He hadn't noticed that, at the foot of the precipice, in the shade of the hill, two basket makers sat on the ground, weaving a mat. Gāmani-Canda fell directly on top of one of the basket makers and killed him on the spot. Speechless from the shock, Gāmani-Canda picked himself up and stood there.

"You v-v-villain!" stuttered the other basket maker. "You have m-m-murdered my father! Here's the k-k-king's officer!" he cried, seizing Gāmani-Canda's hand and dragging him toward the road.

"What's this?" asked the other three.

"This fellow has murdered my father!"

11

"Let's go!" the others shouted, and the four of them dragged poor Gāmani-Canda toward Bārānasi.

As they passed through another village, the headman greeted the old man, "Uncle, where are you off to?"

"To see the king," replied Gāmani-Canda.

"Indeed!" cried the headman. "I've been meaning to send him a message. You see, I have always been handsome, rich, and healthy. Recently, however, I have been miserable and suffering from jaundice. Please ask the king why this is. I've heard that he is a wise man, so I'm sure he'll know. You can give me his answer when you return."

Gāmani-Canda cheerfully agreed to ask the king.

In the next village, the local prostitute called out, "Where are you going, Uncle?"

"To see the king," he answered.

"They say the king is a wise man. Take him a message for me. I used to make plenty of money, but, these days, I'm not getting even the price of a betel-nut. Nobody hires me. Ask the king why this is, and tell me what he says when you come back."

At a third village, a young woman shouted to Gāmani-Canda, "Uncle! Recently, I haven't been able to stay comfortably either with my husband or in my parents' house. Ask the king why this is, and tell me what he says."

A little further on, there was a snake living in an anthill near the road. When he learned that Gāmani-Canda was going to see the king, he said, "When I go out to get my food, I'm famished, but my body fills the hole and I can barely get out of this anthill. When I return after eating, I feel fat, but I can slide easily through the hole, without even touching the sides. Why is this? Please ask the king, and bring me his answer."

Further on, a deer called out, "Uncle, I can't eat grass anywhere but under this tree. Ask the king, and tell me why this should be."

Next, a partridge said, "When I sit at the foot of this anthill and sing, my voice is beautiful, but, anywhere else, it sounds terrible. Ask the king why, and let me know."

As they passed through a forest, a tree deva said, "I used to be highly honored, but now I don't receive any respect, and no one makes offerings to me. Ask the king what has happened."

From a pool of water beside the road, a nāga rose up and said, "The water in this pool was once as clear as crystal. Now it's murky and covered with scum. Ask the king why this has happened."

Not far from the capital, some ascetics called out, "In the past, our park had plenty of sweet fruit, but now the fruit is tasteless and dry. Ask the king why!"

Just outside the gate of Bārānasi, some brahmin students stopped Gāmani-Canda and said, "Previously, we easily understood our lessons, and our subject was perfectly clear. Now we can't memorize anything, and our lessons are like muddy water in a leaky jar. Ask the king why!"

The four men led Gāmani-Canda into the court, and the king recognized him immediately. "This is my father's servant, Gāmani-Canda, who used to dandle me on his knee," the king shouted with joy. "Where are you living now, Gāmani? We haven't seen you for a long time? What brings you here?"

"Sire," Gāmani-Canda began, "when My Lord, your father, died, I retired to the country and began to support myself by farming. This morning, this man accused me of stealing his oxen, and he has brought me here."

"Well, Gāmani," the king shouted with a laugh, "If he had not brought you here, you never would have come, so I am very pleased. Where is that man?"

"Here, Your Majesty."

"You brought our friend, Gāmani?"

"Yes, Sire."

"Why?"

"He refuses to give back my pair of oxen!"

"Is this so, Gāmani?"

"My Lord," Gāmani-Canda replied, "Please listen to my side of the story," and he proceeded to tell the king exactly what had happened.

The king turned again to the neighbor and asked, "Did you see the oxen enter the stall?"

"No, My Lord," the man replied.

"Tell me the truth!" the king commanded.

"W-w-ell," the man stammered, "I'm n-n-not sure."

"Speak honestly! I am warning you," said the king sharply.

"Yes, Your Majesty, I saw them," he admitted.

"Thank you," said the king. "Now, Gāmani, you failed to return the oxen. Therefore, you still owe this man for them. On the other hand, this man just lied to me. Therefore, I order you to pluck out his eyes! Then you must pay him twenty-four coins for the oxen." Courtiers stepped forward as if to seize the neighbor's arms to hold him for punishment.

"If I lose my eyes," he thought, as he started to sweat profusely, "what do I care for the money?" He fell at Gāmani-Canda's feet and begged, "Good neighbor, Gāmani, please keep the twenty-four coins, and take these, as well!" He gave him all the money he had with him, jumped up, and fled as fast as he could.

The king turned to Gāmani-Canda's friend and asked, "My good man, why have you come to see me?"

"Your Majesty," he answered, "this man struck my wife and caused her to miscarry."

"Is this true?" asked the king.

"No, Sire." Gāmani-Canda replied. "I stopped at his house to ask for something to eat, and his wife was going to fix me breakfast."

"Did you strike her and cause her to miscarry?" asked the king.

"No, Sire! She fell from the ladder."

Turning to the accuser, the king asked, "Do you expect me to heal the miscarriage which he has caused?"

"No, Sire, that is not my request."

"Well, what do you want as satisfaction?"

"I expected to have a son, Your Majesty, and ..."

"All right," the king interrupted. "Gāmani, I order you to take the man's wife to your house. When a son is born to the two of you, give the baby to this man, and send back the wife!"

This man also fell at Gāmani-Canda's feet. "Don't take my wife!" he cried. He, too, threw down some money and hurried off.

"Now, my good man," the king said to the stable owner, "what brings you here?"

"This man broke my horse's leg," he replied.

"Is this true?" the king asked, and Gāmani-Canda explained exactly what had happened.

Turning back to the stable owner, the king asked, "Did you ask Gāmani to throw something at the horse to make him turn back?"

"No, Sire, I did not," he replied, but on being pressed, he finally admitted that he had.

"Gāmani," said the king, "this man just lied to me. For that, I order you to tear out his tongue. Then we will pay him one thousand coins for his horse." The terrified stable owner quickly gave Gāmani-Canda a sack of money and fled.

"And what brings you here?" the king asked the basket maker.

"Sire, this man is a murderer. He killed my father!"

"Is this true?" the king asked Gāmani-Canda.

"No, Sire," Gāmani-Canda replied, and he proceeded to explain exactly what had occurred.

"What do you want?" the king asked the basket maker.

"My Lord, I must have my father."

"Gāmani, this man must have a father. Obviously you cannot bring his father back from the dead, so you will have to take his mother to your house, live with her, and be a father to him."

14

"Oh, Master!" the man cried. "Don't break up my dead father's home!" He, too, gave Gāmani-Canda a sack of money and hurried away.

Gāmani-Canda was relieved to have won all his lawsuits. Then he remembered those he had met along the way and their messages for the king. "Your Majesty, "he said, "as we were coming here this morning, many beings asked me to give you messages. May I ask you their questions?"

"Of course, Gāmani. Speak up."

"Where shall I begin?" Gāmani-Canda wondered aloud. "Let me see. Near the city gate there were some students," and he repeated the students' question to the king.

"Where those students live," the king explained, "there used to be a reliable rooster. In the past, when they heard him crow, they got up and repeated their texts until the sun came up. Because they followed this routine, they did not forget what they learned. Now they have a cock that crows erratically— sometimes in the dead of night and sometimes in broad daylight. When he crows at night, they get up, but they are too sleepy to study. When he crows during the day, it is too late for them to study. Because of this, whatever they learn, they soon forget."

When he heard the ascetics' question, he replied, "Formerly, those ascetics were practicing properly; they meditated regularly and performed all the duties of an ascetic. Recently, however, they have become very lax. They are not meditating diligently, and they are neglecting their duties. They give the fruit growing in the park to their attendants. Rather than all going out together, some of them stay at the hermitage, and they take turns begging for alms. Because of this sinful behavior, the trees no longer produce sweet fruit. If they resume their former practices and behave properly, the fruit will become sweet again. Tell those ascetics that there is once more a king in this land and that they should act accordingly."

To the question from the nāgas, King Ādāsamukha replied, "Those nāgas have quarreled with each other, so the water has become murky. If they make peace and live with each other in harmony, the water will become clear again."

To the question from the tree deva, he replied, "That tree deva used to protect people passing through the woods, so she received many offerings. She has stopped protecting travelers, so, of course, they do not give her anything in return. If she starts guarding them as before, she will again receive generous gifts."

To the question from the partridge, King Ādāsamukha replied, "Under the anthill, where the partridge's cry is so pleasant, there is buried a crock of treasure. Dig it up, and keep it for yourself."

15

To the question from the deer, he replied, "In the tree under which the deer grazes is a great honeycomb. He has developed a craving for the grass on which this honey has dripped, and he no longer cares for any other. Retrieve the honeycomb, send the best portion of it to me, and enjoy the rest yourself."

To the question from the snake, he replied, "Under the snake's anthill, there is a great treasure, and he lives there guarding it. When he goes out, because of his greed for this hoarded wealth, his body adheres to the hole. After he has fed, his desire to return to his treasure causes him go back in quickly and easily. Dig up the treasure, and keep it for yourself."

To the question from the young woman, the king replied, "Between her house and her parents' village, that young woman has a lover. Whenever she thinks of him, she cannot stay with her husband. She tells her husband that she is going to visit her parents and, on the way, stays a few days with her lover. After she has been with her parents for a few days, she begins longing again for her lover. She tells her parents that she is going to return to her husband and, on the way, stays a few more days with her lover. Gāmani, tell her that there is a king in the land and that she must stay with her husband. If she refuses, I will have her arrested!"

To the question from the prostitute, King Ādāsamukha replied, "Formerly, that prostitute didn't offer her services to anyone until she had given the man she was with his money's worth. By satisfying one man at a time, she made a good living. Recently, she took on a new style. Without permission from the customer she is serving, she starts taking care of someone else. Now, no one wants her, and she is not making any money. If she returns to her old ways, she will once again become prosperous."

To the question from the village headman, he replied, "That village headman used to make judgments fairly so that men were pleased with him and gave him many presents. That is why he was handsome, rich, and honored. Now he takes bribes, and his decisions are no longer fair. People are unhappy, so he has become miserable and jaundiced. If he decides cases righteously again, he will regain all that he has lost. Tell him that there is a king in the land and that he must be fair and honest in all judgments."

King Ādāsamukha gave Gāmani-Canda many presents, including the village where he had retired. On his return, Gāmani-Canda faithfully delivered all the answers from the king. He dug up the treasure from beneath the anthills and took it home. He got the honeycomb down from the tree and sent the best portion to the king. He stayed in the village until the end of his life and passed away to fare according to his deserts.

King Ādāsamukha continued to rule wisely, to give alms, and to live righteously. After his death, he was reborn in heaven.

Having concluded his story, the Buddha taught the Dhamma, and many attained the first path. Then the Buddha identified the birth: "At that time, Ānanda was Gāmani-Canda, and I was King Ādāsamukha."

100
Defeating the Golden Crab
Kakkata Jātaka

It was while staying at Jetavana that the Buddha told this story about a good and courageous woman.

A landowner of Sāvatthī set out on a journey to collect outstanding debts and took his wife with him. While they were traveling, they were attacked by robbers. When the head of the gang saw the beautiful wife, he threatened to kill the landowner and to take the woman away for himself. The wife fell at the robber's feet and cried, "I will never go with you! Killing him would be useless. I would rather kill myself than give myself to you! I beg you to show mercy!" The robber listened to her and let them both go.

When they got back safely to Sāvatthī, they visited Jetavana to pay their respects to the Buddha. After making their salutations, they sat down at one side. The Buddha asked them where they had been.

"We've been on a trip to collect our debts," they answered.

"Did your journey pass successfully, without mishap?" he asked.

"No, Venerable Sir, we were attacked by robbers," said the husband, "and the leader of the band threatened to kill me, but my wife persuaded him not to do anything rash. I owe my life to her."

"You are not the only one, layman, whose life she has saved. Long ago, also, she saved someone wise." At the man's request, the Buddha told this story.

Long, long ago, when Brahmadatta was reigning in Bārānasi, there was a great lake in the Himavat in which lived a golden crab as big as a threshing floor. Because he lived there, the lake was known as Crab Tarn. This enormous crab survived by catching and eating elephants, and, from fear of it, elephants never dared to browse near the lake.

When the mate of the leader of an elephant herd that lived in the vicinity of Crab Tarn became pregnant, she stayed in the mountains until the baby was born. The young elephant grew up strong and wise. When he came of age, he chose a mate for himself.

This elephant had heard tales of the golden crab, and, although he had never seen the beast, he resolved to destroy it. One day, with his mother and his mate, he sought out his father and told him what he wanted to do.

"No, Son, I forbid you to venture into the lake," his father replied. "You will not be able to do it."

Unwilling to take "No" for an answer, he begged his father again and again, and finally got permission to try.

First, the young elephant gathered information. He asked his elders to tell him everything they knew about the crab. "When does he usually catch an elephant?" he asked. "Is it when the elephant goes down to the lake, while he is eating, or when he comes back?"

"He always attacks when the elephant comes back."

"All right, then," he replied. "Let's all go down to the lake. I will go first. When we finish eating, you come back first. I will follow you."

The young elephant and his mate led the herd to the lake. When all of them had finished eating, the rest of the herd started to go. From the water, the crab was watching. When he saw the elephants leaving, he prepared to attack, and, of course, it was the young elephant at the back of the line that he grabbed. With his powerful claw he seized the elephant's hind leg as tightly as a blacksmith grips a piece of iron in his tongs. The elephant tried to pull the crab toward the shore, but, since the crab was much stronger, the elephant felt himself being pulled into the water. His mate watched in horror as he was being dragged away, but she stayed close beside him. Suddenly, afraid that he might indeed be losing his match with the crab, the young elephant trumpeted wildly. This so frightened the rest of the herd that they stampeded toward the shore. Even his loyal mate was so terrified by the panic in his voice that she began to edge away toward safety.

"My dear," the elephant cried, "this golden creature with protruding eyes and bony shell has caught me fast with his powerful claw, but, please, partner of my life, don't desert me now! I know you love me well!"

When she heard his plea, she turned and cried out, "Noble husband, there is none so dear to my heart as you. I will never abandon you!" Then she whispered softly to her husband, "Let me talk to this crab." Out loud, she called to the creature, in her sweetest voice, "Great Golden Crab! Of all the crabs who live in the sea, in rivers, and in lakes, you are surely the greatest! Magnificent in hue and supreme in power, please hear me, and let my dear husband go!"

The crab was so touched by the beauty of her voice and the gentle pleading of such a mate, that he forgot himself for just a moment and relaxed his grip on the elephant's hind leg. As soon as the elephant felt that his leg was free, he lifted it and stomped with all his might on the crab's back. With a thundering crack, the crab's shell split, and his eyes popped out of his head. Lifting his trunk jubilantly, the young elephant trumpeted a cry of victory. Instantly, the whole herd turned and rushed back. Seizing the crab's body, they dragged it to dry land and trampled it to a pulp. Overjoyed that the monstrous crab would terrorize them no more, the elephant herd returned to the jungle, leaving the two enormous claws lying on the ground next to the smashed body.

Crab Tarn was near the great Gangā, and, every year, when the river flooded, the two bodies of water were joined. When that happened the following year, the two claws were lifted up by the water and floated down the Gangā. One of them was found by ten royal brothers, called Dasarahas, while they were playing in the river. From it, they made a drum called Anaka. The other claw reached the sea, where it was discovered by the asuras, who fashioned it into a drum called Alambara. When the asuras were defeated in battle by Sakka, they abandoned this drum, and Sakka claimed it. Sometimes, when there is thunder, people say, "Listen to the mighty Alambara!"

At the conclusion of this story, both husband and wife attained the first path. Then the Buddha identified the birth: "At that time, this woman was the she-elephant, and I was her mate."

101
The Vanishing Jungle
Vyaggha Jātaka

It was while staying at Jetavana that the Buddha told this story about Venerable Kokālika.

After Venerable Kokālika had abused Venerable Sāriputta and Venerable Moggallāna and driven them from his monastery, the villagers made him promise that he would bring the two chief bhikkhus back.[2] To try to do this, he traveled to Jetavana, paid his respects to the Buddha, and said to the chief bhikkhus, "Friends, the citizens of my country request you to return. Let us go there together!"

"Go by yourself, Friend. We won't go," they answered.

In the Hall of Truth, other bhikkhus were talking about Venerable Kokālika's dilemma. When the Buddha heard what they were discussing, he said, "This is not the first time that Kokālika has not been able to live either with Sāriputta and Moggallāna or without them." Then the Buddha told this story of the past.

Long, long ago, when Brahmadatta was reigning in Bārānasi, there was a jungle which was effectively controlled by two great animals, a lion and

2   The occasion for this story is related in detail in Tale 88.

a tiger. In fear of these two fierce beasts, no human being dared to linger in that jungle. With the lion and the tiger prowling about, no one could think about cutting the trees or plowing the soil. The lion and the tiger killed animals every day. After they had eaten as much as they wanted, they left the remains where they lay. Eventually, the jungle floor was littered with carcasses and the air was filled with a strong odor.

The smell of decaying flesh greatly upset and offended a deva. Although this deva lived in the largest tree in the jungle, truly a great monarch of a tree, the deva himself was rather foolish. One day, he complained to the deva of a nearby tree. "My friend," he said, "this jungle reeks with a foul stench, and it's all because of that lion and that tiger. I am sick of the smell, and I am going to drive them away."

"Good friend," said the other deva, "it is precisely these two creatures who protect our homes. If they were not here, this jungle would disappear! Once men do not see lion and tiger tracks, they will cut down all the trees, clear the land, and turn it into farmland. Please do not drive away those two beasts. They are our protectors! When friends like them guarantee your peace, their lives should be as dear to you as your own!"

In spite of his friend's explanation and warning, the foolish deva was determined to get rid of the two animals. Whenever the lion and the tiger approached his tree, he assumed a terrifying shape and, finally, succeeded in driving them away.

It was not long before villagers noticed that there were no longer any pugmarks of those great cats. The villagers also noticed that the stench of decaying flesh was fading. As soon as they were sure that the lion and the tiger were gone, men arrived with their axes. As quickly as they could, they cut the trees and hauled away the logs. Then they cleared the brush and began plowing the soil.

The foolish deva visited his friend and cried, "Oh, my friend, you were right! I didn't listen, and I didn't follow your advice. I drove away the lion and the tiger, and now men have begun cutting down the trees! The jungle is disappearing, just as you said it would! What can we do?"

"The only way to stop the destruction," the wise deva said, "is to bring back the lion and the tiger. It's up to you to bring them back."

The deva hurried to the jungle where the two animals had gone and begged, "Please come back, Tiger! Please come back, Lion. I'm sorry for the way I treated you. I will never act that way again. Please come back, and live in our jungle. If you don't, it will be completely destroyed! Without you to protect us, all our homes will fall to the axe! Please come back!"

"Go away!" they replied sharply. "Yours is not the only jungle. We are perfectly happy here. We will never return to your jungle!"

The deva returned to the jungle alone, and, in a few days, all the trees had been cut. It was not long before fields were plowed and crops were growing in the sunshine.

Having concluded his story, the Buddha taught the Dhamma. Then he identified the birth: "At that time, Kokālika was the foolish deva, Sāriputta was the lion, Moggallāna was the tiger, and I was the wise deva."

102
The Kuru Virtue
Kurudhamma Jātaka

It was while staying at Jetavana that the Buddha told this story about a
bhikkhu who killed a wild goose.[1]

Two bhikkhus, who came from Sāvatthī, were good friends and usually
went around together. One day, they went to the Aciravatī River. After taking their bath, they stood on the sand, basking in the sunlight and talking
pleasantly together. At that moment, two wild geese flew overhead. One of
the young bhikkhus picked up a stone.

"I'm going to hit that goose in the eye!" he bragged.

"You can't do it," said the other.

"I certainly can, and not only that! I can hit either the left or the right
eye, as I please."

"Impossible!" said his friend.

"Just watch me!" Picking up a triangular stone, he threw it so that it
passed by the bird. When the goose heard the pebble whizzing through the
air, it turned its head. The bhikkhu immediately threw a round stone which
struck the bird's left eye.

---

1   The occasion for this story is the same of that for Tale 42.

The goose gave a sharp cry, tumbled over and over in the air, and fell dead at their feet.

Other bhikkhus standing nearby saw what had happened and hurried over. "You should be ashamed!" they cried. "A bhikkhu must never take the life of a living creature!" They immediately took him to the Tathāgata and explained what had happened.

"Is what they say true?" the Buddha asked. "Have you really killed a living creature?"

"Yes, Venerable Sir," answered the bhikkhu.

"A bhikkhu ought to control himself in deed, word, and thought," the Buddha told him. "Wise men of old, even when there was no Buddha in the world, felt great remorse over mere trifles, but here you are, even though you ordained in this great doctrine, behaving without scruples."

At the bhikkhus' request, the Buddha told this story of the past.

Long, long ago, when Dhanañjaya was reigning in Indapatta, the capital of the Kuru kingdom, the Bodhisatta was born to the queen-consort. After completing his education in Takkasilā, he was appointed as crown prince. After his father's death, he became king and ruled righteously, carefully observing the ten duties of a king. He built six alms-halls, one at each of the four city gates, one in the middle of the city, and one at his own palace door. Daily, he distributed money in alms. His goodness and generosity inspired all of Jambudīpa. The five precepts had long been established in the Kuru kingdom and were widely known as the Kuru Virtue. The Kuru Virtue was kept not only by the king and his courtiers, but by many citizens, both men and women, including even manual laborers and slaves.

At that time, there was a severe drought and famine in the neighboring kingdom of Kālinga. Unable to find food, the citizens of Kālinga wandered about destitute, leading their children by the hand. Suffering from starvation and afraid that the lack of food would result in plague and disease, the people gathered in Dantapura, the capital, and appealed to the king for mercy and assistance.

When the king saw the great crowd from the window of the palace, he asked his advisors what the people wanted.

"Sire, the crops have failed, and everyone is afraid of poverty, disease, and starvation. They have come with their children to plead with Your Majesty to have mercy on them and to cause it to rain."

"What did former monarchs do when the rains failed?" the king asked his advisors.

"In the past, Sire, kings caused rain to fall by giving alms, fasting, and doing penance for seven days on a grass pallet."

"Very well, let us do so!" the king proclaimed, and he did exactly as they had suggested, but still no rain fell.

The king again conferred with his advisors, and they replied, "Sire, in Indapatta, King Dhananjaya has a great state elephant, called Añjanavasabha, the Black Bull. If we could get that mighty elephant here, it would surely bring rain."

"But how can we do that?" the king asked. "King Dhananjaya is strong, and his army will not be easy to overcome."

"Sire, the king is extremely generous. They say that, if anyone asked, he would give up his kingdom, tear out his eyes, or even cut off his magnificent head. There is no need to plead for the elephant, let alone to fight him. If we ask him, he will give it to us without fail."

"But who can we send to ask him?" asked the king.

"Some brahmins to act as emissaries, Your Majesty."

The king summoned eight brahmins, gave them money for their journey, and sent them to Indapatta to request Añjanavasabha.

They traveled quickly and reached Indapatta in a few days. After taking a meal at the king's alms-hall at the eastern gate, they asked when the king would come.

"Tomorrow is the full moon," a citizen answered, "and the king will be here, because he comes every Uposatha day."

Early the next morning, King Dhananjaya, mounted on Añjanavasabha, arrived at that alms-hall. He dismounted and gave food to seven or eight people, solemnly announcing to all, "It is a great joy and a very meritorious thing to give alms personally with one's own hand." Then he remounted the elephant and proceeded to the southern gate. So many people had gathered to greet the king that the brahmins from Kālinga had not been able to get anywhere near him, so they hurried to the southern gate and waited at the front of the crowd for the king. As soon as the king was in sight, the eight brahmins raised their hands in salutation. He guided his elephant toward them and greeted them. "What is it you desire?" he inquired.

"Your Majesty's virtue is widely proclaimed," they replied. "We have come from Dantapura in Kālinga to request your elephant. Only by taking this magnificent beast back to our kingdom can we bring the rains to end the severe drought from which all of our people are suffering. For this, Your Majesty, we have traveled far."

"Brahmins," the king replied, "you have come a great distance for this elephant. My preceptors have taught me that whoever comes must be made welcome. Since you ask for this elephant, I gladly present him to you!"

29

Dismounting, the king continued, "Take him with all his trappings and his mahout, too, and go on your way. If there is any part of his body which is unadorned, let me decorate it before I formally give him to you." He walked around the elephant three times and carefully examined him, but he found not even the smallest spot which was not adorned. Placing the elephant's trunk in the brahmins' hands, the king poured scented water from a golden vase and formally relinquished his treasure.

The brahmins gratefully accepted the gift and, mounting on the back of the elephant, returned to Dantapura. As soon as they had presented Añjanavasabha to King Kālinga, he mounted the elephant and rode in procession around the city, but still no rain fell.

The king again conferred with his advisors, and they replied, "We had heard that Añjanavasabha was powerful, but that power must be inadequate to end our drought. However, King Dhanañjaya practices the Kuru Virtue. It must be the power of this virtue, Sire, which causes it to rain every ten or fifteen days in his kingdom."

"Very well," replied the king. Then, summoning the brahmins once more, he ordered, "Return this elephant to King Dhanañjaya. Ask him to inscribe the Kuru Virtue, which he practices, on a golden plate, and bring that back to me."

The brahmins traveled once more to Indapatta, and, after returning the royal elephant, they said to King Dhanañjaya, "Your Majesty, even though King Kālinga rode your mighty elephant around Dantapura in a grand procession, no rain has fallen in our country. We have heard it said that you practice the Kuru Virtue. Our king wishes to practice this himself. He has sent us here, asking that this Kuru Virtue be written on a golden plate so that he may know it and follow it. May it please Your Majesty to tell us what the Kuru Virtue is."

"Friends," replied the king, "I have practiced this Kuru Virtue, but, recently, I have come to doubt my practice. In fact, my mind is so troubled that I cannot honestly give it to you with complete confidence."

"What is it that has troubled your mind?" the brahmins asked.

"There is a ceremony," the king began, "which is held every third year in the month of Kattikā. In performing this ceremony, the king, dressed in formal robes, shoots arrows decorated with brightly colored flowers in the four cardinal directions. Once, I stood on the bank of the river to shoot these arrows. Three of my arrows could be followed, but the fourth fell into the water. It greatly troubles me that the arrow may have struck some fish. I fear that I may have taken the life of a living creature. If this is so, my virtue is not pure, and I cannot teach it to you."

"But, Sire," the brahmins protested, "when you shot the arrow, you had no intention of taking life. Without any intention of killing in the heart, there is no wrong-doing. Please give us the Kuru Virtue which you have always practiced."

"Very well," King Dhanañjaya replied, "I will give it to you, but, because I have such grave doubt about my own virtue, I am not satisfied, and you should not trust it. Ask the queen mother, who scrupulously practices the Kuru Virtue. You can get it from her."

"Certainly, Your Majesty," the brahmins agreed. We will ask your respected mother, but please give us your own Kuru Virtue."

"One must abstain from slaying any living creature," the king intoned, as the brahmins inscribed his words on their golden plates. "One must abstain from taking what is not given; one must abstain from sexual misconduct; one must abstain from telling lies; and one must abstain from taking strong drink or drugs which cloud the mind. This is known as the Kuru Virtue, but remember that I doubt my own practice, and you must receive it properly from my mother."

"Thank you very much, Your Majesty," said the brahmins as they paid their respects to the king. "Now we will pay a visit to the queen mother."

When the brahmins were admitted to the queen mother's presence, they greeted her and said, "Lady, it is well-known that you practice the Kuru Virtue. Please teach it to us."

"My sons," replied the queen mother, "I have practiced this Kuru Virtue, but recently I have come to doubt my practice. In fact, my mind is so troubled that I cannot honestly give it to you with complete confidence."

"What is it that has troubled your mind?" the brahmins asked.

"I have two sons," the queen mother began. "The elder is the king, and the younger is the crown prince. Recently, a neighboring king sent the king some expensive perfume of fine sandalwood and a golden necklace. Thinking to honor his mother, he sent these presents to me, but, since I neither use perfumes nor wear necklaces, I decided to give them to my daughters-in-law. My first thought was, 'My elder son's wife is the queen, so I will give her the gold necklace. My younger son's wife is a poor timid creature, so I will give her the sandalwood perfume.' After I had given these gifts, I thought, 'I keep the Kuru Virtue. I should not favor one daughter-in-law over the other. It makes no difference whether or not one is poor. Perhaps, I have lapsed in the practice of my virtue.' If this is so, my virtue is not pure, and I cannot teach it to you."

"But, Your Highness," the brahmins protested, "when a thing is in your hands, it can be given as you will. Virtue is not broken by such a small thing.

31

If you have scruples about such a trifling matter as that, what sin would you ever do? Please teach us the Kuru Virtue."

"Very well," the queen mother replied, "I will give it to you, but, because I have such grave doubt about my own virtue, I am not satisfied, and you must not trust it. You must ask my daughter-in-law, the queen-consort, who scrupulously practices the Kuru Virtue. You can get it from her."

"Certainly," Your Highness," the brahmins agreed. "We will ask your daughter-in-law, but please give us your own Kuru Virtue."

The queen mother recited the five precepts exactly as the king had done, and the brahmins inscribed her words on their golden plates.

The brahmins next sought out the queen-consort and asked her to teach them the Kuru Virtue. She responded in the same way as the king and the queen mother had. When asked what troubled her mind, she replied, "One day, as I was watching the king in a procession around the city on the royal elephant, with the crown prince sitting behind him, I suddenly developed a crush on the crown prince. 'What if I struck up a friendship with him?' I thought. 'If the king were to die, the crown prince would become king, he would marry me, and I would become queen!' No sooner had I fantasized in such a way than I became terribly ashamed. 'I am a married woman! My husband is the king. How can I, who practice the Kuru Virtue, look with infatuation on another man? Perhaps, I have lapsed in the practice of my virtue.' If this is so, my virtue is not pure, and I cannot teach it to you."

"But, Your Highness," the brahmins protested, "sin is not a mere thought! Virtue is not broken by such a small thing. If you have scruples about such a trifling matter as that, what sin would you ever do? Please teach us the Kuru Virtue."

"Very well," the queen-consort replied, "I will give it to you, but, because I have such grave doubt about my own virtue, I am not satisfied, and you must not trust it. You must ask the crown prince, who scrupulously practices the Kuru Virtue. You can get it from him."

"Certainly, Your Highness," the brahmins agreed. We will ask the crown prince, but please give us your own Kuru Virtue."

The queen-consort recited the five precepts exactly as the king and his mother had done, and the brahmins inscribed her words on their golden plates.

The brahmins next sought out the crown prince and asked him to teach them the Kuru Virtue. He responded in the same way as the others had. When asked what troubled his mind, he replied, "I go every evening to pay my respects to the king. If I intend to dine in the palace and to spend the night there, I throw the reins and the whip on the yoke of my chariot. That is a sign for my servants to leave and to come again early the next morning to serve me. In that case, my charioteer takes care of the horses and the chariot, and he returns with them the next morning. On the other hand, if I expect to leave that evening, I leave the reins and the whip in the chariot. In that case, my servants wait with the chariot until I come out of the palace. One evening, not expecting to stay long with the king, I left the reins and the whip in the chariot. While I was inside the palace, however, it began to rain, and the king would not let me leave. I took my meal with the king and slept soundly in the palace. The next morning, when I left the palace, I found that all my servants had stayed out in the rain the entire night, expecting me to return to my quarters. I felt terribly ashamed at seeing so many people standing there drenched to the bone. 'I practice the Kuru Virtue,' I said to myself, 'but I have put all of these good people to great discomfort! Perhaps I have lapsed in the practice of my virtue.' If this is so, my virtue is not pure, and I cannot teach it to you."

"But, Your Highness," the brahmins protested, "you never intended to inconvenience those people. What is not intended does not count against one. If you have scruples about such a trifling matter as that, what sin would you ever do? Please teach us the Kuru Virtue."

"Very well," the crown prince replied, "I will give it to you, but, because I have such grave doubt about my own virtue, I am not satisfied, and you must not trust it. You must ask the king's chief advisor, who scrupulously practices the Kuru Virtue. You can get it from him."

When the brahmins agreed, the crown prince also recited the five precepts, and the brahmins inscribed his words on their golden plates.

The advisor responded in the same way as the others had, and, when asked what troubled his mind, he replied, "One day, as I was on the way to the palace to see the king, I spied a magnificent golden chariot. I asked some courtiers who it belonged to and learned that it had been sent as a gift to the king by another ruler. 'I am an old man,' I thought. 'Wouldn't it be wonderful if the king gave me this beautiful chariot? Wouldn't I feel grand riding about in such a magnificent vehicle?' I continued on to the throne room, greeted the king with a wish for prosperity and happiness, and stood respectfully to one side, while the courtiers showed the chariot to the king.

"'That is a fine car,' said the king. 'Give it to my advisor.'

"Even though the king begged me over and over again to accept the gift, I adamantly refused. I was so ashamed that I had coveted it that I could never have accepted it. I had always tried to practice the Kuru Virtue, but I still felt envy for something belonging to my king. Perhaps I have lapsed in the practice of my virtue. If this is so, my virtue is not pure, and I cannot teach it to you."

33

"But, sir," the brahmins protested, "the mere arising of envy is not a stain on your virtue. If you have scruples about such a trifling matter as that, what sin would you ever do? Please teach us the Kuru Virtue."

"Very well," the advisor replied, "I will give it to you, but, because I have such grave doubt about my own virtue, I am not satisfied, and you must not trust it. You must ask the royal surveyor, who scrupulously practices the Kuru Virtue. You can get it from him."

When the brahmins agreed, the advisor also recited the five precepts, and the brahmins inscribed his words on their golden plates.

The surveyor responded in the same way as the others had, and, when asked what troubled his mind, he replied, "Some time ago, I was measuring a field. The owner was standing on one side of the field, holding one end of a string. I tied the other end to a stake and walked to the other side of the field. In exactly the place where I needed to place the stake, I saw a crab's hole in the mud. I was faced with a dilemma. 'This is the exact boundary of the property,' I thought, 'but, if I put this stake in the hole, I will probably hurt the crab. If I put it a little on the other side, the king will lose some land. If I put it a little on this side, I will be cheating the farmer.' I didn't know what to do. 'Perhaps,' I thought, 'the crab is not in the hole. If he were, wouldn't he show himself?' Satisfied with that reasoning, I put the stick in the hole. Suddenly, I heard a crack! 'Oh, no!' I thought. 'The stick has struck the crab and killed him! I have always tried to practice the Kuru Virtue, but I have killed a living creature. Perhaps I have lapsed in the practice of my virtue.' If this is so, my virtue is not pure, and I cannot teach it to you."

"But, Sir," the brahmins protested, "you had no intention of killing the crab. What is done without intent is not a sin! If you have scruples about such a trifling matter as that, what sin would you ever do? Please teach us the Kuru Virtue."

"Very well," the surveyor replied, "I will give it to you, but, because I have such grave doubt about my own virtue, I am not satisfied, and you must not trust it. You must ask the royal charioteer, who scrupulously practices the Kuru Virtue. You can get it from him."

When the brahmins agreed, the surveyor also recited the five precepts, and the brahmins inscribed his words on their golden plates.

The charioteer responded in the same way as the others had, and, when asked what troubled his mind, he replied, "One day, I drove the king to his pleasure garden, and, on the way back in the evening, before we got to the city, the sky grew dark with black clouds. Lightning flashed, and thunder rumbled all around. Fearing that the king would get wet, I flicked the horses with the whip and made them gallop home. Ever since then, whenever the horses reach that spot, they began to run. Because I hit them with the whip at that place once, they suppose that there must be some danger there. It does not really matter, and it is no fault of mine if the king gets a little wet, but, ever since I gave those well-trained steeds a touch of the whip for no reason at all, they gallop needlessly and tire themselves out, and that is my doing. I tried to practice the Kuru Virtue, but perhaps I have lapsed in the practice of my virtue. If this is so, my virtue is not pure, and I cannot teach it to you."

"But, sir," the brahmins protested, "you had no intention to tire the horses. What is done without intent is not a sin! If you have scruples about such a trifling matter as that, what sin would you ever do? Please teach us the Kuru Virtue."

"Very well," the charioteer replied, "I will give it to you, but, because I have such grave doubt about my own virtue, I am not satisfied, and you must not trust it. You must ask the treasurer, who scrupulously practices the Kuru Virtue. You can get it from him."

When the brahmins agreed, the charioteer also recited the five precepts, and the brahmins inscribed his words on their golden plates.

The treasurer responded in the same way as the others had, and, when asked what troubled his mind, he replied, "One day, when I went to my paddy field, I saw a head of rice bursting the husk. I took a handful of rice stalks and tied that head onto a post to keep it from falling. As soon as I had done that, I realized that I had not yet given the king his due from the harvest. I had tried to practice the Kuru Virtue, but I had taken a handful of rice from an untaxed field! Perhaps I have lapsed in the practice of my virtue. If this is so, my virtue is not pure, and I cannot teach it to you."

"But, sir," the brahmins protested, "you had no intention of stealing. Without that intention, there is no theft. If you have scruples about such a trifling matter as that, what sin would you ever do? Please teach us the Kuru Virtue."

"Very well," the treasurer replied, "I will give it to you, but, because I have such grave doubt about my own virtue, I am not satisfied, and you must not trust it. You must ask the master of the royal granaries, who scrupulously practices the Kuru Virtue. You can get it from him."

When the brahmins agreed, the treasurer also recited the five precepts, and the brahmins inscribed his words on their golden plates.

The master of the royal granaries responded in the same way as the others had, and, when asked what troubled his mind, he replied, "One day, I was sitting at the door of one of the king's granaries, measuring the rice which had come in as tax. I took several grains of rice from the heap which had not yet been counted and put them down for markers. At that moment, it began to rain. I hurriedly counted the markers, swept them all together, dropped them on a heap of paddy, and ran inside. I'm afraid I dropped the markers on the measured paddy, in which case, the king's rice was increased, and the owners were charged more than was fair. Because of carelessness, I cheated the owners. I have always tried to keep the Kuru Virtue, but perhaps I have lapsed in the practice of my virtue. If this is so, my virtue is not pure, and I cannot teach it to you."

"But, sir," the brahmins protested, "you had no intention of cheating. Without that intention, one cannot say that you were dishonest. If you have scruples about such a trifling matter as that, what sin would you ever do? Please teach us the Kuru Virtue."

"Very well," the master of the royal granaries replied, "I will give it to you, but, because I have such grave doubt about my own virtue, I am not satisfied, and you must not trust it. You must ask the gatekeeper, who scrupulously practices the Kuru Virtue. You can get it from him."

When the brahmins agreed, the master of the royal granaries also recited the five precepts, and the brahmins inscribed his words on their golden plates.

The gatekeeper responded in the same way as the others had, and, when asked what troubled his mind, he replied, "One night, when it was time to close the city gate, I called loudly three times to announce its closing. Not hearing any response, I began closing the great doors. Suddenly, a raggedly dressed man and woman appeared and asked to be permitted to pass through. I gruffly scolded the man and shouted, 'Don't you know that the king is in the city and that this gate is always closed at sunset? What have you been doing in the woods? Making love?'

"'Master,' the poor man protested, 'I went to the woods to gather bamboo. I tried to get back in time, and I hurried as soon as I heard your cry. I am very sorry. Furthermore, this is not my wife; she is my younger sister.'

"How rude I was to speak to that poor man in that way! It was unseemly of me to address his sister as his wife! I have tried to practice the Kuru Virtue, but perhaps I have lapsed in the practice of my virtue. If this is so, my virtue is not pure, and I cannot teach it to you."

"But, sir," the brahmins protested, "you said what you did because you thought it was true. In that, you did not break your practice of virtue. If you have scruples about such a trifling matter, what sin would you ever do? Please teach us the Kuru Virtue."

"Very well," the gatekeeper replied, "I will give it to you, but, because I have such grave doubt about my own virtue, I am not satisfied, and you must not trust it. There is, however, a courtesan, the most famous in Indapatta, who scrupulously practices the Kuru Virtue. You must ask her. She can give it to you."

When the brahmins agreed, the gatekeeper also recited the five precepts, and the brahmins inscribed his words on their golden plates.

The courtesan responded in the same way as the others had, and, when asked what troubled her mind, she replied, "Once, I received one thousand coins from a young man who told me he would visit me a little later. I waited for him, but he did not come back. Day after day, I waited for him for three years, but, still, he never came. During those three years, in order to preserve my honor, I did not take even so much as a piece of betel nut from another man. I lost all of my wealth. Finally, reduced to penury and unable to survive, I had no choice but to go to the chief justices to report the situation and to obtain permission to accept customers as before. I explained to the court that, three years before, a man had given me one thousand coins, but had never returned. Not knowing whether he was dead or alive, I asked the court to release me from my pledge to him. The justices declared that, since he had not come back for three years, I was free to earn my living as before. As soon as I left the court, another man offered me one thousand coins. I held out my hand to accept his money when, suddenly, the first man appeared. 'I cannot accept your money,' I cried to the second man, pulling back my hand, 'for I am bound to this one, who gave me one thousand coins three years ago! Then the first man abandoned his disguise and revealed his identity. He was Sakka. Shining as bright as the sun, he announced to the crowd that had gathered, 'To test this woman's virtue, I gave her one thousand coins three years ago. All of you should be as honest as she is and maintain your honor as she has done!' Then Sakka followed me to my house and filled it with jewels. 'Continue to be vigilant,' he encouraged me and returned to Tāvatimsa. I have always tried to practice the Kuru Virtue, but I know that I held out my hand to receive money from a second customer before I had satisfied the first. Perhaps I have lapsed in the practice of my virtue. If this is so, my virtue is not pure, and I cannot teach it to you."

"But, madam," the brahmins protested, "merely holding out your hand was not a breach of virtue. Your virtue is certainly the highest perfection! If you have scruples about such a trifling matter as that, what sin would you ever do? Please teach us the Kuru Virtue."

"Very well," the courtesan replied, "I will give you the Kuru Virtue." She too, recited the five precepts, and the brahmins inscribed them on their golden plates.

Finished at last, they took the golden plates back to Dantapura and reported to the king everything that had happened.

The king of Kālinga henceforth practiced the Kuru Virtue as all in Kuru had done. Very soon after the brahmins returned to Dantapura, rain fell in abundance throughout the entire realm. The three fears of starvation, disease, and poverty, which had blighted the lives of the people, were dispelled; the land once more became fertile; and the kingdom again prospered.

As long as he lived, King Dhanañjaya continued to give generous alms and to act righteously. He encouraged his subjects to keep the five precepts, and, as they died, they all went to fill the heavens.

Having concluded his story, the Buddha taught the Dhamma. Some bhikkhus attained the first path, some attained the second, some attained the third, and some became arahats. Then the Buddha identified the birth: "At that time, Uppalavannā was the courtesan, Punna was the gatekeeper, Sāriputta was the treasurer, Kolita was the master of the royal granaries, Mahā-Kaccāna was the surveyor, Anuruddha was the charioteer, Mahā-Kassapa was the advisor, Nanda was the crown prince, Rāhula's mother was the queen-consort, Queen Mahā-Māyā was the queen mother, and I was King Dhanañjaya."

103
Monkeying Around
Mahisa Jātaka

It was while staying at Jetavana that the Buddha told this story about an impudent monkey.

In Sāvatthī, a family kept a tame monkey. It often ran into the royal elephants' stable and climbed onto one of the king's elephants. While the naughty monkey played on the elephant's back, he sometimes even relieved himself. Being patient, the gentle elephant did not complain.

One day, the keepers had put a different elephant in that elephant's stall. The monkey scampered into the stable and, not noticing any difference, jumped onto the elephant's back. Unfortunately, that elephant was a young and quick-tempered beast. He grabbed the unsuspecting monkey with his trunk, dashed him to the ground, and trampled his body.

The story of the monkey's end became well known, and, one day, the bhikkhus were talking about it. When the Buddha heard what they were discussing, he said, "This is not the first time that that impertinent monkey behaved in that way." Then the Buddha told this story of the past.

Long, long ago, when Brahmadatta was reigning in Bārānasi, the Bodhisatta was born as a wild buffalo in the Himavat. He grew up large and strong and freely roamed all through the hills, mountains, and jungles.

One day, as the buffalo was grazing on the sweet grass under a pleasant tree, a boisterous monkey jumped out of the tree onto his back and defecated. Then the monkey jumped on the buffalo's head and swung by his tail from one of the buffalo's great black horns. The monkey continued amusing himself, jumping up and down on the buffalo's back. The buffalo, who was kind and patient, took no offense at this misbehavior.

The buffalo appreciated the grass in that spot, so he returned frequently to graze under the tree, and the monkey always took advantage of the buffalo's good nature.

One day, the deva who resided in that tree scolded the buffalo for tolerating the monkey's rudeness. "That monkey is a nuisance!" he said. "If you don't punish him for his bad manners, no one, not even little children, will respect you! Make him stop! You can trample him under your hooves or toss him with your mighty horns!"

"Friend," the buffalo replied, "if I cannot endure this monkey's abuse, how can my aspiration ever be fulfilled? I am resolved to bear with this foolish monkey patiently. Someday, he will make a mistake, and he will suffer the consequences. When some other buffalo has killed him, he will no longer annoy me, but I will be innocent of any wrongdoing."

A few days later, that buffalo was grazing elsewhere, and another buffalo discovered the tender grass beneath that tree and began grazing. The monkey, not noticing the difference, jumped onto his back and misbehaved as usual. This buffalo, which was a savage beast, shook the startled monkey off his back, drove one of his horns into the monkey's heart, and trampled his body to mincemeat under his sharp hooves.

Having concluded his story, the Buddha identified the birth: "At that time, the quick-tempered elephant was the savage buffalo, the two monkeys were the same, and I was the patient buffalo."

104
Turning Misfortune Around
Seyya Jātaka

It was while staying at Jetavana that the Buddha told this story about a courtier of the king of Kosala.

In Sāvatthī, there was an intelligent and hard-working young man who rose quickly in the court. Because he was skillful in so many fields, the king paid him great honor. Of course, this made many in the court jealous. Some of the other courtiers began slandering him and spreading rumors about him. The king believed these stories and, without any further investigation, ordered that the man be arrested. He was cruelly bound in chains and thrown into prison.

The charges against him were so serious that he was kept in solitary confinement. Rather than resist or object to this treatment, however, the young man trusted in his innocence and maintained his peace of mind. With his mind at peace, he meditated in the silence of his cell, achieved insight into the true nature of existence, and attained the first path. Eventually, the king learned that the young man was innocent and had him released. The king not only restored the man to his old position, but honored him even more than before.

The young man hastened to Jetavana to pay his respects to the Buddha. After offering flowers and incense, he sat respectfully at one side.

"We have heard that ill fortune befell you," the Buddha said, speaking graciously to him.

"Yes, Venerable Sir," he replied, "but I took the opportunity to practice, and, as I sat in prison, I attained the first path."

"Well done, Friend," said the Buddha. "You are not alone in turning misfortune into good. Long ago, too, a wise man did the same." At the man's request, the Buddha told this story of the past.

Long, long ago, when Brahmadatta was reigning in Bārānasi, the Bodhisatta was born as the son of his queen-consort and was named Kamsa. He was educated at Takkasilā and, at his father's death, became king. He ruled wisely, observing the ten duties of a king, giving alms, practicing virtue, and observing the Uposatha days.

Not long after the coronation, a courtier committed adultery with one of the king's wives. Some servants noticed what was happening and reported the matter to the king. The king investigated, determined that it was true, and banished the offender.

In a neighboring kingdom, the man became a trusted confidant of the king and urged his new master to invade Kāsi. At first, the king didn't believe that so large a realm could be conquered, but the courtier was so convincing that the king prepared for war and led his army to Bārānasi.

When King Kamsa was told that a rival king was outside the walls, he refused to allow his generals to fight. "I want no kingdom that must be kept by doing harm," he declared. "Do nothing at all."

The invading army surrounded the city. Again, the generals approached King Kamsa and urged him to let them defend the city and to capture the invader.

"I will not fight! Open the city gates!" he ordered. Then, surrounded by his court, he seated himself on his throne. The invading army entered the city and took complete control. Finding no resistance even at the palace, the invading king ascended the dais and ordered his soldiers to bind King Kamsa and all his ministers in chains and to throw them into prison. Then he sat on the throne and declared himself king of Kāsi.

From the darkness of his prison cell, King Kamsa extended thoughts of loving-kindness to his captor. Meditating on loving-kindness, he attained jhānic concentration, which was so powerful that the invading king began suffering great torment. As he sat on the throne, his body seemed to be on fire, and he cried out in pain. He asked his generals and advisors why this was happening to him.

"It must be because you have cast a righteous king into prison," they replied. "Surely, that injustice is causing this intense pain."

In agony, he hurried to the prison and begged forgiveness from the unoffending king. After being forgiven, he personally escorted King Kamsa to the palace and placed him once more on the throne. "From now on, let us live in friendship," he pledged. "You may leave your enemies for me to deal with!" When he learned of his evil counselor's grudge, he punished the man and returned with his army to his own capital.

Seated on his throne and surrounded by his ministers, King Kamsa declared, "The best course to follow is always virtue and right action. By treating a rival with loving-kindness, I saved hundreds of men from death in battle. By extending loving-kindness to all the world, one will gain rebirth in heaven among the virtuous."

In time, King Kamsa relinquished the white umbrella, retired to the Himavat, and became an ascetic. Meditating intensively on loving-kindness, he perfected the five extraordinary powers and the eight jhānas.

Having concluded his story, the Buddha identified the birth: "At that time, Ānanda was the marauding king, and I was King Kamsa."

105
Stealing Luck
Siri Jātaka

It was while staying at Jetavana that the Buddha told this story about a brahmin who tried to steal luck.

In Sāvatthī there was a brahmin who was well versed in lucky signs and magic. Hearing that Anāthapindika had regained his wealth after having lost everything,[1] the brahmin wondered what made the rich man so lucky. He resolved to find out and to steal whatever it was.

The brahmin went to Anāthapindika's house and was hospitably welcomed. After the usual civilities, the host asked the brahmin why he had come. The brahmin immediately realized that the rich man's luck resided in the red comb of a cock, which had feathers as white as a sun-bleached seashell and was kept in a golden cage. "Noble sir," he replied, "I teach magic charms to five hundred young students. These days, we are troubled by a cock that always crows at the wrong time. I have come to ask for your white cock. Will you give it to me?"

"Yes, of course," Anāthapindika replied, but, at the instant he spoke, his luck left the cock's comb and settled in a jewel. The brahmin asked for the

1   How Anāthapindika lost his wealth is related in the occasion for Tale 22.

jewel, but the luck immediately jumped to a cudgel propped in a corner for protection. The brahmin asked for the cudgel, but the luck instantly jumped to the head of Anāthapindika's wife, Puññalakkhanā. The greedy brahmin realized that he could never ask for the wife and cried, "Noble sir, the truth is that I came to your house to steal your luck. I saw that it resided in your cock's comb, but when you gave me the bird, the luck passed to this jewel. When you gave me the jewel, it passed to your cudgel, and, when you gave that to me, it passed to Lady Puññalakkhanā's head. Surely, your luck is unattainable. I will never be able to steal your luck, so, keep it!" Leaving all that he had been given, the brahmin turned and walked away empty-handed.

Anāthapindika wanted to tell the Buddha what had happened, so he went to the monastery. After paying his respects to the Buddha, he sat down at one side. The Buddha listened to his narration and replied, "Good layman, that brahmin was unable to take your luck from you, but, long ago, the luck belonging to one of small wit slipped away and fell to the wise." At Anāthapindika's request, the Buddha told this story of the past.

Long, long ago, when Brahmadatta was reigning in Bārānasi, the Bodhisatta was born into a brahmin family in Kāsi and received his education in Takkasilā. When his parents died, he left home to become an ascetic in the Himavat, where he practiced concentration meditation and developed psychic powers.

One year, at the beginning of the rainy season, he returned to Bārānasi to get salt and vinegar and to find a proper place to stay. He spent the first night in the royal park. The next morning, as he was walking for alms, he passed the house of an elephant trainer, who was so impressed by the ascetic's demeanor that he gave him food and offered him lodging in his own small garden. From then on, the elephant trainer looked after the ascetic devotedly.

One night, a firewood gatherer failed to get back before the city gates were closed and had to spend the night in a shrine. Using a bundle of sticks for a rude pillow, he slept under a tree. There were a lot of chickens at the shrine, and, at night, they usually roosted in that tree.

Towards morning, one cock, which was perched up high, let fall a dropping on the back of a bird below.

"Who dropped that on me?" the bird below cried.

"I did," said the cock.

Why did you do it?"

"Didn't think," he replied and did the same thing again.

"You nasty old bird!" shouted the bird below.

"What right do you have to call me nasty, you smelly fowl?" retorted the one above.

"You can't talk to me that way! Who do you think you are, anyway?"

"I know who I am, and I know what I can do. Do you think you have any special power?"

"Well, let me tell you," the bird below cried. "Anyone who eats my roasted flesh will receive one thousand coins the next morning! So there!"

"Ha!" cried the cock. "Is that all? One who eats my breast meat will become king. One who eats my dark meat will become either commander-in chief, if a man, or queen, if a woman. One who eats the flesh next to my bones will become either royal treasurer, if a householder, or spiritual advisor, if an ascetic. Now that's something to brag about!"

When the firewood gatherer heard all this, he thought, "Why bother with one thousand coins? Better to become king!" He stealthily climbed the tree, caught the cock, and wrung its neck. Tying the bird in a fold of his dhoti, he exalted to himself, "Imagine! Soon I'll be king!"

As soon as the gates were opened, he hurried home, plucked the fowl, cleaned it, and gave it to his wife, telling her to roast it. She prepared it with rice and served it to her husband.

"Dear wife," he said, "there's magic in this meat. By eating it I will become king, and you will be my queen! Let's take this meal to the bank of Gangā and eat it together."

His wife put the roasted chicken and rice on a tray, and they carried it to the river. Wishing to take a ritual bath before eating, they set the tray down and stepped into the water.

Just then, a stiff breeze whipped up the water, which washed over the bank and swept away the tray with the chicken on it. The firewood gatherer scrambled out of the water, in his panic swallowing a mouthful of sand and water, and raced along the riverbank after the tray, but it was soon out of sight.

The tray floated downstream and was spotted by the elephant trainer, who was giving his elephants a bath. "What have we here?" he asked as he plucked the tray out of the water. "It's a roast fowl and rice!" He wrapped it carefully in a banana leaf and sent it home to his wife with the message that she should serve it to him when he returned.

At that moment, the ascetic was thinking about his patron. With his extraordinary power, he immediately foresaw what was about to happen, and hurried to the house.

When the elephant trainer returned, he greeted the ascetic respectfully and sat down on one side. He asked his wife to serve curries, rice, and water to the ascetic. For his own meal, he asked for the parcel of food he had sent. Rather than accepting the curries and rice, the ascetic said, "Let me divide this chicken, instead." The elephant trainer offered him the entire parcel of chicken and rice. The ascetic carefully separated the meat into portions, the white meat for his patron, the dark meat for his wife, and for himself, the meat next to the bones. After the meal was over, he announced, "Three days from today, you will become king. Take care what you do!" Then he left.

On the third day after that meal, a neighboring king marched with his army on Bārānasi and surrounded the city. King Brahmadatta ordered the elephant trainer to dress in the royal robes, to mount the royal elephant, and to fight in his place. The king himself put on a disguise and mingled with the ranks. Almost immediately, an enemy arrow struck the king and killed him outright. When the elephant trainer heard that the king was dead, he had a great quantity of money brought from the royal treasury and offered it to all who would come forward and fight to save the city. When the people heard this proclamation, so many joined the ranks that the army quickly routed the attackers and killed the enemy king.

After King Brahmadatta's funeral, the royal advisors deliberated over his successor. "While our king was still alive, he put his royal robes on the elephant trainer," one of them said. "This man fought valiantly to protect the kingdom. He deserves to be king!" The other advisors immediately agreed. That same day, the elephant trainer was proclaimed king, and his wife became the queen. The king appointed the ascetic as his spiritual advisor.

Having concluded his story, the Buddha added, "Good sir, these beings had no other resource than the merit which they had gained in previous births. Merit enables one to obtain treasure without having to dig the earth." Then the Buddha identified the birth: "At that time, Ānanda was King Brahmadatta, and I was the ascetic."

106
The Wedding Feast
Sālūka Jātaka

It was while staying at Jetavana that the Buddha told this story about the seduction of a bhikkhu.

In a respectable family in Sāvatthī, there was a plump young woman who seemed to have no prospects for a husband. Wondering what to do, her mother decided to catch a bhikkhu for a son-in-law. She prepared delicious food and, as the bhikkhus walked on their almsrounds, looked them over in order to find one who could be tempted by a craving for delicacies. At first, it seemed that all the bhikkhus who passed by were extremely diligent and self-possessed. Then she spied a young bhikkhu who appeared a little more worldly than the others. His robe looked a little more cared for and slightly more carefully put on. His gait was a bit sprightly, and his eyes glanced here and there. "Here is a man I can catch!" she exclaimed to herself. Taking his bowl, she invited the bhikkhu into the house. She offered him a seat and provided him with the finest curries and rice. After the meal, she asked him to come every day for lunch. The young bhikkhu could not turn down such tasty dishes; he accepted the invitation and, in time, became familiar with the family.

One day, while the bhikkhu was eating, the woman said aloud, "In this house, we are happy enough, but I have no son-in-law to take over the family." At first, the bhikkhu wondered why she would have said such a thing, but then he realized what she meant and felt weak. A little later, the daughter emerged, dressed in her finest clothes and adorned with beautiful jewels. As she moved around the room, talking nicely to him all the while, he felt passion arise within him. By the time he left, he had lost all resolve, and said to himself, "I can remain no longer in the Sangha."

When he returned to the monastery, he put down his bowl and announced his decision to the other bhikkhus. They immediately escorted him to the Buddha and explained what he had said.

"Is it true that you are discontented?" the Buddha asked the young bhikkhu.

"Yes, Master."

"Why?" the Buddha asked.

"I have fallen in love with the plump daughter of a family in Sāvatthī," he confessed.

"Bhikkhu," the Buddha replied, "that girl is the bane of your spiritual life now, but, because of her, you once before met dire destruction." At the bhikkhu's request, the Buddha told this story of the past.

Long, long ago, when Brahmadatta was reigning in Bārānasi, the Bodhisatta was born as an ox named Mahā-Lohita. Both he and his younger brother, Culla-Lohita, belonged to a farming family in a village. The two oxen lived in a small shed. Next to their shed, in a well-ventilated, spacious sty, lived a hog named Sālūka.

One day, Culla-Lohita remarked to his brother, "Dear brother, we work hard for this family, and we help them make their living. Every day, they give us only grass, but I've noticed that, recently, they have been feeding rice porridge to that lazy pig next door. His sty certainly looks more comfortable than our rickety shed. He doesn't do any work, and they get nothing whatsoever in return. It doesn't seem fair to me!"

"Dear Brother," Mahā-Lohita replied, "don't covet Sālūka's porridge. Have you noticed any change in that girl who takes care of us?"

"The farmer's young daughter?" Culla-Lohita asked.

"Yes," his brother answered.

"What about her?"

"Well, she has grown up, and she's getting married soon. They are fattening Sālūka up for the feast. Wait a few days, and you'll see him hauled out of his sty, killed, chopped into bits, and eaten up by the wedding guests! Don't envy Sālūka, for his food is deadly. Better to be contented with our

106 The Wedding Feast

humble fodder, which allows us to live long. Mark my words! It won't be long before the guests come and dine on poor Sālūka."

A few days later, the unsuspecting pig was taken from his sty. Then, despite his ear-splitting squeals, he was slaughtered. The wedding guests came, and Sālūka's flesh was the center of the grand feast. The two oxen solemnly watched, and Culla-Lohita agreed with his brother that their simple grass was, after all, the best fare.

At the conclusion of this story, the love-stricken bhikkhu gave up his infatuation. Then the Buddha taught the Dhamma, and the bhikkhu attained the first path. Finally, the Buddha identified the birth: "At that time, the girl was the same, the lovesick bhikkhu was Sālūka, Ānanda was Culla-Lohita, and I was Mahā-Lohita."

107

The Seven-Cent Fish
Macchuddāna Jātaka

It was while staying at Jetavana that the Buddha told this story about a dishonest merchant.

Long, long ago, when Brahmadatta was reigning in Bārānasi, the Bodhisatta was born as the elder son of a wealthy landowner. After their father died, he and his younger brother had to go to a distant village one day to take care of some family business. They collected a large debt of one thousand coins and started home. While waiting on the bank of the Gangā for the ferry, they ate the lunch packets they had carried in leaf wrappers. The elder brother had some leftover rice, so he dropped it into the river for the fish. As he did so, he shared the merit with the deva of the river. Then he folded his jacket to make a pillow for his head and lay down on the sand to take a nap.

While he was sleeping, his younger brother wrapped some gravel to make a parcel which looked exactly like the parcel of coins. He surreptitiously tucked one parcel into his pack.

When it was time to leave, he woke his brother, and they both boarded the ferry. When they reached the middle of the river, the younger brother stumbled against the side of the boat and let a parcel fall into the river.

"Brother!" he cried, "our money just fell overboard! What shall we do?"

"What can we do?" the elder brother replied. "What's gone is gone. At least, Brother, it was not you falling overboard!"

The river deva saw the parcel falling to the bottom of the river and realized that it was the money and not the gravel as the younger brother believed. Grateful to have received the merit from the elder brother, she resolved to take care of his treasure. She caused a large-mouthed fish to swallow the parcel and sent him into the net which some fishermen had cast at that spot.

As soon as the younger brother got home, he chuckled over his trick and gleefully unwrapped the parcel he had hidden. When he saw the gravel, his heart shriveled up with disappointment, and he fell on his bed in despair.

When the fishermen pulled in their net, they were delighted to find the large fish. As they were carrying it into the city, many people asked what the price was.

"One thousand coins and seven cents," replied the fishermen.

"Amazing! Now we have actually seen a fish costing one thousand coins!" people exclaimed and went off laughing.

The fishermen carried the fish directly to the elder brother's house, and asked him to buy it.

"What's the price?" he asked.

"For you, sir, it is only seven cents," they said.

"How much did you ask from other people for it?"

"For everyone else the price was one thousand coins and seven cents; but you may have it for seven cents," they told him.

He paid the fishermen seven cents, took the fish, handed it to his wife, and returned to his work. When she cut the fish open and found the parcel of money, she shouted with surprise. The elder brother immediately recognized it as his own, but he wondered how it had gotten inside the fish and found its way back to his house.

"These fishermen asked other people one thousand coins and seven cents for this fish!" he exclaimed. "But the one thousand coins inside it were mine, and they let me have it for only seven cents! This is enough to make the most confirmed skeptic believe!"

At that moment, the river deva hovered in the air and declared, "I am the deva of the Ganga. You gave your leftover rice to the fish, and you shared the merit with me. In gratitude for that, I have taken care of your property and brought it back to you. Your brother tried to steal the money and made a parcel of gravel exactly like the parcel of money. He thought that that was what he let fall overboard. Now, he is at home, bemoaning his bad luck. Please take care of this money. Don't give any of it to your brother. He is a scoundrel! Anyone who would cheat his own brother doesn't deserve to prosper."

The elder brother profusely thanked the deva for returning the money but calmly told her, "What you say is impossible. He is still my brother, our parents' son, and their heir. I must give him his fair share, which is half of this money." As soon as the deva had left, he did exactly that.

Having concluded his story, the Buddha taught the Dhamma, and the dishonest merchant attained the first path. Then the Buddha identified the birth: "At that time, this merchant was the younger brother, and I was the elder."

108
The Wishing Cup
Bhadraghata Jātaka

It was while staying at Jetavana that the Buddha told this story about one of Anāthapindika's nephews.

After squandering his entire inheritance of forty crores of gold, this young man appealed to his uncle. Anāthapindika gave him one thousand coins and advised him to trade with it. The fellow wasted that, too, and went back to see his uncle. This time, Anāthapindika gave him five hundred. When that was gone, Anāthapindika gave the youth only two shirts made of coarse cloth. When those wore out, he again begged his uncle for money, but Anāthapindika threw him out of the house with nothing, and, at last, he collapsed in an alley and died. When Anāthapindika learned that he was dead, he told the Buddha about it.

The Buddha said, "How could you expect to gratify such a person? Long ago, I couldn't satisfy him, even with the Wishing Cup?" At Anāthapindika's request, the Buddha told this story of the past.

Long, long ago, when Brahmadatta was reigning in Bārānasi, the Bodhisatta was born as the son of a rich merchant. When his father died, he continued the family business and increased his wealth to forty crores. He lived virtuously, performing many good deeds and generously giving alms. When he died, he was reborn as Sakka, and his son inherited his fortune. The son did not attend to business, but, instead, built a grand pavilion across the road from the great house. He and his friends spent all their time in the pavilion, drinking, dining lavishly, and enjoying the company of attractive women. They were constantly entertained by singers, dancers, jugglers, and acrobats. In no time at all, he had squandered all the family wealth. Without a thought, he mortgaged the entire estate—the property, the house, and all the furniture. Finally, with nothing of value left, he was reduced to wearing rags.

From Tāvatimsa, Sakka saw what had become of his only son. Still feeling love and pity for the boy, he left his heaven and appeared before his heir. "My son," he said, presenting him with a magnificent chalice, "whatever you do, don't break this invaluable Wishing Cup. Take good care of it! It will give you whatever you wish for. As long as you have it, your wealth will never run out." Repeating, "Take good care of it!" Sakka returned to Tāvatimsa.

The young man casually accepted the Wishing Cup. Instantly receiving everything he wished for, he easily regained his wealth. None the wiser, however, he continued the same life of drinking and debauchery. He kept the Wishing Cup filled with the finest liquor and drank from it incessantly. One day, when he was bored, he began amusing himself by tossing the cup into the air and catching it. After a number of throws, because he was so inebriated, he missed, and the immeasurably precious cup crashed to the floor, shattering into a million pieces. Without the cup, his luck vanished, and his friends left him. Again, he went about in rags, begging scraps to eat. Finally, he lay down beside a wall and died.

Having concluded his story, the Buddha identified the birth: "At that time, Anāthapindika's nephew was the wastrel who broke the Wishing Cup, and I was Sakka."

109

In His Majesty's Service
Supatta Jātaka

It was while staying at Jetavana that the Buddha told this story about a serving of red fish.

Once, Venerable Bhaddakaccānā was suffering from stomach troubles. When Venerable Rāhula learned of his mother's condition, he told Venerable Sāriputta about it and explained that an appropriate cure would be a special dish of rice mixed with red fish and ghee. Venerable Sāriputta immediately went to the king and obtained the food. He gave it to Venerable Rāhula, who, in turn, gave it to his mother. As soon as she ate it, the pain subsided. The king sent a messenger to inquire after her and was very pleased to learn that the dish had been efficacious. Thereafter, the king frequently sent this special food to her.

One day, in the Hall of Truth, the bhikkhus were talking about how wonderful it was that Venerable Sāriputta was able to provide the bhikkhunī with that special meal.

When the Buddha heard what they were discussing, he said, "This is not the first time, Bhikkhus, that Sāriputta has given Rāhula's mother what she wanted. Long ago, he did the same." Then he told this story of the past.

Long, long ago, when Brahmadatta was reigning in Bārānasi, the Bodhisatta was born as a crow named Supatta. He became the leader of a flock of eighty thousand crows, which lived near the city.

One day, Supatta and his mate, Suphassā, happened to fly over the royal kitchen just as the king's chef was preparing a great variety of dishes, including a special fish curry. The aroma created in Suphassā a great longing for a taste of that dish, but she didn't say anything at the time.

The next day, when Supatta asked her to go looking for food, she said, "Please go by yourself today. I long for something I can't have."

"What is it?" Supatta asked.

"Yesterday, I smelled the dishes in the palace kitchen. The scent was like ambrosia! Now I crave a taste of the king's food, but I know that I can never get it, so I will just die."

This upset Supatta very much, and he wondered what to do. His captain, Sumukha, noticed that something was bothering his leader, and he asked what it was.

Supatta told Sumukha what his mate had said, and the captain immediately replied, "All right! Both of you must stay here today. I will fetch food from the palace."

Sumukha called a meeting of all crows and explained his mission. He chose eight of the strongest crows as an elite corps to join him on the roof of the royal kitchen. He posted several companies of the others all around the royal kitchen. To the group of eight, he said, "While the food is being taken to the dining room, I'll make the cook drop the dishes. As soon as the dishes fall, four of you must fill your mouths with rice, and four with fish. Take the food back to our king and queen for their meal. Don't pay any attention to me. I don't expect to survive, but, if Supatta asks where I am, tell him that I'm coming."

After the royal chef had finished preparing all the curries, he hung the dishes on a carrying pole and started towards the king's dining room. As he passed through the courtyard, Sumukha signaled to his followers and flew straight toward the chef, striking him on the chest. Startled, the man dropped the pole, and the dishes crashed to the ground. As he tried to swat the crow, Sumukha scratched him with his claws, pecked him all over his face with his sharp beak, and, finally, used his claws to hold the poor man's jaws tightly closed.

The other eight crows swooped down and began scooping up the curry and rice which was strewn on the courtyard pavement. When they had filled their beaks, they flew away, leaving the remains for all the other crows who were watching and waiting.

The king happened to be walking up and down on an upper floor, and, glancing out a large window, he saw the entire drama unfold. "Never mind the dishes!" he shouted to the chef. "Catch that crow, and bring him to me!"

The chef was finally able to subdue the crow. Holding Sumukha tightly at arm's length, he carried him to the king's chamber.

Meanwhile, the eight crows delivered the fish curry and rice to Supatta and Suphassā, and her craving was appeased.

As soon as the chef arrived in the king's chamber with his captive, the king addressed the crow, "You foolish bird! You have shown great disrespect to me! You have broken my chef's nose! You have smashed my dishes! You have spoiled my meal! And you have recklessly thrown away your life! What made you do such a rash thing?"

"Sire," Sumukha calmly replied, "our king, Supatta by name, lives near Bārānasi, and I am his captain, Sumukha. Yesterday, when his wife, Suphassā, happened to smell the delicious dishes your chef was preparing, she conceived a great longing to taste the fish curry. When our king told me about this, I, at once, resolved to sacrifice my life to fulfill her desire. My eight trusty comrades have taken her the food she was hungering for, and I have accomplished my mission. I meant no disrespect to Your Majesty, but my loyalty is to my king, and I would do anything for him or for his queen."

When the king heard this, he remarked, "No matter how much we honor our courtiers, we cannot fully depend on them. Though we shower them with valuable gifts, presents of money, jewels, or even entire villages, we can find no one loyal enough to give his life to please us. Yet here is this crow, a mere bird, sacrificing his life for his king and queen. How admirable! How noble!"

The king was so impressed that he offered Sumukha the white umbrella, but the captain refused the honor, insisting that his king was much more virtuous than he.

King Brahmadatta insisted on meeting this King Supatta, and ordered Sumukha to bring him to the palace so that he, Brahmadatta, might hear his teaching. Sumukha did so, and King Brahmadatta was extremely pleased with the wise instruction. Thereafter, he sent food daily from his own table to Supatta, Suphassā, and Sumukha. He also ordered that an enormous cauldron of rice be cooked every day for the rest of the flock. For the rest of his life, King Brahmadatta, following the teaching of Supatta, the king of the crows, practiced virtue and protected the lives of all creatures.

The teaching of King Supatta was remembered for seven hundred years.

Having concluded his story, the Buddha identified the birth: "At that time, Ānanda was King Brahmadatta, Sāriputta was Sumukha, Rāhula's mother was Suphassā, and I was King Supatta."

110
The Wolf's Fast
Vaka Jātaka

It was while staying at Jetavana that the Buddha told this story about old friends.

Venerable Upasena, the younger brother of Venerable Sāriputta, had been ordained for only one year when he ordained another bhikkhu. When he went with this new young bhikkhu to visit the Buddha, the Master chastised him for this hasty procedure and established the rule that no one who had been a bhikkhu for less than ten years could ordain another. After being rebuked in that way, Venerable Upasena was spurred to earn the Buddha's praise and, practicing meditation with great urgency, soon became an arahat.

Venerable Upasena adopted various dhutangas. He was such a skillful preacher and his eloquence was so persuasive that many bhikkhus joined him in dhutanga practice. In a short time, he had a large number of followers, and the Buddha declared him to be the foremost among the bhikkhus who were altogether charming.

It was an established rule that, during the rains retreat, if the Buddha had declared a period of solitude, no one was to visit him. Nevertheless, Venerable Upasena paid a visit to the Master at this time, and, since the

Buddha wanted to discuss something with him, he amended the rule such that one who was practicing dhutanga be allowed to visit even when the Buddha was observing solitude. When Venerable Upasena reported this to other bhikkhus, some undertook dhutanga practice simply to have the right to visit the Buddha. After practicing dhutanga and completing a short period of seclusion, those bhikkhus discarded their rag-robes and donned new ones. One day, the Buddha asked a dhutanga bhikkhu whether wearing rag-robes pleased him, and the bhikkhu replied that it did not, but that he wore rag-robes out of respect for Venerable Upasena, his teacher. Some time later, when the Buddha went around the monastery, he noticed many rag-robes lying about and asked about them. When he was told the reason, he said, "Bhikkhus, this kind of short dhutanga practice is like the wolf's observance of Uposatha." At their request, the Buddha told this story of the past.

Long, long ago, when Brahmadatta was reigning in Bārānasi, the Bodhisatta was born as Sakka. At that time, a wolf lived near the bank of the Gangā. One Uposatha day, as he lay on a massive rock very near the water's edge, the water suddenly rose in a flash flood, completely surrounding the rock. At first, the wolf panicked to find himself stranded, but then he thought. "Well, here I am with no food and with no way to get any. I may as well observe Uposatha." He sat down and made as if to meditate.

When Sakka heard the wolf's thought, he decided to test the beast's resolve. He took the form of a wild goat and appeared on the rock.

As soon as the wolf saw the goat, he thought, "Well, well, well! I'll keep the fast another day!" He leaped at the goat and tried to catch him, but Sakka evaded him and ran to the other side of the rock. Thwarted by the goat's agility, the wolf lay down again and thought, "Well, I didn't break my fast, so I will continue meditating."

Sakka then assumed his own form, hovered in the air, and proclaimed, "What can fasting mean to one like you? At the earliest opportunity, you were ready to break your fast. Your desire for goat's flesh was much stronger than your pretense of meditation!" Then Sakka returned to Tāvatimsa.

Having concluded his story, the Buddha identified the birth: "At that time, I was Sakka."

111
Over-Confidence
Culla-Kālinga Jātaka

It was while staying at Jetavana that the Buddha told this story about the higher ordination of four female ascetics as bhikkhunīs. The ruling families of Vesāli, the Licchavis, numbering seven thousand seven hundred and seven, were well known for their appreciation of oratory and disputation. Once, two Jain ascetics, one male and the other female, arrived separately in Vesāli. Both were extremely skilled in argumentation. The Licchavi princes were delighted to have these two visit their city at the same time and for them to argue. The lively public debate was well-attended and exciting, but, because the two ascetics were perfectly matched, it ended in a tie. Then the Licchavis had the notion that these two ascetics would produce clever children, so they arranged their marriage. The couple settled down in Vesāli and had five children—four daughters, Saccā, Lolā, Avavādakā, and Patā-carā, and a son, Saccaka. By the time these children grew up, they had each mastered one thousand theses, five hundred from their mother and another five hundred from their father. The couple instructed their daughters, "If a layman defeats you in debate, you should marry him, but, if another ascetic defeats you, join his order."

After the couple died, Saccaka stayed in Vesāli, but his sisters wandered from city to city, seeking debates. When they reached Sāvatthī, they planted their jambu branch in a pile of dirt by the city gate. "If anyone thinks he is equal to debating us," they told some boys playing nearby, "he should trample this branch and scatter this dust." Then they went into the city for alms.

That morning, Venerable Sāriputta, after first sweeping the monastery, refilling the water pots, and tending the sick, also went into Sāvatthī to collect alms. When he saw the branch, he asked the boys what it meant, and they repeated what the four women ascetics had said. He ordered the boys to knock the branch down and to trample on it. "Tell those who left this bough to come and see me at Jetavana when they have finished their meal," he said.

When the women returned, they were delighted to find the branch trampled on. Learning from the boys that Venerable Sāriputta had done it, they set out for Jetavana, eager for a debate. Accompanied by a large crowd, the four ascetics found Venerable Sāriputta waiting for them. Confidently, they proposed their one thousand theses, but Sāriputta successfully refuted all of them and asked if they had any more.

"No, Venerable Sir," they answered.

"All right," he said. "Let me ask you something."

"Ask, sir. If we know it, we will answer you."

"What is the one?" he asked.

None of the four ascetics could answer. They asked him for the answer, and he replied. "All beings subsist on nutriment."[1]

Confounded by this single question, the four admitted defeat and paid their respects to Venerable Sāriputta.

"What will you do now?" he asked.

"Before our parents died," they replied, "they told us, 'If a layman defeats you in debate, you should marry him, but if another ascetic defeats you, join his order.' Venerable Sir, please accept us into your order."

Venerable Sāriputta readily agreed and had them ordained as bhikkhunīs under Venerable Uppalavannā. They studied with Venerable Sāriputta, and all four of them soon attained arahatship.

One day, some bhikkhus were discussing how Venerable Sāriputta had brought the four female ascetics into the order and how, because of him, they had become arahats. When the Buddha heard the subject of their talk, he said, "This is not the first time that Sāriputta has proved a refuge to these women. This time, he brought them into the Sangha, but, long ago, he raised them to the dignity of queens." At the bhikkhus' request, the Buddha told this story of the past.

Long, long ago, when King Kālinga was reigning in Dantapura, he was as strong as an elephant and had a fine army, but he was not contented. He

---

1 This is also the first of ten questions in the Sāmanerapañhā (Questions to a Sāmanera) in the Khuddakapātha, which the Buddha asked the seven-year old novice, Sopāka.

was frustrated because he wanted to wage war, but he could find no one willing to fight with him.

When he told his ministers of his frustration, they replied, "Sire, you have four extraordinarily beautiful daughters. Have them put on their finest clothes, adorn themselves with their most precious jewels, and sit in a splendid carriage. Send this carriage with an armed escort to every other royal city, announcing that any king who wishes to marry your daughters must fight you."

The king did exactly as his ministers suggested, but, out of fear of King Kālinga, no king would allow the carriage to enter his capital. As the carriage was approaching, each king sent precious gifts to the princesses and directed them to the next kingdom. The carriage traversed the length and breadth of Jambudīpa, finally reaching Potali, the capital of Assaka.

King Assaka also ordered the city gates closed and sent gifts to the princesses. However, the king had an extremely wise minister named Nandisena, who thought, "If these princesses can travel throughout this continent without finding anyone willing to fight for them, Jambudīpa is but an empty name. I myself will do battle with Kālinga."

Before the carriage had turned to leave, Nandisena ordered the guards to open the city gate and to escort the princesses to the palace. "Have no fear," he said to King Assaka. "Marry these fair princesses. If there is to be a war, I will take care of everything." Thus, the four princesses were sprinkled with lustral water and installed as queen-consorts. Their attendants were dismissed with instructions to tell King Kālinga that his daughters had been raised to the dignity of queens.

When King Kālinga heard this, he declared, "King Assaka does not know how powerful I am!" and immediately set out with a great army. Hearing of the army's approach, Nandisena sent a message in the name of King Assaka: "Let Kālinga stay on his side of the border and not encroach upon my territory. Let the battle be fought on the frontiers of the two countries." King Kālinga halted at the border and prepared for combat. Nandisena sent King Assaka's army to the border as well.

In the border region between the two kingdoms, there lived an ascetic. While he was waiting for the battle to begin, King Kālinga, in disguise, paid a visit to the ascetic. He sat respectfully on one side and, after polite greetings, said, "Venerable Sir, Kālinga's and Assaka's forces are drawn up on the border, prepared for war. Can you tell me which will be victorious and which will be defeated?"

"Your Majesty," the ascetic replied, "one will conquer and the other will be beaten. I can tell you no more. Tonight, however, Sakka is going to come here, and I will ask him. If you come back tomorrow, I will let you know what he says."

That night, Sakka did, indeed, come to pay his respects, and the ascetic asked him what the outcome of the battle would be. Sakka answered, "Kālinga will conquer, and Assaka will be defeated." In addition, he told the ascetic what omens would appear to determine the battle.

The next day, when King Kālinga returned, the ascetic repeated, "Kālinga will conquer, and Assaka will be defeated." Satisfied that he would be victorious, King Kālinga left without asking about the omens.

The news of this prediction spread rapidly. When King Assaka heard it, he called Nandisena and asked what they should do.

"Sire, no one knows for certain who will win and who will lose," Nandisena replied, trying to comfort the king. "Please do not worry. I will manage everything for you."

Nandisena also visited the ascetic and paid his respects. Sitting respectfully on one side, he asked, "Reverend Sir, who will conquer, and who will be defeated?"

"Kālinga will conquer," the ascetic repeated, "and Assaka will be defeated."

"Will there be any omens to determine the outcome of this battle?" Nandisena asked.

"Yes," the ascetic replied, "the guardian deva of Kālinga will be a pure white bull, and that of King Assaka will be a pitch black bull. The two devas will themselves fight. One will be victorious, and the other will be defeated."

On hearing this, Nandisena thanked the ascetic, stood up, and hurried back to King Assaka's camp. He gathered the king's warriors, totaling one thousand great soldiers, and led them to the top of a nearby mountain. "Would you give your lives for our king?" he asked them.

"Yes, sir, we would!" they answered in unison.

"In that case," Nandisena commanded, "throw yourselves from this precipice!"

Without any hesitation, all of them stepped toward the edge. Before any of them could jump to his death, however, Nandisena shouted, "Stop! You have proved your loyalty to our king. It is better that you show your support by fighting gallantly for him." Promising to do their best, the men marched back to camp.

As the battle was about to begin, King Kālinga was confident of victory. His army was also confident; so much so, in fact, that many of the soldiers felt that they did not even need to make an effort.

The two kings, both mounted on fine horses, approached each other to fight. At the same time, their guardian devas, Kālinga's white bull and Assaka's black bull, began pawing the earth between the two armies, preparing to charge. The two devas were visible only to the two kings.

"Your Majesty," Nandisena asked King Assaka, "can you see the guardian devas?"

"Yes," the king answered, "I can."

"What do you see?" Nandisena asked.

"Kālinga's is a white bull, and ours is black, but he looks distressed."

"Fear not, Sire!" Nandisena encouraged him. "We will defeat Kālinga. You must dismount and slap your horse on the flank to send him away. Then, with your spear in your right hand, lead your men forward. When you are close enough, thrust your spear directly at the white bull. When we see you throw your spear, even though we cannot see the bull, we will throw our spears at the same spot. In this way, Kālinga's guardian deva will perish, and we will be victorious."

"Excellent!" cried the king. Following Nandisena's instructions, he dismounted and sent his horse away. Walking steadily forward, he approached the two bulls and threw his spear at the heart of the white bull. At a signal from Nandisena, the one thousand warriors, following the king's lead, also thrust their spears at that spot. Every one of them pierced the guardian deva of King Kālinga, and the white bull fell dead.

Terrified at this unforeseen outcome, King Kālinga turned and ordered a retreat. He and his army fled as fast as they could. From King Assaka's army a great cry arose, "Kālinga is fleeing!" The soldiers were overjoyed that they had routed the enemy without taking a single human life.

When he felt he was safe and out of harm's way, King Kālinga went to the ascetic's hut. "So much for your wretched prophecy!" the king berated the ascetic. "Aren't you ashamed to have told such a lie?" The ascetic could not answer.

The next time that Sakka paid another visit to him, the ascetic asked how it was possible that the prediction had been wrong.

Without hesitation, Sakka replied, "Devas never begrudge victory to one who is determined. One who shows sufficient courage and strength can overturn even what the devas predict. If Kālinga had used all his resources, he would have won the fight."

King Assaka returned to Potali with all the booty abandoned in Kālinga's retreat. Nandisena sent a stern message to Kālinga, demanding that the king send a dowry for his four daughters. "Otherwise," he added, "I will know how to deal with you."

King Kālinga gladly sent extremely generous dowries, and, from that day onward, the two kings lived in harmony.

Having concluded his story, the Buddha identified the birth: "At that time, these four bhikkhunīs were King Kālinga's daughters, Sāriputta was Nandisena, and I was the ascetic."

112
The Great Horseman
Mahā-Assāroha Jātaka

It was while staying at Jetavana that the Buddha told this story about friendship.

Long, long ago, the Bodhisatta was king of Kāsi. He ruled with justice, gave generous alms, and observed the five precepts.

There was a disturbance on the frontier, and the king led his large army to quell it. One night, the king and some of his men were caught in an ambush and forced to scatter. The king, finding himself alone and lost, rode his horse until he came to a border village early the next morning. There were many men in the streets and in the market, but, when they saw the horseman clad in armor, they were terrified and ran to their homes.

One man, however, stepped forward. "Welcome, my good man," he said to the king. "Are you a royalist or a rebel?"

"Kind sir," the horseman replied, "I am for the king."

"Then come with me," the man said, leading the king to his own house. He gave his guest his own seat and said to his wife, "My dear, bathe our friend's feet and serve him my meal." He also had his wife prepare a bed and, as soon as the king had finished eating, urged him to rest. While the exhausted king slept, the man unsaddled the spent horse, fed and watered

71

him, and rubbed him down with oil. Never imagining who his guest was, the man looked after the king for several days.

"Friend, I must now be off," the king announced when he was thoroughly restored. While the man was saddling the horse, the king continued, "I am called Mahā-Assāroha, the Great Horseman. My house is in the center of Bārānasi. Should you ever come to the capital on business, go to the door on the right of the city gate and ask the porter for Mahā-Assāroha. He will show you to my house." Then the king rode away.

Meanwhile, the army had returned to Bārānasi, but, not knowing where the king was, regrouped outside the city. As the king approached the encampment outside the walls, a cry of joy went up from the army. Officers hurried to greet him and to escort him into the city. As they passed through the gate, the king called the porter and whispered to him, "My good man, in a few days, a man from a border village will come here, and he will ask for Mahā-Assāroha. Bring him immediately to the palace, and you will receive one thousand coins as a reward."

Time went by, but the man failed to come. The king increased the taxes on that village, but still he did not come. The king raised that village's rates a second time and a third time, but even this did not bring the man to Bārānasi.

One day, the villagers gathered in front of the man's house and complained loudly, "Ever since the day that you befriended that soldier, we have been so burdened with taxes that we can't lift our heads. Go to Bārānasi! Ask your friend Mahā-Assāroha to intercede with the king to show us mercy!"

"All right," the man answered, "I will go, but I can't go empty-handed. Our friend mentioned that he had two sons. I must take presents for my friend, for his wife, and for his sons."

The villagers prepared clothes, and his wife fried a cake. With these gifts, he left for Bārānasi.

As soon as he arrived at the city, he went to the door on the right of the gate and asked for Mahā-Assāroha. "Come with me," replied the porter. "I will show you."

When the courtiers announced that the porter had brought the man from the border village, the king got up from his seat. As soon the king saw his friend, he embraced him, and asked about his wife and children. Then the king led the astonished villager to the dais and seated him on the throne beneath the white umbrella.

The king summoned the queen and said, "Wash my friend's feet." While she washed the man's feet, the king sprinkled him with water from a golden bowl and anointed him with scented oil.

"Have you brought anything to eat?" the king asked.

"Yes, Your Majesty," the man replied as he pulled the cake from his bag. "My wife fried this for you."

The king had the cake placed on a golden dish. "Let us eat what my friend has brought," he announced as he took some himself and passed the dish to the queen and the courtiers.

When the man offered the other gifts, the king immediately took off his silk robes and instructed his wife and sons to do the same. Wearing the ordinary clothes from the village, he served a royal meal to his friend and ordered that the villager's beard be trimmed in the fashion of the court. Then the king ordered his servants to bathe his guest in scented water and to dress him in a silk robe worth one hundred thousand coins.

When all this was completed, the king placed a thread of pure vermilion across the center of the royal white umbrella, testifying that he was giving this man half of his kingdom. The king sent for the man's wife and family and had a grand house built for them near the palace. From that day on, they became inseparable friends, sharing everything equally, and eating and drinking together. In fact, they ruled the kingdom in perfect harmony.

The courtiers were resentful of the king's behavior and complained to the crown prince, "Your Highness, we cannot tolerate what your father is doing. He has given half of his kingdom to this stranger. He eats and drinks with him, and he orders us to salute this man's children. We have no idea who he is, where he comes from, or why the king favors him so much. It is impossible for us to say anything to the king. Please talk to your father for us. Find out what this means."

The crown prince approached his father and told him what the courtiers had said. "For everyone's sake, Father," he pleaded, "stop this nonsense! It is not worthy of you!"

"My son," the king replied, "do you remember that some time ago, I was defeated in battle?"

"Yes, Father."

"At that time, I was gone for a few days. Do you have any idea where I was?

"No, Father. I don't."

"I was in a small village on the border. I was almost dead, but this man took care of me. I stayed in his house until I regained my strength. If he had not cared for me, I would have perished. Thanks to him, I was able to return and to regain the throne. How can I not now honor him, my great benefactor?"

"My son," the king continued, "if a man gives gifts to those who are unworthy, but gives nothing to the deserving, when that man is in trouble, he will find no one to help him! Gifts given to the undeserving are given in vain, but even the smallest service to a good man is to your gain. Pay respect to a fool, and you will make no friend, for a fool cannot understand friendship. Show kindness to the wise, and you'll have help when you need it. This man's noble action deserves a throne!"

When the prince reported to the courtiers what his father had so eloquently explained to him, they paid their respects to both the king and his friend, and they complained no more.

Having concluded his story, the Buddha identified the birth: "At that time, Ānanda was the man from the border village, and I was the king."

113

In Complete Secrecy
Sīlavīmaṃsana Jātaka

It was while staying at Jetavana that the Buddha told this story about controlling the defilements.[1]

One night, five hundred bhikkhus, who had ordained together, were harboring sensuous thoughts and decided to return to lay life. To protect them, the Buddha asked Venerable Ānanda to summon all the bhikkhus in Jetavana. After they had gathered, the Buddha said, "Bhikkhus, in former times, a wise man, understanding that wrongdoing can never be kept secret, refrained from it." Then he told this story of the past.

Long, long ago, when Brahmadatta was reigning in Bārāṇasi, the Bodhisatta was born into a brahmin family. When he was old enough, he was sent to study under a renowned teacher, who had five hundred students.

This teacher had a lovely daughter who had just come of age, and the teacher wanted to find a suitable husband for her. "Let me test my bright young students," he thought, "and offer my daughter to the best."

One day, he assembled all the students and announced, "Lads, as you know, I have a grown-up daughter, whom I intend to give in marriage. First,

---

1   The occasion for this story is told in detail in Tale 60.

however, I must have the proper dresses and ornaments for her. I want you to steal these things for me. Anything of value will do, but—and this is most important—it must have been stolen in complete secrecy. If anyone saw you take the thing, I will not accept it. Bring what you steal to me and tell me the details, but make sure that no one else knows you took it."

The students agreed to the conditions and accepted the challenge, believing that success would win them the prize of marriage. At all hours of night and day, they stealthily sneaked around the city furtively stealing dresses, jewels, and other treasures. In secret, they took these items one by one to the teacher who catalogued them carefully under each student's name.

When his storeroom was full, the teacher summoned all his students. He pointed to one student and said, "You alone brought me nothing."

"That is true, Master," the student replied.

"Why is that?" the teacher asked accusingly.

"Master," he replied calmly, "you told us that we had to steal each item in complete secrecy. I believe that there can be no secrecy in wrongdoing. No act of wickedness can be perfectly hidden. The fool may think it is secret, but, at the very least, the devas of the woods will have seen it done!"

Extremely pleased to hear these words, the teacher exclaimed, "Young man, I am a prosperous man of more than ample means. I have no need of these things for my daughter's trousseau. What I was hoping to find was a virtuous man for her to marry. This exercise was a test for all of you, and, obviously, you alone are worthy of her hand!

"As for the rest of you," he said to the other four hundred ninety-nine students, "please retrieve from my storeroom everything you stole and return it to its proper owner."

Shortly thereafter, the teacher had his daughter dressed in robes of the finest silk and gave her in marriage to the honest student.

"Thus, Bhikkhus," the Buddha said in conclusion, "the foolish students, because of their dishonesty, lost the prize they sought, while that wise youth, by his virtuous conduct, won the lovely young woman for his wife."

Having concluded his story, the Buddha taught the Dhamma, and the five hundred bhikkhus attained arahatship. Then Buddha identified the birth: "At that time, Sāriputta was the teacher, and I was the wise and honest youth."

114
A Fruit Seller's Daughter
Sujāta Jātaka

It was while staying at Jetavana that the Buddha told this story about Queen Mallikā.

One day, there was a quarrel between King Pasenadi and Queen Mallikā. The king was so enraged with the queen that he completely ignored her existence.

The Buddha knew all about this quarrel and resolved to make peace between the two.

Early in the morning, he entered Sāvatthī for alms with a following of five hundred bhikkhus and stood at the palace gate. The king took the Buddha's bowl and led the entire party into the dining hall. The king had his servants bring the rice and cakes, but, as he started pouring the Water of Donation, the Buddha put his hand over the vessel and asked, "Sire, where is the queen?"

"What do you have to do with her, Venerable Sir?" the king asked in return. "Her head is turned. She has become intoxicated with the honor she enjoys."

"Sire," the Buddha replied, "since you yourself bestowed this honor on her and elevated her to this rank, it is wrong for you to be so upset that she enjoys it. Rather than cast her aside, you must put up with the small offense that you feel she has committed against you."

The king hearkened to the words of the Teacher and sent for the queen. As soon as she came, she and the king together served the Buddha and the bhikkhus.

After the meal, the Buddha offered anumodana and advised the royal couple, "It is good for husband and wife to live together in peace." Indeed, from that day onward, Pasenadi and Mallikā lived happily together.

Some time later, in the Hall of Truth, the bhikkhus were talking about how the Buddha had reconciled the king and queen with only a few words. When the Buddha heard what they were discussing, he said, "Not now only, Bhikkhus, but, long ago, too, I reconciled them with a few words of admonition." Then he told this story of the past.

Long, long ago, when Brahmadatta was reigning in Bārānasi, the Bodhisatta was his chief advisor.

One day, as the king was standing at an open window overlooking the courtyard, he saw a beautiful young woman with a basket of dates on her head. Not daring to venture into the palace, she stood in the street, crying, "Dates! Delicious, ripe, juicy dates! Who'll buy my dates?"

The king was so overcome by her fresh beauty and her sweet voice that he immediately ordered his courtiers to find out who she was. They reported that her name was Sujātā, that she was the daughter of a fruit seller, and that she was not married. The king sent for Sujātā and made her his chief queen. The king loved her dearly and bestowed great honor upon her.

One afternoon, while the king was eating dates from a golden dish, Sujātā entered the room. "My Lord," she asked, "what are you eating? This is such an interesting fruit!" she exclaimed, picking up one of the dates. "It is so pretty and so red! I wonder where it grows."

When the king heard this, he became very angry. "Daughter of a fruit merchant!" he cried. "Do you not recognize this fruit? These dates are a specialty of your own family. You should be ashamed of yourself! Bare-headed and roughly clad, you once peddled these fruits yourself. Now that you have become queen, you dare to ask the fruit's name! Have you completely forgotten who you are and what you once were, or are you just putting on airs? You are much too proud to be my wife! Begone!"

The advisor heard this and thought, "I must appease the king's anger and prevent him from sending the queen away. He won't listen to anyone else." As soon as the queen had withdrawn, the advisor said softly, "Your Majesty, it was you who transformed this woman from a fruit seller into a queen. This behavior is natural for a woman who is suddenly promoted to such a high position. You must take some responsibility for what you yourself have done. Quench your anger, Sire, and forgive her for this simple fault!"

The king understood the wisdom of his advisor's words and summoned Sujātā. He apologized for his harsh words, restored her to her position as queen, and resolved to overlook the pride she had seemingly developed. They spent the rest of their lives in peace and harmony.

Having concluded his story, the Buddha identified the birth: "At that time, Pasenadi was King Brahmadatta, Mallikā was Queen Sujātā, and I was the royal advisor."

115

The Woodpecker and the Lion
Javasakuna Jātaka

It was while staying at Jetavana that the Buddha told this story about Devadatta's lack of gratitude.

"Not only now is Devadatta ungrateful," Buddha said. "Long ago he was the same." Then he told this story of the past.

Long, long ago, when Brahmadatta was reigning in Bārānasi, the Bodhisatta was born as a woodpecker in the Himavat.

One day, while devouring his prey, a lion got a bone stuck in his throat which made his throat swell so much that he couldn't swallow. He was in severe pain.

From his perch on a large tree, the woodpecker noticed the lion's distress and asked, "Friend, what ails you?"

In a strained voice, the lion told him what was the matter. "I could easily take the bone out of your throat, Friend," the woodpecker replied, "but I don't dare put my head into your mouth."

"Don't be afraid, Friend. Please save my life! I promise not to harm you."

"All right," said the woodpecker. He told the lion to lie down on his side. As he was about to put his head inside the beast's open mouth, the woodpecker thought, "Who knows what this fellow might try!" He found a strong stick and placed it between the lion's upper and lower jaws. Then, certain that the lion could not try to eat him, he put his head into the lion's great mouth. He quickly found the bone, latched onto it with his strong beak, dislodged it from the lion's throat, and let it drop harmlessly on the ground. Once the woodpecker had withdrawn his head from the lion's mouth, he gave the stick a blow with his beak so that it fell out, and he flew back to his tree.

A few days later, the woodpecker noticed that the lion, having fully recovered, was devouring a wild buffalo which he had killed. "Now is a good time to put him to the test," the woodpecker thought. He flew to a tree near the lion and perched just above his head.

"Friend," he said to the lion, "recently, I did you a great kindness, as great a favor as a bird such as I could do. I wonder whether, in return, you would grant me a trifling boon."

"You trusted your head to my mighty jaws, and you are still alive," replied the lion. "That's quite enough of a favor from me to you!"

Seeing the lion's true character, the woodpecker calmly replied, "From such a thankless wretch, I should never have hoped for any gratitude for my good deed. Still, it does no good to give in to bitter thoughts or to reply with angry words. I'm happy that I don't have to keep company with this ingrate in the future." With neither hatred nor regret, the woodpecker flew away.

Having concluded his story, the Buddha identified the birth: "At that time, Devadatta was the lion, and I was the woodpecker."

116
High Seat, Low Seat
Chavaka Jātaka

It was while staying at Jetavana that the Buddha told this story about the Gang of Six.

Once the Buddha sent for these bhikkhus and asked whether it was true that they taught the Dhamma from a low seat while their students sat on a higher seat. They confessed that it was so, and the Buddha scolded them for their lack of respect for the Dhamma. "Long ago," he added, "a teacher was rightly rebuked by the wise for teaching even inferior doctrines while sitting on a low seat." Then he told this story of the past.

Long, long ago, when Brahmadatta was reigning in Bārānasi, the Bodhisatta was born as a candāla, an outcaste. When he grew up, he got married and set up his own household. When his wife became pregnant, she had a great longing for ripe mangoes, and asked him to get her some.

"My dear," he replied, "this is not the season for mangoes. Would you like me to bring you some other acidic fruit?"

"No," she replied, "I must have a mango. If you do not get one for me, I will die."

The poor man loved his wife very much, but he did not know what to do. "Where in the world am I going to find a mango for her?" he moaned. Suddenly, he remembered that he had heard that in the king's garden there was one mango tree which had fruit on it all year round. The only way to relieve his wife's craving was to fetch a ripe mango from that tree.

That night, he quietly scaled the wall and climbed the tree. Moving stealthily from branch to branch, he searched for a ripe fruit. While he was still searching, day began to break.

"If I climb down now," he thought, "the guards will see me. I'll be arrested as a thief and thrown into prison. I'd better wait until dark, so I can get away." He climbed higher and, hidden by the thick leaves, settled into a fork of the tree.

A little later, the king and a brahmin priest entered the garden and walked straight toward the mango tree. Unaware that there was a man in the branches, the king sat on a splendid couch at the foot of the tree. The brahmin sat on a lower seat and began reciting sacred texts.

"How wicked this king is!" thought the candāla as he watched and listened from his perch high above. "There he is, sitting on a high seat and studying sacred texts. His teacher is just as wicked, sitting on a lower seat and teaching him. But who am I to talk? I am just as wicked as they are, for I have fallen under the influence of a selfish woman. Here I am, acting like a thief and risking my life to steal a mango for her!"

He grabbed hold of a strong branch and swung himself down, landing on the ground right beside the king and the brahmin. He stood up and said, "Your Majesty, I know that I am as good as dead, but you are a fool, and this priest is damning himself."

"What do you mean by insulting my teacher and me in this way?!" the king demanded.

"Both of you, teacher and royal scholar, have sinned against the holy law!" the candāla exclaimed. "We respect Your Majesty, and look up to you, but, when you listen to the sacred texts, you should be sitting lower than your teacher, and he who is reciting the texts must know that it is forbidden to do so from an inferior seat."

"My food is fragrant rice from the hills," the brahmin intoned smugly. "It has the delicate flavor of meat. I make a good living, so why should I be fussy about rules intended for saints?"

"Brahmin, your sin makes your little learning useless," the candāla insisted. "Your greed is a disgrace to the very texts you teach, and it will take you straight to hell!"

The king was pleased with this young man's exposition of the law. "Who are you, anyway, and what are you doing in my garden?"

The man bowed to the king and replied, "Your Majesty, I am a caṇḍāla. I secretly climbed your tree hoping to steal a ripe mango to appease my wife's craving."

"Friend," the king said, extending his hand to the astonished man, "if you had been from a family of the warrior caste, I would have made you king in my place, but let it be known that, from now on, I will rule by day, and you shall have power at night." The king removed a garland from his own neck and placed it around the neck of the caṇḍāla. "I hereby appoint you Protector of the City!" he proclaimed. This was the origin of the custom for the Protector of the City to wear a garland of red flowers. The king never forgot the caṇḍāla's wise admonition, and, thereafter, whenever he listened to the sacred texts, he showed his respect for the law by sitting on a lower seat.

Having concluded his story, the Buddha identified the birth: "At that time, Ānanda was the king, and I was the caṇḍāla."

117
Putting up with Youth
Kassapamandiya Jātaka

It was while staying at Jetavana that the Buddha told this story about an elderly bhikkhu.

A young nobleman of Sāvatthī had ordained under the Buddha and, not long afterwards, had become an arahat. After the death of his mother, he admitted his father and younger brother to the Sangha, as a bhikkhu and a sāmanera respectively, and they all stayed at Jetavana.

During the rains retreat, they stayed at a small village monastery. At the end of the rainy season, the three decided to return to Jetavana. They traveled together most of the way, but it was difficult for the father to walk quickly, so they progressed very slowly. A little before sunset, the young bhikkhu instructed his brother, the sāmanera, to continue with their father, and he hurried ahead to prepare their kutis. The sāmanera tried to speed up his father, pulling him and prodding him with his head, but the old bhikkhu refused to be rushed. At one point, he even walked back to the village and had to be goaded to set out again. While the two were quarreling, the sun went down, and darkness set in.

The young bhikkhu finished cleaning and setting out the water pots and wondered why the two had not arrived, so he took a torch and went to look for them.

By the time he got them settled at Jetavana, it was too late to pay his respects to the Buddha. The next day, when the young bhikkhu went to the Buddha, the Teacher asked him when he had arrived.

"Yesterday, Venerable Sir."

"You came yesterday, and yet you pay your respects to me only today?"

"Yes, Venerable Sir," and he explained how much trouble he and his brother had had with their father.

"This is not the first time he has acted in this way. Now it is you that are annoyed by him. It was another wise man that he annoyed long ago." At the bhikkhu's request, the Buddha told this story of the past.

Long, long ago, when Brahmadatta was reigning in Bārānasi, the Bodhisatta was born into a brahmin family and grew up in a town in Kāsi. When his mother died, he performed the funeral rites, and, at the end of the six-week period of mourning, he gave away all the money that was in the house. Wishing to live as an ascetic, he put on bark garments, and, taking his father and younger brother with him, he went to the Himavat, where the three of them lived on roots and wild fruit.

During the months when the rain was incessant in the Himavat, it was impossible to dig up roots or to gather fruit, so, like most ascetics living in that region, they came down and stayed with villagers. At the end of the rainy season, the young ascetic began the trek back to the Himavat with his father and brother. As the sun was going down, they were not far from the hut, so he said, "You can come on slowly. I will go ahead and get the hermitage in order."

The younger brother pulled his father by the arm along the path and butted him with his head to make him go forward, but the old man protested. "I do not like the way you are taking me home!" he cried. He turned around and walked all the way back to the village and started over again.

The young ascetic took a torch and set out to find them. After he had brought them safely to the hermitage, he gave his father a bath and made him comfortable. "Father," he said, as he gently massaged the old man's feet, "young boys are just like earthen vessels and can be broken in a moment. Once broken, they cannot be mended again! When youth become abusive, older folk should bear with them patiently! Forbearance is wiser than foolish reaction." The old man accepted his son's admonishment and began practicing self-restraint.

Having concluded his story, the Buddha identified the birth: "At that time, the old bhikkhu was the elderly father, the sāmanera was the younger brother, and I was the young ascetic who admonished his father."

118
The Doctrine of Patience
Khantivādī Jātaka

It was while staying at Jetavana that the Buddha told this story about a hot-tempered bhikkhu.

When the Buddha learned that a certain bhikkhu often lost his temper, he summoned that bhikkhu and asked, "How is that you, who have been ordained under a teacher who is incapable of any form of wrath, continue to exhibit such displays of anger? Long ago, after suffering one thousand blows and even mutilation of his entire body, the wise showed no anger toward another." Then the Buddha told this story of the past.

Long, long ago, when a king named Kalābu was reigning in Bārānasi, the Bodhisatta was born into an extremely wealthy brahmin family, and his name was Kundaraka. After completing his education in Takkasilā, he returned to Bārānasi and entered his father's business.

When his parents died, he reviewed the family wealth and treasures and reflected, "My kinsmen who amassed all this treasure are all gone. Now it is my turn to take responsibility for it and then to die. What does this accomplish?"

He carefully chose several virtuous people, who, because of their alms-giving, were deserving, and divided all his wealth among them. Taking the name of Khantivādi, he left Bārānasi and went to the Himavat to live as an ascetic. For a long time, he survived on wild fruit and practiced meditation by developing the Four Brahma Vihāras.

Once, at the beginning of the rainy season, Khantivādi left to get salt and vinegar and to find a place to stay. He arrived in Bārānasi and spent the night in the royal park. The next morning, on his almsrounds in the city, he arrived at the house of the commander-in-chief, who was very pleased with his deportment. The commander-in-chief took his bowl and offered him the food from his own table. Then he invited the ascetic to take up residence in the royal park and arranged for him to stay there.

One day, when King Kalābu had had too much to drink in the palace, he announced that he wanted to continue partying outdoors. He led a noisy procession of musicians, singers, dancers, and court women to the royal park. On the great stone dais in the center of the park he had a special couch spread for himself and sat down to enjoy the revelry, which was, he felt, comparable to that of Tāvatimsa. He thoroughly enjoyed all the entertainment, and, at last, fell asleep with his head on the lap of a favorite from the harem.

"Well," the women said to each other, "now that His Majesty is asleep, what is the point of our singing any more? He certainly isn't listening to us!" The musicians put down their instruments, and the women went off together to see the beautiful flowers and to enjoy themselves.

In their wandering, they happened upon the ascetic, who was sitting in meditation at the foot of a flowering sal tree. "Ladies," one of the women cried, "let us sit down and listen to something from this wise man until the king awakes."

The women greeted the ascetic, sat down around him, and said, "Sir, please tell us something worth hearing." With that invitation, the ascetic began preaching to them.

Meanwhile, the royal favorite shifted her body slightly, and her movement woke up the king. He sat up, and, surprised not to see anyone else, he shouted, "Where have those wretches gone?"

"Sire," the favorite answered, "they wandered off some time ago, and now they are sitting over there, listening to an ascetic."

The king grabbed his sword and angrily rushed off, shouting, "I'll give this false ascetic a lesson!"

Some of the women saw the king coming, hurried to him, relieved him of his sword, and tried to calm him down. He strode straight to the center of the group and stood beside the ascetic. "What doctrine do you preach, Ascetic?" he asked.

"I teach the doctrine of patience, Your Majesty," Khantivādi replied.

"What is this patience?"

"It is not being angry when someone abuses you, strikes you, and vilifies you."

"Very well," said the king. "Let me test the reality of your patience." He summoned the royal executioner, who quickly arrived wearing his yellow robe and a red garland. He was carrying a scourge of thorns and an axe, the implements of his office. He saluted the king and asked, "What is your pleasure, Sire?"

"Take this vile rogue of an ascetic!" ordered the king. "Throw him on the ground and give him two thousand lashes, front, back, and both sides!"

The executioner shoved the ascetic to the ground and began beating him. The thorns of the whip cut the skin on all parts of his body, and blood flowed from the thousands of wounds. The ascetic neither resisted nor cried out in pain.

"What doctrine do you preach now?" cried the king.

"I teach the doctrine of patience, Your Majesty," Khantivādi repeated. "You imagine that my patience is only skin deep. No, Sire, it is fixed deep within my heart, where it cannot be seen by one such as you."

"Executioner!" the king shouted.

"What is your pleasure, Sire?" the executioner asked.

"Cut off both hands and feet of this false ascetic."

The executioner lifted his mighty axe and chopped off Khantivādi's hands and feet.

Blood poured from his wrists and ankles like lac juice flowing out of a leaking jar. Still, he remained tranquil, showing no sign of emotion.

"What doctrine do you preach now?" cried the king.

"I teach the doctrine of patience, Your Majesty," he repeated calmly. "Did you suppose, Sire, that my patience dwelt in my hands and feet? No, Sire, it is fixed deep within my heart."

"Executioner!" the king shouted.

"What is your pleasure, Sire?" the executioner asked.

"Cut off his nose and ears."

The executioner used his axe again in obedience to the king. Khantivādi's mutilated face was covered with blood.

"What doctrine do you preach now?" cried the king.

"I teach the doctrine of patience, Your Majesty," he repeated. "Did you suppose, Sire, that my patience dwelt in my nose and ears? No, Sire, it is fixed deep within my heart."

"Begone, vile hypocrite! Preach your doctrine of patience no more in my park!" the king cried, as he gave Khantivādi a strong kick in the chest and departed.

As soon as the king was gone, the commander-in-chief gently wiped the blood from Khantivādi's maimed face and body and tried to stanch the bleeding by bandaging his wounds. Tenderly placing the ascetic on a seat, the commander-in-chief paid his respects to him. "Reverend Sir, if you must be angry with anyone, please let it be only with the king," he pleaded. "We take no part in this, great sage. Please spare our poor land!"

"Long live the king!" Khantivādi replied weakly. "Peace to him who has so cruelly injured this body of mine. I teach patience, and I practice patience. I feel no anger toward him for what he has done."

As the king was leaving the garden, he passed out of the ascetic's line of vision, and, at that moment, the earth opened up, and a mighty flame, rising all the way from hell, issued forth and enveloped the king. Wrapped around by that flame as if it were a macabre scarlet robe of royalty, the king sank into the earth and was reborn in Avīci hell.

That same day, Khantivādi died from his grievous injuries. The women of the palace, the king's servants, and many ordinary citizens honored his broken body with perfumes, garlands, and incense as they reverently performed his funeral rites. For many days, the only topic of discussion was the extraordinary patience that Khantivādi had displayed at the brutal sadism of the king. People marveled that he had endured such torture without a trace of anger. Everyone agreed that the king would surely remain in hell for a very long time to pay for his wickedness in killing such a noble being.

Having concluded his story, the Buddha taught the Dhamma. The hot-tempered bhikkhu attained the second path, and others attained the first path. Then the Buddha identified the birth: "At that time, Devadatta was Kalābu, king of Kāsi; Sāriputta was the commander-in-chief; and I was Khantivādi, the ascetic who taught patience."

119

The Four Cries from Hell
Lohakumbhi Jātaka

It was while staying at Jetavana that the Buddha told this story about King Pasenadi.[1]

One day, as King Pasenadi was leading a procession around Sāvatthī, he saw a beautiful woman and was suddenly smitten by desire. His desire increased even further when he learned that she had a husband. To get rid of her husband, the king ordered him to fetch clay and lotuses from a pond a yojana from the city and to return in time for his bath. To make sure that the man failed, the king had the city gates closed early. When the husband returned with the lotuses and clay, he found the gates closed and sought refuge at Jetavana, where, afraid for his life, he spent a sleepless night.

In the palace, because of his passion, the king also slept badly. Toward morning, he was awakened by dreadful sounds. He heard four very loud and plaintive cries. There were four different voices, but each one uttered only a single syllable: "Du!" "Sa!" "Na!" and "So!" These cries so terrified him that he could not go back to sleep. For several hours, he sat up shivering in his bed, frozen with fear and waiting for the dawn.

---

1   The occasion for this story is the same as that for Tale 160.

When morning finally came, the court brahmins entered his chamber and asked if he had enjoyed a good night's sleep. "How can you ask if I slept well?" the king retorted. "How could I have slept well, when I was frightened out of my wits in the middle of the night? At this point, I am surprised to be alive!"

"Your Majesty," the brahmins replied sympathetically, "whatever happened? Please tell us what troubles you!"

"Some hours ago," the king began, "when it was completely dark and utterly quiet, I heard four piercing screams. There were four different human voices, but each uttered only one horrifying syllable; "Du!" "Sa!" "Na!" and "So!" These voices were so full of menace that it was absolutely terrifying. After hearing them, I could not go back to sleep. I just sat here in my bed, trembling with fear. What were these terrible sounds?" the king asked.

The brahmins wrung their hands, looking very distressed. "What is it, sirs?" the king asked nervously. "Do these sounds mean anything?"

The brahmins looked at each other and shook their heads. "Tell me!" the king demanded, becoming terrified all over again. "Why did I hear these cries? What is going to happen?"

"Your Majesty," the brahmins replied, choosing their words carefully, "these sounds were inauspicious omens. They certainly portend great danger to the kingdom and violence to your royal person."

"Is there any remedy for this?" the king asked desperately. "Can we prevent this disaster in any way? Is there any hope for us?"

"There are those who would say that it was hopeless," they replied grimly, "but, fortunately for you, we are well-trained in such matters, Sire."

"What can be done to avert these evils?"

"Sire, there is only one way to prevent disaster. You must perform the fourfold sacrifice. Only by sacrificing four of every living creature can the evil be averted."

"All right!" shouted the king. "It must be done! Let us do it quickly! Prepare the men, elephants, bulls, horses, all the animals, and all the birds, down to the quail, for the sacrifice. You must restore my peace of mind and save both me and my kingdom!"

The priests immediately withdrew and began gloating among themselves over the feast they would soon enjoy and the wealth they would gain from this huge sacrifice. They ordered that a sacrificial pit be dug and that the numerous victims be tethered to stakes. The brahmins bustled back and forth, making demands, issuing orders, and making sure that everyone accepted the seriousness and the importance of the sacrifice.

Queen Mallikā heard the uproar and saw the brahmins smiling and looking smug, and she asked the king what was happening.

"My dear," the king replied, with more than a hint of reproach in his voice, "why should you care what the brahmins are doing or how they feel, when you haven't noticed my suffering. You must be intoxicated with your own glory, not to see that I have been absolutely wretched all morning!"

"My Lord," Mallikā said, sincerely concerned, "what is the problem? I had no idea that you were upset!"

"Last night," the king began, "I heard dreadful noises. I was terrified all night. This morning, I asked the brahmins what those ghastly cries meant, and they warned me that they threatened danger to my kingdom and my very life. The only way to avert this disaster is to perform the fourfold sacrifice, so they have dug the pit and have tethered the victims. Now they are preparing all the details, and we will very soon make the offerings. We have to do this quickly to restore my peace of mind. I simply cannot go on like this."

"My Lord, have you consulted the chief brahmin as to the origin of these cries?" asked the queen.

"Who, dear lady, do you mean by 'the chief brahmin'?"

"The great Gotama," she replied, "the Supreme Buddha."

"No," he admitted, "I have not informed the Buddha about this."

"Then go," she advised, "and consult with him immediately."

The king hearkened to the queen's words. As soon as he had finished his morning meal, he rode in his chariot to Jetavana. After paying his respects to the Buddha, he said, "Venerable Sir, in middle of the night, I heard four dreadful cries, "Du!" "Sa!" "Na!" and "So!" which terrified me so much that I could no longer sleep. This morning, I conferred with the court brahmins, and they told me that those sounds portend great danger, and that the only way to prevent this is to perform the fourfold sacrifice, which they are preparing at this moment. What do you say that hearing these cries augurs for me?"

"Nothing whatever, Sire." the Buddha said. "You heard the crying of four beings in hell. In their extreme agony, they were trying to tell you of their suffering, and they cried aloud. This has nothing to do with you and represents no danger to you or to your kingdom. Furthermore, Sire, you are not the first to have heard these cries. Long ago, they were heard by royalty, and, at that time, too, court brahmins were eager to slay victims for a sacrifice." At the king's request, the Buddha told this story of the past.

Long, long ago, when Brahmadatta was reigning in Bārānasi, he was terrified one night by the sound of four chilling cries. The next morning, he asked the court brahmins about them, and they told him that the sounds foretold that any one of three great dangers—to his kingdom, to his property, or to his life—would befall him unless he agreed to perform the fourfold sacrifice.

The chief advisor, one of those brahmins, prepared a sacrificial pit, collected a great crowd of victims, and tied them to stakes.

At this time, there was an ascetic in the Himavat who had developed extraordinary powers through the practice of jhānic meditation. From his hermitage, this ascetic surveyed the world with his divine eye and saw what was happening in Bārānasi. Guided by compassion, he resolved to prevent the sacrifice and to save the lives of all those helpless creatures. He immediately transported himself to the king's royal park, sat down on the stone seat, and waited.

As the chief advisor was bustling about the palace, arranging everything for the sacrifice, one of his young students approached him and asked, "Master, is it not written in the ancient texts that there is no happiness for those who take the life of another creature?"

"Hold your tongue!" the advisor hissed. "Just bring me the things I need! Soon we'll be feasting on the finest delicacies and the most delicious meat imaginable. Tomorrow we will be rich! Just keep your mouth shut, and do what you're told! Now, go!"

"I will take no part in this sacrifice!" the student declared to himself. "It is wrong!" He left the palace and went to the royal park, where he saw the ascetic, looking like a golden image. He approached the stone seat, saluted the ascetic in a friendly manner, and took a seat at a respectful distance.

"Young man," the ascetic asked, "does the king rule righteously?"

"Yes, Venerable Sir, he does," answered the student, "but, last night, he heard four cries, and the brahmins have convinced him that they must perform the fourfold sacrifice. The king is so upset that he is going ahead with the sacrifice, and a vast number of victims are already tethered near the sacrificial pit. I would hope that a holy man like you might explain the cause of these noises and save those victims from the jaws of death."

"Young man," the ascetic replied, "the king does not know me, nor do I know the king. I know the origin of these cries, however, and, if the king were to come and ask me, I would gladly resolve his doubts for him."

"Excellent, Venerable Sir. Please wait here, and I will bring the king."

The ascetic silently agreed, and the youth ran to the king's chamber. A few minutes later, he returned to the park with the king. The king saluted the ascetic, sat on one side, and asked him whether it was true that he knew the origin of those noises.

"Tell me exactly what you heard, Your Majesty," replied the ascetic.

"In the middle of the night," the king began, repeating what he had told the brahmins, "I heard four piercing screams. There were four different voices, but each uttered only one horrifying syllable; "Du!" "Sa!" "Na!" and "So!" The voices were full of menace. They were terrifying!"

"Sire," the ascetic said softly, "in their former lives, four men were guilty of gross misconduct with the wives of their neighbors near Bārānasi. Because of their wickedness, their lives were cut short, and they were reborn in hell in iron cauldrons, filled with a thick corrosive liquid and heated over blazing fires. For thirty thousand years, those beings were submerged in that burning liquid. Last night, they happened to rise to the surface like bubbles of foam. For the first time in all those years, each one peered over the edge of his cauldron. Each one tried to utter a complete sentence, a plea for help and a warning, but he had only enough time to utter a single syllable. After uttering the brief cry, he fell back into the corrosive liquid and sank again to the bottom.

"The one who cried, 'Du!' was trying to say, 'Due to lust and greed, my life on earth was short, and suffering here is long!'

"The one who cried, 'Sa!' was trying to say, 'Sour is my fate for what I did! When will I ever be released? The tortures of hell go on for countless eons!'

"The one who cried, 'Na!' was trying to say, 'Now I understand the suffering I brought upon myself! How long will it take to expiate my evil deeds?'

"The one who cried, 'So!' was trying to say, 'So heavy was my sin that I have suffered here so long! If ever once again I attain a human birth, I vow to practice virtue without fail!'

"Fear not, Your Majesty," the ascetic continued. "No harm will come to you because you heard their cries. On the contrary, you can accept them as auspicious messengers advising you to live righteously and to practice generosity."

With this wise explanation and the assurance that the cries foretold no evil, the king cancelled the sacrifice and declared that all the victims should be released and that the sacrificial pit should be filled in.

The ascetic remained for a few days in the royal park as the guest of the king. Then he returned to his hermitage in the Himavat. When he passed away, he was reborn in the Brahma heavens.

Having concluded his story, the Buddha said to King Pasenadi, "Sire, there is no danger at all to you from those sounds. Stop the sacrifice and spare these creatures' lives!" The king immediately did so.[1] Then the Buddha identified the birth: "At that time, Ānanda was King Brahmadatta, Sāriputta was the student, and I was the ascetic.

---

1   This story is also told in the Dhammapada Commentary to Verse 60 (Burlingame, volume 2, pp. 100-107). That version explains that the woman's husband was present when the Buddha told the story and that the king vowed that he would never seek another man's wife again. After concluding the story, the Buddha taught the verse:
Long is the night to the wakeful;
Long is the yojana to the weary;
Long is samsāra to the foolish
Who do not know the Sublime Truth.

120
What Your Words Deserve
Mamsa Jātaka

It was while staying at Jetavana that the Buddha told this story about Venerable Sāriputta providing suitable alms for sick bhikkhus.

Several bhikkhus had been given oil as a purgative and needed some mild food that would be gentle to the stomach. The bhikkhus who were caring for them had walked for alms the full length of the street in the cooks' quarter of Sāvatthī but had not received anything suitable.

Later that morning, when they explained their failure to Venerable Sāriputta, he said, "Come with me," and took them back to the same street. People readily filled his bowl with various bland delicacies. The bhikkhus gave the food to their patients, who were grateful and quickly recovered.

One day, in the Hall of Truth, the bhikkhus were talking about how Venerable Sāriputta was able to obtain the proper food when others had failed. When the Buddha heard what they were discussing, he said, "This is not the first time that Sāriputta obtained better food than others. Long ago, the wise who knew how to speak pleasantly also received generous gifts." Then the Buddha told this story of the past.

Long, long ago, when Brahmadatta was reigning in Bārānasi, the Bodhisatta was born as the son of a wealthy merchant. One day, he and three of his friends went for a stroll outside the city. When they came to a crossroads, they sat down to rest. While they were chatting pleasantly, one of them spotted a deer hunter with a cartload of venison he had butchered and dressed, on his way to the city to sell it.

"I think I'll go and see if that man will give me a piece of venison," the young man said. The others dared him to try, and he strode off. As he approached the man, he shouted, "Hey there, fellow! Give me a piece of meat."

"A man who begs from another ought to speak with a gentle voice. I'll give you something appropriate to your manner of speech!" the hunter replied, and he gave the young man a leg bone with skin but no meat.

When his companions asked him how he had addressed the man, he replied, "I said 'Hey there, fellow!'"

"Well, let me try!" said one of the others. He walked over to the hunter and said, "Elder brother, please give me a piece of venison."

"You will receive the meat that your words deserve," the hunter replied. "'Brother' implies a strong link of kinship, so I'll give you this meaty joint."

When his companions asked him how he had addressed the man, he replied, "I called him elder brother."

"Well, let me try!" said the third young man. He walked over to the hunter and said, "Father, would you please give me a piece of venison?"

"You will receive the meat that your words deserve," the hunter replied. "Since a parent's heart is moved by being called 'father,' I give you the heart of the deer."

When his companions asked him how he had addressed the man, he replied, "I called him father."

"Well, let me try!" said the fourth young man. He walked over to the hunter and said, "My friend, may I please have a piece of meat."

"You will receive the meat that your words deserve," the hunter replied. "A world without friends would be a wilderness. A friend is the greatest and most precious of all possessions, so I give you the whole deer. Let us take this cart full of meat to your house."

The young man took the hunter to his parents' house, and they unloaded the meat. In return, the young man sent for the hunter's wife and son, and settled them on his own estate, thus freeing the family from their cruel occupation. The two men became inseparable friends and spent the rest of their lives together.

Having concluded his story, the Buddha identified the birth: "At that time, Sāriputta was the hunter, and I was the merchant's son who received all the venison."

121
The Rabbit in the Moon
Sasa Jātaka

It was while staying at Jetavana that the Buddha told this story about a gift of all the requisites.

Once, a landowner in Sāvatthī invited the Buddha and all the bhikkhus to his house every day for a whole week. Every day, he seated them on elegant seats in a pavilion in front of his house and offered them a delicious meal. On the seventh day, he presented the Buddha and the five hundred bhikkhus with all the requisites. The Buddha said, "You have done well to give these gifts. This is a tradition of the wise. Once, a being even offered to sacrifice his life to give his own flesh to a beggar." At the request of his host, he told this story of the past.

Long, long ago, when Brahmadatta was reigning in Bārānasi, the Bodhisatta was born as a rabbit living in a forest. On one side of this forest was a mountain; on another side, a river; and on a third side, a village.

The rabbit had three friends, a monkey, a jackal, and an otter. These four good creatures lived together in harmony. Every day, each one got his food in his own way, and in the evening they gathered to talk together. The rabbit, being the wisest, regularly preached the Truth to his three companions. He taught that alms should be given, that the moral precepts should be scrupulously kept, and that the Uposatha days should be observed. The three listened carefully. Then each went to his own part of the forest to sleep.

One evening, the rabbit looked at the sky and realized that the next day was the full moon. "Tomorrow is the full moon," he said to his three companions. "Let all of us observe the Uposatha day and keep the precepts. Remember that alms-giving brings a great reward. Offer food from your own table to any beggars who come to you tomorrow." The friends agreed, and each went to his own home.

Early the next morning, the otter went to the bank of the Gangā to look for fish. It so happened that a fisherman had caught seven red fish, strung them together, and buried them in the wet sand before going downstream to fish some more.

Smelling the fish, the otter dug them up and called out three times, "Does anyone own these fish?" When no one answered, he took the fish in his teeth and carried them back to his den, intending to eat them at the proper time. Then he lay down, thinking how virtuous he was.

The jackal, too, went to look for food. In the empty hut of a field-watcher, he found a roasted lizard on a skewer and a pot of curd. He called out three times, "Does anyone own this food?" When no one answered, he claimed it as his own. He hung the pot of curd around his neck with its string, took the skewer with the lizard in his teeth, and carried everything back to his den, intending to eat it at the proper time. Then he lay down, thinking how virtuous he was.

The monkey went to a mango grove and gathered a number of ripe yellow mangoes. He carried them home, intending to eat them at the proper time. Then he, too, lay down, thinking how virtuous he was.

At the same time, the rabbit came out and began grazing on kusa grass as usual. While he was eating, he thought, "I cannot possibly offer grass to a wandering mendicant! I don't have any rice, oil, or anything else to give. If a beggar comes seeking food, I will have to give him my own flesh!"

As soon as this splendid idea came to the rabbit, Sakka's white marble throne became hot. Sakka realized that the reason for this was the rabbit's virtue, and he decided to test him.

First, though, Sakka thought it would be a good idea to test the other animals. He disguised himself as an old brahmin and stood outside the otter's den. When the otter asked why he was standing there, Sakka answered, "Wise sir, if I could get something to eat, I would perform my priestly duties."

The otter quickly said, "Very well, I will give you some food. I have seven red fish, honestly obtained. Eat your fill, Brahmin. You are welcome to stay in this forest."

The brahmin thanked him and said, "I may come back later."

Next, he went to the jackal's den. The jackal, also, quickly offered him some food, saying, "All I have is a lizard and a jar of curd that I took from the field-watcher's hut. Such as I have I will gladly give to you, and you are welcome to stay in this forest."

The brahmin thanked him and said, "I may come back later."

Then he went to the monkey's tree. The monkey, also, offered him some food. "I have cool water from the stream," he said, "ripe mangoes, and a pleasant place for you to enjoy them in. You are welcome to stay in this forest."

The brahmin thanked him and said, "I may come back later."

Finally, he went to rabbit's warren. The rabbit asked why he was standing there. "Wise sir," Sakka answered, "if I could get something to eat, I would perform my priestly duties."

The rabbit was thoroughly delighted and replied, "Brahmin, you have done well in coming to me for food. I have no rice, oil, or beans to give, but, today, I will give you a gift that I have never given before. I will give what is freely mine to give! Go, Friend, pile up some wood, and kindle a fire. When it is burning well, call me. I will gladly sacrifice myself by jumping into the flames. When my body is roasted, you may eat my flesh. Then you can perform your priestly duties."

Sakka used his extraordinary power to create a heap of burning coals. Then he called the rabbit, who rose from his bed of kusa grass and approached the fire. Three times, he shook himself so that any insects in his fur would be spared. Without hesitation, he leaped directly into the center of the burning coals. Despite the flames which flared up from the embers, not a single hair on his body was even singed. Indeed, it was as if he had jumped into a snowdrift! Amazed, he addressed Sakka, "Brahmin, the fire you have kindled is ice-cold. It doesn't even warm the hair on my body. What does this mean?"

"Wise sir! I am no brahmin. I am Sakka, and I came to put your virtue to the test."

The rabbit declared, "Even if all the inhabitants of this earth were to test me in alms-giving, they would not find in me any unwillingness to give!"

Pleased with this resounding answer, Sakka said, "Wise rabbit, I will make your virtue known throughout this whole eon!" Then he squeezed the mountain, extracting its very essence, which he used to draw the image of the rabbit on the face of the full moon.

After gently placing the rabbit on a bed of young kusa grass, Sakka returned to Tāvatimsa.

The four creatures lived together happily and harmoniously, keeping the precepts and observing the Uposatha days for the rest of their lives until they passed away to fare according to their deserts.

When the Buddha had concluded his story, the householder who had donated all the requisites attained the first path. Then the Buddha identified the birth: "At that time, Ānanda was the otter, Moggallāna was the jackal, Sāriputta was the monkey, and I was the wise rabbit."

122
Alive or Dead, I Don't Want Her!
Kanavera Jātaka

It was while staying at Jetavana that the Buddha told this story about a bhikkhu who was tempted by his former wife.

A young man from a good family in Sāvatthī had left his wife and children to become a bhikkhu. There were so many bhikkhus who were senior to him that he was always at the end of the line. By the time his turn came, all the delicious food had been served. He usually received no more than rice gruel with broken lumps of rice, stale chapatis, or rotting vegetables. Even that was tossed at him hastily, and he had to sit with the sāmaneras. Unable to survive on this fare, he took what he had gotten and went to his old house. His ex-wife took his bowl, emptied it, and served him delicious curries instead. He was so pleased by the succulent dishes that he did not want to leave. Heartened to see this, his former wife decided to test him.

She invited some of her village friends to come for lunch. She also arranged for a bullock cart to be brought to the house. While the friends were eating and enjoying themselves in the main room and the cart was waiting, the bhikkhu, her ex-husband, arrived at the door.

"There's a bhikkhu at the door!" her friends shouted to her. "Greet him kindly, and ask him to pass on!" she shouted back, without emerging.

Her friends did so, but he refused to leave. "He's still here!" the friends shouted again.

When the woman came out of the inner room and saw her husband, she exclaimed, "Oh, it is the father of my children!" She took his bowl and gave him a wonderful meal. When he had finished eating, she sat down respectfully at one side and said, "Sir, you are now a well-disciplined bhikkhu. We have been living here since you left, but there is no proper household without a master, so we have decided to leave and to return to the country. Be steadfast in your practice. Please forgive us if we have done anything wrong by you."

When the bhikkhu heard this, he thought that his heart would break. He struggled with his thoughts for a moment and then cried out. "Please don't go! I cannot live without you! I don't want to be a bhikkhu anymore. I'll take back my robe and bowl today. I'll come back and live with you! Please!" His wife was overjoyed. She welcomed him back with open arms.

He hurried back to Jetavana and told the other bhikkhus what he had decided and tried to give them his bowl and robe. They took him straightaway, against his will, to the Buddha.

"Is it true, Brother," the Buddha asked, "that you are ready to give up the holy life?"

"Yes, Venerable Sir, it is true," the bhikkhu replied.

"What has caused you to feel this way?" the Buddha asked.

"I have met my former wife, and my passion for her has been rekindled," the bhikkhu answered.

"Brother!" the Buddha admonished him. "That woman is an evil threat to you. In former times, she was also a source of great danger for you. Once, because of her, you even had your head cut off." Then the Buddha told this story of the past.

Long, long ago, when Brahmadatta was reigning in Bārānasi, the Bodhisatta was born in a village of Kāsi, and the astrologer who cast his horoscope predicted that he would become a thief. This prediction proved to be correct, for, when he grew up, he made his living by breaking into houses and stealing whatever he could. He often targeted the houses of wealthy merchants and made off with great fortunes. He was notorious for his daring and his great strength, and it seemed that no one could catch him.

The thief had robbed so many houses, and so many people had complained, that the king finally ordered the governor to arrest him without fail. The governor offered a sizable reward for his capture and stationed soldiers in all the likely places. At last, the thief made a mistake, fell into a trap, and was caught red-handed. Without hesitation, the king ordered his execution.

As was the custom in Bārānasi, the criminal's arms were tightly bound behind his back, a wreath of red kanavera flowers was hung around his neck, and brick dust was sprinkled on his head. To the beat of a harsh-sounding drum, he was marched to the execution site at the southern gate of the city. At every crossroads, the procession stopped, and he was beaten with whips. All along the way, townsfolk gathered to watch. Everyone was relieved and overjoyed that the thief who had plagued the city had been captured at last.

As the procession passed the palace, a famous courtesan named Samā, happened to lean out of an open window on the upper floor. When she saw the thief being dragged along, she noticed that, even in fetters, he was extremely handsome, standing head and shoulders above his guards. She immediately fell in love with him and began wondering how she could get him released.

Samā was the most successful courtesan in Bārānasi. She counted among her clients all the important men of the city, including the king. Her favors were so sought after that she regularly received one thousand coins for a single night. After thinking for a few minutes, Samā entrusted one of her female servants with one thousand coins. "Go to the governor," she told the servant. "Tell him that the thief who is being executed is Samā's dearly beloved brother. Give him the money, and ask him, as a favor to Samā, to allow his prisoner to escape."

The servant did as she was told, but the governor replied, "This is a notorious thief. I cannot simply let him go free, but, if I had another man as a substitute, I could put the thief in a covered carriage and send him to Samā." The servant reported this to her mistress.

Early that evening, a rich young merchant, who was quite enamored of Samā and who visited her almost daily, arrived to see her. Samā accepted his one thousand coins, but, as she held them in her lap, she began to weep.

"My dear Samā," the young man asked, "what is the matter? Why do you weep?"

"My Lord," she sobbed, "the thief who was just captured is my brother. He never visited me, because people told him that I follow a low trade, but I love him dearly. I appealed to the governor, and he volunteered to let my brother go free if I gave him one thousand coins. Now I have the money, but I can't find anyone to take it to the governor for me."

"Darling Samā," the young man said passionately, "you know how much I care for you! I would do anything for you. Please let me deliver the money. I can take it and hurry right back."

"Oh, that is so sweet!" Samā replied, drying her tears. "I would be so happy if you took this money to the governor!" She handed the one thousand coins to the unsuspecting young merchant and sent him off.

Delighted with the second bribe of one thousand coins, the governor seized the young man. After having the two men exchange clothes, the governor sent the thief as he had promised to Sāmā and hid the merchant in a secret cell. "Everyone knows what the thief looks like," the governor said to himself, "so I can't send this young man out now. I'll have to figure out how to put him to death after it gets dark." He kept making excuses for the delay of the execution, and, finally, everyone gave up waiting and returned home. Then, with only a few torches lighting the execution site, he had the young merchant beheaded. The next morning, when the populace found the body exposed as a warning, they, of course, assumed that it was the thief and pointed it out to their children as a warning to behave.

From that day, Sāmā refused offers from other men and spent all of her time with the thief. She lavished her affection on him and pampered him with every luxury, but she never let him out of her sight.

"This woman is dangerous," the thief thought. "She says she loves me, but I am in a very precarious position. I know that I can't trust her. If she falls in love with someone else, she will betray me just like she did that other fellow. She would have me killed without a second thought. My only hope is to escape."

As soon as he found the chance, he pilfered some of her jewels and hid them in a bundle so that he would not leave empty-handed. Shortly thereafter, when he had gotten everything ready, he said to her, "My dear, since I arrived here, we have stayed indoors like cockatoos in a cage. Let's go outside and enjoy ourselves in the garden."

"That's a wonderful idea!" she cried. She immediately ordered her servants to prepare a picnic lunch with plenty of delicious dishes. She adorned herself in her most expensive finery, and the two of them rode in an elegant closed carriage to a secluded garden.

Sāmā was enjoying herself immensely, chasing her lover and being chased by him in return. Suddenly, he grabbed her amorously and pulled her into a thicket of kanavera bushes. Pretending to embrace her passionately, he squeezed her so hard that she swooned and lost consciousness. Believing that he had killed her, he threw her body on the ground and stripped off all her jewelry, which he put in his bundle with the rest. As agile as a fleeing deer, he leapt over the wall and disappeared.

When Sāmā regained consciousness, she called her attendants and asked what had become of her lover.

"We do not know, ma'am; we haven't seen the young lord."

"Oh, dear!" she moaned. "He must have thought me dead and, in his panic, run away!"

"Oh, my poor darling," she cried aloud, "I will not lie on my soft couch, and I will live in mourning until I have set eyes on you again!"

True to her word, she gave up her bed and began sleeping on the floor. She wore only rough clothing; stopped using perfumes, lotions, and cosmetics; and limited herself to only one meal a day.

Determined to find her lover and to bring him back, Samā sent for a troop of actors. She gave them one thousand coins and instructed them, "Take your performance everywhere, to every village, town, and city. Everywhere you go, to every crowd, sing this song: 'It was the joyous springtime, with trees and shrubs brightly flowering. From her swoon, Samā has awakened. Now Samā lives, and Samā lives for you alone!' If my husband is in the crowd, he will hear this song, and he will speak to you. When you meet him, tell him I am well, and ask him to come back with you. If you bring him back, I will give you a rich reward. If he refuses, then bring me back his message." After giving them even more for expenses, she sent them off.

From Bārānasi, the actors traveled throughout Kāsi. They performed in even the smallest village and hamlet. At last, they reached the border and set up their stage in a remote village of thieves. As they had done with every performance, they concluded by singing, "It was the joyous springtime, with trees and shrubs brightly flowering. From her swoon, Samā has awakened. Now Samā lives, and Samā lives for you alone!"

As soon as they had finished singing, Samā's thief stepped in front of the troop and said, "You say that Samā is alive, but I do not believe it. The dead do not come back to life!"

"Samā is not dead. Nor was she ever so," one of the actors replied. "She told us to tell you that she has not allowed any man to take your place. Waiting for you, she lives in mourning. She sleeps on the floor and wears rough clothing. She no longer uses any make-up, and she takes only one meal a day. She swears, sir, that she loves you and you alone!"

"Whether she is alive or dead, I don't want her!" the thief declared. "Samā is fickle and has a roving eye. She once cast off a faithful man, and she would have betrayed me, too, if I hadn't fled!"

The actors immediately returned to Bārānasi and reported to Samā exactly what the thief had said.

All hope gone, she regretfully resumed her old way of life.

Having concluded his story, the Buddha taught the Dhamma, and the backsliding bhikkhu attained the first path. Then the Buddha identified the birth: "At that time, this bhikkhu was the rich young merchant, his former wife was Samā, and I was the thief."

123
The Decoy
Tittira Jātaka

It was while staying at Badarika Monastery near Kosambi that the Buddha told this story about Venerable Rāhula.

From the time he was a sāmanera, Venerable Rāhula was always scrupulous in his behavior. One day, the bhikkhus were praising Rāhula because he welcomed instruction and always showed patience whenever he was corrected. When the Buddha heard what they were discussing, he said, "Not only now, Bhikkhus, does Rāhula have all these virtues. Long ago, also, he had them." Then he told this story of the past.

Long, long ago, when Brahmadatta was reigning in Bārānasi, the Bodhisatta was born into a brahmin family. After receiving his education in Takkasilā and returning to Bārānasi, he renounced the world to become an ascetic in the Himavat. There, he stayed in a pleasant grove, practicing austerities and meditating.

Once, at the beginning of the rainy season, the ascetic traveled to a frontier village to get salt and vinegar and to find a place to stay. The villagers were so impressed with his demeanor that they invited him to remain nearby. They built him a simple hut of leaves and provided him with all that he required.

In that village, there was a fowler who had trained a partridge to act as a decoy. Every day, he took the trained bird in its cage to the forest. When other partridges heard its cry, they came in great numbers, and the fowler could easily trap them with his net. He stuffed all the birds into a basket and carried them home. In this way, the fowler made a good living.

The decoy partridge watched this happen every day and became upset. "It seems that, because of me, many of my relatives are lured to their death," he worried. "I'm afraid that this is evil behavior on my part." As a test, he refused to cry and sat quietly in his cage. Of course, no birds came, and the fowler became angry. He took a piece of bamboo and beat the poor decoy until he cried out in pain. At that, many birds came to his aid, and the fowler was able to snare them all with his wide net.

"When I am silent, no birds come. When I cry, they come and are captured," the decoy reasoned. "I am definitely the cause of their suffering and death. I certainly don't mean them any harm. Sometimes I do my best not to cry, but I can't help it. I wonder whether I will suffer any consequences from this action of mine. Am I really responsible? Is it evil on my part? Am I guilty?" No matter how much he thought about this, he could not answer these questions. He was greatly troubled. "Who can help me understand this?" he wondered.

One day, the fowler trapped a great many partridges. He stuffed them all into his basket and began walking back toward the village. As he was passing the ascetic's hermitage, he felt thirsty, so he paused to ask for a drink of water. The fowler put down the heavy basket, placed the decoy's cage near the ascetic, drank some water, and lay down to rest.

The partridge became excited. "Now is my chance," he thought. "This ascetic should be able to answer my questions."

As soon as the fowler was asleep, the bird called out, "Venerable Sir."

"What can I do for you, Friend," the ascetic replied.

"My life is happy enough,' the partridge began. "I am well taken care of, and I get plenty of food, but I am forced to serve as a decoy. I'm afraid that I am in great danger. Am I responsible for the death of all the birds who come when they hear my cry? What will my future be?"

"If there is no evil in your heart, leading you to do a wicked deed," the ascetic answered, "you are not guilty."

"There is no evil in my heart," the partridge continued, not completely convinced, "but when I cry, they come. If I don't cry, they don't come. Then my master beats me, and I cry in pain. Then many birds come to help me, and they are all trapped and later killed. Am I not guilty of causing their suffering? If I didn't cry, they might still be alive and free! I really worry about this. Please resolve this question for me."

"The important consideration here is intention. If no wicked intention lurks in his heart, the doer will not suffer as a consequence. He who plays a passive part is innocent."

At last, the bird was convinced and was freed from remorse. After the ascetic and the partridge had finished their discussion, the fowler woke up, paid his respects to the ascetic, picked up the decoy's cage, shouldered the basket of birds, and returned home.

Having concluded his story, the Buddha identified the birth: "At that time, Rāhula was the partridge, and I was the ascetic."

124
Intractable
Kutidūsaka Jātaka

It was while staying at Jetavana that the Buddha told this story about Venerable Mahā-Kassapa's wayward sāmanera.

Venerable Mahā-Kassapa was staying in a hermitage in the forest near Rājagaha with two sāmaneras who looked after him. One of the sāmaneras was very diligent, but the other was cunning and lazy. The second sāmanera managed to take credit for every task that the first completed. If the first sāmanera prepared toothsticks and water, the second went to Venerable Mahā-Kassapa and said, "Venerable Sir, everything is ready for you to brush your teeth now." If the first got up early and swept out the teacher's room, the second waited and, when the teacher appeared, moved a few things around, as if he'd just finished the job by himself.

The diligent sāmanera saw what was happening and thought, "This rascal takes credit for everything I do. Let me expose his tricks." One day, while the lazy sāmanera was sleeping after his meal, the diligent sāmanera heated water for the bath and hid it in a back room, leaving only a small amount of hot water in the pot over the fire.

When the lazy sāmanera awoke, he noticed the steam rising from the pot and thought, "No doubt, my friend has heated water and prepared the teacher's bath." He hurried to Venerable Mahā-Kassapa's kuti and announced, "Sir, the water is ready. Please, take your bath." Venerable Mahā-Kassapa followed the sāmanera to the bathroom, but there was no water there. "Where is the water?" the bhikkhu asked the sāmanera.

"I'm sorry, sir!" the sāmanera cried in surprise. "It's hot. I'll bring it!" He ran to the fire and put the ladle in the pot to dip water, but it rattled like a gong when it struck the empty pot. At that moment, the diligent sāmanera appeared, carrying the hot water. "Venerable Sir," he announced, "please take your bath."

Thereafter, the lazy sāmanera became known as Ulunkasaddaka, which means "noisy ladle."

That evening, Venerable Mahā-Kassapa said to Ulunkasaddaka, "Someone under religious vows is allowed to say, 'I did that,' only if he himself has actually done it. To take credit for another person's work is to tell a deliberate lie. In the future, you must not do that."

The next morning, still upset that he had been scolded, Ulunkasaddaka refused to go for alms with Venerable Mahā-Kassapa and the other sāmanera. After they had left, he went in a different direction, to the house of some of Venerable Mahā-Kassapa's devotees. When the family asked where Venerable Mahā-Kassapa was, the sāmanera said that he was sick. They asked what sort of food he needed, and the sāmanera mentioned various delicacies that he himself liked. The family promptly filled his bowl, and the sāmanera left. He took the bowl to a secluded place, ate his delicious meal, and returned to the hermitage, thoroughly pleased with himself.

The next day, when Venerable Mahā-Kassapa visited that family, they expressed concern about his health, saying that they hoped that the special food that they had given the sāmanera for him had proved beneficial. Venerable Mahā-Kassapa smiled and nodded. After he had finished his meal and offered anumodana, he returned to the monastery.

That evening, Venerable Mahā-Kassapa scolded Ulunkasaddaka again. "Yesterday," he said, "you went for alms to my devotees' house and told them that I was not well and that I should have such and such delicacies to eat. They gave you those curries, and you ate them yourself. Asking for alms like that is highly improper, and it is another way of telling a lie. Make sure that you are never again guilty of such misconduct."

This was more than Ulunkasaddaka could stand. His anger turned into a bitter grudge against Venerable Mahā-Kassapa. "The other day," he fumed, "he scolded me merely on account of a little water. Now he's angry because I ate a handful of rice from his devotees. I'll fix him!"

The next morning, after Venerable Mahā-Kassapa and the other sāmanera had gone to the city for alms, Ulunkasaddaka took a hammer and broke up all the furniture. Then he set fire to the kuti and ran away, but his name and his evil deed became well-known throughout the country.

For the rest of his life, Ulunkasaddaka lived like a ghost and gradually withered away. When he died, he was reborn in Avīci hell.

One day, shortly after the fire, some bhikkhus came to Sāvatthī to visit the Buddha. After they had paid their respects, the Buddha asked where they had come from.

"From Rājagaha, Venerable Sir."

"Who is your teacher there?" the Buddha asked. "Mahā-Kassapa, Venerable Sir."

"Is your teacher well, Bhikkhus?"

"Yes, Venerable Sir, he is well, but, recently, a young sāmanera got so angry after he was corrected that he set fire to Venerable Mahā-Kassapa's kuti and ran off."

"Friends," the Buddha replied, "if you do not meet your equal or your better, it is better to continue on alone. Truly, there is no companionship with the foolish![1] For Mahā-Kassapa, solitude would have been better than keeping company with a fool like that. This is not the first time, however, that this youth has destroyed the dwelling of one who reproved him." At their request, the Buddha told this story of the past.

Long, long ago, when Brahmadatta was reigning in Bārāṇasi, the Bodhisatta was born as a singila bird in the Himavat. Being skillful and resourceful, this bird was able to build a sturdy nest which was both warm and well-protected from the rain.

One day, in the middle of the rainy season, during a particularly heavy downpour, a monkey sat down near the singila bird's nest. The monkey was drenched to the bone. His teeth were chattering, and he was miserable.

Feeling sorry for the monkey, the bird struck up a conversation with him. "You are quite similar to a human being," the bird said. "Your hands and feet appear to be dexterous. How is it that you do not build for yourself some sort of shelter from the bad weather?"

"Although my face, hands, and feet are similar to those of a man," the monkey replied, "I lack the wisdom of a human being."

Wishing to offer sound advice to the monkey, the bird said, "One whose mind is fickle won't find happiness. Be steadfast, my friend. If you want to improve yourself, you should at least try to make some sort of shelter to keep you warm and dry."

The monkey, however, took umbrage at this remark. "Just because this bird has such a cozy nest," he thought, "he despises me. I'll show him a thing or two!" He leapt at the bird, trying to catch him, but the bird was too quick and flew away unharmed. To vent his anger, the monkey smashed the nest, completely destroying it, and went on his way.

Having concluded his story, the Buddha identified the birth: "At that time, the sāmanera who burned down Mahā-Kassapa's kuti was the monkey, and I was the singila bird."

125

The Sound the Hare Heard
Duddubha Jātaka

It was while staying at Jetavana that the Buddha told this story about ascetics of different sects.

One morning, while some bhikkhus were on their almsrounds in Sāvatthī, they passed some ascetics of different sects practicing austerities. Some of them were naked and lying on thorns. Others sat around a blazing fire under the burning sun.

Later, while the bhikkhus were discussing the ascetics, they asked the Buddha, "Lord, is there any virtue in those harsh ascetic practices?"

The Buddha answered, "No, Bhikkhus, there is neither virtue nor any special merit in them. When they are examined and tested, they are like a path over a dunghill or like the sound the hare heard."

Puzzled, the bhikkhus said, "Lord, we do not know about that sound. Please tell us what it was." Then the Buddha told them this story of the distant past.

Long, long ago, when Brahmadatta was reigning in Bārānasi, the Bodhisatta was born as a lion in a forest near the Western Ocean. In one part of that forest there was a grove of palms mixed with bael trees. A hare lived in that grove beneath a palm sapling at the foot of a bael tree.

One day, the hare lay under the young palm tree, idly thinking, "If this earth were destroyed, what would become of me?" At that very instant, a ripe bael fruit happened to fall and hit a palm frond making a loud "Thud!"

Startled by this sound, the hare leapt to his feet and cried, "The earth is collapsing!" He immediately fled, without even glancing back.

Another hare, seeing him race past, as if for his very life, asked, "What's wrong?" and started running, too.

"Don't ask!" panted the first. This frightened the second even more, and he sprinted to keep up.

"What's wrong?" he shouted again.

Pausing for just a moment, the first hare cried, "The earth is breaking up!" At this, the two of them bolted off together.

Their fear was infectious, and other hares joined them until all the hares in that forest were fleeing together. When other animals saw the commotion and asked what was wrong, they were breathlessly told, "The earth is breaking up!" and they, too, began running for their lives. In this way, the hares were soon joined by herds of deer, boars, elk, buffalos, wild oxen, rhinoceroses, a family of tigers, and some elephants.

When the lion saw this headlong stampede of animals and heard the cause of their flight, he thought, "The earth is certainly not coming to an end. There must have been some sound which they misunderstood. If I don't act quickly, they will be killed. I must save them!"

Then, running as fast as only he could run, he got in front of them and roared three times. At the sound of his mighty voice, all the animals stopped in their tracks. Panting, they huddled together in fear. The lion approached them and asked why they were running away.

"The earth is collapsing," they all answered.

"Who saw it collapsing?" he asked.

"The elephants know all about it," some animals replied.

When he asked the elephants, they said, "We don't know. The tigers know."

The tigers said, "The rhinoceroses know."

The rhinoceroses said, "The wild oxen know."

The wild oxen said, "The buffaloes know."

The buffaloes said, "The elk know."

The elk said, "The boars know."

The boars said, "The deer know."

The deer said, "We don't know. The hares know."

When he asked the hares, they pointed to one particular hare and said, "This one told us."

The lion asked him, "Is it true, sir, that the earth is breaking up?"

"Yes, Your Majesty, I saw it," said the hare.

"Where were you when you saw it?"

"In the forest in a palm grove mixed with bael trees. I was lying there under a palm at the foot of a bael tree, thinking, 'If this earth were destroyed, what would become of me?' At that very moment, I heard the sound of the breaking up of the earth, and I fled."

From this explanation, the lion realized exactly what had really happened, but he wanted to verify his conclusions and to demonstrate the truth to the other animals. He gently calmed the animals and said, "I will take the hare and go to find out whether or not the earth is coming to an end where he says it is. Until we return, stay right here!"

Placing the hare on his tawny back, he raced with great speed back to that grove. Then he put the hare down and said, "Come, show me the place you meant."

"I don't dare, My Lord," said the hare.

"Don't be afraid," said the lion.

The hare, shivering with fear, would not risk going near the bael tree. He could only point and say, "Over there, sir, is the place of dreadful sound."

The lion went to the place the hare indicated. He could make out where the hare had been lying in the grass, and he saw the ripe bael fruit that had fallen on the palm frond. Having carefully ascertained that the earth was not breaking up, he placed the hare on his back again and returned to the waiting animals. He told them what he had found and said, "Don't be afraid. The earth is not breaking up." Reassured, all the animals went back to their usual places and resumed their routines.

Those animals had placed themselves in great danger because they listened to rumors and unfounded fears rather than trying to find out the truth themselves. Truly, if it had not been for the lion, all of them would have rushed into the sea and perished. It was only because of the lion's wisdom and compassion that they escaped death.

Having concluded his story, the Buddha identified the birth: "At that time, I was the lion."

126
Noble Reticence
Brahmadatta Jātaka

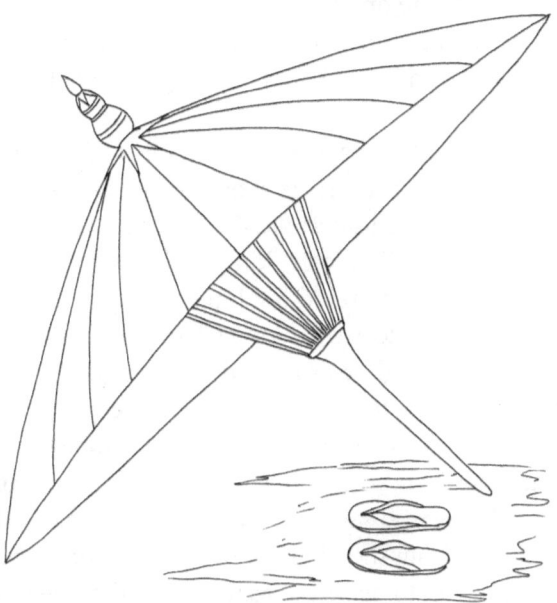

It was while staying at Aggālava Cetiya near Ālavi that the Buddha told this story about bhikkhus asking for requisites.

The bhikkhus of Ālavi had asked for building materials for their monastery so aggressively and so frequently that the mere sight of a bhikkhu was enough to cause householders to flee. When Venerable Mahā-Kassapa reported the unhappy situation to the Buddha, the Master reproved the bhikkhus for requesting such things from laypeople. "Long ago, the wise, being scrupulous, even though the king had offered to grant any wish, hesitated to say a single word of petition." Then the Buddha told them this story of the past.

Long, long ago, when a Pañcāla king was reigning in Uttarapañcāla,[1] the capital of the Kampilla kingdom, the Bodhisatta was born into a brahmin family in a market town. After he had finished his education in Takkasilā, he became an ascetic in the Himavat.

---

1   It seems that the region called Pañcāla and Kampilla was not clearly defined. Sometimes Kampilla was the capital of Dakkhinapañcāla (South Pañcāla), and sometimes it was the capital of Uttarapañcāla (North Pañcāla). At other times Uttarapañcāla was the capital of Kampilla. The region was continually under contention between the Pañcālas and the Kurus.

At the beginning of the rainy season, he left his hermitage to get salt and vinegar and to find a place to stay. He walked to Uttarapañcāla and spent the night in the royal park. The next morning, he went into the city for alms. When he arrived at the palace, the king was so impressed with his demeanor that he seated him on the dais and offered him food from his own table. After the ascetic had finished eating, the king invited him to stay in the royal park. The ascetic accepted, and the king provided a proper lodging and all the requisites.

For the next three months, the ascetic received food at the palace every day. At the end of the rainy season, he thought, "It is time for me to return to the Himavat, but if I am to undertake the journey, I must have a pair of sandals and an umbrella. I will ask the king for these things."

Shortly thereafter, he encountered the king sitting in the garden and saluted him. The ascetic started to ask the king for the sandals and the umbrella, but, before he could say a single word aloud, he thought, "One who asks for something from another may become emotional. Likewise, the person being asked, if he refuses, may also become emotional. It would be embarrassing for both of us if anyone were to see this. I should ask him in private."

"Your Majesty," the ascetic said, "I would like to speak with you in private." At a slight signal from the king, all the royal attendants withdrew.

The ascetic again began to make his request, but then he thought, "If the king refuses my request, our friendship will become strained. I should not ask a favor from him after all!" Aloud he said, "Your Majesty, please excuse me. I will bring this up at another time."

A few days later, the ascetic again encountered the king sitting in the garden. Again, he started to make his request, but the same thing happened. In fact, exactly the same thing happened periodically for twelve years.

One day, the king thought, "For twelve years this ascetic has been saying that he wants to speak with me in private, but, even after my courtiers withdraw, he never has the courage to speak. After living the religious life for so many years, perhaps he regrets leaving the world. He is probably eager to experience the pleasures he has so long denied himself. Perhaps he is keeping silent because he wishes for sovereignty, but is unable to say the word 'kingdom.' In any case, today I will give him whatever it is he desires, even my kingdom!"

With that resolve, the king went to the garden to find the ascetic. As soon as the ascetic saw the king, he again asked to speak with him in private. The courtiers withdrew, and the ascetic again started to excuse himself, but the king interrupted him and said, "For twelve years you have asked to speak to me in private, but even then you have never said a word. Now, let me be the first to speak. I declare that I will grant any request you make. Please do not be afraid. Ask me for anything you want, and I will give it to you, even my kingdom. Please just make your request."

"Your Majesty," the ascetic asked, "will you really give me what I need?"

"Yes, Venerable Sir, I will."

"Your Majesty, in order to return to the Himavat, I must have a pair of sandals and an umbrella."

"What?" the king cried in astonishment. "Is that all that you have been unable to ask me for twelve long years?"

"That's right, Your Majesty."

"Tell me why you acted this way?"

"Sire, one who asks for something from another may become emotional," the ascetic replied, saying aloud the reasoning that he had repeated to himself for twelve years. "Likewise the person being asked, if he refuses, may also become emotional. It would be embarrassing for both of us if anyone were to see this, so I asked to speak to you in private.

"Then I was afraid that, if you refused my request, our friendship would become strained, so I decided to remain silent."

The king was so impressed with the ascetic's sensitivity that he immediately offered him one thousand head of cattle.

"No, Your Majesty," the ascetic protested, "I don't want wealth. Please just give me only that which I have asked for. I truly need a pair of sandals and an umbrella."

"I will gladly offer you sandals and an umbrella," the king replied, "but please stay here in my park. Do not deny us your presence!"

"Sire," the ascetic persisted, "for twelve years, I have enjoyed your hospitality, but, as an ascetic, my practice requires solitude. I wish to return to my hermitage in the Himavat."

At last, the king agreed and gave him the sandals and the umbrella. The ascetic exhorted the king to rule righteously, to keep the moral law, and to observe the Uposatha days. Then he returned to the Himavat and intensively practiced meditation on the Four Brahma Vihāras. When he passed away, he was reborn in the Brahma heavens.

Having concluded his story, the Buddha identified the birth: "At that time, Ānanda was the king, and I was the modest ascetic."

127

The Leather Ascetic
Cammasātaka Jātaka

It was while staying at Jetavana that the Buddha told this story about an ascetic wearing leather garments.

One day, the bhikkhus were talking about an ascetic who had been killed in Sāvatthī. When the Buddha heard what they were discussing, he said, "Long ago, exactly the same thing happened to that ascetic." At their request, the Buddha told this story of the past.

Long, long ago, an ascetic, wearing both upper and lower garments of leather, was walking on his almsrounds. As he was passing the rams' fighting ground, a large ram lowered his head and began pawing the ground. When the ascetic saw this, he concluded that the beast was paying its respects to him. "In the whole world," he exclaimed, "this ram alone recognizes my merits. What a wonderful animal to pay humble obeisance to the brahmin versed in ancient lore! Good creature, I return your greeting." Thus, instead of stepping back, the ascetic stood there and raised his joined hands in a polite salutation.

A merchant, who was sitting in his storeroom nearby, observed this scene and shouted, "Sir, do not be so hasty in trusting this animal. The ram is going to attack!"

Before the merchant was able to finish his warning, the ram charged at full speed. The enraged brute struck the ascetic such a terrific blow that it knocked him down and broke his legs.

The ascetic lamented weakly, "All who pay respect to the unworthy will share my fate." With his last breath, he moaned, "Here I die, butted by a ram in whom I placed my confidence, and, for my foolishness, I pay with my life."

Having concluded his story, the Buddha identified the birth: "At that time, the ascetic in leather was the same, and I was the wise merchant."

128
Fragrant Wreaths
Kakkāru Jātaka

It was while staying at Jetavana that the Buddha told this story about Devadatta.

One day, in the Hall of Truth, the bhikkhus were talking about Devadatta. Some described how a stream of hot blood had gushed from his mouth after he had uttered falsehoods. When the Buddha heard what they were discussing, he said, "This is not the first time, Bhikkhus, that Devadatta has suffered great pain as a result of his lies." Then he told this story of the past.

Long, long ago, when Brahmadatta was reigning in Bārānasi, there was a great festival in the city. Many nāgas and garulas, as well as all the local devas, came to enjoy the festival. Most unusual, however, was the presence of four devas from Tāvatimsa. These four devas were wearing wreaths of heavenly kakkāru flowers, whose exquisite smell filled the city. People looked here and there, wondering where the heavenly fragrance could be coming from.

The four devas flew high up over the royal court and made themselves visible. The king and his courtiers emerged from the palace and gazed, along with the multitude, at these splendid deities standing there in mid-air.

"Where are you from?" they asked the devas.

"We have come from Tāvatimsa," the devas replied. "Why have you come here?"

"To enjoy your marvelous festival."

"What are those flowers you are wearing? Their heavenly fragrance fills our city!"

"These flowers are called kakkāru."

"Great sirs," the people shouted, "in your heaven there must be many more flowers which you can wear. Please give those fragrant flowers to us."

"These divine flowers," the leader of the devas replied, "are only suitable for one possessed of great virtues. A being in this human realm who is base, foolish, faithless, or wicked must never wear these flowers."

Holding his flowers aloft, the leader proclaimed, "Only one who refrains from stealing, lying, and excessive pride should dare to wear these blooms."

When the king's chief advisor heard this, he thought, "If I can get these flowers, everyone will think that I am exceptionally virtuous. What an honor that would be! I'm sure I can trick these devas into giving them to me."

Aloud he said, "Great sir, I am endowed with those virtues!" The flowers were presented to him, and he put them on.

Holding his flowers aloft, the second deva proclaimed, "Only one who earns his living honestly, who never practices deceit, and who lives simply, is entitled to wear these heavenly flowers."

"Great sir, I am endowed with those virtues!" the advisor stated once more. Those flowers, too, were presented to him, and he put them on.

Holding his flowers aloft, the third deva proclaimed, "Only one who is steadfast and generous may justly claim these flowers."

"Great sir, I am endowed with those virtues!" the advisor said again. Those flowers, too, were presented to him, and he put them on.

Holding his flowers aloft, the fourth deva proclaimed, "Only one who never speaks ill of others and whose actions match his words may safely wear these flowers."

"Great sir, I am endowed with those virtues!" the advisor declared for the fourth time. Those flowers, too, were presented to him, and he put them on.

Then the four devas disappeared and returned to Tāvatimsa. While everyone was gazing into the sky at the spot where the devas had been, the advisor suddenly placed his hands on his head and screamed in pain. It seemed to him that his head was caught in a tightening vise and that a sharp iron spike was being driven into his skull. Maddened with pain, he continued screaming as he fell and frantically rolled around on the ground.

"What's wrong?" the attendants demanded. "What can we do?" the guards shouted.

The advisor tried to speak. "I l-l-lied when I asked for the wr-wreaths," he stuttered. "I d-don't have those v-v-virtues. Take these flowers off me!"

Many tried, but no one could remove the wreaths from the advisor's head. They were attached to him as if by an iron band. The attendants carried him home, where he lay in agony, thrashing about and screaming in pain.

After several days with no relief in sight, the king became worried. "If this goes on much longer," he said to his other advisors, "my chief advisor will die. What can we do?"

"Sire," they answered, "let us hold another festival. Perhaps the devas will come again. If they do, they may be willing to help us."

The king agreed and declared that a second festival would be held exactly one week from the first. Once more, the city was filled with the fragrance of the heavenly kakkāru flowers, and everyone knew that the devas had again arrived. The king ordered that the suffering advisor be carried out on a litter and placed in the courtyard of the palace.

Lying on his stomach on the litter, still writhing with pain, the advisor beseeched the devas, "My Lords, please spare me! Take back your flowers! Please! I beg you!"

"We told you that these flowers were not to be given to one who is wicked. They are suitable only for the virtuous. You lied to us and to all the citizens here. For your evil words and deeds you have been properly punished. In the future, be truthful and honest." Having chastised the advisor and exposed his hypocrisy to everyone, the chief deva effortlessly removed the flowers from the advisor's head, and his pain instantly disappeared.

The devas faced the crowd and encouraged them always to practice virtue, generosity, and honesty. Then, once again, they disappeared and returned to their home in Tāvatimsa.

Having concluded his story, the Buddha identified the birth: "At that time, Devadatta was the chief advisor; Kassapa, Moggallāna, and Sāriputta were three of the deities; and I was their leader."

129
Why Should I Weep?
Ananusociya Jātaka

It was while staying at Jetavana that the Buddha told this story about a landowner who had lost his wife.

This landowner was so overcome with grief that he completely neglected himself. He ignored his business, never took a bath, and forgot to eat. Every day, he wandered aimlessly around the charnel ground, mourning his deceased wife.

Early one morning, when the Buddha surveyed the world, he beheld that landowner and thought, "I am the only one who can relieve that man's sorrow. I must show him the way to end suffering. I will be his refuge."

After finishing his meal, the Buddha went with an attendant bhikkhu to the landowner's house. As soon as the man realized that it was the Buddha, he welcomed him, gave him a seat, paid obeisance, and sat to one side.

"Layman, why are you so silent?" the Buddha asked. "Venerable Sir," the man replied, "I am grieving for my late wife."

"Friend, that which is breakable is broken," the Buddha taught him, "but, when that happens, one should not grieve. Long ago, when a sage lost a wife, because he knew this truth, he did not mourn." At the man's request, the Buddha told this story of the past.

Long, long ago, when Brahmadatta was reigning in Bārānasi, the Bodhisatta descended from heaven and was born into a brahmin family. After completing his education in Takkasilā, he returned to Bārānasi. His parents insisted that he marry, but, remembering his previous birth, he told them he was not at all interested. "When you are gone," he told them, "I will become an ascetic, so there is no point in my getting married."

They begged him so much to get married that, finally, he had a golden image of a woman made. This image was as beautiful as a deva. "Dear parents," he said one day, showing them the image, "if you can find me a maiden like this, I will make her my wife."

His parents placed the golden image in a splendid covered carriage and ordered several servants to take it all over Jambudīpa in search of a young girl who resembled the statue. When they found her, they were to present the golden image to her family as a dowry and to bring the maiden back to Bārānasi.

The servants had not even left Kāsi, when, upon entering a certain town, citizens asked them, "Why is Samīllabhāsinī riding in that carriage?"

"Who is Samīllabhāsinī?" the servants excitedly asked in return.

"She is the daughter of a brahmin of this town. Her family is worth more than eighty crores, and she looks exactly like your golden image."

The servants asked where this family lived, and the citizens took them to the house. The servants told the couple that their masters, a brahmin family in Bārānasi wished to have Samīllabhāsinī as a bride for their son, and they offered the golden image as a dowry. The parents immediately accepted the proposal and informed their daughter.

Sixteen years before, however, Samīllabhāsinī had descended from heaven and, remembering her previous birth, had no interest in marriage whatsoever. "When you are gone," she told them, "I will become an ascetic, so there is no point in my getting married."

"Nonsense!" the parents replied angrily, and, accepting the golden image, they sent Samīllabhāsinī to Bārānasi with the servants.

The marriage ceremony took place against the wishes of both the bride and the groom. Although they shared the same bed, they had no passion whatsoever and lived like two ascetics in a hermitage.

When the young man's parents passed away, he dutifully performed their funeral rites. Then he summoned Samīllabhāsinī and said, "My dear wife, my parents' property amounts to eighty crores, and your estate is certainly worth the same. I want you to take all of it. As for me, I intend to become an ascetic."

"Sir," she replied, "I have no wish to continue living the household life. I, too, will become an ascetic."

"Very well," he agreed, "let us go together and live in the forest." They quickly disposed of their entire estate, placing no more personal value on it than if it were phlegm to be spat out. Of course, their method of disposal was to donate all their wealth and property to the needy and the worthy. Unencumbered, they left Bārānasi, walked to the Himavat, and built a hermitage with two rooms where they could abide safely and quietly and practice meditation.

Once, at the beginning of the rainy season, they left to get salt and vinegar and to find a place to stay. They arrived in Bārānasi and established themselves in the royal park, but, while they were there, Samīllabhāsinī developed dysentery. Unable to get proper medicine, she grew extremely weak.

One day, before going for alms, the ascetic carried Samīllabhāsinī to a public hall and laid her on a bench. Taking his bowl, he left to seek food for them both. He had scarcely gone, when she breathed her last. People gathered around her body and, moved by her beauty, wept openly.

When the ascetic returned, he saw the crowd around the bench and wondered what had happened. When someone informed him that a beautiful woman had died, he replied simply, "That which has the nature to dissolve has dissolved. All such existence is impermanent." He sat down on the bench next to Samīllabhāsinī's body, ate the food he had brought for the two of them, and rinsed out his mouth. When he had finished his meal, the onlookers asked, "Reverend Sir, what was this female ascetic to you?"

"When I was a layman," he replied, "she was my wife."

"Reverend Sir," they continued, "unable to control our feelings, we weep. Why is it that you do not weep for her?"

"While she was alive," he replied calmly, "one could say that she belonged to me in some way. Now that she has gone to another realm, she belongs to no one. Why should I weep for fair Samīllabhāsinī? She has gone the way she had to go, and now she is lost to me. Why should a person, himself subject to death, weep for that which is only lent to him? Who can know how long it will be until his own death. At some place, at some time, in the twinkling of an eye, when least expected, death will come to claim him! Life is unstable. The loss of friends is inevitable. It is better to cherish those who are alive than to grieve for those whom you survive."

The citizens performed the funeral rites for Samīllabhāsinī, and the ascetic returned to the Himavat. Living alone, he resumed his practice of concentration meditation and, when he died, was reborn in the Brahma heavens.

Having concluded his story, the Buddha taught the Dhamma, and the landowner attained the first path. Then the Buddha identified the birth: "At that time, Rāhula's mother was Samīllabhāsinī, and I was the ascetic."

130
The Court Favorites
Kālabāhu Jātaka

It was while staying at Veluvana that the Buddha told this story about Devadatta's loss of honor.

When it became well-known that Devadatta had tried to kill the Buddha by releasing the fierce elephant Nalagiri, intoxicated with toddy, many people were outraged and stopped supporting him. Even King Ajātasattu withdrew his patronage.

One day, in the Hall of Truth, bhikkhus were talking about Devadatta's inability to keep the fame and honor that he had worked so hard to gain. When the Buddha heard what they were discussing, he said, "This is not the first time, Bhikkhus, that Devadatta has lost his honor." Then he told this story of the past.

Long, long ago, when Dhanañjaya was reigning in Bārānasi, the Bodhisatta was born as a parrot named Rādha, and his younger brother was named Potthapāda. While these two birds were still quite young, a fowler trapped them and presented them to the king. The king put the two handsome parrots in a golden cage and took good care of them. Every day, they ate parched corn flavored with honey from a golden dish, and their water was always slightly sweetened with sugar. As court favorites, they were constantly honored and pampered.

One day, a forester brought a big black monkey named Kālabāhu and presented it to the king. This monkey, who could perform many tricks, quickly became the court favorite. The king and his courtiers brought him many delicacies and paid attention to his every whim. The two parrots were all but forgotten. Their corn, if it came at all, was no longer mixed with honey. Their water dish was often empty.

Potthapāda became upset with this state of affairs. "Dear brother," he complained one day, "it used to be that we received special treatment and delicious food here in the palace, but now we get nothing. All attention goes to Kālabāhu. Most of the courtiers have even forgotten that we exist. Why should we stay here any longer? Let's go back to the forest!"

Rādha, who was older and much wiser than his brother, replied, "Dear brother, you must be patient. Gain and loss, praise and blame, pleasure and pain, fame and dishonor—these are all just transient conditions of the world. Don't fret, dear Potthapāda! All good things come to him who waits."

"All right, Brother, since you are so wise and know the future," Potthapāda retorted, still begrudging the monkey his popularity, "tell me, if you can, when that vile creature will go back to where he came from and how we can make sure he does."

"Just watch!" Rādha replied, calmly. "We don't have to do anything at all. That monkey's popularity won't last much longer. He will perform some foolish trick, and his puckered face will frighten the young princes and princesses. When that happens, he'll be gone soon enough."

A few days later, Kālabāhu shook his ears, screeched shrilly, and, wanting to play, leaped toward the children. The princes and princesses, however, thought the monkey was attacking them, and they ran wailing to the king.

When the king heard what had happened, he immediately ordered his servants to drive Kālabāhu back to the forest.

With the monkey gone, Rādha and Potthapāda were restored to their former place of respect and honor.

Having concluded his story, the Buddha identified the birth: "At that time, Devadatta was Kālabāhu, Ānanda was Potthapāda, and I was Rādha."

131

An Untimely Word
Kokālika Jātaka

It was while staying at Jetavana that the Buddha told this story about Venerable Kokālika.[1]

Long, long ago, when Brahmadatta was reigning in Bārānasi, the Bodhisatta was his trusted minister. King Brahmadatta was extremely loquacious, and his minister was always hoping for a way to break him of his bad habit. "Somehow, I must end the king's excessive talkativeness before it causes a disaster!" he resolved as he waited and watched for the right opportunity.

In King Brahmadatta's park stood a large mango tree which shaded the royal stone slab, a favorite sitting place of the king. In the branches of that tree, there was a crow's nest in which a black cuckoo had stealthily laid her egg.[2] The crow patiently sat on the eggs in her nest. When the chicks hatched, she fed the cuckoo chick along with her own offspring, stuffing food into its open beak.

---

1 The occasion for this story is related in more detail in Tale 88.

2 Cuckoos are negligent parents. They try to trick other birds into brooding their eggs and rearing their young.

One fine day, the king went with his full entourage to the park and sat at ease on his great stone seat.

Unheard by any of the people below, the baby cuckoo uttered its characteristic call, which shocked the foster mother crow. "This young bird makes a terrible sound!" she thought. Alarmed by the chick's cry, and, realizing that it was not one of her own, she began fiercely pecking the helpless chick, until she killed it. Then she pushed its body out of the nest.

The bloody and lifeless chick fell at the feet of the startled king. "Friend!" he cried, jumping up. "What does this mean?"

The minister saw the crow's nest and understood immediately what had happened. "This is what I have been waiting for!" he thought. Aloud, he said, "Sire, this young cuckoo was being raised by a crow. Still having its pin feathers and unable to fly, it uttered a premature cry and gave itself away. As soon as the crow realized that it was not her own offspring, she killed it and pushed it out of the nest. This baby bird met its end for speaking at the wrong time. A similar fate awaits all those who are too talkative. Neither poison nor sword, Your Majesty, is as dangerous as an ill-spoken, untimely word!"

Brahmadatta realized that the wise words of his minister applied to himself, and he resolved to be more moderate in speech. Grateful for the excellent lesson, he generously rewarded the minister.

Having concluded his story, the Buddha identified the birth: "At that time, Kokālika was the young cuckoo, and I was the wise minister."

132
The Four Charms
Thusa Jātaka

It was while staying at Veluvana that the Buddha told this story about Prince Ajātasattu.

Long, long ago, when Brahmadatta was reigning in Bārānasi, the Bodhisatta was a renowned teacher at Takkasilā, where he trained many young princes and brahmin youths in the arts and sciences. One of his students was the son of King Brahmadatta. When this prince had mastered all the arts and sciences, he prepared to leave his master and to return to Bārānasi.

Being gifted in prophecy, the teacher realized that this prince, after he became king, would be in great danger from his own son. He resolved to save the boy from this threat. He summoned the prince and told him, "Dear prince, I am going to teach you four charms which I have composed. You must memorize them. You will not need them until your own son is sixteen years old. At that time, while you are seated for dinner, just as the rice is being served, recite the first charm. During a great reception for visitors, recite the second charm. As you are ascending to the palace roof, just as you stand at the head of the stairs, recite the third charm. When entering the royal chamber, just as you stand on the threshold, recite the fourth charm."

145

Not at all understanding their meaning, but trusting his teacher implicitly, the prince memorized the four charms, promised to recite them exactly as instructed, saluted his teacher, and departed.

On his return to Bārānasi, he was anointed crown prince and served until his father's death, when he ascended the throne. His own son watched him receiving honor, enjoying himself in the royal park, and wielding regal power, and he grew increasingly jealous of his father. He felt an overwhelming desire to become king himself immediately. Secretly, he sounded out some of his attendants, and they encouraged him. "Your Highness," they said, "it is true that you are fit to be king! What is the point of waiting until you are old? Kill the king now, and take the throne!"

"I was sure you would support me!" the prince replied enthusiastically. "Tonight I will poison the king's rice!" He prepared a vial of a subtle but deadly concoction and went to take his evening meal with his father. While they were sitting together, the king realized that his son had just turned sixteen and recollected his teacher's words. When the bowl of steaming rice was brought in, he recited the first charm: "With senses refined, rats discriminate the worthless husk from the tasty rice. Ignoring the husk, they consume the fragrant rice grain by grain."

"What? Rats! My plot has been discovered!" thought the prince in a panic. "My father knows that I mean to poison the rice!" Not daring to carry out his plan, the prince abruptly stood up, bowed to the king, and left without eating anything.

The prince met with his attendants secretly in the garden and explained to them that his father had discovered his plot and that he had been afraid to carry it out. He asked them what he should do next. "You still have a chance," they said. "There is going to be a great reception. Put on your sword, and stand among the councilors. As soon as you see the king off his guard, strike him with your sword, and kill him." The prince readily agreed to this plot.

When the king was holding a great reception, the prince entered the hall with his sword strapped around his waist and moved about among the councilors. He carefully watched the king, waiting for an opportunity to strike.

Just then the king recollected his teacher's words and recited the second charm: "The secret counsel taken in the wood, I clearly understand. The sinister plot whispered softly in the ear, that, too, I hear!"

"My father knows my plan!" thought the prince in a panic. "He must have heard us in the garden!" He unceremoniously left the levee and hurried to tell his attendants what had happened.

For the next week, he and his attendants listened and watched carefully to find out how much the king knew. At the end of the week, they met again.

"Your Highness, your father has done nothing," his attendants told him. "He must not know anything about our plans. Nor does he have any suspicions about your feelings towards him. You're imagining things. Let's go through with it! Kill him, and seize the throne!"

Their words renewed the prince's courage and determination. That evening, he strapped on his sword and hid in the closet at the top of the stairs leading to the roof of the palace. As he had expected, he heard his father mounting the stairs alone, and he waited silently. When the king reached the top step, he recited the third charm: "Once a monkey had to resort to cruel measures to render his offspring impotent."

"Oh, no! My father knows, and he is going to arrest me!" He remained perfectly still in the closet, hoping his father would not find him. As soon as the king had passed, he sneaked out and fled. Once more, he told his attendants that his father was aware of his plot and had threatened him.

After the lapse of a fortnight, the attendants again chided him for his cowardice. "Prince, if the king knew your plans," they said, "he would have acted by now. It's merely your imagination. Get on with it! Murder him, and take the throne!"

That evening, the prince again took his sword and hid under the couch in the royal bedchamber on the floor of the palace, intending to slay the king as soon as he lay down.

After his evening meal, the king dismissed his retinue and retired to the royal chamber. As soon as he stepped on the threshold, he uttered the fourth charm: "Your cautious, creeping ways are like a one-eyed goat that strays into a mustard field. I know that you are lurking in the shadows here."

"Heaven help me!" the prince thought. "My father knows everything! He will have me executed for sure!" Trembling with fear, he crawled out from beneath the couch, and threw his sword at the king's feet.

"Forgive me, Your Majesty," he begged, groveling before his father.

"Foolish boy!" the king cried. "You thought that no one knew what you were plotting. Too soon did you aspire to be king!" He told his son of the virtuous teacher with whom he had studied many years before in Takkasilā, and he explained how his teacher, foreseeing this very danger, had given him the four charms. Then he summoned his soldiers and ordered them to bind the prince and to take him away. He had a special prison built where the prince was kept under constant guard.

After a long and righteous rule, the king died. At the end of the funeral rites, the councilors brought the crown prince out of prison and set him on the throne.

Having concluded his story, the Buddha said to King Bimbisāra, "Thus, you see, Sire, that that king suspected treachery, and his suspicion was justified." Bimbisāra, however, gave no heed to the Buddha's warning. Then the Buddha identified the birth: "At that time, I was that famous teacher in Takkasilā."

133
The Birds of Bāveru
Bāveru Jātaka

It was while staying at Jetavana that the Buddha told this story about ascetics of other sects.

Before the Buddha's Enlightenment, these ascetics were greatly honored and received plenty of support. After the Buddha began teaching, they lost a great deal of that honor, their support fell away, and they were like fireflies at sunrise. One day, some of the bhikkhus were talking about this in the Hall of Truth. When the Buddha heard what they were discussing, he said, "Bhikkhus, not now only, but formerly, too, one without virtue was honored until the truly virtuous appeared and deprived him of his glory." Then the Buddha told this story of the past.

Long, long ago, when Brahmadatta was reigning in Bārānasi, some merchants sailed from Kāsi to the kingdom of Bāveru.[3] These merchants were very fond of birds, and they always had some kind of bird aboard their ship. On this particular journey, they were traveling with a black crow. It seems that there were no birds in Bāveru. Therefore, when the inhabitants saw the crow perched on the top of the mast, they shouted, "Look at that beautiful

---

3 Perhaps Babylon.

shiny black creature. With a sharp beak for a mouth and eyes like jewels, it is a sight to behold! We have never seen anything like it! Please, sirs, give us this bird," they begged the merchants. "We have nothing like this, and you can easily get another in your own country."

"This bird is very useful to us," the merchants replied, "but we might part with it for a price."

"We will pay you a gold coin," they offered.

"Oh, no!" the merchants protested. "This bird as black as charcoal is worth at least two hundred coins."

The two sides began bargaining, and the local people gradually increased their offer to one hundred coins.

"All right," the merchants agreed, "for the sake of friendship, you may have it for one hundred coins."

The people of Bāveru took the crow and put it in a golden cage. Every day, they fed it fish, meat, and fruit. In a place where no other birds lived, even a crow endowed with ten vices[4] received the highest honor and glory.

The next time the merchants sailed to Baveru, they carried on board a royal peacock. They had trained the bird to cry when anyone snapped his fingers and to dance when anyone clapped his hands. When the ship arrived, a huge crowd gathered to see the magnificent bird. As soon as the vessel was securely moored to the pier, the merchants had the peacock perform on deck. People were entranced by the peacock's cry and the brilliance of its beautiful tail. Everyone was enraptured by the spectacle of the peacock's dance.

"This is certainly the king of the birds!" someone cried. "He is both beautiful and well-trained!" cried another.

"We must have this bird here in Baveru! Sell it to us!" many cried at once.

"First we brought a crow, and you demanded that," the merchants protested. "Now we have a royal peacock, and you are demanding that, too. If you take every bird from us, it will be impossible to visit here again!"

"Never mind that, sirs," the local people replied. "Just let us have this beautiful bird. You can easily replace it in your own country."

After very hard bargaining back and forth, the two sides finally agreed to a price of one thousand coins. The peacock was placed in an elegant cage decorated with the seven precious things. Within hours of its arrival, this royal bird was receiving the highest glory and honor. Every day, many citizens brought it fish and wild fruit, honey, parched corn, and sugared water. Those who had previously paid respect to the crow now gave their

4   The crow is (1) destructive, (2) reckless, (3) greedy, (4) gluttonous, (5 rough, (6) merciless, (7) weak, (8) noisy, (9) forgetful, and (10) wasteful..

full attention to the peacock. Day by day, fewer and fewer people visited the crow, until, finally, no one gave the poor bird a second glance.

The neglected crow no longer received any food at all. One day, he cried plaintively, "Caw! Caw!" Then he flew away and settled on a dunghill.

Having concluded his story, the Buddha added, "Just as the crow was honored until the peacock arrived, in the same way, the various ascetics were respected and supported until I attained Enlightenment and began teaching the Truth. Then the Buddha identified the birth: "At that time, Nigantha Nātaputta was the crow, and I was the royal peacock."

134
Alms Without Limit
Visayha Jātaka

It was while staying at Jetavana that the Buddha told this story about Anāthapindika,

Anāthapindika valued nothing more than the Triple Gem.[1] He had spent over fifty-four crores to build Jetavana Monastery. Whenever the Buddha was staying there, this pious layman visited at least three times every day—at daybreak, after breakfast, and in the evening. Thinking that the sāmaneras and boys might need something, he never went empty-handed. When he went in the early morning, he took rice-gruel; after breakfast, he took ghee, butter, honey, jaggery, and other medicines; in the evening, he offered incense, flowers, and robes. His generosity knew no bounds.

The Buddha told Anāthapindika, "Your devotion to giving is not surprising, but what is remarkable is that a wise man of old continued giving alms, even when urged to stop by Sakka himself." At the merchant's request, the Buddha told this story of the past.

Long, long ago, when Brahmadatta was reigning in Bārānasi, the Bodhisatta was a great merchant named Visayha, worth eighty crores, who

---

1   The occasion for this story is the same as that for Tale 22.

always kept the five precepts. Being generous and devoted to generosity, Visayha had alms-halls built at the four city gates, in the heart of the city, and at the door of his own house. He regularly went on foot to offer alms with his own hand. Every day, he gave food, exactly the same as his own, to thousands of ascetics and mendicants.

One day, Sakka noticed that his white marble throne was shaking and becoming hot. "Who is trying to oust me and to win my place in heaven?" Sakka wondered. Looking around, he saw Visayha going on foot from place to place to offer alms with his own hand. "With his alms-giving, this merchant is stirring up all Jambudīpa," Sakka exclaimed. "I must stop him before he dethrones me and becomes Sakka in my place!"

Sakka waved his hand, and, in one stroke, all of Visayha's jars of oil, honey, ghee, and molasses vanished. All the grain disappeared from his storerooms. All the bags of gold evaporated from his treasury. All of his servants, slaves, and workmen disappeared, as well.

Those who were dependent on his charity marched in a procession to his house and cried loudly, "My Lord, the alms-halls have disappeared. There are now only empty lots."

"Instead of food, then, take money," Visayha replied. He summoned his wife and instructed her to distribute money to all who had come to beg. His like-minded wife searched the whole house, even the darkest corners, but couldn't find a single coin.

"Husband," she cried, "except for the clothes we are wearing, I find nothing! The whole house is empty!"

Visayha rushed from room to room. He opened the storerooms and inspected the treasury. He could not find anyone or anything either. "My dear," he said to his wife, "although everything seems to be gone and we are alone, we must not stop our alms-giving. Search the whole house once more. You must find something!"

In a small doorway at the side of the compound, she found a sickle, a carrying pole, and some rope which a grass cutter had left there. She gave these things to Visayha and said, "Husband, this is all I could find."

"Well, dear, in my whole life I have never cut grass before, but today, since we must continue giving alms, I will try." The merchant picked up the sickle, the pole, and the rope, and walked out of the city. When he came to a place with plenty of grass, he cut it, and tied it up in two large bundles. "One is for us," he declared, "and with the other we will give alms." Hanging the bundles of grass on his carrying pole, he walked to the city gate and sold the grass for two coins. He gave one coin to some beggars who were nearby, but many others cried out, "Give something to us! Please help me, too!" Unable to restrain himself, Visayha gave them the second coin. Without any money for themselves, he and his wife fasted that day.

Six days passed in this way. During this time, Visayha and his wife had no solid food. The merchant was weak from hunger, and, because he was not used to physical labor, his entire body ached. On the seventh day, Visayha began working even though the sun was particularly bright and hot, without a breeze for relief. After a few minutes, he became dizzy and collapsed, scattering the grass he had cut.

As soon as Visayha fell, Sakka, who had been watching for the entire week, appeared, standing in mid-air, and called out, "Visayha! You offered alms without limit! Through giving too much, you lost your wealth. I urge you to show a little self-restraint, thus enjoying greater joy as long as you live."

As he regained his senses, Visayha asked weakly, "Who are you?"

"I am Sakka!"

"You? Sakka? What hypocrisy!" Visayha cried. "It was by giving alms that you were reborn in heaven. You attained your exalted position by giving alms, by keeping the moral precepts, by observing the Uposatha days, and by fulfilling the seven vows. How can you now forbid me to practice the very same virtues that gave you your own greatness? Truly, you should be ashamed of yourself for stooping so low! As for us, we will give alms as long as we have life. We will never repress a generous thought!"

"All right," Sakka relented, "but, please, my good man, tell me why you give alms so steadfastly."

"My Lord," Visayha replied, "do not assume that I give alms because I desire rebirth in your heaven. My goal is neither Tāvatimsa nor the Brahma heavens. I give all that I can because I seek omniscience!"

Delighted to hear those words, Sakka extended his hand and touched the merchant on the shoulder. The instant Visayha enjoyed this divine favor, his whole being was filled with exquisite joy. At that very same moment, Sakka not only restored to Visayha and his wife everything he had taken away, but he increased their wealth one-thousandfold.

"Virtuous sir!" Sakka exclaimed, before returning to Tāvatimsa, "As long as you live, continue to give alms without limit. May your aspiration be fulfilled!"

Having concluded his story, the Buddha identified the birth: "At that time, Rāhula's mother was the merchant's wife, and I was Visayha."

135

The Monkey's Heart
Vānara Jātaka

It was while staying at Veluvana that the Buddha told this story about Devadatta's attempts on his life.

Long, long ago, when Brahmadatta was reigning in Bārānasi, the Bodhisatta was born as a monkey and lived on the banks of the great Gangā in the Himavat. In the river near his home, there lived two crocodiles. One day, the female crocodile developed a craving for the monkey's heart. She told her husband what she wanted to eat, and he immediately resolved to kill the monkey in order to satisfy his wife's longing.

The crocodile swam near where the monkey was sitting in a tree and called out, "Friend! Not far from here is a lovely island where the fruit is ripe and extremely sweet. Let's go and enjoy it."

"I'd love to go," the monkey replied, "but how can I get there?"

"Jump on my back, and I'll carry you there," the crocodile offered.

Not suspecting the crocodile of any ill-will, the monkey jumped on his back and sat there comfortably as the crocodile swam smoothly on the surface of the river. As soon as they were in the middle of the deep river, the crocodile began his dive.

"What are you doing?" the monkey cried. "Don't go under the water like that! I can't swim!"

"I know," the crocodile replied with a smirk. "I'm going to drown you and give your heart to my wife to satisfy her longing."

"Foolish fellow!" the monkey retorted sharply. "Do you suppose I carry my heart with me all the time?"

"Don't you? Where have you left it?"

"I didn't want to risk getting it damaged. Don't you see it hanging on that big tree?" The monkey pointed to a tree far away on the riverbank where a bright red fruit was hanging from a bough.

"Sure, I can see it, but how can I get it?"

"Just take me over there, and, because you are my good friend, I will give it to you."

The crocodile swam toward that great tree. As soon as he was near the bank, the monkey sprang from the crocodile's back, scampered up the tree, and called out, "Now that I'm safe on dry land, I'll be satisfied eating the fruit at hand. There's no need to sail to mythical islands if the fare of passage is my heart. When danger comes, I'm quick-witted, so I have nothing to fear from a gullible fool like you!" As he disappeared into the jungle, he shouted, "Good-bye, my friend!"

Having concluded his story, the Buddha identified the birth: "At that time, Devadatta was the crocodile, and I was the monkey."

136
The Best of Seasonings
Kesava Jātaka

It was while staying at Jetavana that the Buddha told this story about food given in friendship.

Anāthapindika, the devout merchant, regularly fed five hundred bhikkhus in his house. The doors of his mansion were always open to the Sangha. Their yellow robes brightened the halls, and their noble virtues perfumed the passageways.

One day, while making a procession around the city, the king happened to catch sight of the assembly of bhikkhus in the merchant's house.

Also wanting to grant perpetual alms to the Buddha's order, the king went to Jetavana. After greeting and paying his respects to the Buddha, the king invited five hundred bhikkhus to receive their meal in the palace daily.

Beginning the next day, the best rice and curries were prepared in the king's kitchen, and five hundred bhikkhus went to the palace every day, but neither the king nor anyone in his family offered the food with his own hand. The food was dispensed by the king's servants, who were ordered to do so. The bhikkhus accepted the food, but, instead of sitting down at the palace, they took the delicious offerings to the houses of other devotees, where they handed over their bowls and accepted whatever was set before them.

One day, a great quantity of ripe fruit was brought to the king. "Give it to the bhikkhus for their dessert," he ordered his servants.

Servants carried the fruit to the dining hall but returned immediately and informed the king that not a single bhikkhu was there.

"What, is it not time yet?" asked the king.

"Yes, Sire, it is the time," other servants told him, "but the bhikkhus take the food we give them to the houses of other devotees. The bhikkhus give your food to the devotees and accept whatever is set before them.

"Our food is scrumptious," the king thought, "and of the highest quality. I wonder why the bhikkhus neglect it and eat the common fare provided in other houses. I'll have to ask the Buddha about this." At the proper time, he went to Jetavana, paid his respects, and told the Teacher what was happening.

"The best food is that which is given affectionately by the hand of the donor," the Buddha replied. "Since no one in your palace distributes the food hospitably, the bhikkhus prefer to eat in a place where they feel more welcome. There is no seasoning, Sire, equal to that of friendship. A dish given without friendship, even though it contains the four sweet things, is not worth as much as coarse wild leaves served with affection. Long ago, a wise man, who was afflicted with disease, forsook the comfort of the king's palace and the care of royal physicians to be cured on a diet of wild rice and millet eaten among his intimate friends."[1] At the king's request, the Buddha told this story of the past.

Long, long ago, when Brahmadatta was reigning in Bārānasi, the Bodhisatta was born into a brahmin family in the kingdom of Kāsi and was named Kappa. After completing his education at Takkasilā, he became an ascetic. In the Himavat, Kappa studied under an ascetic named Kesava and soon became the chief of Kesava's five hundred students. The two ascetics became close friends.

At the beginning of the rainy season, Kesava and his students left the Himavat to get salt and vinegar and to find a place to stay. They arrived in Bārānasi and spent the first night in the royal park. The next morning, they went into the city for alms. As they filed past the palace, the king saw them and invited all of them to take lunch in the palace. He also invited them to stay in the royal park for the rainy season and provided food for all of them every day. When the rains were over, Kesava went to the king to take leave.

"Venerable Sir," the king replied, "you are elderly. Our royal park and our palace are comfortable for you. Please send your students back to the Himavat, and stay here."

---

1   More about this is found in the occasion of Tale 179.

After some persuasion, Kesava agreed to the king's invitation and told Kappa to take the students back to the Himavat and to continue teaching them. Alone in the capital, Kesava grew increasingly unhappy. He longed for Kappa's companionship and became so depressed that he could not sleep well. Unable to meet Kappa and to discuss his ideas with him, Kesava's appetite suffered. Food no longer tasted good nor sat well on his stomach. Eventually, he developed dysentery and experienced severe pain.

The king summoned the royal physicians who carefully attended to the ascetic, but his illness did not subside. Indeed, his symptoms worsened.

Finally, the weakened ascetic asked the king, "Sire, do you wish me to die or to recover?"

"To recover, sir, of course!" the king replied without hesitation.

"In that case, Sire, please send me back to the Himavat," the ascetic requested.

"As you wish, sir," said the king. He immediately summoned one of his ministers, a man named Nārada, and ordered him and a group of foresters to escort Kesava to the hermitage in the Himavat. When he had accomplished his task, Nārada returned to the capital.

Despite the rigors of the journey, as soon as Kesava saw Kappa, his depression ended, and he was able to smile again.

Kappa prepared some broth made of millet, wild rice, and leaves, with neither salt nor spices, for the elderly ascetic, and that simple meal cured the dysentery.

Some time later, the king asked Nārada to visit Kesava and to ascertain his condition.

Nārada traveled once more to the Himavat. When he arrived at the hermitage, he was surprised to find Kesava completely recovered and sitting peacefully with Kappa.

"Reverend Sir, five of the king's own physicians treated you, but they could not cure your sickness. How did Kappa manage to restore your health?"

"You see, Nārada," Kesava replied, "everything here makes me happy. Just the sight of Kappa and the sound of his pleasing words cheer me up. As soon as I arrived, Kappa gave me some broth made of millet, wild rice, and leaves. That simple unsalted and unseasoned broth eased my pains and soothed my stomach."

"But, sir," Nārada objected, still quite puzzled, "in Bārānasi, the king provided you with the purest rice delicately boiled and flavored with meat. How is it that you prefer insipid millet and wild rice, which is an ascetic's fare?"

"It doesn't matter whether the food is simple or refined, scanty or abundant," Kesava explained. "If the meal is served with affection, it is delicious and restorative. Truly, affection is the best of all seasonings."

Nārada took note of the wise ascetic's words. He returned to Bārānasi and reported to the king, "Kesava told me that friendship lifted his depression and that he was cured by food served with affection by his companions."

Having concluded his story, the Buddha identified the birth: "At that time, Ānanda was the king, Sāriputta was Nārada, Baka-Brahmā was Kesava, and I was Kappa."

137
Antidote for Grief
Sujāta Jātaka

It was while staying at Jetavana that the Buddha told this story about grief.

When his elderly father died, a landowner in Sāvatthī was overcome with grief and completely distracted by sorrow. The Buddha knew that the landowner had the capacity for spiritual attainment, so, one morning, he went on almsrounds along that street. As he passed the door, the landowner invited him to enter.

"Layman, are you grieving?" the Buddha asked his host.

"Yes, Venerable Sir, I am," the landowner replied. "Friend, long ago, a man who had lost his father listened to words of wisdom and overcame his grief." At his host's request, the Buddha told this story of the past.

Long, long ago, when Brahmadatta was reigning in Bārānasi, the Bodhisatta was born into the house of a wealthy landowner and was named Sujāta. When Sujāta was still quite young, his grandfather died. Sujāta's father was overcome with grief. He took the old man's bones from the cremation pyre and made a cetiya for them in the garden. He decorated the cetiya with flowers and spent virtually all his waking hours mourning there. He was so distraught that he neglected himself. He ignored his business, stopped bathing, and often forgot to eat.

"Father has not been himself at all since grandfather died," Sujāta thought. "I must help him. I am sure that no one else can assuage his grief."

That afternoon, as he was walking just outside the city gate, Sujāta found exactly what he needed—a dead ox lying beside the road. He brought a bowl of water, gathered some grass, and placed both at the ox's head. Kneeling beside the dead animal, Sujāta began chanting mournfully. "Eat and drink! Eat and drink!"

Passers-by stared at this strange sight, and those who recognized him asked anxiously, "Sujāta, have you lost your mind? Why are you offering grass and water to a dead ox?" Without answering, Sujāta continued his chanting.

Friends hurried to his house and told his father. "Sir, your son has gone mad! Sujāta is offering grass and water to a dead ox near the city gate!"

The landowner immediately forgot about his father and began worrying about his son. He rushed there, saw what was happening, and cried, "Sujāta, my boy! What's wrong with you? What are you doing? That ox is dead! It cannot eat! It cannot drink!"

Sujāta turned to look at his father's worn and grizzled face and slowly replied. "I think this beast just might come to life again. After all, its head, four feet, and tail are still intact. My grandfather's head, arms and legs are gone! There's nothing left of him but charred bones. Some fool, however, still weeps constantly over his grave."

These simple sentences, bluntly spoken by his son, utterly shocked the landowner and brought him to his senses. "My son is right," he thought. "He is wise and has done this to console me." Aloud he said, "Sujāta, my dear son, you are wise, and I have been foolish. I will stop grieving. I know that everything is impermanent. Everyone should be so blessed as to have a son like you to ease his sorrow!"

Having concluded his story, the Buddha taught the Dhamma, and the landowner attained the first path. Then the Buddha identified the birth: "At that time, I was Sujāta."

138
The Worn-Out Skin
Uraga Jātaka

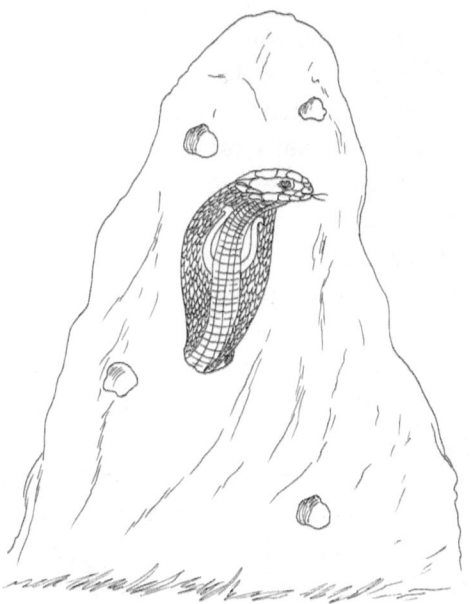

It was while staying at Jetavana that the Buddha told this story about a landowner whose son had died.

When he went to the house of a landowner one day, he found the man grieving and asked why.

"Venerable Sir," the man replied, "I have been in mourning since my son's untimely death."

"Sir, that which is subject to dissolution has dissolved; that which is subject to destruction has been destroyed," the Buddha taught him. "This doesn't happen to only one family, nor to a single village. It happens in countless spheres. All beings are subject to death. No creature is exempt from dying, and nothing can endure unchanged. Long ago, when the wise lost a son, they said, 'That which is subject to destruction is destroyed,' and shed not a tear." At the landowner's request, the Buddha told this story of the past.

Long, long ago, when Brahmadatta was reigning in Bārānasi, the Bodhisatta was a brahmin farmer in a village outside Bārānasi. He had two children, a son and a daughter. When his son became of age, he was married to a girl of similar status who came to live with the family. It was a happy and affectionate household of six: the farmer, his wife, the son, the daughter-in-law, the daughter, and a servant girl.

The farmer regularly exhorted the others to be generous, to keep the five precepts, and to observe the Uposatha days. He also urged them to be mindful and to ponder often on the thought of death. "For creatures like us," he taught his family, "death is certain; only life is uncertain. All things are impermanent and subject to decay. Therefore, be mindful day and night." The entire household listened attentively to his advice and lived virtuously, frequently recollecting the certainty of death.

One day, the farmer and his son went to work in the field. While the father was plowing, the son raked the brush, weeds, and stubble into a pile and set fire to it. Not far from where he was working, a snake lived in an anthill. The thick smoke irritated the snake's eyes, and it emerged from its hole in a great fury. Seeing the young man, the snake thought, "My pain is due to that fellow!" It reared up, spread its hood wide, struck the youth with its fangs, and crawled away. The venom did its work swiftly, and the son fell dead beside the fire.

As soon as the farmer saw his son fall, he left his oxen and ran to help him. Kneeling down, however, he realized that the boy was already dead. The farmer picked up his son's body, carried it to the edge of the field, laid it at the foot of a tree, and covered it with a shawl. "That which is subject to dissolution has dissolved," he recited softly. "That which is subject to destruction has been destroyed. All living beings are subject to death." With neither tears nor lamentation, he returned to his plowing.

When a neighbor happened to be walking past the field, the farmer called to him, "Friend, are you going home?"

"Yes, I am," the other answered.

"Please give this message to my wife, 'Today, do not prepare food for two; for one is enough. Rather than sending the maid with the lunch, all four must put on clean clothes and come with incense and flowers.'"

The neighbor agreed, went to the house, and repeated that exact message to the man's wife.

"Who asked you to give this message to me?" she asked. "Your husband, lady," he replied.

She immediately understood that her son was dead, but she did not so much as tremble. With great calm and self-possession, she told the rest of the family to put on clean clothes and prepared her husband's lunch as he had directed. Then she herself put on white clothes and gathered up incense and flowers. With the wife at the head, they all walked to the field. Although they all realized why they were going to the field, not one of them shed a tear.

The farmer sat silently in the shade beside his son's body and ate his simple lunch. When he had finished, they all collected fire-wood. After placing the body on the funeral pyre, they made offerings of incense and flowers and lit the fire. Solemnly reflecting on death, none of them shed a single tear.

As this was happening, Sakka's throne became hot. "Who is trying to take my throne?" asked the king of the devas, as he surveyed the world. He immediately realized that the cause was that family's moral excellence and self-restraint. Highly pleased, he resolved to extol their virtues with a lion's roar and to reward them for their virtuous conduct.

Appearing beside the funeral pyre, Sakka asked the family what they were doing.

"We are cremating the body of a man, My Lord," answered the farmer.

"That cannot be a man that you are burning," Sakka retorted. "I suspect you are roasting the flesh of some beast you have slain."

"Not so, My Lord," they replied in unison. "This is the body of a man."

"He must have been an enemy," Sakka remarked provocatively.

"No, My Lord, not an enemy," the farmer said. "He was my own son."

"This son could not have been very dear to you."

"He was much beloved, My Lord."

"If that is so, why aren't you weeping?"

The farmer replied calmly, "Each man abandons his body, much as a snake casts off its worn-out skin. No lamentation can touch one who has died. Why should I grieve? He fares along the path he had to tread."

Then Sakka turned to the wife and asked, "Dear lady, what was this dead man to you?"

"I carried him for ten months in my womb and nursed him at my breast. I rejoiced when he learned to walk and to talk. He was my only son, My Lord."

"I grant you that a father, being a man, may not weep, but, surely, a mother's heart is soft and tender. Why aren't you weeping?"

She replied calmly, "Uninvited he came; uninvited he went. What cause is there for tears? No lamentation can touch one who has died. Why should I grieve? He fares along the path he had to tread."

Then Sakka turned to the farmer's daughter and asked, "Miss, what was this dead man to you?"

"He was my brother, My Lord."

"Sisters are usually loving towards their brothers. Why aren't you weeping?"

The young girl replied calmly, "I could fast and weep for my brother, but what profit would that bring? That would only make my family suffer more. No lamentation can touch one who has died. Why should I grieve? He fares along the path he had to tread."

Then Sakka turned to the farmer's daughter-in-law and asked, "Lady, what was this dead man to you?"

"He was my husband, My Lord."

"When a husband dies, the widow is pitiful and helpless. Why aren't you weeping?"

The young woman replied calmly, "As children cry in vain to grasp the moon, mortals mourn in vain when those they love are gone. No lamentation can touch one who has died. Why should I grieve? He fares along the path he had to tread."

Then Sakka turned to the maid and asked, "Lady, what was this dead man to you?"

"He was my master, My Lord."

"He must have so abused you and beaten you that you are glad that he is dead!"

"Don't say that, My Lord. I will not hear you speak ill of him. My young master was full of kindness and affection for me. He was like a son to me."

"If that is so, why aren't you weeping?"

The maid replied calmly, "Just as none can piece together again a smashed pot, one mourns the dead in vain. No lamentation can touch one who has died. Why should I grieve? He fares along the path he had to tread."

Sakka was greatly pleased with what each had to say. "Wisely has this family reflected on death. As Sakka, I am aware that all of you have also lived virtuously. For this, I wish to reward you. Henceforth, you need not work so hard to earn a living. I bestow upon your house an abundance of the seven precious things. As you give alms with this wealth, I urge you to continue keeping the precepts, observing the Uposatha days, and being mindful in all you do." After filling their house with treasure as he had promised, Sakka returned to Tāvatimsa.

Having concluded his story, the Buddha taught the Dhamma, and the landowner attained the first path. Then the Buddha identified the birth: "At that time, Khujjuttarā was the maid, Uppalavannā was the daughter, Rāhula was the son, Khemā was the mother, and I was the farmer."

139
To Level the Earth
Kārandiya Jātaka

It was while staying at Jetavana that the Buddha told this story about Venerable Sāriputta.

Whenever people, such as hunters or fishermen, who were following wrong livelihood, came to visit Venerable Sāriputta, he urged them to keep the five precepts. Because of their respect for him, they took the precepts, but, continuing the same occupation, they invariably failed to keep them.

When Venerable Sāriputta mentioned this to other bhikkhus, they replied, "Good sir, you preach the law to them against their wishes. You ask them to take the precepts, and, because they dare not disobey you, they do. You should not urge the precepts on men like that." Sāriputta was offended by what they said.

Later, in the Hall of Truth, some bhikkhus were talking about this. When the Buddha heard what they were discussing, he said, "This is not the first time, Bhikkhus, that Sāriputta has preached the Dhamma to everyone he chanced to meet." Then he told this story of the past.

Long, long ago, when Brahmadatta was reigning in Bārānasi, the Bodhisatta was born into a brahmin family and was named Kārandiya. When he was old enough, his parents sent him to Takkasilā to study with a re-nowned teacher, and Kārandiya soon became the teacher's best student. This teacher was so famous that many people paid their respects to him wherever he went, and he insisted on preaching the moral law, particularly the five precepts, to everyone. Some people, of course, were not inclined to listen to his preaching, but they had no choice. Many, such as fishermen and hunters, whose livelihood involved killing, found it impossible to keep the precepts and broke them as soon as they returned home. This laxity on the part of his followers bothered the teacher greatly, and he complained about it to his students.

"Great teacher," they replied, "these people don't keep the precepts because you give them against their wishes. You should not preach to those who are not prepared to listen. You should give the precepts only to those who are willing to undertake them."

In spite of this good advice, the teacher did not change his ways in the slightest. He preached and gave the precepts to everyone he met.

One day, some donors invited the teacher and his students to participate in a large offering of cakes.

The teacher called Kārandiya and said, "My dear boy, I won't be going to that alms-giving, but I want you to go in my place with the other students. Please bring my portion back for me."

Kārandiya went with the students as his teacher had instructed. On the return, he noticed a cave near the road and had an idea. He told the other students to sit comfortably and to eat their cakes. He set his bowl on the ground, walked to the mouth of the cave, and began throwing large stones inside. While the others ate quietly, he stood there and threw as many stones as he could find. After a few minutes, the other students demanded to know what he was doing, but Kārandiya did not answer. Nor did he stop. The others hurried back and told their master that Kārandiya was behaving very strangely.

The teacher immediately rushed to the cave. "Why are you heaving all those stones into that cave, Kārandiya?" he asked. "Do you think you can fill in the cave?"

"I intend to make the whole country as smooth as the palm of my hand. I will level the hills and raise up the valleys. In order to accomplish this task, I must fill each hole and cave with stones."

Suspecting that his best student had lost his mind, the teacher gently said, "Kārandiya, it is impossible for one of mortal birth to level this great earth. I'm afraid it is beyond your power to fill even this single cave, which isn't particularly large."

"Why can't I level the whole earth?" Kārandiya asked calmly. "You seem to think that you can make the whole world moral. Venerable Sir, if I lack the power to level the earth, you lack the power to make all sinners keep the precepts."

The teacher immediately understood what Kārandiya was saying. "My dear boy, you are quite right," he said, paying due respect to his student's wisdom. "Just as the earth cannot be leveled, so not all people can keep the precepts. I will give up trying to reform everyone I meet. How fortunate I am to have a student as wise as you!"

Having concluded his story, the Buddha identified the birth: "At that time, Sāriputta was the teacher, and I was his student Kārandiya."

140
The Quail's Revenge
Latukika Jātaka

It was while staying at Veluvana that the Buddha told this story about Devadatta.

One day, the bhikkhus were talking about the Buddha's cousin. "Devadatta is harsh and violent," they said. "He doesn't have the slightest pity for others." When the Buddha heard what they were discussing, he said, "Bhikkhus, not only now, but also long ago, he was pitiless." Then the Buddha told this story of the past.

Long, long ago, when Brahmadatta was reigning in Bārānasi, the Bodhisatta was born as an elephant. He grew up to be a fine beast and became the leader of a large herd in the Himavat. At that time, a quail laid her eggs in a nest on the ground. In due time, her young broke out of their shells. While the chicks were still unable to fly, the herd of eighty thousand elephants came that way, looking for food.

On seeing them, the quail thought, "These elephants might trample on my young ones and kill them. I will beg their leader for his righteous protection for my babies." She stood in front of him, raised her wings, and cried out,

"Great elephant, lord of the forest, I am only a tiny bird. I appeal to you, as leader of this vast herd, to spare my little ones."

"Mother quail," the elephant replied, "don't worry. I will protect your children." While the entire herd passed by, he stood directly over the nest to guard it. After all the elephants had gone, he warned the quail, "Not far off, coming along behind us, there is a solitary rogue elephant. He will not pay any attention to anything I say. When he comes near, you must beg him, also, not to harm your babies." After giving her this advice, he followed his herd.

Very soon, just as the elephant leader had predicted, the rogue elephant approached that spot. The quail went forward to meet him. With wings raised respectfully, she asked him not to harm her chicks.

When this mighty elephant heard her plea, he laughed loudly. Mocking her, he cried, "You are nothing but a puny quail. How could you possibly stop me? Why shouldn't I kill your babies? Your nest is in my way! With only my left front foot, I could easily smash one thousand birds like these! In fact, I think I will!" At that moment, he brought his foot down with a resounding "Thud!" and crushed the entire nest with all the baby birds. Then he stood over the flattened nest and washed their remains away in a flood of urine. Proud of himself, he went off trumpeting loudly.

"Go ahead and trumpet as much as you like," the quail said softly. "You will soon see what I can do. You don't know the difference between strength of body and strength of mind. I will teach you a lesson. The fool abuses power and suffers the consequences! Monster! You killed my helpless little ones! Somehow I will punish you," she vowed grimly.

A few days later, the quail did a favor for a crow, who gratefully asked: "What can I do for you in return?"

"Nothing much," said the quail, "but do you know the rogue elephant that roams in this area?"

"Yes," the crow replied, "I see him often."

"Well, the next time you see him, use your sharp beak to peck out his eyes."

The crow readily agreed. That same day, the quail did a favor for a blue fly. "How can I repay you?" the fly asked.

"Do you know that rogue elephant?" the quail asked. "Of course, I do," answered the fly.

"Well," continued the quail. "Very soon, the crow is going to peck out his eyes. After she has done it, I would like you to lay your eggs in the bloody sockets."

The fly immediately agreed and flew off to find the elephant.

A little later, the quail kindly helped a frog.

"How can I possibly repay you?" asked the frog.

"Very soon," replied the quail, "a blind elephant will come crashing through here in search of water. Go to the top of that hill," she said, pointing a short distance off. "As soon as you hear him, start croaking loudly. Then, when he has climbed to the top, come down, and croak again at the bottom of the cliff. That's all I ask of you."

The frog willingly agreed.

The crow found the rogue elephant with no difficulty, landed on his head, and quickly pecked out both of his eyes. Coming right behind her, the fly dropped her eggs into the sockets. It was not long before the eggs hatched, and the elephant, tormented by maggots, was maddened with pain. Tortured by thirst and wanting to wash his bloody and infected wounds, he trumpeted loudly. He thrashed wildly, left and right, in search of water. The frog, hearing his cue, began croaking as loudly as he could from the top of the hill.

"Aha!" cried the elephant. "Frogs live in water. There must be water there." He slowly climbed the hill, following, as carefully as he could, the sound of the frog. As soon as the elephant had reached the top, the frog hopped down the steep cliff and croaked again at the bottom. "Yes," sighed the elephant. "I can still hear the frog. He must be in the water. Surely there is water right there." Unable to see where he was, he continued to follow the croaking, stepped off the edge of the cliff, and fell to his death.

The quail, who had been waiting nearby and watching this drama unfold, approached the dead elephant and proclaimed, "I have seen the back of my enemy!" Then she triumphantly ran up and down the elephant's broken body.

Having concluded his story, the Buddha added, "Bhikkhus, one should not anger anyone. By cooperating, these four weak creatures brought about the destruction of a powerful elephant." Then the Buddha identified the birth: "At that time, Devadatta was the rogue elephant, and I was the leader of the herd of elephants."

141

The Jealous Rage
Culla-Dhammapāla Jātaka

It was while staying at Veluvana that the Buddha told this story about Devadatta's attempts to kill him.

One day, the bhikkhus were talking about Devadatta's violent nature. "Friends," they said, "Devadatta is always scheming to slay the Buddha. First, he arranged for archers to shoot him. Then he rolled a boulder down to crush him. Finally, he released the Nalagiri elephant to kill him in the street."

When the Buddha heard what they were discussing, he said, "Bhikkhus, long ago, also, Devadatta sought to kill me, but he never excited a particle of fear in me before, nor does he do so now." Then he told this story of the past.

Long, long ago, when Mahā-Patāpa was reigning in Bārānasi, his queen-consort was named Candā, and the Bodhisatta was born as their son. They named the baby Dhammapāla.

One day, when Dhammapāla was seven months old, he was bathed in scented water and handed to the queen. While she was sitting in her chamber playing with the baby, the king entered. Queen Candā was so engrossed with the boy and so filled with a mother's love for her child that she failed to rise.

The king was furious at this affront and thought, "Already this woman is filled with pride on account of her son and no longer respects me at all. As the boy grows up, she will think, 'I have a man in my son,' and she will ignore me completely. I must have the baby put to death at once."

Without even greeting the queen, the king returned to the throne room and summoned the executioner. This man arrived almost immediately wearing his yellow robe and a crimson wreath. His axe was on his shoulder, and he was carrying a block and a bowl, the tools of his trade. He stood before the king and asked, "What is your pleasure, Sire?"

"Go to the queen's chamber, and bring Dhammapāla to me," ordered the king.

The queen had realized that the king had left her in a jealous rage, and she was holding the infant tightly to her bosom and weeping when the executioner entered. This heartless man gave her a sharp blow on the back and snatched the boy out of her arms. He returned with the baby to the king and asked again, "What is your pleasure, Sire?"

The king had his servants bring a board and placed it in front of the throne. "Put the boy on the board," he ordered the executioner. As the executioner laid the baby on his back on the board, Queen Candā, who had hurriedly followed them to the throne room, stepped forward. She stood weeping at the baby's head.

"What is your pleasure, Sire?" the executioner asked. "Cut off Dhammapāla's hands," ordered the king.

"Your Majesty!" Queen Candā cried. "My son is merely an innocent baby, seven months old! He knows nothing! He has done nothing! If there is any fault, it is mine. Let Mahā-Patāpa's wretched queen take all the blame. Cut off my hands, and spare the child!"

"What is your pleasure, Sire?" the executioner asked again. "Cut off his hands," said the king coldly.

The executioner swung his sharp axe and, with two swift strokes, cut off the boy's hands as easily as if they had been tender young bamboo shoots.

The baby uttered no cry. Filled with loving-kindness, he bore the pain with patience. Queen Candā knelt and picked up the tiny hands. First, she put the tips of his fingers to her lips. Then she sank to the floor at the head of the board and placed the bloody hands in her lap. Soon her dress was smeared with blood.

"What is your pleasure, Sire?" the executioner asked again. "Cut off his feet!" ordered the king.

"No!" Queen Candā cried. "Dhammapāla is innocent! Let Mahā-Patāpa's wretched queen take all the blame! Cut off my feet, and spare the child!"

"What is your pleasure, Sire?" the executioner asked again. "Cut off his feet," replied the king.

The executioner swung his sharp axe and cut off both of the baby's feet with one swift stroke. Queen Candā placed his tiny blood-stained feet in her lap and sobbed, "My Lord Mahā-Patāpa, his feet and hands have been cut off. A mother is bound to support her children. I will work for wages and support my son. Please give him to me."

"Is the king's pleasure fulfilled?" the executioner asked. "Is my service finished, Sire?"

"Not yet," replied the king.

"What is your pleasure, Sire?"

"Cut off his head!" ordered the king.

"No!" cried the queen. "Dhammapāla is innocent! Let Mahā-Patāpa's wretched queen take all the blame! Cut off my head, and spare the child!"

"What is your pleasure, Sire?" the executioner asked again.

"Cut off his head," replied the king.

The executioner swung his sharp axe again and cut off the baby's head.

"Is the king's pleasure fulfilled now?" he asked.

"Not yet," replied the king.

"What is your pleasure, Sire?"

"Encircle the body with a garland of cuts from your sword!" ordered the king.

The executioner picked up the headless body of the baby and threw it spinning into the air. As it fell, he held out his sword and let the body roll along the sharp edge, etching a bright red garland of blood around the torso and scattering bits of flesh on the dais.

Queen Candā gently picked up the mutilated body of her son and placed it in her lap. "Why is there no wise councilor to advise the king not to slay the heir that he begat?" she wailed. "Why is there no loving relative to urge him not to slay his only son?"

Gazing at the heap of bloody flesh that filled her lap, she moaned in a soft voice, "Dear Dhammapāla, by right of birth, you were lord of this great land. Your little arms, once bathed in oil of sandalwood, are now steeped in darkening blood. I cannot bear this grief. My heart breaks at losing you so needlessly!" At that moment, her heart did indeed break, just as bamboo snaps in a forest fire, and she fell dead.

The king, too, fell from his throne. As his body hit the dais, an abyss opened in the earth, and the flames of Avīci Hell flared up. King Mahā-Patāpa plunged into the abyss and vanished from sight. The royal councilors performed the joint funeral rites for Queen Candā and her son, Dhammapāla.

Having concluded his story, the Buddha identified the birth: "At that time, Devadatta was King Mahā-Patāpa, Mahā-Pajāpati Gotamī was Candā, and I was Prince Dhammapāla."

142
The Golden Deer
Suvanna-Miga Jātaka

It was while staying at Jetavana that the Buddha told this story about a young woman.

In Sāvatthī, a householder and his wife, who were devout followers of Venerable Sāriputta and Venerable Moggallāna, had a daughter, who, from childhood, was also deeply devoted to the Buddha. As she grew up, she regularly gave alms, delighted in performing good deeds, and developed wisdom.

When she came of age, another family in Sāvatthī, who were of equal rank but were not followers of the Buddha, wanted to arrange a marriage between her and their son.

"Please choose another young woman," her parents suggested. "Our daughter is a faithful follower of the Buddha, and she is devoted to giving alms. Since you and your son hold divergent beliefs, she would not be able to give alms, to visit the monastery, to hear the Dhamma, and to observe the Uposatha days. Therefore, we cannot give her to you."

"Quite the contrary!" the young man's parents protested. "If your daughter marries into our house, she will be free to practice her beliefs in any way she wishes. We will not prevent her from doing any of these things. Please let her marry our son."

"In that case," they said, "we can agree to the marriage."

The marriage was celebrated with a great feast at an auspicious time, and the young woman became a devoted wife and daughter-in-law.

One day, she said, "Husband, I would like to give alms to my family's bhikkhus."

"Certainly, my dear, "he replied. "You may give them whatever you please."

The next day, she invited the two chief disciples and prepared a great feast of delicious curries. After the bhikkhus had finished, she said to them, "Venerable Sirs, this family is ignorant of the value of the Triple Gem. Until my husband and my in-laws develop confidence in the Buddha and appreciate the Triple Gem, please continue to receive your food here."

The chief disciples agreed and thereafter took their meals every day at the young woman's house.

Sometime later, she said, "Husband, my family's bhikkhus come here daily. Won't you see them?"

Her husband agreed and, the next morning, after the bhikkhus had finished their meal, he came, sat respectfully on one side, and talked with them cordially.

Venerable Sāriputta taught the Dhamma to her husband, and he was so pleased with the chief disciples' demeanor and with Venerable Sāriputta's teaching that, from the next day, he himself prepared mats for the chief disciples and strained their water. Every day, he listened attentively to the exposition of the Dhamma. Gradually, he gave up his heretical views, and, one day, after Venerable Sāriputta had finished teaching, both the husband and wife attained the first path. Not long afterward, the entire household, including the servants, took refuge in the Buddha, Dhamma, and Sangha.

One day after this, the young woman said, "Husband, I am no longer satisfied with the household life. I wish to become a bhikkhunī."

"Very well, my dear," he said, "I, too, am no longer satisfied with the household life. I will become a bhikkhu."

First, he conducted her with great grandeur to a monastery and had her admitted. Then he went to the Buddha and asked to be ordained.

Not long after they had ordained, both of them attained arahatship.

One day, in the Hall of Truth the bhikkhus were talking about these two. "This woman's faith was so strong," they said, "that she was able to bring her husband and all his family into the Buddha Sāsana. How wonderful that both of them not only entered the Sangha, but have now attained arahatship!" When the Buddha heard what they were discussing, he said, "Bhikkhus, this time she set her husband free from the bonds of passion, but, long ago, she freed a wise and great being from the bonds of death." At the bhikkhus' request, the Buddha told this story of the past.

Long, long ago, when Brahmadatta was reigning in Bārānasi, the Bodhisatta was born as a deer the color of gold. He grew up to be a handsome and graceful stag. His hooves were as shiny as black lacquer. His mouth was crimson, his eyes were like jewels, and his horns were like a silver wreath around his head. His mate was a beautiful doe, and they lived harmoniously together. This golden deer was the leader of one hundred sixty dappled deer.

One day, a hunter set a snare on the path that these deer always used. As the golden deer was leading the herd along that path, he did not see the snare, and his foot was caught. He pulled at the rope, trying to break it, but it cut his skin. He pulled again, but the rope tightened and cut the flesh. The third time he pulled, the rope damaged the tendon and cut to the bone. Unable to break the rope and in fear of death, he uttered a cry of alarm. The rest of the herd immediately panicked and fled. As the leader's mate was running, she searched for the golden deer. When she realized that he was not among those fleeing, she thought, "This panic must certainly have something to do with my lord!" She raced back and found him trapped. "My Lord," she cried, as she licked his wound and washed it with her tears, "you are strong! Make an effort," she urged him, "and break this snare! Use your great strength to snap the rope! Unless you are with me, my dear, I will find no happiness in roaming the woodland."

"My dear," the golden stag replied weakly, "I have exerted all my strength, but I cannot break the rope. The more I struggle, the tighter the rope on my leg becomes, and the deeper it cuts my flesh."

"Do not fear!" the doe comforted him. "I will plead with the hunter. I will offer my life in exchange for yours." She stood calmly and firmly beside her blood-stained mate and comforted him as the hunter approached with his spear.

Fearlessly, the doe stepped forward to meet the hunter. Stopping at a respectful distance, she bowed her head and greeted him. "Sir," she began softly, "as you can see, my husband is the color of gold. He is endowed with innumerable virtues and is the great king of a herd of one hundred sixty deer. Please spare his life. I offer my life in his place. I beg you to release him and to kill me instead."

"I have heard a deer speak!" the hunter exclaimed in amazement. "This doe speaks valiantly with a sweet voice. In the realm of men, no one would willingly give up his life even for the king, but this animal is offering her life for her mate! What can this mean?" Addressing the doe directly, he continued, "Gentle deer, I grant you the life of your magnificent mate, and I will spare your life, as well. I could never harm either of you." To the stag, he declared, "Golden king of the deer, you will never again have cause to fear me."

The doe bowed again and thanked the hunter for his mercy. "I rejoice to see my husband free," she told him. "Soon, the entire herd will rejoice to have our king restored to us."

As soon as he was free, the golden deer thought, "Now that this hunter has restored my freedom and spared my life, that of my mate, and, indeed, the lives of my herd, I must help him. One should always repay one's benefactor." He presented the hunter with a magic jewel which he had found in their feeding ground. "With this jewel," he said, "you can support your family without killing. You will also be able to give alms and do many good deeds. From now on, my friend, please refrain from taking the life of any creature." With another bow of respect and gratitude, the golden deer and his mate disappeared into the forest.

Having concluded his story, the Buddha identified the birth: "At that time, Channa was the hunter, this bhikkhunī was the doe, and I was the golden deer."

143
The Eternal Law of Peace
Dīghiti-Kosala Jātaka

It was while staying at Jetavana that the Buddha told this story about quarrelsome bhikkhus in Kosambi.

At one time, a strong disagreement arose between two groups of bhikkhus in Kosambi. The two factions refused to listen to reason and continued arguing. The Buddha left them and spent the rains retreat in a forest where he was looked after by the elephant Pārileyya and a monkey. After the monks, pressured by their lay followers, had reconciled their differences, they went to Sāvatthī to ask the Buddha's forgiveness.

"Bhikkhus," the Buddha admonished them, "you are my heirs in this Sāsana. Children should not go against the counsel given them by their father, but you did not follow my advice. Long ago, a wise young prince, having resolved, 'I will not trample on the counsel given me by my father,' did not kill the one who had slain his parents and seized their kingdom. Even when the culprit, who was undeniably guilty, fell into his hands, the wise young man remembered his father's advice and refrained from violence." Then the Buddha told this story of the past.[1]

---

1   In the Jātaka, this story is briefly told. The version related here has been

Long, long ago, when Brahmadatta was reigning in Bārānasi, the capital of the kingdom of Kāsi, Dīghiti was the king of Kosala. At that time, Kāsi was rich and powerful, but Kosala was very weak. When Brahmadatta attacked Kosala, Dīghiti fled with his wife, and Kosala fell without a fight.

King Dīghiti and his queen wandered incognito, finally ending up in a potters' village just outside Bārānasi. Not long afterwards, the exiled queen gave birth to a son whom they named Dīghavu. When Dīghavu was old enough to look after himself, his parents sent him to live and to study in a safe place.

A few years later, King Dīghiti's former barber, who had come to serve King Brahmadatta, happened to see the exiled king in the potters' village and recognized him in spite of his disguise. He hurried to inform King Brahmadatta about his enemy.

King Brahmadatta immediately ordered soldiers to arrest King Dīghiti and his queen, to bind them tightly, to march them through the town, and to execute them at the southern gate.

It so happened that, on that same day, Prince Dīghavu returned to visit his parents, whom he had not seen for a long time. As he entered Bārānasi, he heard the beat of a harsh-sounding drum and saw his dear parents cruelly tied with ropes and being marched to the southern gate. Of course, he started toward them. King Dīghiti saw his son coming and stopped him, shouting with a clear voice: "Dear Dīghavu! Don't be far-sighted! Don't be near-sighted. Vengeance is not settled through vengeance. Vengeance is settled through non-vengeance."

The people in the crowd heard King Dīghiti's words and mocked him, shouting, "Have you gone crazy? You're talking nonsense. Who is Dīghavu? What do you mean?"

The king replied, "I'm neither crazy nor talking nonsense. He who knows will understand."

Then a second time and a third time, he cried, "Dear Dīghavu, don't be far-sighted! Don't be near-sighted. Vengeance is not settled through vengeance. Vengeance is settled through non-vengeance."

The people jeered. "This King Dīghiti has gone crazy. He's talking gibberish!"

Again the king retorted, "I'm not crazy, nor am I talking gibberish. He who knows will understand."

When the soldiers reached the southern gate, they executed the king and queen, cut their bodies into four pieces, and buried the pieces in four different holes.

expanded with material from the Vinaya, Mahāvagga 10.

That night, Prince Dīghavu bought some liquor and got the guards drunk. Solemnly he gathered sticks and pieces of wood to make a funeral pyre. He exhumed his parents' bodies and respectfully cremated them.

King Brahmadatta happened to be standing on the balcony of his palace, and he saw the prince circumambulating a fire where the king and queen had been executed. The king wondered who it was but gave it no more thought.

A few days later, the prince went to the king's elephant stable in the palace compound and said to the chief mahout, "Sir, I want to learn your craft."

The mahout accepted him and was pleased with his new helper.

One night, Prince Dīghavu was sitting near the stable and singing as he accompanied himself on the lute. The king heard him and called his page, "What an incredibly sweet voice that is! Who is singing and playing the lute in the elephant stable? I've never heard that before."

"Your Majesty, it is a young man who came recently. The elephant trainer has taken him on as an apprentice."

"Bring him to me."

The page fetched Prince Dīghavu. The king was impressed with the young man and asked him to serve in the palace. Prince Dīghavu soon gained such favor that he became a personal attendant to the king. Never revealing his background, the prince always spoke politely to the king and faithfully did whatever the king ordered. It was not long before King Brahmadatta gave the prince a position of trust and kept him by his side almost constantly.

One day, King Brahmadatta said to Prince Dīghavu, "Harness the chariot. I'm going hunting."

"As you wish, Your Majesty."

King Brahmadatta mounted the chariot but gave the reins to the prince and asked him to drive. At first, the hunting party stayed together, but, then the prince turned the horses aside so that the chariot became separated from the rest. After they had ridden quite a while, the king said that he was tired and wanted to rest. He ordered Prince Dīghavu to stop and to unharness the horses.

"As you wish, Your Majesty."

The king lay down and put his head in the prince's lap. Soon, he was fast asleep.

The prince looked at the king and thought, "This King Brahmadatta has done us great harm. He seized our kingdom and executed my parents. Here he lies, completely in my power. Now is my chance for revenge! I will slay the villain who killed my dear mother and father and cut their bodies into pieces!" Silently, he drew his sword. As he raised his weapon to strike the king, however, he remembered what his father had said, "Dear Dīghavu,

187

don't be far-sighted! Don't be near-sighted. Vengeance is not settled through vengeance. Vengeance is settled through non-vengeance."

Quietly, he replaced his sword in its sheath. "Even though I lose my own life," he vowed, "I will not disobey my father's words."

A few minutes later, as the king continued sleeping quietly, the prince again drew his sword. Again he remembered what his father had said, and he put away his sword. A third time he pulled out his sword. A third time he recollected his father's words and put away his sword.

Suddenly, frightened and alarmed, King Brahmadatta jumped to his feet.

"What is the matter, Your Majesty?" asked the prince,

"Just now I dreamed that the son of Dīghiti, king of Kosala, killed me with his sword."

The prince quickly grabbed King Brahmadatta by the hair with his left hand and with his right hand drew his sword. "Your Majesty," he shouted, "I am Prince Dīghavu, son of Dīghiti, king of Kosala. You did great harm to my family. You seized our kingdom and killed my dear parents. Now I will have my vengeance!"

King Brahmadatta wept, helpless before the prince. "Please don't kill me, Dīghavu! Please spare my life, Prince Dīghavu!"

"In the hour of death, Sire," Dīghavu replied softly, slightly relaxing his grip on the king's hair, "one's wealth is of no use at all! Only good deeds done and good words spoken can bring any comfort. 'This man abused me. That man struck me. That other man robbed me long ago.' Those who harbor such thoughts will never overcome their anger. Only by giving up such thoughts can we appease our anger and hatred. Hatred is never appeased by hatred. Hatred is appeased only by love. This is the eternal law of peace."

The prince released his hold on the king and held out his sword. "Take my sword, Your Majesty," he said. "Who am I to give you your life? Slay me, or give me my life."

"In that case, Dīghavu," the king replied in a tremulous voice, as he grasped the prince's hand, "you have given me my life, and I give you your life."

King Brahmadatta and Prince Dīghavu embraced and vowed never to harm one another.

"Now, my dear Dīghavu," the king said, "harness the chariot. We will go back."

They rejoined the hunting party and returned to Bārānasi.

The king summoned his court and asked, "If you were to see Prince Dīghavu, son of King Dīghiti, what would you do?"

From various corners the cries went up, "We would cut off his hands, Your Majesty!" "We would cut off his feet!" "We would execute him at the southern gate!"

"This," the king announced, "is Prince Dīghavu, the son of King Dīghiti, You are not to harm him in any way. He gave me my life, and I have given his life to him."

"Now, Prince," the king continued, turning to Dīghavu, "as your father was about to die, he kept repeating these sentences: 'Dear Dīghavu, don't be far-sighted! Don't be near-sighted. Vengeance is not settled through vengeance. Vengeance is settled through non-vengeance.' Please tell us what he meant by that."

"When my father said, 'Don't be far-sighted,' he was telling me not to hold a grudge for a long time, not to seek revenge. When he said, 'Don't be near-sighted,' he was telling me not to be quick to break with a friend. When he said, 'Vengeance is not settled through vengeance. Vengeance is settled through non-vengeance,' he was expressing an eternal law. He knew that if I were to kill you as you killed my parents, your friends would kill me. Then my friends would kill your friends. In this way, vengeance, hatred, and killing would go on endlessly. But, by swearing friendship, you have given me my life, and I have given you your life. Hatred and vengeance have ceased."

"Wonderful! Wonderful!" King Brahmadatta exclaimed. "It's amazing how wise this Prince Dīghavu is! He was able to understand in full what his father said in brief!"

To demonstrate to all that he was sincere in his vow of friendship, King Brahmadatta restored to Prince Dīghavu the entire kingdom of Kosala—capital, palace, army, fields, villages, and all its wealth. He also offered his own daughter to the prince in marriage.

The prince accepted all the gifts and established himself as the king of Kosala with his new queen. The two kings lived the rest of their lives in harmony and peace.

Having concluded his story, the Buddha identified the birth: "My parents were King Dīghiti and his queen, and I was Prince Dīghavu."

144
Mount Neru
Neru Jātaka

It was while staying at Jetavana that the Buddha told this story about some fickle laypeople. Once, a bhikkhu who had received a meditation subject from the Buddha went to a remote frontier village. The people there were pleased with the bhikkhu's deportment and invited him to stay. They built him a hut in the forest and promised to take care of his needs. Despite their offer of support, however, it was not long before they forgot about him and began following one who taught Eternalism. Shortly thereafter, they abandoned that teacher and followed another who denied immortality. Soon, they were listening to the teaching of some naked ascetics.

The bhikkhu became thoroughly disgusted by those villagers, whose minds bent whichever way the wind blew, with no concept of truth or falsity, good or evil. After the rains retreat, he returned to the Buddha and told him what had happened. The Buddha chastised that bhikkhu for staying so long with those who couldn't distinguish between good and evil. "Long ago, the wise, even though only animals, refused to stay for a day among such creatures. You, too, should have left immediately!" Then the Buddha told this story of the past.

Long, long ago, when Brahmadatta was reigning in Bārānasi, the Bo-dhisatta was born as a golden goose. He lived with his younger brother in the Himavat on a hill called Cittakūta, and they fed on wild paddy.

One day, as they were flying back to Cittakūta, they landed on the summit of Mount Neru, which shone with a golden luster. The younger golden goose looked around and asked, "Brother, how is it that all the birds—the black ravens, the white paddy birds, the drab sparrows, the colorful peacocks, and we noble geese—and all the animals—the mighty lions, the playful monkeys, and the mean jackals—all appear golden? What mountain is this that has such a powerful effect?"

"This great mountain is called Neru," the elder goose replied. "While rest-ing here, all creatures take on the luster of the mountain itself and appear beautiful and golden."

"Dear brother," the younger goose retorted, "a place where the good find no greater honor than the most contemptible, where the dull and the clever, the brave and the cowardly, are all respected equally, is not the place for us. The wise should not stay with such indiscrimination! Since Mount Neru cannot distinguish the mean, the indifferent, and the good, let us leave immediately!"

The elder goose heeded his brother's words, and the two golden geese flew away to Cittakūta.

Having concluded his story, the Buddha taught the Dhamma, and that bhikkhu attained the first path. Then the Buddha identified the birth: "At that time, Ānanda was the younger golden goose, and I was the elder."

145

The Merit of the Virtuous
Nandiya-Miga Jātaka

It was while staying at Jetavana that the Buddha told this story about a bhikkhu who was caring for his parents.

Once, some bhikkhus criticized a bhikkhu for supporting laypeople with donations from devotees and escorted him to the Buddha. "Is it true, Bhikkhu, that you are giving to laypeople the alms you receive?" the Buddha asked him directly.

"Yes, Lord, it is true."

"Who are they?"

"They are my father and mother, Lord."

"Well done! Well done, Bhikkhu! You are maintaining a tradition of the wise. Long ago, even an animal risked his own life for his parents." Then the Buddha told this story of the past.

Long, long ago, when King Kosala was reigning in Sāketā, the Bodhisatta was born as a deer, named Nandiya. The virtuous Nandiya faithfully looked after his father and mother.

The king loved hunting. Every day, he went into the countryside with a great retinue. His passion for hunting deer kept the citizens so busy that they could not do their own work.

One day, the people gathered to discuss the king's excessive demands on their time. "Friends, the king is destroying our business and disturbing our home life!" one man declared. "Let us plant grass in Anjanavana, dig a tank for water, and enclose the entire park with a sturdy fence. Then we can drive all the deer from the forest into the park. Whenever the king wants to hunt, he can chase the deer in Anjanavana without disturbing any of us. The king will be satisfied, and we can get on with our farming and our trades."

Everyone agreed that this was an excellent idea, and they all began working enthusiastically in the park. When they had finished, they opened the gate wide and surrounded the forest. As they began closing in on the forest, they shouted and beat on shields with spears. The noise frightened the deer, and they ran toward the apparent safety of Anjanavana. The men marched through the forest, continuing their racket and searching the bushes to flush out as many deer as they could find.

Nandiya was fully aware of the scheme these men had devised, and he had taken his father and mother into a little thicket, where the three of them were hiding. When he saw the men approaching, he realized that their hideout was discovered. "I must save my parents, even if it means my own life!" he thought. He stood up, saluted his parents, and said, "Dear Father and Mother, if these men search this thicket, they will find all three of us. If I run out before they come, they will think that there was only one deer here, and they will pass it by. This is the only way that you will be safe." Tearfully, they agreed to his sacrifice.

As soon as the men reached the thicket where the three deer were hiding, Nandiya ran out. The men were fooled and did not search inside the thicket.

Nandiya joined the other deer in Anjanavana. When the sturdy gate was closed, the people, pleased that their plan had succeeded, informed the king that he could thenceforth hunt in the park, and they returned to their own homes.

Delighted with this arrangement, the king went every day with his bow and arrow to Anjanavana. Each morning, the deer drew lots. When the king arrived, most of the deer were hiding, but the animal whose turn it was to die would run out, trembling in fear, to be stalked by the king. The king thoroughly enjoyed the pursuit, which always ended with his shooting the deer. Servants carried the carcass back to the palace, and the royal cooks prepared the venison.

Day after day, Nandiya drank water from the tank, grazed on the sweet grass, and wondered when his turn would come.

Meanwhile, his parents grew lonely and longed to see him "When Nandiya was with us here in the forest, he was strong and always in perfect health," they recalled. "If our dear son is still alive, he can certainly leap over the park fence. Let us send him a message so that he will come and visit us." They stood near the road and waited for a suitable messenger. Before long, a brahmin passed by. "Good sir, where are you going?" they asked.

"I'm on my way to Sāketā," he replied.

"Would you please go to Anjanavana and inform our son Nandiya that we are anxious to see him again?"

The brahmin agreed and continued on his way. When he reached Sāketā, he hurried to Anjanavana and asked for Nandiya.

The noble deer approached and identified himself, and the brahmin conveyed his parents' message.

"Don't misunderstand me, brahmin. I could easily go. I would have no difficulty whatsoever leaping over this fence, but, since I have accepted food and drink from the king, I feel I owe him a debt. It would be improper for me to leave without repaying this king. Furthermore, having lived with these deer for such a long time, it would be unfair of me to abandon them to their fate. Surely, my turn will come soon, and then I must show my strength. After I have fulfilled my virtuous act, I hope to go and see my parents."

Unable to grasp what Nandiya was telling him, the brahmin shook his head and went about his own business.

A few days later, the lot fell to Nandiya. When the king arrived at Anjanavana, Nandiya was standing boldly in a clearing. The king fitted the arrow into his bow and aimed, but Nandiya did not run. He stood steadfast, his side with its mighty ribcage exposed to the king's arrow. Showing no fear of death, he continued breathing normally and radiated loving-kindness. The power of that loving-kindness reached the king, and he hesitated.

"Sire, why do you not shoot your arrow?" Nandiya calmly asked.

"King of the deer, I cannot!"

"Sire!" Nandiya exclaimed. "Observe the merit of the virtuous!"

These words thrilled the king, and he lowered his bow. "Noble animal," the king replied, "this senseless length of wood knows your virtue. How could I, an intelligent being, not know it? Forgive me for even attempting to take your life! I grant you safety for as long as you live."

"Your Majesty, you grant me security, but what of the other deer in the park?"

"They, too, will be spared!" proclaimed the king.

"Your Majesty, what of the other creatures—the animals, fish, and birds—in your kingdom?"

"All of them, too, will be spared!" proclaimed the king. Then Nandiya established the king in the five precepts and taught him, "Your Majesty, a monarch should rule with generosity, morality, sacrifice, honesty, kindness, self-control, freedom from ill-will, harmlessness, patience, and uprightness. These ten duties of a king will enable you to rule well so that both you and your people will be happy."

After staying with the king for a few more days, instructing him in virtue and generosity, Nandiya advised, "Be heedful, Your Majesty!" and then bounded into the forest to be reunited with his parents.

Having concluded his story, the Buddha taught the Dhamma, and the bhikkhu who was caring for his parents attained the first path. Then the Buddha identified the birth: "At that time, my father and mother were the deer parents, Sāriputta was the brahmin, Ānanda was the king, and I was Nandiya."

146

The Secret Charm
Kharaputta Jātaka

It was while staying at Jetavana that the Buddha told this story about a bhikkhu and his former wife.

When the bhikkhu confessed that he was longing for the wife of his lay life, the Buddha told him, "That woman is hindering you now, and, long ago, she was willing to send you into the fire." Then the Buddha told this story of the past.

Long, long ago, when a king named Senaka was reigning in Bārānasi, a nāga king left his watery kingdom to wander about the earth, looking for food. Some village boys spotted him, shouted, "Snake! Snake!" and began throwing clods of earth at him, and beating him with sticks.

King Senaka happened to be passing by on his way to his pleasure garden and saw what was happening. "Drive those urchins away!" he ordered his soldiers. "Don't let them harm the snake!"

That night, at midnight, the nāga king appeared at the royal bedchamber and presented King Senaka with many beautiful jewels from his nāga palace. "Thank you, Your Majesty," he said. "You saved my life, and I am extremely grateful!"

King Senaka and the nāga king became good friends, and the nāga king frequently visited Bārānasi. Because the nāga king could not stay away from his realm too long, he assigned a nāga maiden to stay with King Senaka and to protect him. The nāga king also taught a charm to his friend, instructing him, "If for some reason, you cannot see the maiden, repeat this charm."

One day, King Senaka went to the royal garden to bathe and to amuse himself in the lotus-tank. The nāga maiden spied a water-snake and, abandoning her human shape, made love with him.

The king wondered where the maiden had gone and recited the charm. Instantly, he saw her with the snake. He was upset at her misbehavior and struck her with a piece of bamboo. She immediately vanished and returned to the nāga realm. When the nāga king asked her why she had returned, she showed him the mark of the blow and replied, "Your friend hit me on the back because I did not do what he wanted."

The nāga king became so angry at King Senaka that he sent four nāgas youths to the royal bedchamber in Bārānasi to kill him with their poisonous breath. When they entered the bedchamber, they heard the king and queen talking.

"Lady," the king said, "do you know what that nāga maiden did?"

"No, Sire," replied the queen, "I do not."

"While we were bathing in the tank today, she assumed her nāga form and misbehaved shamelessly with a common water snake. To make her stop, I hit her lightly with a piece of bamboo, but I'm afraid she got angry and went back to the nāga realm. To excuse herself and turn my friend against me, she may have lied to the king about what happened."

The four young nāgas hurried back to inform their king about this. He realized that he had been too hasty in judging King Senaka and went himself to Bārānasi to apologize. "Friend," he said as soon as he entered the king's chamber, "I am sorry that I mistrusted you. I was foolish to believe the story of that maiden. Allow me to make amends by giving you a special charm. This will allow you to understand the voices of all creatures, even the smallest. I must warn you, however, that you must never give this charm to anyone else. If you do, you will instantly be consumed by fire. Sire, this charm is priceless. Guard it well!"

"Friend," King Senaka replied, "I am grateful. Thank you for this precious gift. I fully understand its conditions, and I promise to keep it secret." The nāga king taught King Senaka the charm and returned to his own realm. King Senaka used it often and found it fascinating to understand what various animals were saying to each other.

One day, while he was sitting on the throne and eating a delicious pastry covered with honey and molasses, a morsel fell on the dais. As soon as a tiny ant found the crumb and the drops of honey and molasses, he shouted to his friends, "The king's honey jar has broken! His molasses cart has spilled! Someone has dumped the pastry basket! Come and enjoy a feast!"

When the king heard this, he laughed aloud.

The queen was sitting beside him, but, of course, she heard nothing. "What has made the king laugh?" she wondered, but said nothing.

A little later, after the king had taken his bath, he was sitting on a couch, and a fly settled beside him. "Come, dear lady!" the fly called to his mate. "Let us enjoy some lovemaking."

The female fly, still buzzing around, replied, "Wait a little, Husband. Servants will soon bring perfumes to the king. After he powders himself, I will perfume myself with the powder that falls at his feet. Then we can make love on the king's back while he is sleeping."

The king again laughed aloud.

The queen was passing by the couch, but she had heard nothing. Wondering once more why the king had laughed, she kept silent.

Still later, while the king was eating his supper, a lump of rice fell on the floor, right beside an ant who was scurrying around. "Rice!" the ant cried. "A wagon of rice has spilled in the king's palace! Rice for everyone!" The king laughed aloud for the third time.

At that time, the queen was serving soup to the king with a golden spoon, but she had heard nothing. "Is it the sight of me that makes the king laugh?" she wondered, but she remained silent.

That night, in the royal bed-chamber, she said, "Sire, today, with me beside you, you laughed three times. May I ask why you laughed so heartily?"

"My dear," the king replied, "what is it to you if I laugh?"

"I fear, Sire, that I was the cause of your laughter."

"No, no, my dear!" the king said, chuckling as he remembered the voices of the insects. "It had nothing to do with you!"

"My Lord," the queen insisted, "you are unkind not to tell me what amuses you."

Remembering his promise to the nāga king, King Senaka refused to let the queen know that he could understand the voices of animals, but the queen was so persistent, that, finally, he told her about the charm.

"How fascinating!" the queen exclaimed. "Please teach me this charm!"

"I cannot!" the king replied firmly. "I promised the nāga king that I would not divulge this secret to anyone!"

"But, My Lord," the queen begged, "I am your wife. You should not keep secrets from me."

"I was told that, if I teach this priceless charm to anyone, I will die," replied the king, feeling himself weakening and fearing death. "I will be consumed by fire!"

"My Lord, if you love me, teach me this charm!" the queen implored.

"But what if teaching it to you means that I die?" pleaded the king.

"Teach me the charm!" the queen demanded again.

"All right!" the king said, relenting, at last, because he was so enamored of the queen. "I will teach it to you tomorrow in the royal park."

Sakka heard the king agree to the queen's demand and thought, "The besotted king is throwing away his life for his selfish wife! He knows what he is doing, but he cannot help himself. Fortunately, I can. I must save his life!"

The next day, King Senaka was in his chariot on the way to the royal park, repeating to himself over and over, "By teaching her the charm, I am condemning myself to the fire!" At the same time, Sakka, in the form of a billy goat, and his wife Sujā, in the form of a nanny goat, were descending from Tāvatimsa. They appeared in the roadway and began coupling right then and there. Sakka made sure that the two of them were visible only to King Senaka and the Sindh horses harnessed to his chariot. When the horses saw the pair of goats making love in the middle of the road, one of them shouted, "Friend goat, we had heard that goats were stupid and shameless! We did not believe it, but now that we see what you are doing, we know that it is true! Are you not ashamed to be doing here in public that which should be done only in a private place?"

"Great steed," the billy goat replied, "you think we are stupid, but think about yourself. There you are, tied with reins and harness, bridled with a bit between your teeth. You could be running through the fields and eating the sweetest of grasses, but you pull the king's chariot and allow yourself to be whipped if you don't gallop fast enough. Even when you're set loose, you don't escape. That, sir, is what I call 'stupid'! Furthermore, that King Senaka whom you pull around is even stupider than you are!"

"All right, Mister Goat," replied the horse, "I think you are stupid, and you think I am stupid, but tell me, why do you say that King Senaka is so stupid?"

"When someone has a priceless treasure," the goat proclaimed loudly and clearly, "and gives it away to a wife who doesn't care whether he lives or dies, that's real stupidity! What kind of fool is he to throw away his life so carelessly?"

"King of the goats!" cried the king, who had been closely following the exchange. "Surely you are doing all of this for my benefit! Please tell me what I should do!"

"Sire, that which every creature holds most dear is himself. It is wrong to destroy oneself and to abandon one's honor merely for the sake of another whom you hold dear. If the price for satisfying a desire is your life, renounce that desire! Life is a precious thing! It must be cherished! Do not throw it away lightly!"

"King of the goats!" the king cried again. "You are right! I have been a fool! Please tell me where you have come from."

Assuming his natural form, Sakka declared, "I am Sakka! I have come here to save you from your folly!"

"Sakka, I am grateful, but what can I do?" cried King Senaka. "I have promised to give the queen the charm."

"Your Majesty, the queen would not use this charm wisely. If she had it, she would surely make a fool of herself. Teaching it to her would, therefore, destroy both of you. That's sheer lunacy! A little beating is all that is required, and it would be for her own good. Just tell her that a beating is part of the ritual, and she will give up soon enough! Spare yourself from the fire!"

Overjoyed at this wise advice, the king agreed, and Sakka returned to Tāvatimsa with Sujā.

King Senaka proceeded to the garden, seated himself on the royal stone, and summoned the queen. When she arrived, he greeted her and asked, "Lady, are you still determined to have the charm?"

"Yes, Lord."

"Then let us begin the ritual."

"What ritual, My Lord?"

"One who receives this charm must first receive one hundred lashes of the whip across the back. During this ordeal, the recipient must not make a sound."

"Very well, My Lord, if this is required, I accept. I must have that charm!" The queen bared her back and lay down on the grass. The king ordered his servants to begin whipping her. Gritting her teeth and biting her tongue, the queen endured three lashes in silence, but then she cried out, "Stop! Keep your charm! I don't want it! Make them stop!"

"You would have killed me to get the charm," the king observed dryly. "Can't you endure a little pain?" He ordered the servants to continue to whip her until her back was bloody. Then he sent her back to her chamber. After that, the queen never again mentioned the spell.

Having concluded his story, the Buddha taught the Dhamma, and the discontented bhikkhu attained the first path. Then the Buddha identified the birth: "At that time, this bhikkhu was the king, his former wife was the queen, Sāriputta was the Sindh horse, and I was Sakka."

147
Sutana and the Royal Regalia
Sutana Jātaka

It was while staying at Jetavana that the Buddha told this story about a bhikkhu who supported his mother.[1]

Long, long ago, when Brahmadatta was reigning in Bārānasi, he was fond of hunting. One day, he went with a large party to an area of great forest. Determined to catch a deer, he posted men all around the forest and announced, "If a deer escapes past any man's post, that man will be fined the value of the deer!" The king took his position in a blind near the road, and servants beat their drums to rouse the animals. A deer immediately ran past the king's blind, and the king sent an arrow flying, but the clever beast, anticipating the arrow, wheeled around and fell as if wounded.

"I've hit him!" the king cried. As he rushed to retrieve his game, however, the beast leapt up and fled like the wind. The ministers laughed, but the king pursued the deer for so long that the animal finally fell exhausted, whereupon the king killed it with his sword. He cut the deer into pieces which he tied to a pole to balance on his shoulder. Carrying his prize, he headed back to

---

1   The occasion for this story is the same as that for Tale 210, where it is related in detail.

join his party. He was himself exhausted from the chase and stopped to rest under a banyan tree. He was soon fast asleep. This great banyan tree was inhabited by a fierce yakkha called Makhādeva, to whom Vessavana had granted permission to seize and to eat all living beings who ventured into its shade. When the king awoke, he started to get up, but he heard a voice shout, "Stay! You are my food," and something grabbed his arm.

"Who are you?" asked the king.

"I am a yakkha, and this is my banyan tree. I devour all who enter its shade."

"Do you eat only today," the king asked boldly, "or do you need to eat often?"

"I'd like to eat every day, but sometimes I don't get anything," the yakkha replied candidly.

"Then eat this deer today, and let me go," the king suggested. "I promise you that, starting tomorrow, I will send you, every day, a man with a plate of rice."

"All right," the yakkha agreed. "But be careful! If you ever fail to send me someone, that day, I will find you and have you!"

"Don't worry! I will keep my promise. After all, I am the king of Kāsi. There is nothing I cannot do."

The yakkha accepted the deer and released the king on his own recognizance.

As soon as the king returned to the palace, he conferred with his chief advisor and asked what should be done.

"Was a limit of time fixed, Sire?" the man asked. "No," replied the king.

"That was a mistake, but, never mind. I will take care of it, Sire."

"Excellent!" exclaimed the king. "I leave it entirely in your hands, but make sure you never fail to send someone. My life is at stake!"

"You have nothing to worry about, Sire," the advisor assured him, and the king retired to his chamber.

Every day, after that, the advisor chose a prisoner from the jail and sent him to the yakkha with a plate of rice.

Soon, however, the jail became empty. When the king heard this, he began shaking with fear. "Don't worry, Sire," the advisor comforted him. "For some men, the desire for wealth is stronger than the desire for life. Let us offer one thousand coins to anyone who will carry the plate of rice into the forest."

The king agreed, and a sack with one thousand coins was placed on the back of an elephant. As the elephant marched through the streets to the beat of a drum, a proclamation was read: "This wealth goes to anyone who will carry a plate of rice to a yakkha in the forest!"

In Bārānasi, there was a youth named Sutana. All his life, he had been working for wages to support his family. His father died, and the boy had to continue doing manual labor to provide for his mother. When he heard the proclamation, he thought, "I work myself to the bone and get only one and a half coins a day. Even then, I can hardly support my mother. This wealth is more than I could earn in five years. Let me claim the sack of coins and give it her. If I defeat the yakkha, so much the better, but, even if I don't, my mother will be able to live comfortably for a long time."

He told his mother of his plan, but she begged him not to do it. "We have enough, dear!" she cried. "I don't need wealth! What good would money do me without you?" Twice, she forbade him to go, but, without asking a third time, he went to the palace.

"Sirs," he announced, "give me the one thousand coins, and I will take the rice!"

"Certainly!" the king's soldiers replied. They carried the sack of money to his house, where he gave it to his mother. "Don't fret, Mother dear," Sutana said. "The yakkha will not eat me! You'll see! I will overcome the yakkha, satisfy the king, and return to put a smile on that tearful face of yours!" After allowing him to pay his respects to his mother one last time, the king's soldiers escorted him back to the palace to bind him to his contract.

When he was taken before the king, Sutana paid his respects, and the king greeted him, "My dear lad, they tell me that you will you take the rice to the yakkha."

"That is correct, Sire. I will."

"What do you want to take with you?"

Sutana replied boldly and without hesitation, "Sire, I will need your golden slippers, your royal umbrella, your sword, and your golden bowl. If you will lend these things to me, I promise that I will return them to you shortly."

"How can you be so sure the yakkha will not eat you?" asked the king.

"Protected by your royal regalia, the yakkha will not be able to touch me!" declared Sutana.

Giving the youth the benefit of the doubt, the king entrusted him with all the things he asked for.

The king's soldiers gave Sutana directions to the tree, but none dared accompany him further than the edge of the forest.

When Sutana got close to the banyan tree, he stopped. Setting down the golden bowl, he put the golden slippers on his feet, buckled the king's sword around his waist, and raised the royal umbrella. Then, once more picking up the bowl, he walked boldly with his head held high, right up to the tree.

The yakkha was watching him and thought, "This youth does not approach like the others. He shows no fear. I wonder why."

Sutana placed the bowl on the ground and pushed it toward the trunk of the tree with the king's sword. "The king has sent rice seasoned well with meat from his own table," Sutana shouted. "If Makhādeva is at home, let him come forth and eat from the king's own bowl!"

Makhādeva wanted to attack the boy and eat him, but, seeing the sword, he hesitated. He felt it would be better to frighten his victim. "This is my tree!" he shouted. "All who stand on the ground beneath it are mine to eat!"

"Good Makhādeva," Sutana replied calmly, "that may be so, but I am not standing on the ground. I am standing on the king's golden slippers!"

"But you are standing in the tree's shade! That is enough!" the yakkha insisted.

"Makhādeva," Sutana answered in a friendly voice, "do you not see that I am standing under the shade of the royal umbrella? Think before you lose a great prize for a trifle. I have brought you food such as you have never had before. The king's jail is empty. If you eat me, no one will ever bring you food again!"

"Young man," Makhādeva replied, his anger completely dissolved, "what you say makes sense. You have very clearly stated my interests, and it seems that you truly have my interests at heart. I respect your wisdom and your bravery. Return to your mother in peace; you have my permission to go. Take your slippers, your sword, your umbrella, and your golden dish, and be on your way."

Sutana was pleased. "My task is accomplished," he rejoiced quietly. He faced the yakkha and saluted him, "Makhādeva, I declare that the king has hereby fulfilled his promise to you. His debt is paid. I thank you that, through this mission, my mother and I have become wealthy. Makhādeva, may you and all your relatives be happy!"

Out of compassion for the yakkha, Sutana offered to teach him, and Makhādeva sat down to listen.

"Friend," Sutana began, "long ago, you committed many evil deeds. You were cruel and harsh, and you ate the flesh of many. That is why you were born as a wretched yakkha. If you continue as you are doing, you will never escape from this state. Abstain from killing, and win yourself a better future."

Sutana further expounded the blessings of virtue and established Makhādeva in the five precepts. "Now, my friend," he continued, "why stay in the forest any more? Come with me. I will settle you near the city gate, and you will be provided with the best rice."

Makhādeva agreed. Sutana asked him to carry all the royal paraphernalia, and together they returned to Bārānasi. When the king heard of their arrival, he went out to meet them. Just as Sutana had promised, Makhādeva was set-tled near the city gate, and, every day, he was given a plate of excellent rice.

Once more, to the beat of a drum, the king made a proclamation, but, this time, he summoned all his subjects to a grand meeting in which he praised Sutana and appointed him commander-in-chief of the army. Sutana also established the king in the five precepts, and, for the rest of his reign, King Brahmadatta gave alms generously and performed many good deeds. When he passed away, he was reborn in heaven.

Having concluded his story, the Buddha taught the Dhamma, and the bhikkhu who was supporting his mother attained the first path. Then the Buddha identified the birth: "At that time, Angulimāla was Makhādeva, Ānanda was King Brahmadatta, and I was Sutana."

148

The Jackal's Judgment
Dabbhapuppha Jātaka

It was while staying at Jetavana that the Buddha told this story about the Sākyan, Venerable Upananda.

Venerable Upananda had forsaken the virtues of contentment and had become extremely greedy. One year, at the beginning of the rains retreat, he visited several monasteries and received permission to stay. At each one, he left an umbrella, a shoe, a water pot, or a walking stick before going to the next. At the rural monastery where he actually spent the retreat, he praised contentment with bare necessities and expounded on the nobility of having few wants. "Bhikkhus must live contentedly!" he proclaimed. Swayed by his eloquence, which seemed to make the moon rise in the sky, his fellow bhikkhus threw away their fine robes and vessels and began wearing robes of rags and using rough clay bowls.

Venerable Upananda collected all the choice items and kept them in his own lodging. At the end of the rains retreat, he attended the kathina ceremony in each monastery as though he had stayed there. With a cart filled with the robes he had accumulated, he set out for Jetavana. On the way, he happened to pass a forest monastery. He stopped behind the monastery and wrapped his feet with creepers, thinking "Surely there's something to be gotten here." He entered the monastery and found two elderly bhikkhus who had spent the retreat there and had received two coarse cloaks and one fine blanket. The two were pleased to see Venerable Upananda.

"Sir," they said, "we cannot divide these things. We are having such a disagreement about them that we would be very grateful if you would divide them between us."

Venerable Upananda quickly agreed. He gave a coarse robe to each of them and took the fine blanket for himself. "This falls to me for knowing the rules of discipline," he said and went away.

Those two bhikkhus, who loved the blanket, followed him to Jetavana and explained the matter to the senior bhikkhus who knew the rules. "Is it right," they asked, "for one who knows the rules to take so much away from us in this way?"

When the bhikkhus saw the pile of robes and bowls which Venerable Upananda had brought, they said, "Sir, you must have great merit to have gained so many robes and bowls.

"Sirs," he countered, "it is not a question of merit." Then he proceeded to tell them exactly how he had gained everything.

The bhikkhus were surprised to learn of Venerable Upananda's behavior. Later, in the Hall of Truth, they said to each other, "The Sākyan Upananda is very covetous and greedy."

When the Buddha heard what they were discussing, he said, "Bhikkhus, Upananda's deeds are not suited for progress. A bhikkhu should act suitably himself before he preaches to others about progress. As for Upananda," he added, "this is not the first time that he has been covetous. Long ago, he plundered others' property in the same way." Then he told this story of the past.

Long, long ago, when Brahmadatta was reigning in Bārānasi, there was a jackal named Māyāvī, who had taken a mate and lived near a riverbank. One day, his wife said to him, "Husband, I suddenly feel a very strong craving for fresh rohita fish."

"All right, my dear," he said. "Just wait, and I'll bring you some." Then he went to the river, wrapped his feet in creepers, and crept along the bank.

Not far from that place, two otters, named Gambhīracārī and Anutīracārī, were standing on the bank looking for fish. At that moment, Gambhīracārī saw a great rohita fish. He jumped into the water and grabbed it by the tail. The fish was strong and swam away, dragging the otter with it. Gambhīracārī called to his friend, "Quick! Come and help me, Anutīracārī! This enormous fish will be enough for both of us."

Rushing to help him, Anutīracārī shouted, "How lucky you are, Gambhīracārī! And strong, too! Hold the fish as tight as you can, and like a garuḍa lifting a snake, I'll snatch it from the water."

Then the two together hauled and pushed the rohita fish onto the riverbank, laid it down, and killed it.

"You have caught a great fish," Anutīracārī said. "Please divide it."

"No," protested Gambhīracārī, "I could not have caught it without your help. You must divide it."

In this way, the two of them quarreled, both refusing to divide the fish. At last, they sat down with the fish lying in front of them. As soon as they had sat down, the jackal emerged from his hiding place and approached them. The otters saluted him and said, "Welcome, lord with a coat the color of gray grass! Please help us. Together we have caught this fish, but we cannot decide how to divide it between us. Please cut it fairly, and give us each an equal part."

"Certainly," the jackal answered. "I have settled many cases such as this, and I have always acted fairly, maintaining peace and friendship between the parties."

Then, as cleanly as if he had a butcher's knife, he bit the fish into three pieces. "Anutīracārī, take the tail," he said. "And you, Gambhīracārī, keep the head! Eat your shares without quarreling. The middle part will be my payment for settling your dispute." In a flash, he grabbed the plump middle portion of the fish and ran off.

The two otters sat stunned as though they had lost a purse of one thousand coins.

"What fools we are!" they cried. "If we had not argued over this fish, it would have been enough for a delicious feast for us both. But now the jackal has taken the fish and left us with no more than the bony head and tail!"

The jackal was very proud of himself as he carried the rohita fish to his wife. When she saw him coming, she saluted him and cried, "My Lord, how happy I am to see you with such a prize! You are like a king who has just conquered a neighboring kingdom. Pray, tell me, how did you catch this fish? I know you cannot swim."

Māyāvī placed the fish before his wife and explained, "Strife causes weakness and decay. Because of strife, the otters lost their prize, and I, Māyāvī, brought it home to you."

A tree deva dwelling nearby, who had observed all this, added, "So it is among men as well. When strife arises and men seek an arbiter, he gains the upper hand. They lose their wealth, but the king grows richer still."

Having concluded his story, the Buddha identified the birth: "At that time, Upananda was the jackal, the two old bhikkhus were the otters, and I was the tree deva who witnessed the scene."

149
The Most Difficult Feat of All
Dasannaka Jātaka

It was while staying at Jetavana that the Buddha told this story about a bhikkhu and his former wife.

When the bhikkhu confessed that he was longing for his former wife, the Buddha told him, "That woman is hindering you now. In the distant past, because of her, you almost died from mental illness." At the bhikkhu's request, the Buddha told this story of the past.

Long, long ago, when the great king Maddava was reigning in Bārānasi, the Bodhisatta was born into a brahmin family and was named Senaka. He received his education in Takkasilā, and, after he returned to Bārānasi, he became King Maddava's chief advisor.

One day, the son of the king's personal priest saw the chief queen in one of her most alluring gowns and was bewitched by her beauty. He was so overwhelmed by desire that he could think of nothing else. He went home and lay down. For several days, he stayed at home, eating nothing and seeing no one. When some friends visited and asked him what was wrong, he told them everything.

The king asked those friends where the lad was, and they told him the truth. The king immediately summoned him and said, "My boy, I hear that you are infatuated with my chief queen. I give her to you for seven days. Take her to your house, and enjoy yourself. On the eighth, send her back to the palace."

"Very well, Sire," replied the young man, and he went to his house with the queen. During that week, the queen fell in love with the young man. The two of them fled from the capital and began living secretly in a neighboring kingdom.

The king was very upset when the queen did not come back. He longed for her and ordered his soldiers to search for the queen in every quarter of the city and throughout the kingdom, but no one knew where the couple had gone. The longer she was gone, the more the king missed her. His sense of loss was so great that his heart became inflamed. Every time he thought of her, he felt faint, dizzy, and weak. Overcome by his longing for her, he took to his bed, but the royal physicians could not find anything wrong with him.

Senaka carefully observed the king's behavior, understood the root of the problem, and concluded that he was the only one who could restore the king's health.

He summoned two of the king's other advisors, named Ayura and Pukkusa. "My friends, I have figured out what ails our king," he told them. "He is not physically ill, but he is suffering from severe mental distress over the queen's disappearance. The king deserves our loyal support, and we must cure him. I have an idea, and I'm confident that it will work. I'll set up some entertainment in the courtyard. As the king watches from the window, he will be fascinated. I can predict precisely what he will ask you, and here's what you must answer." Senaka then told them what was going to happen and exactly what they were to reply to the king. "When it is my turn to speak, I will know what to say. You'll see that this will restore the king to health." The two advisors agreed to Senaka's plan and memorized their lines.

The advisors gathered dancers, musicians, jugglers, acrobats, and magicians and asked them to display their skills in the courtyard. Directly below the window, they stationed a sword swallower.

When all was ready, the advisors went to the king and announced, "Sire, there is a festival in the courtyard. It is said that one who watches these entertainers cannot help but find enjoyment and that any sorrow he has will turn to joy. Let us watch the entertainment together." The king listlessly agreed and went with them to the window.

He immediately caught sight of the sword swallower. He was a tall man, and he was holding aloft a glistening steel blade thirty-three inches long. He opened his mouth and repeatedly slid the entire length of the blade down his throat. "Amazing! Marvelous!" the king exclaimed.

"Ayura," he said, turning to his advisor, "That superb Dasanna sword[1] with its perfectly honed edge thirsts for blood, yet that man stands there in the middle of a great crowd, calmly thrusting it down his throat without shedding a drop of blood. Is there any feat more difficult to accomplish than that?"

"Sire," Ayura promptly replied, "a man may swallow a sword from greed for glory or money, but it would be much more difficult, indeed, for a man to say, 'I give this freely!' Compared to that, Sire, swallowing a sword seems a very simple task!"

The king listened to this and thought, "My advisor tells me that more difficult than swallowing a sword is saying 'I give this freely!' Several weeks ago, I said to the son of the priest, 'I give you my queen.' That was a very difficult thing that I did." With that realization, his burden of sorrow decreased.

"Pukkusa," he said, turning to his second advisor, "Ayura tells me that saying, 'I give this freely,' is more difficult than swallowing a sword. I can agree with him, but is there any feat more difficult than that?"

"Sire," Pukkusa replied readily, "it is fine to say, 'I give this freely!' but actually to mean what one says and to give that thing is, indeed, much more difficult!"

The king listened to this and thought, "Pukkusa tells me that actually giving away what you have promised to give is a difficult feat. To the son of the priest, I said, 'I give you my queen.' Then I actually gave her to him. I kept my word. That was an even more difficult thing that I did." With that realization, his burden of sorrow decreased even more.

"Senaka," the king said, turning to his third advisor, "you are my chief advisor. We all admire you for your superior wisdom. Ayura tells me that saying, 'I give this freely,' is more difficult than swallowing a sword. Pukkusa tells me that actually giving that thing is a more difficult feat. I can agree with both of them, but is there any feat more difficult than that?"

"Sire," Senaka replied, choosing his words with great care, "A man may say, 'I give this freely,' and he may actually give that thing, great or small, but, afterwards, to have no regret is, indeed, the most difficult feat of all."

The king listened intently to this and reflected, "I said, 'I give you my queen,' and I actually gave her away, but look at me now! I'm pining away, and I can't control my thoughts. My mind is full of regret! If the queen loved me, she would not have run away! Obviously, she doesn't! Why should I care? What is she to me? I do not regret my gift! Such behavior is unworthy of me! Now I have, indeed, accomplished the most difficult feat of all!" With

---

1   Dasanna was a kingdom apparently famous for making excellent swords.

that determination, his burden of sorrow completely disappeared. It rolled away as a drop of water rolls off a lotus leaf, and his strength returned. Once again, he felt well and happy.

"Senaka!" he exclaimed. "Both Ayura and Pukkusa answered my question well, but your answer was supreme." To show his gratitude to his chief advisor, the king rewarded him with many gifts and a great deal of wealth.

Having concluded his story, the Buddha taught the Dhamma, and the bhikkhu who was longing for his former wife attained the first path. Then the Buddha identified the birth: "At that time, this bhikkhu was the king, his former wife was the queen, Moggallāna was Ayura, Sāriputta was Pukkusa, and I was the wise Senaka."

150

The Skin Bag
Sattubhasta Jātaka

It was while staying at Jetavana that the Buddha told this story about the Perfection of Wisdom.[2]

Long, long ago, when a king named Janaka was reigning in Bārāṇasi, the Bodhisatta was born into a brahmin family and was named Senaka. After he had received his education in Takkasilā and returned to Bārāṇasi, he became the king's chief advisor. Senaka was highly respected for his wisdom and his virtue. Under his teaching, King Janaka observed the ten duties of a king and unfailingly observed the Uposatha days. Peace and prosperity prevailed throughout the kingdom.

In Kāsi, there was an old brahmin who had received one thousand coins as alms and had deposited the entire sum with a brahmin family in Bārānasi for safe keeping while he continued seeking more donations. While he was away, the family used all the money for their own needs. When the brahmin returned, they could not give him back his money, so they offered their daughter instead. The brahmin agreed, married the girl, and took her to a village near Bārānasi.

2   The occasion for this story is the same as that for Tale 216, where it is told in detail.

Still quite young, the girl was dissatisfied with the old brahmin for a husband and soon began a love affair with a much younger man. Scheming to get her husband out of the way, she feigned sickness and went to bed. When her husband asked what was wrong, she replied, "Husband, the housework is too much for me. I really must have a maid."

"Wife, I have no money," he protested. "How can we afford a maid?"

"In the past, you were able to collect more than one thousand coins by begging for alms. Why don't you do that again? We could use the money to hire a maid."

"All right. If you insist, I'll try," he agreed. "Prepare something for my journey."

She filled a catskin bag with dry rations, gave it to him, and sent him on his way.

After several days of walking from village to village and from town to town, he managed to collect seven hundred coins. "This is enough to hire several servants!" he thought and decided to return home. On his way back, he stopped, opened his bag, and ate some more of his provisions. When he was finished, he went to a nearby spring to drink some water. While he was gone, a venomous black snake, smelling the food, crawled in and coiled up inside the bag. When the brahmin returned, he fastened the bag, put it on his shoulder, and headed home.

A tree deva, who had seen the snake enter the bag, called out a warning, "Brahmin, if you stop on your way home, you will die! If you go straight home, your wife will die!"

Terrified by this, the brahmin turned around, but he could not see anyone. He continued walking toward Bārānasi, but, the whole way, he was trembling with fear, and his mind was in turmoil trying to understand the dire message.

As he was passing the city gate, hordes of people were streaming through with flowers and incense. He asked several young men where everyone was going.

"Today is an Uposatha day," they replied, "and the wise Senaka is going to deliver a sermon in the palace courtyard. His voice is so beautiful, and his teaching so wonderful, that we all want to hear it. You must be a stranger here not to know this!"

"These people say Senaka is wise. He can probably help me understand the riddle," the brahmin thought "I am afraid of death, mine or my wife's. At least, I can hear the teaching." With some hope, he followed the crowd.

In the courtyard, a great throng of people gathered around Senaka and the king. The brahmin stood at the edge of the crowd, with his bag on his shoulder, his mind agitated, and his knees trembling.

Senaka preached as if he were showering his listeners with ambrosia. When he finished speaking, he surveyed his audience. "These people are pleased with my teaching," he thought, but then he noticed the brahmin. "That one man is scowling, nervous, and ill-at-ease. There must be some problem nagging him and preventing him from listening to me attentively. Let me free him from his trouble and ease his mind."

"Brahmin," he called out, "I am Senaka. You seem to be confused or upset. I see that your eyes are brimming with tears. What have you lost, or what do you wish to gain by coming here?"

"Wise sage," the brahmin answered, "I am indeed upset. I have just come from the forest, where I heard a voice—a yakkha or a deva—saying: 'Brahmin, if you stop on your way home, you will die! If you go straight home, your wife will die!' I looked around, but there was no one there. Now I'm scared to death and don't know what to do. Since you are wise, can you explain this riddle to me?"

"There are many causes of death in this world," Senaka reflected quietly. "One may drown in the sea, be seized by a crocodile, fall from a tree, or be pierced by a thorn. One may be struck by lightning or by a weapon. One may die by hanging, by poison, by cold, or by sickness. What could possibly kill this brahmin if he stopped on the road, or his wife if he went home?"

Then he noticed the brahmin's skin bag and thought, "Of course! If he stopped, he would open the bag. If he went home, his wife would open it." At once, he understood exactly what had happened, and he knew that the brahmin had been warned by a deva.

'Brahmin," he called, "is there any food in that bag on your shoulder?"
"Yes, sir, there is."
"Did you eat some of it for breakfast this morning?"
"Yes, sir, I did."
"At that time, were you sitting at the foot of a tree?"
"Yes, sir, I was."
"When you finished, did you go to get a drink of water?"
"Yes, sir, I did."
"When you went to get the water, did you leave the bag open?"
"Yes, sir, I did."
"When you returned, did you fasten the bag without looking inside?"
"Yes, sir, I did."
"Brahmin, you have no reason to be afraid. I know what happened, and I can solve your riddle."

"I'm sure you can, sir, for you seem to know exactly what I did this morning as if you were watching me."

"Brahmin, there is a venomous snake in your bag. He crawled in there when he smelled your food. After you closed the bag and made him a prisoner, he coiled up and settled down. The voice you heard was a deva of the forest. He was warning you. He knew that, if you stopped, you would open your bag to get some food, and the snake would bite you. If you went directly home and put the bag down, your wife would open it, and the snake would bite her. Now that snake has been bumped and jostled in your bag for a long time, but he has not moved. Even in the midst of this crowded assembly, he exhibits no fear. It must be a brave and fearless black snake. Brahmin, put your bag down carefully, and open it. Then stand back, and prod it with a stick."

The brahmin did as Senaka instructed, and the black snake crawled out of the bag, rose up, spread his hood, and looked unblinkingly at the crowd.

Overjoyed at this proof of the sage's wisdom, the crowd waved scarves and snapped their fingers in approval. Many showered the teacher with precious stones, and everyone cried, "Well done! Well done! Well done!"

A snake charmer stepped forward and offered to make a mouthband for the snake. Then he easily caught the snake and took him to be released in the forest.

The brahmin approached the king, paid his respects, and said, "Sire, it is your great fortune to have one as wise as Senaka to enhance your kingdom! To him I owe my life and the welfare of my wife." Taking out the seven hundred coins he had collected, he continued, "This is all I have, but I wish to give them to this wise man in gratitude."

"For telling the truth, a wise man cannot accept a wage," Senaka replied. "Instead, let us give you something to help you on your journey home." He presented the brahmin with one thousand coins and continued, "Now, please tell us, Brahmin, who sent you to beg for money?"

"It was my wife, sir."

"Is she old or young"

"She is very young."

"In that case, Brahmin," Senaka replied, "I am afraid that she is misbehaving with someone. She sent you away so that she could continue her affair unhindered. If you go directly home with all this money, she will give it to her lover. I suggest that you hide it in a safe place before you get there."

Following Senaka's advice, the brahmin hid the money at the foot of a tree just outside the village. When he arrived home in the evening, his wife was in the house with her lover.

The brahmin stood at the door and called, "Wife, I am home!"

She immediately put out the light and hurried to open the door. As soon as her husband was inside, she hustled her lover out and closed the door. Then she relit the lamp and greeted her husband properly. After looking in the sack, she asked, "Husband, didn't you get any money on your journey?"

"I collected over one thousand coins."

"Where is the money, then?"

"I left it under the big tree just outside the village, but never mind about that. We will get it tomorrow."

She quickly made up an excuse and ran to tell her lover about the money. He immediately went and got it as if it were his own.

The next morning, the brahmin went to get the money, but, of course, it was not there, so he went to see Senaka.

"What is the matter, brahmin?" the sage asked.

"Sir, I hid the money as you suggested, but this morning it was not there."

"Did you tell your wife where you had hidden it?"

"Yes, sir, I did."

Sure that the wife had told her lover, Senaka asked, "Brahmin, is there a brahmin who is a good friend of your wife's?"

"Yes, sir, there is."

"Is there a brahmin who is a good friend of yours?"

"Yes, sir, there is."

Senaka gave the brahmin a week's expenses and said, "Tomorrow, you and your wife should each invite seven brahmins for lunch. Each day, for a week, you should each invite one fewer, until, on the last day, you each invite only one. Next week, come and tell me whether the man your wife invited on the last day was also in your home every day."

The brahmin agreed and did as instructed. The next week, he returned to the palace and told Senaka, "There is one man that my wife invited every day."

Senaka asked who that man was and sent some of his men to bring him to the palace. With the two brahmins in front of him, Senaka asked the second. "Did you take the coins belonging to this brahmin from under the large tree by the road just outside your village?"

"No, sir," he replied, "I did not."

"I am Senaka the wise. Just as I knew that there was a snake in this man's bag, I know what you have done. If you do not tell me the truth, you will suffer severely. Now tell me, did you take that money?"

Afraid of what Senaka might do to him, the man quickly confessed "Yes, I took the coins," he said.

"What did you do with them?"

"I put them in a box in my room, sir."

Senaka asked the first brahmin, "Do you want to keep your wife or take another?"

"Let me keep her, sir."

Senaka sent his men to fetch the money and the brahmin's wife. He punished the thief and banished him from the city. He punished the wife and warned her not to stray again. He returned the money to the brahmin, gave him great honor, and established him in a new house near his own.

Having concluded his story, the Buddha taught the Dhamma, and many who were listening attained the first path. Then the Buddha identified the birth: "At that time, Ānanda was the brahmin, Sāriputta was the deva, my followers were the assembly, and I was Senaka."

151
Baka-Brahmā
Baka-Brahmā Jātaka

It was while staying at Jetavana that the Buddha told this story about Baka-Brahmā.

In a previous birth Baka-Brahmā had practiced meditation and was reborn in the Vehapphala heaven.[1] After staying there for five hundred eons, he was reborn in the Subhakinna heaven. After sixty-four eons there, he was reborn in the Abhassara heaven, where the life span is eight eons. While he was there, he forgot that he had been born in and passed away from those higher Brahma heavens. He came to believe, "This is permanent, this is stable, this is eternal, this is complete, this is imperishable. Indeed, this is where one is not born, does not age, does not die, does not pass away, and is not reborn; and there is no escape superior to this."

One day, the Buddha became aware of Baka-Brahmā's mistaken and pernicious view, and, just as easily as a strong man can straighten his bent arm, the Buddha disappeared from Jetavana and appeared in the Abhassara Heaven.

When Baka-Brahmā saw the Buddha, he greeted him warmly. "Come here, My Lord!" Baka-Brahmā said. "Welcome, My Lord. It is a long time since

1   See The Thirty-one Planes of Existence in Volume III

you have taken an opportunity to visit. This is permanent, this is stable, this is eternal, this is complete, this is imperishable. Indeed, this is where one is not born, does not age, does not die, does not pass away, and is not reborn; and there is no escape superior to this."

"Baka-Brahmā has become ignorant!" the Buddha replied. "It is ignorance which leads him to say that a thing which is not permanent is permanent, that a thing which is not stable is stable, that a thing which is not eternal is eternal, that a thing which is not complete is complete, that a thing which is not imperishable is imperishable. It is ignorance which leads him to say that one is not born where one is born, that one does not age where one ages, that one does not die where one dies, that one does not pass away where one passes away, that one is not reborn where one is reborn. It is ignorance which leads him to say that there is no escape superior to this."

When Baka-Brahmā heard this, he thought, "This one presses me hard. He pins me down and holds me to exactly what I say!" Then, like a thief who, when caught red-handed, tries to excuse himself by naming others just as guilty, he declared, "There are seventy-two of us, Gotama. We are righteous and great; from birth and aging we are free. This heaven of ours is eternal, and there is nothing above. Indeed, there are many who share this view."

"Actually, Baka," the Buddha corrected him, "your existence in this realm has been short, not long! On the other hand, you have experienced various existences in many other realms, and all those, extending more than one hundred thousand eons into the past, are all well known to me."

"Gotama!" Baka-Brahmā exclaimed, trying to maintain his self-esteem. "I am infinite, and my wisdom is infinite. I am untouched by birth, aging, and sorrow. All those changeable things lie far beneath me. Nevertheless, if you know something that I should know, please tell me."

Then the Buddha revealed to him the events of the past through which he had gained rebirth in the Brahma heavens.

"Once, there was a caravan stranded in the desert. You saved all those people dying of thirst by diverting a river into that desert. This was your virtuous practice long ago. I remember it as if just waking from a dream.

"On another occasion, while staying near a village on the banks of the River Eni, you discovered that the village was under attack by highwaymen. You created the illusion of a troop of royal soldiers, which drove away the gang of thieves. Then you set free the villagers who had been tied up by the gang. This was your virtuous practice long ago. I remember it as if just waking from a dream.

"On another occasion, there was a boat on the River Gaṅgā, filled with people. A mighty nāga seized the boat and threatened to devour all the passengers. You rescued all those people by assuming the form of a great garula and chasing away that nāga. This was your virtuous practice long ago. I remember it as if just waking from a dream.

"You did all this when you were the ascetic Kesava, and, at that time, I was your brightest student, Kappa. I remember all these virtuous deeds of yours as if just waking from a dream. Because of them, for many eons, you have enjoyed the glory and majesty of birth in these Brahma heavens."

Baka-Brahmā expressed great gratitude to the Buddha for revealing to him his deeds in previous existences. Then the Buddha taught the Dhamma, and ten thousand Brahmās attained the paths. Thus, did the Buddha become the refuge for a multitude of devas.

After returning to Jetavana, the Buddha identified the birth: "At that time, Baka-Brahmā was the ascetic Kesava, and I was his wise student Kappa."

152
To Remain Silent Would Be Unrighteous
Gandhāra Jātaka

It was while staying at Jetavana that the Buddha told this story about storing medicine.

One day, while Venerable Pilinda Vaccha was walking for alms in a village, he heard a young girl crying because she had no jewelry to wear to a festival. Taking pity on the child, he used his extraordinary powers to create a gold necklace, earrings, and bangles for her to wear. When the king's men learned about such a display of unexplained wealth, they suspected the child's father of stealing and, without investigating, threw the whole family into jail.

The next day, Venerable Pilinda Vaccha found out what had happened and visited the palace to obtain the release of the innocent family. To prove to the king that he was responsible for the girl's ornaments, he transformed the entire palace into pure gold. After this, Venerable Pilinda Vaccha's fame spread quickly. Devotees were so pleased that they offered him vast amounts of the five medicines, which he distributed to other bhikkhus. The donations were much more than the bhikkhus could consume immediately, so they stored the medicines in pots.

When laypeople saw those pots, they cried, "Look at that! Those greedy bhikkhus are hoarding butter, ghee, oil, honey, and jaggery in their rooms."

When the Buddha heard about this, he established a rule that bhikkhus could keep medicine they received for only seven days. "Bhikkhus," he added, "even ascetics of old, when there was no Buddha in the world, were careful not to store even salt for the next day, but here you are, ordained in such a liberating discipline, hoarding medicine." Then he told this story of the past.

Long, long ago, when King Videha was reigning in Mithilā, the Bodhisatta was the king of Gandhāra. Although the two kings had never met, they corresponded, exchanged presents, had confidence in each other, and considered each other friends.

Once, while the king of Gandhāra was observing the Uposatha day, as he was sitting on the dais near an open window and delivering a learned discourse on the law to his ministers, there was an eclipse of the moon. It was the belief that an eclipse was caused by Rāhu. This caused the king to think, "The moon has lost its light because of external trouble. I, too, am subject to external troubles. It would be better for me to give up my kingdom and to become an ascetic than to lose my light like the moon seized by Rāhu. One should be detached from kith and kin. Rather than trying to control and to admonish others, I should control and admonish myself." Without any hesitation, the king turned to his ministers and handed over responsibility for the kingdom to them. Having renounced his throne, he donned the garb of an ascetic and went to the Himavat to practice meditation.

Shortly after this, when some merchants returned from Gandhāra, the king of Videha asked about his friend and learned that he had become an ascetic. The king was deeply moved by that news and thought, "Since my friend has taken up the religious life, what do I want with a kingdom?" He, too, turned his back on his throne. Abandoning his wealth, his glory, his queens, his sons, and his daughters, he donned the garb of an ascetic, left Mithilā, and went to the Himavat to practice meditation.

The two ascetics met in the Himavat, but they did not recognize each other. They built a hermitage and lived there in tranquility, meditating and subsisting on fruit, roots, and berries. The Videhan ascetic paid due respect to the other as his senior.

One night, as the two ascetics were sitting at the root of a tree, discussing the law, by the light of the full moon, there was an eclipse. "Master, what has happened to the moon?" asked the Videhan ascetic.

"Friend, Rāhu, in his jealousy, has swallowed the moon and prevents it from shining. Once before, when I saw the moon seized by Rāhu, I thought, "The moon has lost its light because of external trouble. I, too, am subject to external troubles. It was at that moment that I resolved to undertake the religious life so that my kingdom would not engulf me as Rāhu engulfs the orb of the moon. That is why I became an ascetic."

"Master, were you king of Gandhāra?"

"Yes, I was."

"Master, I was your friend, King Videha in Mithilā!"

"Why did you become an ascetic?" the Gandhāran ascetic asked.

"When I heard that you had abandoned your throne to undertake the religious life, I was sure that you had understood something important. It was because of you that I resolved to become an ascetic."

After this, the two became even closer. Once, at the beginning of the rainy season, they left the Himavat to get salt and vinegar and to find a place to stay.

In a frontier village, the inhabitants were so impressed by the deportment of the two ascetics that they gave generous alms and invited them to stay. The villagers built huts for the ascetics in a pleasant spot and provided alms every day.

Sometimes, the villagers gave the ascetics salt on a leaf, but there were days when they received no salt at all. One day, when the Videhan ascetic received a large amount of salt, he used some himself at meal time, gave some to his companion, and stored the rest. "This will do for a saltless day," he thought as he put away the leaf.

The next day, the Videhan ascetic retrieved the leaf and said to his companion, "Here is some salt, Master. Please take some."

"The people gave no salt today," the Gandhāran ascetic replied. "Where is this from?"

"They gave us a lot of salt yesterday, so I kept the extra, thinking 'This will do for a saltless day.'"

"You foolish man!" the Gandhāran ascetic chided. "You forsook your great kingdom, three hundred yojanas in extent, to take up the religious life and to attain freedom from attachments, but here you are, longing for salt! Having thrown away all your wealth and power, how can you now hoard this miserable salt!"

The Videhan ascetic bristled at this reprimand and retorted, "Look to yourself, Master! You see my faults clearly, but you are blind to your own! Didn't you leave your own kingdom, saying, 'Rather than trying to control and to admonish others, I should control and admonish myself!' Now here you are, scolding me! You resolved never again to give orders, but you are certainly ordering me around today!"

"What I am saying is righteous," the Gandhāran ascetic replied calmly, "and I speak because I cannot abide what is unrighteous. Wherever immorality is found, it must be pointed out. To remain silent would itself be unrighteous!"

This angered the Videhan ascetic even more. "Master, when one has angered another, it is not appropriate to keep talking, even though what he says is correct. You are speaking very harshly to me as if you were shaving me with a dull razor! Those words which, if spoken, cause offense should be left unspoken by a wise man. In such a case, silence is best."

The Gandhāran ascetic adamantly replied, "Whether or not you take offense, what I say is correct, so there is no fault on my part in speaking out. What I am saying is the truth, and the truth will endure. I am not trying to shape you as a potter beats and shapes wet clay. Rather, I seek to add the finishing touches to a well-fired vessel. If none were trained in wisdom and good conduct, many would wander uselessly like blinded buffalos. Fortunately, there are some wisely trained in moral conduct, who can discipline and lead others along the path of virtue."

The Videhan ascetic immediately understood his companion's wisdom, and apologized. "Master, please admonish me whenever it is necessary!" he begged humbly. "Forgive me for speaking to you so insolently and impetuously." He paid his respects to his senior and was granted pardon.

At the end of the rainy season, the two ascetics returned to the Himavat and continued living in harmony. The Gandhāran ascetic instructed his companion in meditation, and both of them were reborn in the Brahma heavens.

Having concluded his story, the Buddha identified the birth: "At that time, Ānanda was the Videhan ascetic, and I was the Gandhāran ascetic."

153
The Great Monkey King
Mahākapi Jātaka

It was while staying at Jetavana that the Buddha told this story about helping one's relatives.

Some bhikkhus were talking about the good that the Buddha did for his relatives. When the Buddha heard what they were discussing, he said, "Bhikkhus, this is not the first time the Tathāgata has done good deeds to benefit his relatives." Then he told this story of the past.

Long, long ago, when Brahmadatta was reigning in Bārānasi, the Bodhisatta was born as a monkey in the Himavat. When he was fully grown, he was extremely strong and vigorous and became the leader of a troop of eighty thousand monkeys.

On the bank of the Gangā there was an enormous mango tree, with two massive branches so thick with leaves it looked like a mountain. Its sweet fruit was of exquisite fragrance and flavor. One branch spread over the bank of the river, and the other branch extended over the water. One day, while the monkey king was eating the succulent fruit, he thought, "If any of this fruit ever fell into the river, great danger could come to us." To prevent this, he ordered the monkeys to pick all the mango flowers or tiny fruit from that

231

branch. One fruit, however, was hidden by an ant's nest and escaped the monkeys' attention. When it ripened, it fell into the river.

At that time, King Brahmadatta was bathing and amusing himself in the river. Whenever the king bathed in the river, he had nets stretched both upstream and downstream from where he was. The mango floated down the river and stuck in the net upstream from the king. That evening, as the king was leaving, the fishermen pulled in the net and found the fruit. As they had never seen a fruit like this before, they showed it to the king.

"What is this fruit?" the king asked.

"We do not know, Sire," they answered. "Who will know?"

"The foresters, Sire."

The king summoned the foresters, who told him that the fruit was a mango. The king cut it with a knife and, after having the foresters eat some, tasted it himself. He also gave some of the fruit to his ministers and to his wives.

The king could not forget the magnificent flavor of the ripe mango. Obsessed with the taste of the new fruit, he called the foresters again and asked where the tree stood. When he learned that it was on the bank of the river, he had many rafts joined together and rowed upstream to find it. In due course, the king and his retinue arrived at the site of the huge tree.

The king went ashore and set up a camp. After having eaten some of the delectable mangoes, he retired for the night on a bed prepared at the foot of the tree. Fires were lit, and guards set on each side.

At midnight, after the men had fallen asleep and all was quiet, the monkey king came with his troop. The eighty thousand monkeys moved from branch to branch, eating mangoes. The noise woke the king, who roused his archers.

"Surround those monkeys eating mangoes and shoot them," he ordered. "Tomorrow, we will dine on mango fruit and monkey's flesh."

The archers readied their bows to obey the king. The monkeys saw the archers and realized that all means of escape had been cut off. Shivering in fear of death, they ran to their leader and cried, "Sire, there are men with bows all around the tree preparing to shoot us. What can we do?"

"Do not fear," he comforted them. "I will save your lives." Then he climbed onto the branch stretching over the river. Springing from the end of it, he jumped one hundred bowlengths and landed on the opposite bank of the Gaṅgā. Judging the distance he had jumped, he thought, "That is how far I came." Then he found a long vine and cut it, thinking, "This much will be fastened to a tree, and this much will go across the river." He secured one end of the vine to a sturdy tree and the other around his own waist. Then he again leaped across the river with the speed of a cloud blown by the wind. In his calculation, however, he had forgotten to include the length to be tied around his own waist, so he could not reach the trunk of the mango tree. He reached out and grabbed the end of a branch firmly with both hands. He signaled to the troop of monkeys and cried, "Quick! Step on my back, and run along this vine to safety. Good luck to you all!"

The eighty thousand monkeys, each in turn, respectfully saluted the monkey king, asked his pardon, and escaped in this way.

The last monkey in the troop, however, had long resented the leader and wished to overthrow him. When he saw the king hanging there, he exulted, "This is my chance to see the last of my enemy!" Climbing onto a high branch, he flung himself down on the monkey king's back with a dreadful blow which crushed his heart and caused him excruciating pain. Satisfied that his rival would die, the wicked monkey triumphantly escaped and left the monkey king to suffer alone.

Having seen all that had happened as he lay on his bed, the king thought, "This noble monkey king, not caring for his own life, has ensured the safety of his troop. It would be wrong to destroy such an animal. I will have him brought down and carefully nursed." He ordered his men to lower the monkey gently down to a raft on the Gaṅgā. After the monkey had been brought ashore and washed, the king anointed him with the purest oil. Spreading an oiled skin on his own bed and laying the monkey king on it, the king covered him with a yellow robe. After the noble animal had been given sugared water to drink, the king himself took a low seat and addressed him. "Noble monkey, you made yourself a bridge for all the other monkeys to pass over to safety. What are you to them, and what are they to you?"

The monkey explained, "Sire, I guard the troop. I am their lord and chief. When they were filled with fear of your archers, I leapt a great distance to save them. After I had tied a vine around my waist, I returned to this mango tree. My strength was almost gone, but I managed to hold the branch so that my monkeys could pass over my back and reach safety. Because I could save them, I have no fear of death. Like a righteous king, I could guarantee the happiness of those over whom I used to reign. Sire, understand this truth! If you wish to be a righteous ruler, the happiness of your kingdom, your cities, and your people must be dear to you. It must be dearer than life itself."

After teaching the king in this way, the noble monkey died. The king gave orders that the monkey king should have a royal funeral. He ordered his wives to carry torches to the cremation ground with their hair disheveled. The ministers sent one hundred wagon loads of wood for the funeral pyre. When the regal ceremony was over, the ministers took the skull to the king. The king built a cetiya at the cremation site and made offerings of incense and flowers. He had the skull inlaid with gold, raised on a spear, and carried in front of the procession returning to Bārānasi. There he put it at the royal gate and paid homage to it with incense and flowers. The whole city was decorated, and the skull was honored for seven days. For the rest of his life the king revered the skull as a relic, offering incense and garlands. Established in the wonderful teaching of the monkey king, he gave alms and performed other good deeds. He ruled his kingdom righteously and became destined for heaven.

Having concluded his story, the Buddha taught the Dhamma. Then he identified the birth: "At that time, Ānanda was the king, this assembly was the monkey retinue, Devadatta was the wicked monkey, and I was the monkey king."

154

The Potter
Kumbhakāra Jātaka

It was while staying at Jetavana that the Buddha told this story about controlling the defilements.[1]

One night, five hundred bhikkhus, who had ordained together, were harboring sensuous thoughts and decided to return to lay life. To protect them, the Buddha asked Venerable Ānanda to summon all the bhikkhus in Jetavana. After they had gathered, the Buddha said, "Bhikkhus, one must not tolerate unwholesome thoughts. If allowed to grow, an unwholesome thought can bring ruin in its wake. Long ago, wise men of old restrained their defilements as soon as they arose and became Pacceka Buddhas." Then he told this story of the past.

Long, long ago, when Brahmadatta was reigning in Bārānasi, the Bodhisatta was born into a potter's family in a suburb of the city. When he grew up, he became a householder, had a son and daughter, and supported his family by his craft.

At that time, a king named Karandu was reigning in Dantapura, the capital of Kālinga. One morning, as this king was going by elephant with a great

---

1   The occasion for this story is told in detail in Tale 60.

235

retinue to his royal park, he saw a mango tree, laden with ripe golden fruit. He reached out and took several of the succulent mangoes. He ate one in the garden, and gave the rest to his favorites in the court.

As soon as the king had taken his mangoes, everyone else felt free to take what they wanted. Some climbed the tree and picked the fruit, but others broke off whole branches. In a short time, they had not only stripped it of every mango, but had also mutilated the tree itself.

The king enjoyed himself all day in the garden, and, in the evening, as he returned by the same road, he saw the tree again. "This morning this tree stood majestic and beautiful with its burden of fruit," the king marveled. "Now it is battered and broken, without a single mango remaining."

Not far from that tree, there was another mango tree, but this one was barren. The king noticed that it was unharmed and thought, "That mango tree, for its barrenness, is still beautiful, but the other, from its fruitfulness, was brutally maimed and stripped bare. The householder's life is like that fruitful tree, while the religious life is like a barren tree. The wealthy have worries; the ascetic has no fear. I would prefer to be like the barren tree."

Standing under the mango tree, he took the tree as his subject and began meditating. Perfecting his insight into the Three Characteristics, he became a Pacceka Buddha. "Rebirth is ended for me!" he realized. "The ocean of tears is dried up! There is no more to be done."

One of his ministers called to him, "Sire, you have been standing here a long time!"

"I am not a king," he replied. "I am a Pacceka Buddha."

"Pacceka Buddhas are not like you, Sire."

"Then what are they like?"

"A Pacceka Buddha is clean-shaven, wears a yellow robe, is not attached to family or kingdom, is as free as clouds in the sky, and stays in Nandamūla Cave in the Himavat. That, Sire, is what a Pacceka Buddha is like."

The king touched his head, and, instantly, his royal appearance disappeared. He took on the features of a Pacceka Buddha and traveled to the Nandamūla Cave in the Upper Himavat.

At the same time, a king named Naggaji was reigning in Takkasilā, the capital of Gandhāra. One day, as the king was sitting on a couch on the terrace, a servant was sitting on the floor nearby and grinding perfume for the queen. The king noticed that the servant had a single jeweled bracelet on each wrist and thought. "Being separate, her bracelets do not jingle." Then, in order to collect the perfume she had ground without damaging the bracelet, she removed the bracelet from her right wrist and placed it on the left. As she gathered the perfume, the two bracelets jangled against each other. "When that bracelet touched nothing, it made no sound. Now it hits the second and makes a noise. In the same way, when a person is on his own, he is quiet. When two or more are together, they create a din. I would prefer to be like the single bracelet. Rather than ruling the inhabitants of Kashmir and Gandhāra, I should rule myself!" Taking the jangling of the bracelets as his subject, he began meditating. Perfecting his insight into the Three Characteristics, he became a Pacceka Buddha. "Rebirth is ended for me!" he realized. "The ocean of tears is dried up! There is no more to be done." He, too, took on the features of a Pacceka Buddha and traveled to the Nandamūla Cave.

At the same time, a king named Nimi was reigning in Mithilā, the capital of Videha. One morning, after breakfast, as King Nimi, surrounded by his ministers, stood looking down at the street through an open window of the palace, a hawk swooped down on a butcher's stall and caught a chunk of meat in its talons. As the hawk was flying back into the sky, several vultures and a gang of crows attacked it on each side, striking it with their beaks and beating it with their wings, trying to make it give up the meat. Unable to endure the blows of the other birds, the hawk dropped the meat. Another bird quickly swooped down and caught the meat in mid-air. The vultures and crows immediately abandoned the hawk and attacked the bird with the meat. The second bird soon relinquished the meat, and a third snatched it in the same way. Just as quickly, the other birds left the second bird and attacked the one with the meat. Watching these birds, the king thought, "Trouble befell the one who took the meat, but peace returned to the one who let it go. Whoever indulges in the five sense pleasures finds suffering; whoever gives them up finds happiness. I would prefer to be like the bird who relinquished the meat. I have sixteen thousand women in my palace. I should abandon the five sense pleasures and live happily." Taking the fighting birds as his subject, he began meditating. Perfecting his insight into the Three Characteristics, he immediately became a Pacceka Buddha. "Rebirth is ended for me!" he realized. "The ocean of tears is dried up! There is no more to be done." He, too, took on the features of a Pacceka Buddha and traveled to the Nandamūla Cave.

At the same time, a king named Dummukha was reigning in Kampilla, the capital of Uttarapañcāla. One morning, after breakfast, as King Dummukha, wearing all his royal jewels and surrounded by his ministers, stood looking down on the courtyard from an open window, men opened the gate of a cattle pen. The bulls became excited over one cow who was

237

fresh and in season. One huge bull with sharp horns, seeing another bull approach, gored him so brutally that his entrails spilled out, and he died.

When the king saw this, he thought, "All living beings, from beasts to man, experience suffering because of the power of lust. Because of lust, that strong bull is dead. I should abandon the lust that disturbs all beings!" Taking the dead bull as his subject, he began meditating. Perfecting his insight into the Three Characteristics, he became a Pacceka Buddha. "Rebirth is ended for me!" he realized. "The ocean of tears is dried up! There is no more to be done." He, too, took on the features of a Pacceka Buddha and traveled to the Nandamūla Cave.

These four Pacceka Buddhas lived together in harmony. One day, after having cleaned their mouths by chewing toothsticks at Lake Anotatta, they took their bowls and outer robes and left Nandamūla. Arriving in a suburb of Bārānasi, they began walking for alms.

When the potter saw them outside his door, he was delighted and invited them into his house. He seated them, rinsed their bowls, and served them with excellent food. Then, sitting on one side, he paid respects to the eldest, saying, "Sir, your religious life appears very satisfactory. Your senses are calm, and your complexion is clear. Please tell me the subject you took when you became an ascetic."

He posed the same question to each Pacceka Buddha, and each explained what had prompted him to renounce his kingdom and had led him to enlightenment. "A mango tree was punished for its fruitfulness," said the first. "Two bracelets jangled against each other," said the second. "Other birds attacked the one with the chunk of meat," said the third. "A bull was attacked and killed because of lust," said the fourth.

After each answer, the potter replied, "Good sir! What a worthy topic!" All of this wise conversation made him feel inclined to leave home himself and to become an ascetic. As soon as the Pacceka Buddhas had left, he called his wife and said, "Wife, those four Pacceka Buddhas renounced their kingdoms to become ascetics, and now they live pure lives, without hindrances. They are enjoying the bliss of the religious life, while I struggle to earn a livelihood. What do I want with a householder's life? Take the children, and stay at home. I will become an ascetic!"

"Husband," she replied, "I, too, heard the discourse of the Pacceka Buddhas. I understand how you feel, but wait a few minutes. Please look after the children while I get some water from the tank." She balanced a water pot on her head as if she were going to the tank to fetch water for the family and left the house. As soon as she was outside the house, she put down the pot and ran away. Meeting some female ascetics outside the city, she asked to join them and began her life as a religious wanderer.

Since his wife did not return, the potter cared for the children himself. As they became older, he tried to teach them to be self-reliant. One day, he cooked the rice a little too much; the next day, not enough. One day, he added too much water; the next day, not enough. One day, he added too much salt; the next day, none at all. Each day, the children told him that the rice was too hard or too soft; too wet or too dry, too salty or not salty enough. Each day, he would explain why it was that way so that they would learn how to cook it properly themselves. The potter was very patient in his teaching. When he was satisfied that they could manage by themselves, he told them that he was going to become an ascetic. After taking the children to live with their relatives, he left the home life and went to stay in the forest outside the city.

One day, both ascetics, formerly husband and wife, happened to be walking for alms in Bārānasi. As soon as she recognized her former husband, the female ascetic said to him, "Sir, you must have killed the children."

The male ascetic replied calmly, "Lady, I don't kill children. I took care of them until they were able to manage for themselves. Then I became an ascetic. You, on the other hand, were careless of them and pleased yourself by ordaining when you wished. Now let us go our own ways." The female ascetic accepted his admonishment and turned to walk in the other direction.

The two ascetics never saw each other again. He practiced meditation on loving-kindness and was reborn in the Brahma heavens.

When the Buddha concluded his story, the five hundred bhikkhus became arahats. Then the Buddha identified the birth: "At that time, Uppalavanna was the daughter, Rahula was the son, Rahula's mother was the female ascetic, and I was the male ascetic.

155

Forgotten Heroes
Dalhadhamma Jātaka

It was while staying in the Ghosita forest near Kosambi that the Buddha told this story about the elephant Bhaddavatikā.[2] One morning, as the Buddha was entering the city with a group of bhikkhus for alms, this aged she-elephant saw him and knelt before him. "Lord, when I was young and able, the great King Udena loved me," Bhaddavatikā lamented. "He honored me as a great favorite. Every day, I ate the most delicious food. Frequently, I was adorned with costly trappings and led grand processions. The grandeur of my stable was something to behold, with a fine carpet to stand on, colored hangings on

---

2 Bhaddavatikā originally belonged to King Pajjota of Avanti, and was famous for her speed. King Pajjota was jealous of King Udena's splendor. One thing in particular that King Pajjota wanted was an elephant-taming charm that only King Udena knew. Once, King Pajjota captured King Udena, but the latter refused to teach the charm to anyone unless the student would bow to him as a teacher. King Pajjota told King Udena that he would send a student, but that she would be a hunchback, too ugly to be seen, and that she would sit behind a curtain. The "student" he sent was his beautiful daughter, Vasuladattā. To complete the ruse, he told his daughter that the teacher was a leper with whom she should have no contact. When Vasuladattā had trouble memorizing the charm, King Udena called her a hunchback, and Vasuladattā retorted,

the walls, and a perfumed oil lamp burning day and night. He told everyone, 'I owe Bhaddavatikā my life, my kingdom, and my queen!'

"The years have past, and, now that I am old and unable to work, the king has cut off all my honors, leaving me poor and unprotected. I am neglected and forgotten, and no one cares for me. All I have to eat is whatever poor fruit I can manage to find in the forest. Venerable Sir, I have no other refuge. Please remind King Udena of my merits, and ask him to restore my former honor to me, Lord."

"Bhaddavatikā," said the Buddha gently to the poor elephant, "go on your way. I will speak to the king and see that your honor is restored to you."

When they arrived at the palace, the Buddha and the bhikkhus were invited to enter and were served a lavish meal.

When the meal was over, the Buddha offered a blessing. Then he asked, "Sire, where is Bhaddavatikā?"

"Venerable Sir, I do not know."

"Sire, after giving honor to a loyal servant, it is wrong to take that honor away when the servant becomes old. It is always right to be grateful. Bhadda-vatikā was of great service to you, Sire. She saved your life, restored you to your kingdom, and gave you your queen. Now, worn-out with age, the poor elephant is barely surviving. She is unprotected, and no one cares for her. She subsists on whatever wild fruit she can forage in the forest. It is not appropriate for you to have abandoned her like that in her old age. Please restore the honor she enjoyed when she served you so faithfully!"

The king promptly did as the Buddha had advised. Soon everyone in the city knew how the Buddha had restored Bhaddavatikā to the king's favor.

Not long afterwards, bhikkhus in Ghosita were talking about it. When the Buddha heard what they were discussing, he said, "Bhikkhus, this is not the first time that, by telling of her merits, I have gotten her former honor restored." Then he told this story of the past.

Long, long ago, when a king named Dalhadhamma was reigning in Bāra-nasi, the Bodhisatta was born as the son of the king's chief advisor. When

---

(Continued) calling him a leper. They raised the curtain, realized that they both had been lied to, and instantly fell in love. Vasuladattā, in turn, tricked her father and was given permission to use Bhaddavatikā. One day, when King Pajjota was away from the palace, the two lovers filled one bag with gold coins and another with silver and fled on that swift elephant. With King Pajjota's guards in pursuit, King Udena spilled the coins, first the gold and then the silver, on the road. The soldiers scrambled to get the money and let the eloping couple escape. When King Udena arrived back in his capital Kosambi, (Continued) installed Vasuladattā as his chief queen, and Bhaddavatikā was given great honor. (Dhammapada Commentary to verses 21-23, Burlingame, Volume 1, pp. 270-274).

he grew up, he also began serving the king and succeeded his father in the same position.

King Dalhadhamma had a remarkably intelligent and strong she-elephant that could travel one hundred yojanas in one day. In battle, she was formidable and fearless, and, in peacetime, she served as chief royal elephant. In return for her service, the king honored her greatly. Her trappings were extremely elaborate and covered with expensive ornaments. Her stall was lavishly decorated, and her food was especially prepared from the finest ingredients. The king never failed to praise her virtues.

As time passed, the elephant lost her strength and speed. The king removed her from her magnificent stable, withdrew her honors and special privileges, and sent her back to the forest. The poor elephant was reduced to living on rough grass and leaves she could forage.

One day, the king was informed that there were not enough storage jars and pots in the palace. A potter was summoned and told to make a large number of pots of various sizes and to deliver to the palace.

"Sire," the potter replied, "in order to make that many pots, I would need a lot of cow dung to fire my kiln. I don't know how I could get enough dung because I don't have any oxen to pull a cart."

Suddenly the king remembered his old elephant and asked one of his men, "Where is that old she-elephant we used to have?"

"Sire, she is wandering loose in the forest," the man replied. "Potter!" the king exclaimed, more on impulse than anything else. "In the forest, there is an old she-elephant. Yoke her to your cart, and fetch cow-dung for your kiln."

Some time later, the elephant happened to see the chief advisor on the road, and she bowed at his feet. "Lord," she cried in a pitiful voice, "when I was young, the king was very proud to use me. He gave me great honor. Now that I am old, he has no regard for me. After he evicted me from his stables, I managed to survive on grass and leaves in the forest. That was hard, but now he has given me to a hard-hearted potter who yokes me to a cart to haul dung. I am miserable, and I have no refuge but you. You know how well I served the king. I carried the king's weapons and faced all his enemies. Wasn't he satisfied with me? Has he forgotten how bravely I fought for him? How could I have fallen so low as to haul dung for a potter? I am helpless, and I feel that death must be near. Please restore to me the honor I once had!"

The advisor felt sorry for the poor elephant and tried to comfort her. He promised to speak to the king.

The next day, when he waited on the king after his morning meal, he mentioned the elephant. He reminded the king of various battles in which she had distinguished herself and important messages she had carried for him.

He praised her strength, loyalty, and bravery. He spoke of the honor she had enjoyed as the chief royal elephant and how magnificent she had appeared in the royal processions. "Where is that she-elephant now, Sire?" he asked.

"Oh," the king replied off-handedly, "I gave her to a potter to haul his cow-dung."

"Is it right, Your Majesty," the advisor asked, "to allow a former royal elephant to be harnessed to a potter's cart hauling dung? Selfish men throw away their worn-out slaves. They are miserly with their honors. That's how you have treated that poor elephant. Those who forget the help they've received from others will reap failure in other endeavors. Those who remember and reward those who have helped them will succeed in everything they do. Be grateful to those who have served you. In this way, you will prosper and also win heaven!"

The advisor elaborated further on the importance of gratitude, and he taught a great lesson to all who were gathered in the court. The king listened carefully to this profound discourse and restored to the she-elephant all the honor she had previously enjoyed. Firmly established in virtue by the advisor's instruction, the king ruled wisely, gave generous alms, and did many meritorious deeds. After a long and good life, he was reborn in heaven.

Having concluded his story, the Buddha identified the birth: "At that time, Bhaddavatikā was the she-elephant, Ānanda was the king, and I was the wise advisor."

156

The Messenger
Susīma Jātaka

It was while staying at Jetavana that the Buddha told this story about the Great Renunciation.

One day, in the Hall of Truth, bhikkhus were praising the Buddha's renunciation. When the Buddha heard what they were discussing, he said, "Bhikkhus, it is hardly strange that I retired from the world after practicing the Ten Perfections for hundreds of thousands of eons. Long before, I even gave up my Kāsi kingdom, three hundred yojanas in extent, and renounced the world." Then he told this story of the past.

Long, long ago, when Brahmadatta was reigning in Bārānasi, the Bodhisatta was born as the son of the king's chief advisor and was named Susīma. On the same day that he was born, the queen gave birth to a boy, named Brahmadatta after his father. Since the two babies shared the same birthday, the king had Susīma raised with his own son. Both of them were as handsome as devas. They studied together in Takkasilā, and, even after Prince Brahmadatta became crown prince, they continued living together. After the old king died, Prince Brahmadatta became king and appointed Susīma as his chief advisor.

One day, during a festival, the city was decorated like Tāvatimsa. The king, dressed like Sakka himself and seated on the royal elephant's shoulders, with Susīma riding behind him on the elephant's back, led a procession around the city. Eager to see her son, the queen mother stood at a palace window and watched for the procession. As soon as the royal elephant came into sight, her eyes fastened on Susīma, and she suddenly developed an infatuation for him. Overcome with desire for her son's advisor, she retired to her chamber. She lay down, moaning, "If I cannot have him, I will surely die!" For several days, she refused to get up and lost all interest in food.

Not seeing his mother, the king asked after her and learned that she was ill. He went to her room to ask what ailed her. She was embarrassed to admit that she was in love with Susīma, so she said nothing. Still worried, the king sent his own queen to find out what the matter was. Women do not hide secrets from each other, so, as the queen sat stroking her mother-in-law's back, the queen mother confessed her secret. As soon as the queen told her husband about this, he replied, "Dear wife, go to my mother, and comfort her. I will make Susīma king, and she can be his queen."

The king sent for his advisor and told him, "Susīma, my friend, my mother is in love with you. Therefore, you must become king and make her your queen. I will serve as crown prince once more."

"Your Majesty, that is impossible!" Susīma protested.

King Brahmadatta asked him again and again, pointing out that this was the only way to save his mother's life. Finally, Susīma consented, very reluctantly, to this unusual proposition.

For a while, this new arrangement seemed harmonious enough, but Susīma, who had never been interested in marriage or the life of a householder, began to feel like an inmate in jail or a bird in a cage. He showed no interest in the affairs of the kingdom and took no delight in worldly pleasures.

"Susīma avoids me," the queen sighed. "He dines alone and sleeps in his own chamber." As she pondered the reasons for this, she concluded, "He is young and fresh, but I am old and gray. I wonder whether I could get him to think that he is not so young. If he thinks he is aging, he might seek my company."

One day, as she was stroking the king's head, she suddenly stopped and cried, "Here's a gray hair! Your Majesty is getting old!"

"Pull it out and put it in my hand." the king replied. She pulled out a black hair from the king's head, and quickly replaced it with a gray hair from her own head, which she showed to the king.

As soon as King Susīma saw that gray hair, the fear of death rose up in him, and sweat broke out on his forehead. "Susīma, you have become old without realizing it," he declared, reproving himself. "Your hair has always been black, but this white one is a messenger. From birth until now, you've been living sunk in the mud of desire, like a village pig wallowing in filth. It is high time for you to abandon your desires and to become an ascetic."

"Lady!" he cried, "I must take up the religious life in the Himavat!"

The queen realized she had made a terrible blunder. Instead of getting him to love her, she had given him reason to leave. "No, Your Majesty!" she cried. "That silver hair was not from your head! It is mine! You are still young! You are strong and handsome! Keep your kingdom, Sire! Smile at me. There's no need for you to be thinking already about what old age will bring! This is the springtime of your life!"

"Your Majesty," Susīma replied calmly, "you have foretold what is to come. As age ripens, these black hairs will turn gray. I have observed the change and the breaking up of the body that comes with time. Royal maidens, as tender as lotus flowers, as fair as gold, and intoxicated with the pride of their glorious youth, bewitch men with their charms. As the years pass, they walk less steadily, they become palsied, they walk with a cane, and, in the end, they are bent like a rafter. Without exception, this is the natural course for all living beings. It is the dreary, but natural, end for all! My life has been privileged. As king, every desire has been fulfilled, but, lying alone at night, I have pondered the untrustworthiness of sense pleasures and the power they wield. The life of a householder, rooted as it is in the gratification of those sense pleasures, leads to certain disappointment. The wise man renounces that and goes his own way!"

He sent for Brahmadatta, announced his decision to become an ascetic, and returned the kingdom to its rightful heir. For a while, Susīma stayed in the palace, teaching everyone in the court. He explained the delight and the misery of sense pleasures and exhorted his listeners to practice virtue. Then, amid cries of lamentation from relatives, courtiers, and friends, he donned the robes of an ascetic, left Bārānasi, and made his way to the Himavat. For the rest of his life, he intensively practiced meditation on the Four Brahma Vihāras. When he died, he was reborn in the Brahma heavens.

Having concluded his story, the Buddha taught the Dhamma. Then he identified the birth: "At that time, Ānanda was the young King Brahmadatta, Rāhula's mother was his mother, and I was King Susīma."

157

The Banyan Seed
Kotisimbali Jātaka

It was while staying at Jetavana that the Buddha told this story about controlling the defilements.[1]

One night, five hundred bhikkhus, who had ordained together, were harboring sensuous thoughts and decided to return to lay life. To protect them, the Buddha asked Venerable Ānanda to summon all the bhikkhus in Jetavana. After they had gathered, the Buddha said, "Bhikkhus, one must not tolerate unwholesome thoughts. If allowed to grow, an unwholesome thought can bring ruin in its wake. Unwholesome thoughts spring up around a man as banyans and creepers grow up around a tree. Long ago, a wise deva clearly saw this danger." Then he told this story of the past.

Long, long ago, when Brahmadatta was reigning in Bārānasi, the Bodhisatta was a tree-deva dwelling in the top of a silk cotton tree growing near the ocean. One day, an enormous garula king flew over the ocean and, with the sweep of his vast wings, parted the waters below, exposing a nāga king, whom he seized by the tail. After forcing the nāga to disgorge the huge

---

1   The occasion for this story is told in detail in Tale 60. It is the same as that
for Tales 113 and 154.

stones he had swallowed, the garula carried him toward that silk-cotton tree. On the way, the garula flew over the tops of some other trees. Seeing a chance to escape, the huge nāga king stuck his head into the branches of a great banyan tree and coiled his body around the trunk. He held tightly to the banyan tree, expecting that the garula would have to release him. The garula and nāga, however, were evenly matched. The nāga would not let go of the tree, and the garula would not let go of the nāga. Finally, the banyan tree was uprooted, and the garula continued his flight, now carrying both the nāga and the banyan tree. When the garula reached the silk-cotton tree, he laid the nāga on a thick branch and slit open his belly. After consuming the fat, he threw the rest of the carcass, with the banyan tree still attached, into the ocean.

There had been a small bird feeding in the banyan tree when it was up-rooted. This bird had remained in the branches of the banyan tree, but, as it was being thrown into the ocean, the bird flew out and perched in a bough at the top of the silk cotton tree. The deva immediately began trembling with fear. As the deva trembled, the mighty tree shook to its very roots. The garula noticed this and said, "You steadfastly supported my weight, the weight of the nāga, and the weight of great banyan tree, as well. Why are you now quaking at the sight of that tiny bird which weighs almost nothing?"

The deva replied, "Mighty garula, you eat flesh, but that little bird eats fruit! He will drop seeds of the banyan fruit on my branches and around my trunk. When those seeds sprout, their roots will completely engulf my home. That is why I quake at the sight of that small bird!"

"You have indeed seen the danger that that small bird portends," the garula said in praise of the deva, "and your fear is well-founded. Let me protect you by driving him away."

Having concluded his story, the Buddha declared, "It is right to mistrust where mistrust is warranted. Even a small thing can be a dire threat," and with those words, the five hundred bhikkhus became arahats. Then the Buddha identified the birth: "At that time, Sāriputta was the garula, and I was the tree deva."

158
When the Novelty Wears Off
Dhūmakāri Jātaka

It was while staying at Jetavana that the Buddha told this story about paying undue honor to newcomers.

Once, King Pasenadi welcomed some new officers into his army and showed them such honor that some of his senior generals felt slighted. The next time trouble flared up on the border, the senior generals did not take any initiative, leaving the field open to the young officers who had received so much attention. At the same time, the young officers hesitated, expecting the senior generals to lead the attack, so the battle was lost.

When the king returned to Sāvatthī, he went to Jetavana and asked the Buddha whether he was the only king to have been defeated because of showing favor to newcomers.

The Buddha answered, "Sire, yours is not the only case; former kings were defeated for the same reason." At the king's request, the Buddha told this story of the past.

Long, long ago, when Dhanañjaya was reigning in Indapatta, the Bodhisatta was the king's chief advisor, and he was called Vidhurapan-dita, Sage Vidhura.

King Dhananjaya acted exactly the same as King Pasenadi did, and the same thing happened. The king asked Vidhurapandita the same question that King Pasenadi asked the Buddha.

Vidhurapandita replied, "Your Majesty, consider your present disappointment to be a mere trifle compared to that of the brahmin Dhūmakāri, who was caring for a huge flock of goats. Dhūmakāri took his goats to the forest and made a pen for them there. He milked them every day and lived on the milk, curd, and cheese. He constantly kept a fire smoking to keep off the gnats.

"Soon after he had settled down, a small herd of golden deer came down from the mountains because of the monsoon rains. Dhūmakāri was fascinated by these lovely deer and developed an affection for them. Completely neglecting his own goats, he lavished all his care and attention on the golden deer. When autumn came, the herd of deer returned to the Himavat. By this time, all the goats were dead, and the brahmin was left with nothing. Alone in the forest, he came down with jaundice, and died.

"Because he paid honor to newcomers and neglected his own herd, he lost everything. Because of his sorrow, he became sick and died. He certainly suffered one hundred, or even one thousand times, more than you. One who, disregarding his old friends and loyal servants, excessively admires strangers is like that foolish Dhūmakāri and will shed many bitter tears!"

King Pasenadi was comforted by the story, and, from that time onwards, he was careful never to neglect his faithful ministers and soldiers in favor of newcomers. Then the Buddha identified the birth: "At that time, Ānanda was King Dhananjaya, King Pasenadi was Dhūmakāri, and I was the wise Vidhurapandita."

159
Right Is Dead
Kaccāni Jātaka

It was while staying at Jetavana that the Buddha told this story about supporting one's mother.

In Sāvatthī, there was a young man from a very respectable family who was supporting his mother. Against his wishes, his mother arranged a marriage for him. His wife, trying to turn her husband against his mother so that he would kick the old woman out of the house, surreptitiously mistreated her mother-in law.

When the wife gave her husband an ultimatum, he calmly replied, "Wife, you are still young, and you can make a living wherever you go. My mother is old and weak. I am her only support. You had better go back to your own family."

Such a response completely shocked the young wife, and she was thoroughly frightened. She realized how much her husband loved his mother and that he would never abandon her. She also realized that, if she went back to her old home, her life would be miserable. "I will reconcile myself with my mother-in-law," she decided, "and I will take care of her." From that moment on, she did everything she could to please her mother-in-law and to make her comfortable.

Soon afterward, the young man, who was a devotee of the Buddha, went to Jetavana to hear the teaching. After paying his respects to the Buddha, he stood at one side. When the Buddha asked him if he was dutiful in tending his mother, he replied, "Yes, Lord. Against my wishes, my mother brought me a young woman to marry. After a while, my wife mistreated my mother and blamed her for all sorts of things. She tried to get me to get rid of my mother, but, when I refused, she stopped her mischief and completely changed her ways. Now she is looking after my mother with all respect."

"This time you resisted your wife," the Buddha replied, "but, long ago, you did indeed throw your own mother out of the house. I intervened, however, and you took her back and cared for her properly." At the man's request, the Buddha told this story of the past.

Long, long ago, when Brahmadatta was reigning in Bārānasi, there was a woman named Kaccāni, whose husband had died. She was living with her devoted son, who took very good care of her. One day, Kaccāni said, "My dear son, you should marry a suitable young woman who will look after me. Then you will be free to do your own work."

"But Mother," the young man answered, "it makes me happy to take care of you. Who else would look after you as well as I do?"

"Son, you need to devote yourself to improving the family fortunes."

"To tell you the truth, Mother, I am not really interested in the house-holder's life. I will, of course, take care of you as long as you live, but, when you are gone, I intend to become an ascetic."

Although she repeatedly encouraged him to get married, he never changed his mind. Despite that, however, and without his approval, she arranged a match with a girl from a good family. Unwilling to oppose his mother, he married the young woman.

His young wife noticed the attention her husband lavished on his mother and, following his example, took very good care of her mother-in-law. Pleased with his wife's devotion to his mother, the young man gave his wife small gifts.

After a while, the young woman began to think, "My husband is always giving me presents. He really loves me. He must love me more than he loves his mother. He would love me even more if she weren't around. I'll find a way to get rid of her."

One evening, she said, "Husband, every day, as soon as you leave the house, your mother starts scolding me." He said nothing in reply.

"He didn't object, so I know he's listening to me," the young woman thought. "Now I will irritate the old woman and make her upset him, too." The next day, she served Kaccāni rice gruel which was very hot, and Kaccāni complained. The next day, the daughter-in-law gave her cold rice gruel. When Kaccāni complained again, the daughter-in-law cried, "Before you said it was too hot, and now you say it's too cold! Who can satisfy you?" The same was repeated with salty food and food with no salt.

One day, in the bath, the daughter-in-law threw some very hot water on Kaccāni's back. "Daughter, my back is burning!" she cried. The young woman threw cold water on her back, and Kaccāni cried, "Oh, that's too cold!"

The daughter-in-law shouted so loud that the neighbors could hear, "A few minutes ago, you screamed that the water was too hot, but now you complain that it is too cold. I ask you, who can endure this abuse?"

When Kaccāni complained that her mattress was full of fleas, the daughter-in-law shook her own mattress over it and said, "I've given it a shake." This gave poor Kaccāni twice as many fleas as before, and she lay awake the entire night scratching. The next morning, she complained of being bitten all night, and, in front of her husband, the daughter-in-law retorted, "Your bed was shaken yesterday and the day before. Who can please such a demanding woman?"

For several days, the young woman scattered gray hairs around the house and spat phlegm here and there. When her husband asked why the house was so dirty, she answered, "It is your mother, but, when I ask her not to make such a mess, she gets angry and shouts at me. I can't stay in the same house with such an old witch. You must decide whether she stays or I stay."

"All right," he replied, and he went to see his mother. "Mother," he said firmly, "you are always causing strife in the house. I'm afraid that you are going to have to leave. You'll have to find somewhere else to live. Go wherever you want."

Kaccāni wept, but she obeyed her son. She went to a friend's house and worked for a meager living as a servant. Soon after Kaccāni had left her own house, her daughter-in-law conceived a child. She let everyone know that such a thing could never have happened if "the old witch" had stayed at home. After she delivered a son, she reminded her husband, "While your mother was here, I was never able to have a child, but now we have a wonderful son! You can see what a hag she was."

When Kaccāni heard about this, she thought, "Surely Right must be dead in the world. If it weren't, those two would not have had a son, and they would not be living a comfortable life after mistreating their mother and throwing her out. I will make an offering to the dead Right." She took some ground sesame, some rice, a little pot, and a spoon to the charnel ground and built a cooking fire using three skulls. She put her things down near the fire and went to the river to bathe and to wash her hair. When she returned, she put the rice and sesame in the pot with a little water, placed the pot on the skulls, and began stirring it with her spoon.

At that time, the Bodhisatta had been reborn as Sakka. He wondered why his throne suddenly became hot and realized immediately that Kaccāni was making an offering to Right as if Right were dead. Disguised as a brahmin, Sakka descended from Tāvatimsa, entered the charnel ground, and said to Kaccāni, "Mother, people do not cook food in charnel grounds. What are you going to do with that sesame and rice when it is done?"

"I am not preparing this rice and sesame for food," she answered. "It is an offering to Right, which is dead in this world."

"Madame, who told you such a lie? Right still prevails in the world. It is well and strong. Right can never die!"

"Brahmin, I have proof that Right is dead. Those who follow Wrong flourish, prosper, and thrive. My son's once-barren wife beat me and threw me out of the house. Then she bore a son. Now, with the blessing of my son, she is lady of our house, and I am an outcast. That is my proof that Right is dead."

"Not so, Kaccāni!" declared Sakka, revealing his true identity. "I live, and Right shall prevail. It was for your sake that I came here. Your daughter-in-law mistreated you, but she and her infant son will soon be ashes in my punishing flame!"

"Oh no!" Kaccāni cried. "Do not say such a thing, Your Majesty! Please don't harm my grandson! Sakka, if, indeed, you have come on my behalf, allow my children and their son to live with me in harmony!"

"Noble lady," Sakka addressed her in praise, "you were cruelly treated, but still you rely on Right. You are the proof that Right is alive in the world. By my power, your son and your daughter-in-law will soon come here and beg for your forgiveness. Go home with them, and live together in peace and harmony!" His purpose accomplished, Sakka returned to Tāvatimsa.

At that instant, the son and his wife recollected their mother's goodness and asked the neighbors where she had gone. They bundled up the baby and rushed to the charnel ground, calling her name as they ran. As soon as they saw her, they fell at her feet and apologized profusely for their offences. Kaccāni promptly forgave them and fondled her grandson. They all returned home, and, from that time on, they lived happily together.

Having concluded his story, the Buddha taught the Dhamma, and the young man attained the first path. Then the Buddha identified the birth: "At that time, the young man and his wife were the same, and I was Sakka."

160

The Case of the Eight Sounds
Atthasadda Jātaka

It was while staying at Jetavana that the Buddha told this story about the king of Kosala.[1]

At one time, King Pasenadi became infatuated with a beautiful woman and threatened her husband with death in order to secure her for himself. Shortly after that, in the middle of the night, the king heard four very loud and plaintive cries. They so frightened him that he could sleep no more. When dawn came, he asked his brahmins about the sounds, and they told him that the sounds foretold great danger, from which the only escape was a great sacrifice of living beings. The king immediately told them to prepare the sacrifice. When his queen, Mallikā, heard about this, she suggested that the king seek advice from the Buddha. Thus, the king went to Jetavana and asked the Buddha whether these sounds betokened any danger to him or to his kingdom.

"Sire, do not be afraid!" the Buddha replied. "No danger will befall you or your kingdom because of those sounds. Long ago, similar dreadful sounds were heard by a great king. Then, as now, brahmins prepared the fourfold

---

1 The occasion for this story is told in detail in Tale 119.

257

sacrifice, but after seeking advice from a wise man, that king canceled the sacrifice and set free all the tethered animals." At the king's request, the Buddha told this story of the past.

Long, long ago, when Brahmadatta was reigning in Bārānasi, he was terrified one night by eight different, mysterious, and fearful sounds in rapid succession. Not having slept a wink afterwards, as soon as the sun was up, he consulted his brahmin advisors, who gravely announced that the sounds foretold that at least one of three great dangers—to his kingdom, to his property, or to his life—would befall him unless he agreed to perform the fourfold sacrifice. His chief advisor, one of those brahmins, got busy overseeing the preparation of a sacrificial pit and the collection of a great number of creatures to be slain, which he had tied to stakes nearby.

At that time, there was, in the Himavat, an ascetic, who had developed psychic powers through his long practice of jhānic meditation. From his hermitage, this ascetic surveyed the world with his divine eye and saw what was happening in Bārānasi. Guided by compassion, he resolved to prevent the sacrifice and to save the lives of all those helpless beings. He immediately transported himself to the king's royal park, sat down on the stone seat, and waited.

As the chief advisor was bustling about the palace, arranging everything for the sacrifice, one of his young students approached him and asked, "Master, is it not written in the ancient texts that there is no happiness for those who take the life of another creature?"

"Hold your tongue!" the advisor hissed. "Just bring me the things I need! Soon we'll be eating the finest delicacies and the most delicious meat imaginable. Tomorrow, we will be rich! Just keep your mouth shut, and do what you're told! Now go!"

"I will take no part in this sacrifice!" the student declared to himself. "It is wrong!" He left the palace and went to the royal park, where he saw the ascetic, looking like a golden image. He approached the stone seat, saluted the ascetic in a friendly manner, and took a seat at a respectful distance.

"Young man," the ascetic asked, "does the king rule righteously?"

"Yes, Venerable Sir, he does," answered the student, "but, last night, he heard eight sounds, and the brahmins have convinced him that they must perform the fourfold sacrifice. The king is so upset that he is going ahead with the sacrifice, and a vast number of victims are already tethered near the sacrificial pit. I would hope that a holy man like you might explain the cause of these noises and save those victims from death."

"Young man," the ascetic replied, "the king does not know me, nor do I know the king. I know the origin of these cries, however, and, if the king were to come and ask me, I would gladly resolve his doubts for him."

"Excellent, Venerable Sir. Please wait here, and I will bring the king."

The ascetic silently agreed, and the youth ran to the king's chamber. A few minutes later, he returned to the park with the king. The king respectfully greeted the ascetic, sat on one side, and asked him whether it was true that he knew the origin of these noises.

"Tell me exactly what you heard, Your Majesty," replied the ascetic.

"I heard eight distinctly different sounds," the king replied. "I could not tell where they were coming from, but each seemed to emanate from a different place. I couldn't identify what sort of sounds they were or who or what might have made them. I was mystified. Each sound filled me with more fear."

"Sire, there is no danger whatsoever connected with these sounds. They were made by eight different beings in your palace grounds, each one seeking your assistance.

"So they weren't all caused by the same thing?" asked the king.

"No, Sire. Let me explain them to you one by one so that you can deal with each appropriately.

"The first sound you heard was a crane, crying, 'This pond, where my ancestors resided, was once deep and full of fish. Even though I'm reduced to eating frogs, I will never leave my home!'

"Sire, do you have an old, unused, royal garden?" the ascetic asked.

"Yes, I do," replied the king.

"In that old garden, there is a crane who is half-dead from hunger because the pond where he lives is dried up. That crane cried out in hunger because there is neither water nor fish in the pond."

The king ordered his gardener not only to clean the pond, refill it with water, and restock it with fish, but to return the entire garden to its original beauty.

"The second sound you heard was a crow, crying, 'Help! That wicked one-eyed Bandhura is going to destroy my nest and my little ones!'

"Sire, do you have a mahout named Bandhura?" the ascetic asked.

"Yes, I do," replied the king.

"Does he have only one eye?" the ascetic asked.

"Yes, that's right," replied the king.

"Over the entrance of your elephant stable, Sire, a female crow has repeatedly built her nest and laid her eggs. Each time, as soon as the eggs have hatched out, your chief mahout, Bandhura, who has but one eye, has destroyed the nest with his hook and has killed all the baby crows. That female crow cried out because her babies are in danger."

The king summoned Bandhura, reprimanded him for destroying the crow's nest, and dismissed him. The king was careful to promote a kindlier mahout to manage his elephant stable.

"The third sound you heard was a woodworm, crying, 'I have eaten all the softwood! I cannot eat the hardwood! I'm going to starve to death!' In the pinnacle of the roof of your palace, Sire, there is a woodworm who has eaten all the softwood of a beam, but, not being able to eat the hardwood, is trapped. That woodworm cried out in fear of dying high up in the pinnacle of your palace."

The king ordered his carpenter to tear out the ceiling of the palace, to find the beam in the pinnacle where the woodworm was imprisoned, and to release the insect.

"The fourth sound you heard was a cuckoo, crying, 'Oh, to regain my freedom, to fly in the woods, and to build my nest in a tree!'

"Sire, is there a tame cuckoo in your palace?" the ascetic asked.

"Yes, there is," replied the king.

"That tame cuckoo is yearning for freedom. He cried out when he remembered the joy of flying free in the forest."

The king ordered that the cuckoo be taken to the forest and released in the same place where he had been captured.

"The fifth sound you heard was a deer, crying, 'I was the leader of my herd, but now I am confined to this small pen! Would that I could regain my freedom and drink pure water from the mountain spring!'

"Sire, is there a tame stag in your royal park?" the ascetic asked.

"Yes, there is," replied the king.

"That stag is yearning for freedom and longs to be with his doe. He cried out when he remembered the joys he shared with her when he was the king of the deer."

The king ordered that the deer be taken to the forest and released in the same place where he had been captured.

"The sixth sound you heard was a monkey, crying, 'My beautiful wives were all my joy as I frolicked in the forest before Bharata carried me away!'

"Sire, do you have a hunter named Bharata?" the ascetic asked.

"Yes, I do," replied the king.

"Is there a tame monkey in the palace, and did he bring it?" the ascetic asked.

"Yes, Bharata recently brought a monkey that I have put in a cage," the king replied.

"That monkey had many mistresses when he lived in the forest, and he misses them. He cried out when he remembered how happy he was with them in the forest."

The king summoned Bharata and ordered him to take the monkey back to the forest and to release him in the same place where he had been captured.

"The seventh sound you heard was a kinnara, crying, 'As it was getting dark on the mountaintop, she warned me, "Be careful, dear, not to stumble on this narrow rocky path!"'

"Sire, is there a kinnara in your palace?" the ascetic asked.

"Yes, there is," replied the king.

"That kinnara is longing for his mate. Last night, he remembered how he had once gathered flowers with her to make garlands and how she had carefully led him down from the mountaintop. That kinnara cried with the pang of love for his beautiful kinnarī."

The king ordered that the kinnara be transported back to the Himavat and released in the same place where he had been captured.

"The eighth sound you heard was a Pacceka Buddha, crying, 'Truly, have I seen my last birth. No more shall I enter a womb. My last existence, with all its misery, is finished!' Last night, in the Nandamūla cave, a Pacceka Buddha realized that the conditions for his life were at an end, and, knowing that Your Majesty would honor his bodily remains, he decided to enter Parinibbāna under a sal tree in full bloom in your royal park. That Pacceka Buddha cried out in ecstasy as he threw off the burden of life."

The ascetic showed the king the place in the royal park where the Pacceka Buddha had entered Parinibbāna.

The king immediately canceled the fourfold sacrifice and ordered the release of all the creatures which had been tethered to be killed. He made a great proclamation that there should be no more slaughter of animals anywhere in the kingdom.

He then ordered his servants to prepare an elaborate funeral pyre and proclaimed a seven-day festival to honor the Pacceka Buddha. The entire court offered incense and flowers. To enshrine the relics, the king had a cetiya erected at an auspicious intersection in the city.

The ascetic stayed a few more days in Bārānasi, preaching righteousness and exhorting the king to be diligent. Then he returned to the Himavat and continued meditating on the Four Brahma Vihāras. When he passed away, he was reborn in the Brahma heavens.

Having concluded his story, the Buddha said to King Pasenadi, "Sire, there is no danger at all to you from those sounds. Stop the sacrifice, and spare these creatures' lives!" The king immediately did so. Then the Buddha identified the birth: "At that time, Ānanda was King Brahmadatta, Sāriputta was the student, and I was the ascetic."

161
The Last Embrace
Sulasā Jātaka

It was while staying at Jetavana that the Buddha told this story about Puññalakkhaṇā, a maid of Anāthapindika's wife.

Once Puññalakkhaṇā borrowed a precious necklace from her mistress and wore it to a festival in the public garden. While she was there, she met a young man who seemed very friendly and attentive, staying near her for a long time. After a while, realizing that he was a thief and that he intended to kill her to steal the necklace, Puññalakkhaṇā asked him to draw some water for her from a nearby well. As he was leaning over the edge of the well, she pushed him in and threw a stone down on him.

When Anāthapindika related Puññalakkhaṇā's adventure to the Buddha, the Master replied, "Householder, this is not the first time that that servant girl has used her wits to escape death. Long ago, she did the same." At Anāthapindika's request, the Buddha told this story of the past.

Long, long ago, when Brahmadatta was reigning in Bārāṇasi, a thief named Sattuka[2] had a successful criminal career, breaking into the houses of

---

2 Except for the names of the characters, part of this story is identical to part of Tale 122. The narration has been shortened here. This story is also similar to the events

wealthy merchants and stealing vast sums. He was notorious for his daring and strength, and no one could bring him to justice.

So many influential people had complained that the king ordered the governor to arrest him with no more excuses. The governor offered a sizable reward for his capture and stationed soldiers in likely places. At last, Sattuka made a mistake, fell into a trap, and was caught red-handed. Without hesitation, the king ordered his execution.

To the beat of a drum, the condemned man was marched to the execution ground at the southern gate of the city. At every crossroads, the procession stopped, and he was beaten with whips. All along the way, townsfolk gathered to watch. Everyone was relieved that Sattuka had been captured.

The procession passed the house of Sulasā, the most famous courtesan of Bārānasi, who regularly received one thousand coins a night for her favors. Just as Sattuka passed under her window, Sulasā glanced out, and, seeing him, immediately fell in love with him. "If I can free that sturdy fighting man," she thought, "I will give up this bad life and live respectably with him." Sulasā gave one of her maids one thousand coins. "Go to the governor," she said. "Tell him that the thief who is being executed is Sulasā's dearly beloved brother. Give him the money, and ask him, as a favor to Sulasā, to allow his prisoner to escape."

The maid did as she was told, but the governor replied, "This is a notorious outlaw. I cannot simply let him go free. If I had a substitute, I could send the thief to Sulasā." The servant reported this to her mistress.

Early that evening, a rich young merchant, who was enamored of Sulasā, arrived. Sulasā accepted his fee, but then began to weep.

"My dear Sulasā," the young man asked, "what is the matter?"

"My Lord," she sobbed, "the thief who was just captured is my brother. I appealed to the governor, and he agreed to let my brother go for one thousand coins. Now I have the money, but I can't find anyone to take it to the governor for me."

"Darling, you know how much I care for you! Please let me take the money and hurry right back."

"I would be so happy if you took this money to the governor!"

Delighted with the second bribe, the governor locked the young merchant in a cell and sent the thief to Sulasā. He waited until after dark to carry out the execution, so no one was the wiser.

For several months Sattuka and Sulasā lived happily together. Then Sattuka began thinking, "I have never been able to stay in one place very long.

in the life of Venerable Bhadda-Kundalakesā before she ordained. At that time, Sattuka was also the name of the thief. [See Kundalī in Glossary of Personal Names in Volume III.]

It's time for me to move on, but I don't want to go empty-handed. Why don't I kill Sulasā and take her jewelry, which is worth at least one hundred thousand coins?"

One day, he said to Sulasā, "Dear, as I was being led away to be executed by the king's men, I made a vow to the deva of a tree on the mountaintop that, if I survived, I would make an offering. That deva is now complaining that I have not yet fulfilled my vow. I want to make that offering now."

"Very well, husband, prepare it and send it," she replied.

"Dear, we can't just send it. It must be offered in person. Let's go together, dressed in our best clothes and jewelry, and make the offering."

"Very well, Husband. We'll do just that."

As soon as the offering was ready, Sulasā summoned her servants, climbed into her carriage and sat down next to Sattuka, who was wearing all his weapons. They headed out of the city. At the foot of the mountain, Sattuka said, "Dear, the deva might not appreciate this big crowd of people. Please ask the servants to wait here, while just the two of us go up and make the offering."

Sulasā agreed and took the offering from one of her servants, and the couple began climbing the mountain. When they reached the top, Sattuka took the offering from her and placed it at the foot of a tree which stood at the edge of the precipice. "Dear," he said menacingly, "Please, take off all your jewelry and make a bundle of it in your cloak."

"Why should I take it off?" she asked.

"We have not come here to make an offering," he replied. "I am going to kill you and take your jewelry."

"Husband, why would you kill me?"

"I need your money!"

"Why do you need my money?' she asked in tears. "As long as we are together, all that I have is yours."

"That's just the point," he replied. "It's time for me to leave!"

"Husband!" she cried. "Remember all that I have done for you! When you were being dragged away in chains, I gave up a rich man's son for you! I paid a large ransom to save your life! I could still be getting one thousand coins a day, but I never look at another man now. I have been good to you. I saved your life. Why are you leaving? Please do not kill me! I'll give you whatever you want. I'll be your slave!" With these entreaties she offered him her golden necklace, emeralds, and pearls and asked only to serve him.

"Stop crying!" Sattuka ordered brutally, "just take off your jewels, and put them over there. I'm going to kill you."

"This criminal is really going to try to murder me," Sulasā thought, as she started removing her jewelry and putting it in a pile. "Fortunately, I'm cleverer than he is!"

When she had finished putting all her gems in a pile, she said, "Truly, Husband, I have never loved another man as much as I love you. I have been extremely happy with you. Before you kill me, Dearest, please accept my last salute, my last embrace, for we'll never again meet face to face in this world! Just stand here beside the tree and let me pay my respects to you."

"All right," he replied, stepping near the tree and keeping his eye on the jewels. "I suppose you deserve at least that much."

Sulasā respectfully walked around him three times in salutation. "Now, husband, let me make obeisance to you on all four sides." She knelt in front of him and touched her head to his feet. She bowed again on his right side and again on his left. Then she stepped behind him, and, with strength born of desperation, she grabbed his back and pitched him headfirst to his death over the steep cliff.

The deva of the tree had been watching this drama and observed, "Wisdom is not only for men. Women, too, can show remarkable cleverness! Sulasā quickly saw how to protect herself! One mindless of peril will fall as the thief fell from the precipice. One mindful of peril will be saved as was Sulasā."

When Sulasā returned from the summit alone, her attendants asked where her husband was. "Don't ask!" she said, as she climbed into her carriage to return to the city.

Having concluded his story, the Buddha identified the birth: "At that time, Puññalakkhanā was Sulasā, the thief who tried to steal Puññalakkhanā's necklace was Sattuka, and I was the deva."

162
Until Anger Is Appeased
Sumangala Jātaka

It was while staying at Jetavana that the Buddha told this story about King Pasenadi.

Long, long ago, when Brahmadatta was reigning in Bārānasi, the Bodhisatta was born as the son of his chief queen. When his father died, he became king. He ruled wisely and delighted in giving abundant alms.

One day, a Pacceka Buddha had left the Nandamūla Cave in the Himavat and arrived in Bārānasi, where he spent the night in the royal park. The next morning, as the Pacceka Buddha was walking for alms in the city, the king was so impressed by his demeanor that he invited him into the palace and served him from his own table. After the Pacceka Buddha had finished and given anumodana, the king asked him to stay on in the pleasance. As soon as the king had finished his own breakfast, he went personally to arrange everything. Then he asked his gardener, Sumangala, to be the Pacceka Buddha's attendant.

The Pacceka Buddha stayed comfortably in the royal park and took his meals in the palace. Sumangala looked after him respectfully.

One day, the Pacceka Buddha announced to Sumangala that he was going to visit a village for a few days. Sumangala informed the king so that alms were not prepared during his absence.

A few days later, the Pacceka Buddha returned, but, since it was after sunset, Sumangala had already gone home. The Pacceka Buddha put away his bowl and outer robe and began meditating, first walking, then sitting on a stone slab.

That evening, some guests came to Sumangala's house unexpectedly, and he had no meat for curry. He took his bow to the royal park, intending to kill a deer. In the gathering darkness, he mistook the Pacceka Buddha for a deer and shot him with a hunting arrow. Calmly uncovering his head, the Pacceka Buddha called out, "Sumangala."

"Venerable Sir!" cried Sumangala, utterly shocked and devastated, "I did not know you had come back! I mistook you for a deer. Forgive me!"

"You meant no harm. Come, pull out the arrow," replied the Pacceka Buddha. Sumangala paid obeisance and extracted the arrow as gently as he could. In great physical pain, but with a calm voice, the Pacceka Buddha asked the gardener, "What will you do now? Take care." Then he breathed his last and passed into Parinibbāna.

Sumangala was sure that the king would not forgive him for killing the Pacceka Buddha, even though it had been an accident. With his wife and children, he fled Bārānasi that very night.

The next morning, the king was informed that Sumangala had killed the Pacceka Buddha and had run away. The king ordered his servants to prepare an elaborate funeral pyre and proclaimed a seven-day festival to honor the Pacceka Buddha. The entire court offered incense and flowers. To enshrine the relics, the king had a cetiya erected at an auspicious intersection in the city, where he frequently stopped to pay his respects.

One year later, Sumangala wondered how the king felt about him. He slipped secretly into Bārānasi and asked one of the king's ministers to find out. The next time the minister was with the king, he casually mentioned Sumangala and praised the gardener. The king acted as if he had heard nothing.

The minister told Sumangala that it seemed that the king was not pleased with him.

After another year had passed, Sumangala tried again, but the answer was the same.

The next year, Sumangala returned to Bārānasi with his family and asked the minister to try yet once again. This time, the king indicated that he would like to meet the gardener.

The minister escorted Sumangala to the palace, and the king invited him in. After exchanging friendly greetings, the king asked, "Sumangala, why did you kill the Pacceka Buddha, through whom I was gaining merit?"

"Sire, I did not mean to kill him!" Then he explained how he had accidentally shot the Pacceka Buddha and why he had run away.

The king told him not to worry about the incident and reinstated him as royal gardener.

Puzzled, the minister asked, "Your Majesty, twice before, when you heard me praise Sumangala, you did not say anything, but, the third time, you sent for him and forgave him completely. Why is that?"

"Sir," the king replied, "for two years, I was silent because I was still upset and angry. The third time you mentioned Sumangala, sure that my anger was appeased, I sent for him. It is one of the duties of a king to be aware of his own feelings and never to act hastily in anger. To do so would make him unworthy of his crown! Only when he has become completely calm, can he understand a case, safely make a clear judgment, and fix a proper penalty. If he acts in this way, he will not harm others, nor will he harm himself. Even though a king has great power, he must be led by virtue, not by emotion. A reckless king, who metes out harsh punishments remorselessly, will be notorious and hated and will earn his reward in hell! A king who is virtuous, calm, wise, pure in thought, word, and deed, and filled with kindness, will be renowned and respected and will win his reward in heaven! Since I am king, I must never make a judgment when anger colors my mind. Instead, compassion must prompt the punishments I mete out."

The entire court was delighted to hear the king proclaim his own virtues. "Such excellence in moral practice is worthy of Your Majesty!" exclaimed the minister.

"Sire, your words are true, and your actions are noble!" Sumangala declared. "Your reign is like a welcome cloud bringing gentle rain! Such is your glory and your power! May you never relax them even for a moment! Free from anger and free from fear, may you reign in health, prosperity, and joy for one hundred years! Calm and wise, firm in virtue, but full of compassion, may you rule with righteousness! When, at last, you are freed from this earth, may you be reborn in heaven!"

Having concluded his story admonishing King Pasenadi, the Buddha identified the birth: "At that time, the Pacceka Buddha passed into Parinibbāna, Ānanda was Sumangala, and I was the king."

163

The Half-Penny King
Gangamāla Jātaka

It was while staying at Jetavana that the Buddha told this story about observing Uposatha days.

One day, the Buddha said to some devout laymen who were observing the Uposatha, "Laymen, it's good that you observe Uposatha. You should practice generosity, avoid getting angry, develop loving-kindness, and keep the eight precepts. Long ago, a wise man gained great glory by observing only half of an Uposatha day." At their request, the Buddha told this story of the past.

Long, long ago, when Brahmadatta was reigning in Bārānasi, there was a rich merchant named Suciparivara, who had a fortune of eighty crores and delighted in good deeds, such as giving generously. His entire household, from wife and children to his servants, including even the cowherds, observed the Uposatha days.

At that time, the Bodhisatta had been born into a poor family and lived a hard life as a manual laborer. One day, hoping to get work, he went to Suciparivara's house. He paid his respects to the rich man and explained, "I want to work for you for wages."

"Very well, my good man," answered the merchant, "you can work for me and make arrangements for your wages." When other men had approached the merchant for work, he had said to them on the first day, "In this house everyone keeps the moral precepts. If you can keep them, you may work for me." He forgot, however, to mention anything about it to the new worker.

From that time on, the young man worked for Suciparivara obediently and whole-heartedly, without a thought for his own fatigue. Every day, he began work very early in the morning and returned in the evening.

One day, a festival was announced in the city. The merchant called one of his maidservants and said, "Today is an Uposatha day. Cook rice early for the workers. They will eat before noon and keep the fast."

The young man got up early and went to his work. No one had told him that he should observe the Uposatha that day. Everyone else in the entire household ate in the morning and proceeded to keep the fast. Each person went to his own room, sat down, and reflected on the precepts. The young man alone worked the full day. When he returned at sunset, the cook gave him water to wash his hands and scooped some rice in a bowl for him.

"On other days, it was always very noisy at this time," the young man observed. "Where is everybody today?"

"They are all in their own rooms, keeping the precepts."

Hearing this, he thought, "In the midst of all these people keeping the precepts, I refuse to be the only one not to do so." He went and asked the merchant, "Is it possible for me to observe Uposatha by taking the precepts now?"

"Yes, but, because you did not take the precepts in the morning," the merchant replied, "it will not be a full Uposatha, but it will be half."

"Let it be that much," declared the young man. In the merchant's presence, he took the precepts and began fasting. Then he went to his room and lay down, reflecting on the precepts. Because he had not eaten the whole day, however, at the beginning of the last watch of the night, he felt excruciating pain like a knife in his stomach. Learning that he was ill, the merchant brought him various kinds of medicinal foods and encouraged him to eat them.

The young man answered, "I will not break Uposatha. Even if it costs my life, I will keep the precepts."

The pain increased, and, at dawn, he was losing consciousness. The other servants realized that he was going to die soon and carried him outside the house. Just then the king of Kāsi happened to ride by in his royal chariot surrounded by a grand retinue. Seeing the king, the young man felt a craving for royal grandeur and made a wish to be reborn a king himself. He died and, through the merit of observing half of an Uposatha day, was conceived in the womb of the chief queen, who in due time gave birth to a son. He was named Udāya.

The prince grew up and became proficient in all the arts and sciences. Because he had the special ability to recall his previous births, he remembered the merit he had made in his last existence. He frequently expressed his joy by singing, "Oh, what a great reward for such a small action!" At his father's death he became king. Observing his own majesty, he sang the same song of joy again and again.

One day, a festival was announced. In this city, there was a poor man, a water carrier, who had married a poor woman, another water seller, and moved in with her near the southern gate.

"My dear," the woman said to her husband, "there is a festival in the town. If you have any money, let us enjoy ourselves."

"I have," he answered. "How much?"

"A half-penny."

"Where is it?"

"I hid it near where I used to live. It's concealed between two bricks in the city wall near the northern gate, twelve yojanas from here. What about you? Do you have anything saved up?"

"Yes, I do."

"How much?"

"A half-penny, also. So yours and mine together make a whole penny. With one part of it, we'll buy some flowers. With another part, perfume. With the third, we'll buy some liquor. Go and get your half-penny from its hiding place. We'll have a wonderful time!"

He was exhilarated at his wife's suggestion. "Don't worry, dear, I'll go and get it," he assured her as he set out. By midday, the sand was as hot as burning coals. The man was as strong as an elephant, but he was barefoot and wearing only the poorest dhoti. In his ear, he had stuck a palm-leaf in place of a proper earring. Even though he had already run more than six yojanas in the searing heat, he was so filled with desire that he was singing as he went by the palace court on the way to retrieve his treasure. At that moment, King Udāya opened his lion-carved window and looked out. He saw the man passing and wondered, "How can this man be so indifferent to the terrible heat that he is singing merrily as he goes by? I'll ask him." The king sent a servant to bring the man to him.

"The king is calling you," the servant informed the poor man.

"What's the king to me?" he retorted. "I don't know the king." The servant grabbed him and took him by force before the king.

"The earth is like coals, and the sand is like burning embers," the king said to him. "The sun is beating down, and the thin dhoti you're wearing doesn't protect you at all. Still you sing so cheerfully. Tell me, don't you feel hot?"

"A craving for my treasure and for my wife has set my heart ablaze with a fire much hotter than the sun. I have so many things to do that I can't be bothered by the sun's heat."

"What is it you have to do?" asked the king.

"Sire," the man answered, "I live near the southern gate with a poor woman. This morning, she said to me, 'Let's enjoy the festival!' When she asked whether I had any money, I told her, 'My wealth is stored in a wall near the northern gate,' 'Go and get your treasure from its hiding place,' she said. 'We'll have a wonderful time!' Those words of hers never leave my heart. Whenever I recall them, hot desire inflames me. That's what I have to do."

"But you were singing so lightheartedly," the king persisted. "How can you be so oblivious to the hot wind and the sun?"

"Sire," the man answered. "I sing because I'm thinking how much I'll enjoy myself with her after I get my treasure."

"Then, my good man," the king asked, "is the treasure you have hidden by the northern gate one hundred thousand coins?"

"Oh no, Sire!" cried the man.

The king then asked successively if it were fifty thousand coins, forty thousand, thirty thousand, twenty thousand, ten thousand ... five hundred, four hundred, three hundred, two hundred, one hundred, fifty, forty, thirty, twenty, ten, five, four, three, two, one silver coin, a half coin, a quarter coin, four pennies, three pennies, two pennies, one penny?

"No!" the water carrier answered emphatically each time. At last, the king asked, "Is it is a half-penny?"

"Yes!" cried the man. "My treasure is one half-penny, and I am going to fetch it to enjoy myself with my wife. The thought of the pleasure I'm going to have keeps the wind and sun from bothering me now."

"My good man," the king said, "don't go there in this heat. I will give you a half-penny."

"Sire," answered the man, "I will take you at your word and accept your half penny, but I won't lose the other. I won't give up going to get the other one."

"My good man," urged the king, "stay here! I'll give you a whole penny, two pennies, four pennies!" The king continued doubling his offer up to a ten million coins, one billion coins, and even boundless wealth, if the water carrier would give up going.

Each time, however, the man answered, "Sire, I'll take your money, but I'll retrieve my half-penny, too."

Then the king tempted him by offering him the post of treasurer and even higher positions, including that of crown prince. "All right," the king said at last, "I'll give you half the kingdom if you will give up going."

At this, the man agreed.

The king turned to his ministers and said, "Have my friend's hair and beard trimmed. Have him bathed and dressed in the finest clothes, and bring him back here." The servants did as the king commanded.

Then the king divided his kingdom in two and gave half to the water carrier. It is said that out of love for his half penny, the man took the northern half. He was called King Addhamāsaka (Half-Penny). From then on, the two kings ruled the kingdom together in friendship and harmony.

One day, they went to the royal garden together. When King Udāya felt tired, he lay down with his head on Addhamāsaka's thigh. As soon as he fell asleep, the attendants wandered off to enjoy themselves in the park.

King Addhamāsaka looked down at King Udāya and wondered, "Am I going to be king of only half a country forever? I can kill this man and be the only king," he reasoned. "I'll cut off his head!" He drew his sword to strike the king, but then he considered further, "When I was just a poor man, this king made me his partner and gave me great power. Killing such a great benefactor would be shameful." Returning to his senses, he sheathed the sword. This happened three times. "If this same thought arises again," he realized, "it will provoke me to commit this evil deed!" He immediately threw his sword on the ground, woke the king, and fell at his feet.

"Forgive me, Sire," King Addhamāsaka cried.

"Friend, there is nothing wrong between us, is there?"

"Oh yes, Sire," King Addhamāsaka cried, "there is!" Then he related all that had just happened.

"If this is true," King Udāya reassured him, "I forgive you. Be the sole king if you wish. I will become a prince and serve under you."

"Sire," King Addhamāsaka replied, "I don't want to be a king. In fact, such a desire will cause me to be reborn in one of the four lower realms. Please rule by yourself. I will become an ascetic. I have seen the root of desire. It is nurtured by our thoughts. From this moment, I will have no such thoughts any more."

Then, turning to the crowd of people who had gathered there and who were themselves caught up in the desire he was forsaking, he proclaimed, "Little desire is never enough. Great desire is never satisfied. Foolish men are always saying, 'my' and 'mine.' By striving, desire can be overcome, and wisdom can be won!"

After teaching this truth, King Addhamāsaka returned his half of the realm to King Udāya, took leave of the weeping crowd, went to the Himavat, and became an ascetic. After some time, he attained the four jhānas and acquired supernatural powers.

King Udāya again uttered the verse expressing his own joy, "Oh, what a great reward I received for such for a little action!" but he added another verse extolling the greatness of his friend's renunciation, "Now Udāya has great glory, but greater by far is the glory of the ascetic, who overcame all desire." No one understood the meaning of this verse, but the king would not tell even the queen.

One day, the king remarked to the queen, "My dear, our court barber, Gangamala, is a fool!"

"What do you mean?" she asked.

"When he trims my beard," the king explained, "he always uses the razor first and then plucks the stray hairs with his tweezers. The first operation is very pleasant, but the second is extremely painful. At first, I feel like giving him a reward, but, when he starts plucking, I feel like cutting off his head. He should use the tweezers first and shave with the razor afterwards."

As soon as the queen was alone, she sent for the barber. "My good man," she said, "the next time you are trimming the king's beard, you should use your tweezers first, and then shave him with your razor. If the king offers you a reward, you must say, 'Sire, I don't want anything except to learn the meaning of your verse.' If you do this, I will give you a lot of money." Gangamala readily agreed.

The next day, just as he had been told to do, the barber began by using the tweezers. "Gangamala," the king asked, "is this a new style of yours?"

"Sire," he answered, "we barbers have developed a new routine." He continued to pluck the king's whiskers with the tweezers, and afterwards used the razor. The king was so pleased, he offered Gangamala a reward.

"Sire, I do not want anything. Just tell me the meaning of your verse."

The king felt ashamed to talk about what he had done in those days of poverty in his previous life, so he said, "My good man, what is the use of such a reward to you? Choose something else."

"That is all I want," insisted Gangamala.

Afraid to break his word, the king relented. "All right," he said, "I'll explain, but not to you alone. If I must answer, it will be to everyone." He sent a drum around the whole city to announce that he was going to explain his verse. He summoned the entire court and seated himself on a jeweled throne.

"Gangamala," he began, "in a previous birth in this very city, I performed an act of merit by observing half of an Uposatha day." Then he proceeded to tell that whole story.

"That explains half the stanza, Gangamala" the king continued. "Now, my friend has become an ascetic, but I remain heedless and attached to my throne. That," he concluded, "explains the second half."

When Gangamala heard the king's revelation, he was astonished. "So the king gained his greatness by keeping only half of an Uposatha day," he thought. "Indeed, one must perform meritorious acts. I, too, should become an ascetic and work out my own liberation."

With the king's permission, the barber left his family and his possessions and went to the Himavat to become an ascetic. Through Vipassana meditation, he gained perfect insight into impermanence, suffering, and non-self, thus becoming a Pacceka Buddha with bowl and robes. After spending five or six years on Mount Gandhamadana, he wished to see the king of Kāsi again. He passed through the air to the king's garden and sat on the royal stone seat.

The gardener recognized him as soon as he saw him and went to tell the king. "Sire," he said, "Gangamala has become a Pacceka Buddha and is now sitting in the park."

"I will pay my respects to the Pacceka Buddha," announced the king, and he left the palace immediately, accompanied by his mother. The king entered the park along with his retinue and a crowd of citizens that had gathered, paid homage to the Pacceka Buddha, and sat down in a proper place.

The Pacceka Buddha spoke kindly to the king, "Brahmadatta," he asked, calling him by his family name, "are you diligent? Are you ruling the kingdom righteously? Are you practicing generosity and performing other meritorious actions?"

When the queen mother heard this, she became very angry. "This filthy low-caste son of a barber does not know his place!" she cried. "He dares to call my son, the king, ruler of the country, and one descended from a royal family, by name: 'Brahmadatta'!" She turned to the Pacceka Buddha and retorted, "Through austerities, men may cleanse themselves of their bad deeds and escape their caste of barber, potter, or whatever. But you, Gangamala, are taking advantage of your asceticism. You presume to surpass my son and to call him by his name."

The king tried to restrain his mother by proclaiming the qualities of the Pacceka Buddha. "Mother, please look at what is right before your very eyes. All people, kings like me and ministers, as well, must worship this Pacceka Buddha. Through patience and morality, he attained this fruit."

The people, however, agreed with the king's mother. "Sire," they protested, "it is not decent that such a low-caste person should speak to you by name like that."

The king scolded them and again declared the dignity of the Pacceka Buddha: "Gangamala is now a perfectly restrained sage. Don't say anything more to him. He has crossed the ocean of samsāra and is free from all sorrow."

Then the king bowed down to the Pacceka Buddha and entreated him to forgive his mother and all the people.

"Sire," the Pacceka Buddha replied, "I forgive them all."

The king asked the Pacceka Buddha to promise to stay in the kingdom and to depend upon him for food and robes, but the Pacceka Buddha would not agree to that. While the king and the crowd watched respectfully, he rose into the air, gave advice to the king, and returned to Mount Gandhamadana.

Having concluded his story, the Buddha added, "In this way, laymen, you should observe the Uposatha days." Then he identified the birth: "At that time, the Pacceka Buddha entered Parinibbāna, Ānanda was King Addhamāsaka, Queen Mahā-Māyā was the king's mother, Rāhula's mother was the king's wife, and I was King Udāya."

164
The First Lie
Cetiya Jātaka

It was while staying at Jetavana that the Buddha told this story about Devadatta.

One day, the bhikkhus were talking about how Devadatta, because he had spoken falsely, had been swallowed by the earth and had been reborn in Avīci Hell. When the Buddha heard what they were discussing, he said, "This is not the first time that he has sunk into the earth." Then he told this story of the past.

Long, long ago, in the first eon, a king named Mahā-Sammata reigned in Sotthivati, the capital of Ceti. Mahā-Sammata, who had an immeasurably long life-span, was succeeded by his son Roja, who was succeeded by his son Vararoja. After Vararoja, the succession of kings was Kalyāna, Varakalyāna, Uposatha, Varuposatha, Mandhāta, Varamandhāta, Cara, and Upacara.[1] King Upacara was endowed with four supernatural qualities: he could pass through the air; four devas protected him; his body had the fragrance of sandalwood; and his breath had the fragrance of lotuses.

---

1   Also called Apacara, who is regarded as one of the ancestors of the Sākyans

Upacara had grown up with Korakalambaka, the younger brother of his father's chief advisor, a brahmin named Kapila. Upacara and Korakalambaka had been playmates and had studied together under the same teacher. The prince had promised that, as king, he would appoint Korakalambaka his chief advisor. When he became king, however, he discovered that it was impossible to remove Kapila from his position. Because the advisor was so much older than he was, King Upacara treated him with deference. Kapila noticed this and was not comfortable with such a situation. He felt that the king would be happier with an advisor more his own age.

Actually, Kapila had been thinking about becoming an ascetic. He asked the king's permission to resign and to appoint his son as his successor, and the king assented. Kapila instructed his son in all he needed to know to serve the king faithfully and wisely and had him installed as chief advisor. Confident that he had fulfilled all responsibilities, Kapila donned an ascetic's robe and, wishing to stay near his son, retired to the royal park, where he attained proficiency in meditation. Disappointed at not becoming chief advisor, Korakalambaka developed a strong grudge against his brother.

One day, while the king and Korakalambaka were engaged in friendly conversation, the king asked, "My friend, how is it that you are not my chief advisor?"

"Sire, my brother arranged otherwise."

"Hasn't your brother already become an ascetic?"

"Yes, he has, but the post went to his son."

"Well, why don't you arrange things for yourself?"

"Sire, the post is hereditary, and I am the younger brother."

"In that case, I will make you elder and him the younger."

"How will you do that, Sire?"

"With a lie."

"Sire, that would be extremely dangerous. My brother has great supernatural powers! He will destroy you for sure!

"Don't worry. I'll take care of it!"

"When are you going to do it, Sire?"

"Exactly one week from today."

Since the world was very young at this time, no one knew what a lie was. The news spread quickly around the city: "The king is going to make the senior the junior! The younger will become the elder! The post will go to the younger! He's going to do it with a lie!" As this was repeated from person to person, the question everyone was asking was, "What is a lie?" People wondered, "Is it yellow?" "Is it blue?" "How big is it?" "Will we be able to see it?" "Will it have a smell?"

When the chief advisor heard the news, he went to the royal park and spoke to his father. "Father," he said, "people are saying that the king is going to make you the younger brother and to give my post to my uncle. They say he's going to do this with a lie."

"My son," the ascetic replied, "the king would not be able to do that with a lie! When do they say this will happen?"

"In seven days."

"Remind me when the time comes," the ascetic told his son and returned to his meditation.

On the day which the king had specified, hoping to see a lie and to discover what it was, a huge crowd gathered in the palace courtyard. The king dressed himself in full royal regalia and, using his supernatural powers, stood in the air above the multitude. The chief advisor informed his father that the time had come, and the ascetic, using his own supernatural powers, appeared in front of the king. He spread his antelope-skin rug and seated himself in mid-air.

"Is it true, Your Majesty," the ascetic asked, "that, with a lie, you intend to make me the younger brother and to give Korakalambaka the post of chief advisor?"

"Yes, Master, that is true."

"Your Majesty, a lie is a grievously dangerous thing," the ascetic cautioned. "A lie utterly destroys all virtue and can cause rebirth in the four lower realms. With a lie one destroys Right and will himself be destroyed. With a lie, your supernatural qualities will disappear. Trust me, Sire, if you tell a lie, you will doom yourself!"

These dire pronouncements instilled great fear in the king. He glanced at Korakalambaka for reassurance. "Be strong, Your Majesty!" his friend whispered. "I told you my brother would try to use his magical powers. He just wants to change your mind. Use your own supernatural powers, and defeat him!"

This support from his friend, though mild, gave the king enough encouragement to defy Kapila's warning. "Sir," the king shouted, "I declare that Kapila is the younger and that Korakalambaka is the elder!" At that moment, his four guardian devas declared that they would not protect a liar. They threw down their swords and vanished. The king's breath became fetid, and his body reeked like a sewer. He fell crashing to the ground, and everyone understood that his supernatural powers had, indeed, disappeared just as Kapila had predicted.

"Sire!" the ascetic called out from his seat in the air. "This was a warning, but be not afraid! If you speak the truth now, everything will be restored to you."

"Kapila," the king replied, "you are just trying to trick me, aren't you? I declare that Kapila is the younger and that Korakalambaka is the elder!" As soon as he had repeated this lie, he sank up to the ankles in the earth.

"Your Majesty!" Kapila shouted. "To one who intentionally speaks a falsehood, drought comes in the rainy season, and rain falls when it should be dry! Because of your lie, you have sunk in the earth up to your ankles. I implore you! Speak now the truth, and you will regain your four supernatural qualities! All will be restored! If you maintain your lie, you will sink even deeper into the soil of Ceti."

Defiantly, the king repeated even louder, "Kapila is the younger, and Korakalambaka is the elder!" Instantly, he sank up to his knees.

"Sire!" Kapila called out once more. "If you persist in lying, you will sink deeper into the earth! One word of truth will restore all your gifts! It is not too late, Your Majesty!"

Completely ignoring Kapila's warning, the king stubbornly repeated, "Kapila is the younger, and Korakalambaka is the elder!" Instantly, he sank up to his hips.

"Your Majesty!" Kapila shouted. "One who tells a lie will be abandoned even by his own children! No one will support a liar! You still have time to save yourself! Proclaim the truth, and all your glory will return! Lie, and you will sink deeper! Think carefully, Your Majesty!"

A fifth time, the king declared, "Kapila is the younger, and Korakalambaka is the elder!" Instantly, he sank up to his navel.

"Sire!" Kapila shouted once more. "He who speaks an intentional lie will father no sons! If you maintain your lie, I assure you that you will sink even deeper, but it is still not too late! Declare the truth, and all will be restored!"

The king paid no attention. For the sixth time he shouted, "Kapila is the younger, and Korakalambaka is the elder!" Instantly, he sank up to his chest.

"Your Majesty!" Kapila pleaded. "This is your final warning! Your Majesty, consider your five sons! If you persist in lying, you will lose everything, including your own life! Quickly! Speak the truth, and all will be regained! Save yourself before it is too late! Forego your lie, and speak the truth!"

Maintaining his support for his jealous friend and ignoring the advice of the wise, King Upacara declared a seventh time, "Kapila is the younger, and Korakalambaka is the elder!" Suddenly, a great chasm opened wide, the flames of Avīci leaped up, and the king fell into that dreadful hell.

A cry of fear arose from the multitude: "Avīci! Now we have seen the power of a lie! With his lie, the king maligned a wise man! He has fallen into hell!"

The king's five sons prostrated themselves in front of the ascetic and said, "Sir, we appeal to you for refuge!"

"By persisting in falsehood and forsaking the truth, your father doomed himself to hell," replied the ascetic. "In destroying Right, your father also renounced his great lineage. The line of kingship has been broken, and you must no longer stay here."

To the eldest prince he said, "Dear boy, leave the city by the eastern gate, and continue walking straight in that direction until you find a royal white elephant in the seven-point prostration.[2] That will be your sign, and, on that site, you are to lay out and build the capital of your kingdom. Your city will be called Hatthipura."

To the second prince he said, "Dear boy, leave the city by the southern gate, and continue walking straight in that direction until you find a pure white royal horse. That will be your sign, and, on that site, you are to lay out and build the capital of your kingdom. Your city will be called Assapura."

To the third prince he said, "Dear boy, leave the city by the western gate, and continue walking straight in that direction until you find a maned lion. That will be your sign, and, on that site, you are to lay out and build the capital of your kingdom. Your city will be called Sīhapura."

To the fourth prince he said, "Dear boy, leave the city by the northern gate, and continue walking straight in that direction until you find a wheel-frame made of jewels. That will be your sign, and, on that site, you are to lay out and build the capital of your kingdom. Your city will be called Uttarapañcāla."

To the fifth prince he said, "Dear boy, build a great cetiya in this city, and go away toward the northwest. Continue walking straight in that direction until you find two mountains striking against each other and making the sound, 'Daddara!' That will be your sign, and, on that site, you are to lay out and build the capital of your kingdom. Your city will be called Daddarapura."

The five princes left the city as the ascetic had instructed, discovered their signs, built their capitals, and ruled their respective kingdoms..

Having concluded his story, the Buddha identified the birth: "At that time, Devadatta was King Upacara, and I was the ascetic Kapila."

---

2   With the tusks, trunk, and four legs touching the ground.

165
Impossible Conditions
Atthāna Jātaka

It was while staying at Jetavana that the Buddha told this story about a discontented bhikkhu.

When the Buddha asked the bhikkhu why he was discontented, the bhikkhu replied that he was enamored of a woman. "Bhikkhu," the Buddha said, "women can be ungrateful and treacherous. Long ago, a wise man could not satisfy a woman even after giving her one thousand coins a day." Then the Buddha told this story of the past.

Long, long ago, when Brahmadatta was reigning in Bārānasi, his son, Prince Brahmadatta, had a friend named Mahā-Dhana, who was the son of a rich local merchant. When King Brahmadatta died, the prince became king, and Mahā-Dhana visited the palace three times a day.

For many years, beginning even before he took over his father's business, Mahā-Dhana also visited, every day, the house of the most famous courtesan in Bārānasi, a beautiful woman who charged one thousand coins a night for her favors.

One evening, when Mahā-Dhana left the palace, it was already quite dark. As he was on his way home, he thought, "It is too late for me to go home and to come out again. Better that I go straight to the courtesan's house." He dismissed his attendants and entered her house alone.

As soon as she saw him, she asked for her fee. "My dear," he replied, "today I was very late at the palace. I came straight here without going home, so I don't have any money with me. I've already sent my attendants away, but, tomorrow, I will give you two thousand coins."

"If I allow him to get away with this today," she thought, "he'll start coming empty-handed whenever he wants, and he'll probably stop paying me altogether!"

"Sir, have you no respect for me?" she asked him sharply. "Do you think I give my favors away for nothing? If you want to come in, give me my fee!"

"Please, dear, make an exception just this once," he begged.

"You know the rules!" she retorted.

"I will bring twice the amount tomorrow!" he promised.

"No!" was all she answered.

He continued begging, but she refused to listen. Finally, she shouted to her servants, "Don't allow this man to stand there gaping at me! Throw him out, and shut the door!" The maids rushed at him and pushed him out.

Back in the street, he reflected bitterly, "I have spent more than eighty crores on that woman, but, on the one day I come empty-handed, she has me evicted! Women like her are shameless, ungrateful, and treacherous wretches!" As he stood there, pondering the treatment he had just received, his discontent grew into a complete disgust for the life of a layman. "Why should I continue to lead such an existence?" he cried. "What is the point? I will become an ascetic!"

Without going home and without informing the king, Mahā-Dhana went straight to the forest, where he made a rude hut on the bank of the Gangā. Wearing only rough ascetic's garments, he contented himself with roots, berries, and fruit, and spent his time in meditation.

The king soon missed his friend and asked about him. "Sire, haven't you heard?" his attendants responded. "The entire city is saying that Mahā-Dhana was so shamed by a courtesan that he became an ascetic and is now living in the forest."

The king summoned the courtesan and asked her whether what he had heard was true. She admitted that she had thrown Mahā-Dhana out of her house and that she had not seen him since.

"Foolish woman!" the king shouted angrily. "Go and bring him back! If you don't bring him back immediately, I'll have you executed!"

Terrified by the king's threat, the courtesan rode as fast as she could with a large retinue to search for Mahā-Dhana. Stopping often to ask the way, she finally reached his humble hermitage and paid her respects to him. "Venerable Sir," she cried, falling at his feet, "please forgive my foolishness! I was wrong to mistrust you! Now I can see that what I did in my ignorance was, indeed, evil! I swear I will never do such a thing again."

"Very well, madam," Mahā-Dhana replied calmly. "I have already forgiven you. I have no anger whatsoever toward you."

"Thank you, Venerable Sir!" she cried with joy. "You are very noble! Now, please come back to Bārānasi with me! I will give you all the money I have!"

"Madam, I cannot go with you right away, but, if certain conditions are met, I may be able to go."

"Please tell me what those conditions are," she replied hopefully.

"If you can make the Gangā as still as a lotus pond, if you can make cuckoos as white as pearls, and if you can make dates grow on apple trees, I may go with you!"

"Sir, you are joking with me!" she replied with an uncertain laugh. "Please come with me to Bārānasi. I really must be going back."

"I may go," Mahā-Dhana calmly told her.

"When?" she asked.

"When you can make warm winter clothes from tortoise hair, when you can build a sturdy tower from mosquito's teeth, when, from the horns of hares, you can make a ladder to reach the heavens and let mice climb this ladder to eat the moon and to return with mighty Rāhu, and when I see swarms of flies freely drinking liquor from pitchers and building their houses amid burning coals, I may go with you.

"When asses sing and dance with beautiful faces and bright red lips, when crows and owls talk and flirt with each other, when leaf umbrellas protect from heavy monsoon rain, when sparrows pick up the great Himavat in their tiny beaks, and when a little boy can carry a fully rigged sailing ship, I may go to Bārānasi with you.

"I have forgiven you. Please inform the king that I cannot return to Bārānasi unless those conditions are fulfilled."

The courtesan returned to Bārānasi and told the king exactly what Mahā-Dhana had said. She begged the king to spare her life, and the king granted her request.

Having concluded his story, the Buddha taught the Dhamma, and the discontented bhikkhu attained the first path. Then the Buddha identified the birth: "At that time, Ānanda was the young King Brahmadatta, and I was Mahā-Dhana."

166
Intoxication of Youth
Gijjha Jātaka

It was while staying at Jetavana that the Buddha told this story about a disobedient bhikkhu.

In Sāvatthī, there was a bhikkhu who continually resisted discipline by his teachers and fellow bhikkhus. Whenever they told him how to walk, how to wear his robe, or how to hold his bowl, he invariably felt that he was being criticized. "I don't find fault with you!" he would shout. "Why do you treat me like this? I know what is good for me and what is not!" They tried to teach him how to behave toward other bhikkhus, how to guard his senses, how to show moderation, and how to exercise mindfulness. They explained the fourteen sets of rules for daily life, the eighty rules for a bhikkhu under probation, and the thirteen dhutanga practices. They taught him all of this for his own benefit, but he refused to listen.

Several bhikkhus told the Buddha about this disobedient bhikkhu, and the Buddha summoned him. The Buddha asked him whether it was true that he disobeyed his teachers, and the bhikkhu admitted that it was. "Bhikkhu," the Buddha admonished him, "having ordained in this liberating order, why don't you listen to the voice of your seniors who have your best interests at heart? Long ago, too, you disobeyed the wise." Then he told this story of the past.

Long, long ago, the Bodhisatta was born as a vulture on Mount Gijjhakūta, and he had a son named Supatta, who was the leader of many thousands of vultures. When his parents became old, Supatta took responsibility for feeding them. Because Supatta was strong, he was able to fly great distances and to soar at great heights. Supatta's father was concerned about this and warned his son. "My dear boy," he said, "there is a particular point beyond which you must not fly. When you can see the plains, mountains, and forests, surrounded by the great oceans, you will know that you have reached that point. When you can see, with your keen and piercing eyesight, from far above, the sphere of the earth, you will know that it is dangerous. You must not go any higher. That is the limit. As soon as you can see that, dear son, turn back! I implore you!"

Supatta politely listened to his father and replied, "Yes, Father! I understand!" but he did not take the lesson to heart. One day, when it was raining, Supatta flew out with the other vultures. After a while, he left them and started circling higher and higher. Soon, he could see the mountains all around the plains and the forests below. Then he saw the oceans in the distance in every direction. He kept flying higher until the earth appeared a sphere, suspended in space. Ignoring his father's earnest warning of dire peril, he continued circling higher. Soon he felt the force of the deadly Veramba wind. This mighty wind swept him away. Unable to escape from the terrific blast, he was blown apart into one billion pieces.

"Supatta's disobedience was fatal," the Buddha told his listeners. "He perished because he was too proud to heed the warnings of his elders. Intoxicated by his youth, he did not recognize the limits set by the wise. Bhikkhu, do not be like this vulture!" After being thus admonished by the Buddha, the young bhikkhu became obedient and respectful.

Having concluded his story, the Buddha identified the birth: "At that time, this disobedient bhikkhu was Supatta, and I was his father."

167
The Withered Fig Tree
Mahāsuka Jātaka

It was while staying at Jetavana that the Buddha told this story about a young bhikkhu who was discontented with his situation.

After receiving meditation instruction from the Buddha, this young bhikkhu had gone to stay in a border village in Kosala. The villagers provided him with a comfortable dwelling place near the main road, and they were very generous in offering alms.

Unfortunately, less than a month after the rains retreat had begun, the entire village was destroyed by fire. The villagers lost everything, including their stock of seed. Of course, they were not able to provide the bhikkhu with the same savory food they had given before. He was so distressed for alms that he did not make any progress.

At the end of the rains retreat, he went to visit the Buddha. After polite and kindly greetings, the Buddha asked about his residence and his alms. The bhikkhu told the Buddha about the fire. He explained that his residence had indeed been very comfortable but that the alms had not been plentiful.

"Bhikkhu," the Buddha replied, "with such comfortable quarters, you should have been contented with whatever food you were offered. Long ago, out of gratitude, a wise one survived on just the powdered dust of the decayed tree that was his home. Why have you abandoned a pleasant residence, just because the food was scanty and coarse?" At that bhikkhu's request, the Buddha told this story of the past.

Long, long ago, a great flock of parrots lived in a grove of fig trees in the Himavat on the banks of the Gangā. When the fruit was gone, the other parrots flew away to find fruit, but the parrot king, grateful that the tree had provided him with such a comfortable dwelling place, stayed on. He ate whatever was available—shoots, leaves, and even bark. With the mighty Gangā nearby, he had plenty of water, and he was contented to remain there.

Because of the parrot king's profound contentment, Sakka's throne grew hot. When he discovered the cause, the king of the devas decided to test the parrot's virtue. Using his supernatural power, he withered the fig tree to a barren stump. When the hot wind blew, dust blew out of its many holes. The parrot king was reduced to eating that dust and drinking water from the river, but he was still contented. Paying no attention to the sun and wind, he perched on what was left of the dead tree and went nowhere else.

Sakka was impressed with the parrot's contentment and his faithfulness to the tree which had sheltered and fed him. Resolving to have the parrot declare his own virtue, Sakka assumed the form of a royal goose, and, accompanied by his wife Sujā, he descended from Tāvatimsa. He landed on another tree in the grove and struck up a conversation with the parrot. "Friend," he said, "wherever there are trees laden with fruit, one would expect to find a flock of hungry birds, but, when the fruit is gone and the trees wither, the birds move on. Why, if I may ask, are you staying here? Are you daydreaming? This dead stump has nothing to offer you! Why cling to it?"

"Friend goose," the parrot replied, "this tree has always been my home. I can remember its branches and leaves sheltering me when I was newly-hatched. I feel great gratitude to this tree. How could I turn my back on the one who has been my friend for so long? The claims of friendship cannot be overlooked! That's why I don't forsake it, even though it is now dead. I would enjoy a feast of fruit, but I do not have the heart to leave this tree."

"Your friendship and your gratitude are virtues which the wise acclaim!" Sakka declared. "Let me offer you a boon! Wise Parrot King, choose whatever you desire! Tell me what would make you the happiest, and it shall be yours!"

"That which would give me the greatest joy," the parrot king replied confidently, "is for this tree that I love to be restored to its old vigor. My heart would sing to see it strong and bearing delicious fruit once more!"

Sakka and Sujā suddenly abandoned their disguises and appeared in their normal form, standing in all their glory in mid-air above the grove. Sakka dipped a handful of water from the Gangā and threw it over the stump of the fig-tree. Instantly, the stump became a sturdy trunk. Branches, stems, and leaves sprouted in an abundant array. Every branch was laden with honey-sweet fruit. "My friend, here is your tree, once again noble, fruitful, and suitable to be your dwelling place!" Sakka declared.

The parrot king was overjoyed. "May Sakka and all those loved by Sakka be blessed," he cried, "just as I am blessed to see this miraculous sight!"

Having attested to the virtue of the parrot king, Sakka returned with Sujā to Tāvatimsa.

Having concluded his story, the Buddha declared, "You, too, Bhikkhu, should be free from craving for elaborate and succulent dishes. Return to that village, and stay there!" The bhikkhu did so and, in no long time, became an arahat. Then the Buddha identified the birth: "At that time, Anuruddha was Sakka, and I was the parrot king."

168
Footprints in the Air
Padakusalamānava Jātaka

It was while staying at Jetavana that the Buddha told this story about a young boy with a rare talent.

One day, in Sāvatthī, a man left his house without telling anyone where he was going and went to a friend's house. A short time later, his seven-year-old son, who had been at home when he left, joined his father. "How did you know I was here?" his father asked.

"I followed your footprints," the boy replied.

"But, son," the father questioned, "there are many footprints in the street. How did you know which ones were mine?"

"I can't explain it, Father," the boy replied, "but I am clever at this."

The man wanted to test his son's remarkable ability, so, the next morning, immediately after breakfast, he went to his next door neighbor's house. Then he walked to a house on the next street. From there, he went in a different direction to a third house and returned home. Then, leaving the city by the western gate, he walked to Jetavana, where he paid his respects to the Buddha and sat down to listen to the teaching.

When the boy finished his breakfast, he asked where his father had gone, but no one knew, so he traced his father's path. Starting from the next-door neighbor's house, he followed the same zigzag route his father had taken to Jetavana. He too paid his respects to the Buddha and sat down beside his father.

Surprised to see his son so soon, the man asked, "How did you find me?"

"I followed your footprints to all the houses you visited, followed you back home, and followed your footprints here," the boy replied matter-of-factly.

"Layman, what are you talking about?" the Buddha asked.

"Venerable Sir, this son of mine is skillful at recognizing footprints. This morning, I came to Jetavana by a circuitous route. My son followed my footprints to all the places I went and has arrived here by the same route."

"Your son may be skillful at following footprints on the ground, but that is not a great marvel. In the past, a wise young man could recognize and follow footprints even in the air." At the request of the man and his son, the Buddha told this story of the past.

Long, long ago, when Brahmadatta was reigning in Bārāṇasi, his queen committed adultery. When the king discovered it and confronted her with it, she swore she was innocent. "If I have sinned against you, Sire," she cried, taking an oath, "let me become a yakkhinī with the face of a horse!"

Soon after that, the queen died and was, indeed, reborn as a horse-faced yakkhinī in a rock-cave in a huge forest at the foot of a mountain. After serving Vessavana for three years, she was given the right to eat anyone she found in the vicinity of her cave, within an area thirty yojanas long and five yojanas wide. Running through this domain was the road from Bārāṇasi to the western border of Kāsi, and the yakkhinī caught and devoured many travelers on this route.

One day, the yakkhinī noticed a handsome and wealthy brahmin with a large retinue traveling on that road. Thinking how good he would taste, she gave a loud laugh like a horse's whinny and rushed at him. All his attendants panicked and fled in terror. As quick as the wind, she grabbed the man, threw him over her shoulder, and carried him back to her cave. On the way to the cave, perhaps just from carrying him, she developed an affection for him. Instead of devouring him, she made him her husband and kept him in the cave. Whenever she went out, she sealed the mouth of the cave with a huge stone to prevent him from escaping. The yakkhinī also changed the way she worked. Previously, she had been interested only in procuring human victims. In order to provide for her husband, she began collecting their clothing and their supplies of rice, oil, lentils, and other foodstuffs, as well.

In this way, the yakkhinī and her husband lived together fairly amicably. At this time, the Bodhisatta passed away from his former existence and was conceived in the yakkhinī's womb. After ten lunar months, he was born a normal human child. The yakkhinī loved her son very much and cared for him devotedly. Nevertheless, whenever she went out to look for food, she kept both the child and her husband sealed in the cave.

As the boy grew up, he became as handsome as his father and as strong as his mother. One day, after his mother had left, he pushed the stone away from the mouth of the cave. When the yakkhinī returned and asked who opened the cave, he replied, "I did, Mother. We can't sit here in darkness!" Because she adored her son, she didn't say anything more.

Not long after that, the boy asked his father why their mouths were different from his mother's.

"My son," the man answered, "your mother is a yakkhinī. She lives on human flesh, but you and I are humans."

"If we are humans, Father, why do we live here?" the boy asked. "Let's go away and live with other humans!"

"Dear boy, if we try to escape, your mother will kill us both."

"Don't be afraid, Father." he said reassuringly. "I'll take care of you, and I will get you back to the realm of men!"

The next day, after his mother had gone out, the boy took his father by the hand, and they started walking away from the cave.

When the yakkhinī returned, she rushed out to find them. She caught up with them and asked, "Husband, why are you leaving? Is there anything that you want that I haven't given you?"

"My dear," the man replied, "don't be angry with me. Your son asked me to come away with him."

Because she loved her son so much, she did not say anything. She took them back and tried to make them even more comfortable than before.

The boy thought, "My mother is powerful, and she controls this area, but there must be a limit. I need to find out how far her authority extends. If we can get past the boundary of her territory, we will be free."

One day, he sat respectfully near his mother and said, "Mother dear, whatever belongs to a mother belongs to her son. Please tell me how far our authority extends."

Pleased that her son was interested in the domain he would inherit, the yakkhinī described the landmarks—each mountain, river, and rock formation—that marked her territory.

To allay his mother's suspicions, the boy let several days lapse after this conversation. Then, one morning, as soon as his mother had gone into the forest, he picked up his father, placed him on his shoulder, and left the cave. This time, he ran faster than before, hoping to get away before she could catch them. Following the directions his mother had given him, he headed for the river she had said was the boundary of her area.

When the yakkhinī returned, she again rushed out in pursuit. By the time she reached the bank of the river, the boy was in midstream with his father still on his shoulder. Realizing that they were beyond her authority, she stood on the bank and shouted, "My dear son, please come back with your father! What have I done wrong? Aren't you satisfied? Come back home with me!" The boy continued a little further, put his father down in the shallow water, and urged him to climb up on the far side of the river. Then he turned back to talk with his mother.

"My dear son," she cried, "I love you dearly! You may have anything you want. One day, my entire domain will be yours. Please come back."

"Mother," the lad replied gently, "we are humans. You are a yakkhinī. We cannot live with you forever. It is time for us to find the realm of men."

"My son, are you really determined not to return?"

"Mother," he declared. "I will not return."

"In that case, my son," she replied, "I must warn you that it is difficult to live in the realm of men. It will be impossible for you to survive without a craft, and you have had no training. I know a secret charm by which one can trace footprints after a lapse of up to twelve years. You will be able to make a good living by using this charm. Let your mother give you this invaluable charm as her legacy. It is the only thing I have to give you!"

Standing in the middle of the river, he folded his hands and memorized the charm as his mother intoned it. Then he saluted her and called out, "Good-bye, Mother!"

"My son!" the yakkhinī cried wildly, "Without you, I have no will to live!" Overwhelmed by sorrow, she struck her breast with a blow that broke her heart, and she fell lifeless.

Seeing that his mother was dead, the boy summoned his father, and together they built a funeral pyre and cremated her body. After extinguishing the flames, he wept for her and offered wild flowers. Then he and his father started for Bārāṇasi.

The boy went straight to the palace and asked to see the king. An attendant announced to the king, "Sire, there is a youth here who claims that he is skilled in tracking thieves."

The king allowed him to enter and asked, "Friend, what is your skill and your craft?"

"Your Majesty, I am able to follow the footprints of any person. I can even track a thief twelve years after he has stolen something!"

"All right, you are welcome to enter my service," said the king.

"Thank you, Sire! I will serve you for one thousand coins a day."

"Very well, Friend. If that is your fee, I will pay it."

The young man immediately began receiving the salary he had been promised, and he settled down to a comfortable life in the king's service in the capital.

One day, a royal advisor said to the king, "Sire, this youth is receiving an enormous salary, but, so far, he has done nothing to earn it. We have no idea whether or not he can do what he says. We should test him!"

The king readily agreed, and the two of them secretly went to the treasure house. They hid several of the most precious royal jewels in their robes and descended the stairs from the terrace. After zigzagging around the palace, they placed a ladder against the wall and climbed out. They walked to the Hall of Justice and sat for a few minutes. Then they used the ladder again to climb the outer wall of the city. They proceeded to the tank and, without anyone seeing them, they dropped the jewels in the water. Then they returned to the palace.

The next day, the keepers of the treasure house sent up a great cry: "Royal jewels have been stolen!" The king feigned ignorance and summoned the young man. "Friend, several extremely valuable jewels have been stolen from the treasure house. You must find them, restore them to me, and determine who took them."

"My Lord, for one who can follow the footprints of robbers and recover treasure stolen twelve years ago, there is absolutely no difficulty in solving a robbery after a single day and night. Have no fear! I will find your jewels, and I will solve the mystery."

"Proceed, Friend," ordered the king.

"Very well, Sire." Saluting his mother's memory, the young man softly repeated the spell she had given him. "My Lord, the prints of two thieves are to be seen," he said as soon as he had reached the treasure house. From the terrace, he descended the stairs and followed the footprints around the palace in exactly the same course as the king and his advisor had taken. Walking straight to the wall, he said, "My Lord, I see footprints here in the air, but in order to follow them, I need a ladder." As soon as a ladder had been brought, he climbed over the wall and walked to the Hall of Justice. From there, he walked to the outer wall, and, at exactly the same spot where the king and the advisor had climbed the outer wall, he asked for the ladder again. He followed the footprints to the tank and said, "Your Majesty, the two thieves went down into this tank." Reaching into the water, he pulled out the jewels as confidently as if he had placed them there himself. As he handed the jewels to the king, he said, "Sire, these two thieves are men of distinction. They returned to the palace by this route." He led the king and his courtiers back to the throne room. The entire court had been following him during the whole investigation, and the courtiers and ministers snapped their fingers and waved scarves in delight and appreciation.

The king was impressed, but he thought, "This young man was certainly able to follow the footprints and to recover the treasure, but I'm sure he can't figure out who the thieves are." Aloud, he said, "Friend, you have returned the stolen jewels, and we are grateful, but, now, can you catch the thieves and bring them to justice?"

"Sire," the young man replied, "the thieves are here. They are not far off."

"Who are they?" the king challenged him.

"Sire, you have recovered your treasure," he replied softly. "Why should you care about the thieves? Please do not ask me about that."

"Young man, I pay you one thousand coins a day. Find the thieves!" the king commanded.

"Sire, when the property is restored, what is the point of pursuing the thieves?" the young man repeated, trying to placate the king.

"On the contrary," shouted the king, "catching the thieves is more important than recovering the treasure!"

"Your Majesty," the young man replied calmly, "I will not name the thieves, but let me tell you about something that happened long ago. If you are wise, you will understand what it means.

"Long, long ago, not far from Bārānasi, in a village on the bank of the Ganga, there lived an entertainer named Pātala. One day, he went into the city with his wife. After earning some money with his singing and dancing, he got some rice and liquor. On the way home, he sat down on the riverbank to watch the water flow and began drinking heavily. After several large draughts, blithely unaware of his inebriation, he tied his lute around his neck and said to his wife, 'My dear, come with me into the water.' Taking his wife by the hand, he began walking toward the middle of the river. The water poured into the instrument and made it very heavy. Under the weight of his lute around his neck, he sank into the water. Feeling herself being pulled in as well, his wife let go of his hand and retreated to the riverbank.

"Pātala bobbed to the surface, gulping mouthfuls of water and gasping. 'Oh, dear!' his wife thought. 'My husband is going to drown, and he has never taught me any of his songs!'

"'Husband!' she cried. 'Before you sink for the last time, teach me one of your songs! Just one is enough! I'll need it to earn a living after you're gone! Just sing one of your most famous songs now, and I'll memorize it. Quick! Before you are swept away by the Ganga!'

"'My dear,' Pātala gasped, 'how can I sing right now? I'm drowning! This water offers sustenance and life to many people, but, to me, it offers only death!'

"Sire, just as water is the refuge of the people," the young man explained, "so, too, is the king. Who can avert a danger which arises from the king? Sire, my story, with its secret message, should be intelligible to the wise. Please consider its meaning."

"Friend, no one can understand an obscure tale like that!" the king complained "Just name the thieves!"

"Here is another story, Sire." the young man replied. "Please try to grasp the meaning."

"Long ago, in a village near Bārānasi, there lived a potter who fetched clay every day from the same spot in a mountain cave. Eventually, his digging created a deep pit at that spot. One day, while he was shoveling clay from the bottom of the pit, there was a sudden and unseasonable downpour which flooded the cave. The sides of the pit collapsed and buried the potter up to his neck. In desperation, he cried out, 'My sole means of livelihood has buried me alive! My refuge has proved to be my bane!'

"Just as the great earth, Sire, is the refuge of the people," the young man explained, "so, too, is the king. Like the great earth which buried the potter, when the king becomes threatening, who can avert the danger? Sire, do you detect the thief in my story?" he asked.

"Friend, we do not want a hidden meaning. Point out the thief, and hand him over to me!"

"Sire," the young man replied, still trying to avoid openly identifying the king as the thief, "here is another story which points to the thief.

"Once, right here in Bārānasi, a house caught on fire. The owner of that house ordered another man to go into the blazing structure and to bring out his treasure. The man went into the house, but, as soon as he stepped inside, the door slammed shut. As the man was being consumed by the flames, he cried out, 'That which combats the winter cold and cooks our food is now burning me alive! My refuge has proved to be my bane!'

"Sire," the young man tried to explain, "someone who, like the fire, is a refuge stole the jewels. Do not ask the identity of the thief!"

"Listen, Friend!" the king insisted. "Stop telling cryptic stories, and produce the criminal!"

"Sire, here is a simple tale," replied the young man.

"Once, right here in Bārānasi, a man ate too much, and developed indigestion. In severe pain, he cried, 'Food, upon which our very life depends, is now killing me! My refuge has proved to be my bane!'

301

"Sire," the young man again tried to explain, "as food is a refuge for man, someone who is a refuge stole the jewels. Since they have been recovered, why ask about the guilty one?"

"Friend, please stop your nattering, and, if, indeed, you can, just name the thief!"

"Sire," the young man persisted, "perhaps you will understand this story.

"Once, here in Bārānasi, a sudden wind knocked a man down, and, in his fall, he broke his legs. In his pain, he cried out, 'Wind, which, in the hot season, I would have blessed, has broken my legs! My refuge has proved to be my bane!'

"Sire," the young man once more tried to explain, "danger is arising from my own refuge. Understand my meaning!"

"Friend, just give me the thief!" the king demanded.

"Sire, perhaps, you will see the thief in this story," the young man replied.

"Once upon a time, in the Himavat, there was a tree which was home to countless birds. Two large branches of this tree forked from the trunk and grew close together. When the wind blew, these two branches rubbed against each other and produced enough friction to create a spark. That spark fell on some dead leaves which had collected in the fork and grew into a fire. When the leader of the flock saw the fire, he cried, 'Our tree is burning! Flee, my friends! Our home has become our affliction. Our refuge has proved to be our bane!'

"Sire," the young man explained, "As the tree protected the birds, the king protects the people. When the king endangers his people, disaster looms! Take note of this, Sire!"

"Just bring me the thief!" shouted the king, apparently exasperated.

"Sire, please try to understand this story," the young man said.

"In a village near Bārānasi, beside a river full of savage crocodiles, there lived a family with only one son. When the father died, the son looked after his mother, who, against his will, brought a young woman for her son to marry. At first, the wife showed affection for her mother-in-law, but, later, after she had many children of her own, she brought her own mother to live with her and wanted to get rid of her mother-in-law. She began complaining to her husband about her mother-in-law, trying to prejudice him against her. One day, she declared, 'Your mother is impossible. I cannot take care of her any longer. We must do away with her.'

"'It's not easy to murder someone,' her husband responded. 'How shall we kill her?'

"'Tonight, after she falls asleep,' the wife replied, 'we can take her, bed and all, and throw her into the river. The crocodiles will finish her off.'

"'What about your mother?' he asked. 'She sleeps in the same room.'

"'She's a sound sleeper,' the wife assured him. 'She won't notice a thing.'

"'All right,' her husband replied, 'but it is dark in that room. Fasten a rope to my mother's bed so we'll know which one it is.'

"The wife marked the bed and told her husband that everything was ready.

"'Let's wait a little to make sure the two women are both sleeping soundly,' he suggested. They, too, went to bed, and he pretended to doze off. As soon as his wife had fallen asleep, he slipped into the room the old women shared and switched the rope from one bed to the other. Then he woke his wife. Without lighting a lamp, they went quietly into the women's bedroom, lifted the bed with the rope, carried it outside and threw it into the river. The crocodiles quickly ate the woman, and the bed floated away.

"The next day, the wife said, 'Husband, last night, we killed my mother by mistake. Tonight we must kill yours.'

"'All right,' he replied. 'I'll build a funeral pyre in the charnel ground, and, tonight, we can throw her into the fire and kill her that way.'

"That night, after his mother fell asleep, the couple carried her bed to the charnel ground and set it down. 'Give me the fire,' the man said to his wife.

"'I don't have it,' she replied. 'Didn't you bring it?'

"'I thought you had it,' he said. 'Go back and get it!'

"'Husband,' she replied, 'I don't dare go back alone, but I'm afraid to stay here alone, too. Let's go back together and get it.'

"After they both left, the old woman was awakened by the cold wind. Realizing that she was in the charnel ground and seeing the funeral pyre, she reasoned, 'They intend to kill me. They've gone back to fetch the fire. Fools! They do not know how strong I am.'

"She picked up a corpse, laid it on her bed, and covered it over with the blanket. Then she ran away and hid in a nearby cave.

"The couple came back with fire. Assuming that the corpse was indeed his mother, they burned it and returned home.

"A little while later, a thief went to the cave to retrieve the loot, tied in a bundle, that he had left in the cave. When he saw the old woman, he cried, 'Oh, no! There's a yakkhinī in the cave! I'll have to hire a sorcerer to help me get my treasure back.' He ran to fetch a magician he knew and brought him back to the cave.

"The sorcerer entered the cave, chanting his spells, and the old woman said to him, 'Sir, I'm not a yakkhinī. Why don't you run away with me? We can enjoy this treasure together.'

"'How can I believe you?' he asked.

"'Kiss me, and you'll see how passionate I am,' she told him. "The sorcerer kissed her with his mouth open, but the crafty old lady bit off a piece of his tongue and spat it out on the ground. 'Help!' the sorcerer screamed. 'I've been bitten by a yakkhinī!' With blood dripping from his mutilated tongue, he ran away, screaming.

"The next morning, the old woman tidied herself up, picked up the bundle of gold and jewels, and went home. Her daughter-in-law was shocked to see her, but asked only, 'Mother, where did you get that treasure?'

"'My dear,' the old woman replied calmly, 'everyone who is cremated on a pyre in that cemetery gets a package like this.'

"'Really, Mother?' the wife asked. 'Could I get the same treasure?'

"'If you become like me, you certainly will,' the woman replied.

"Without a word to her husband, the greedy wife hurried to the charnel ground, built a great fire, and threw herself into it.

"When her husband came home, he asked, 'Dear mother, isn't your daughter-in-law usually here at this time of the day?'

"'Shame on you, wicked man!' his mother cried. 'Do you think the dead come back to life? I brought a lovely maiden here to be your wife and to reign in my home. I expected her to take care of me, but, instead, she drove me out and tried to kill me. My refuge proved to be my bane!'

"Sire," the young man again explained, "just as a daughter-in-law is a refuge to a woman, a king is a refuge to his people. If danger arises from there, what can be done? Take note of this, Sire."

"Friend, I do not understand any of your chatter. Just bring me the thief," demanded the king.

Still trying to protect the king, he related yet another story. "Long ago, in this very city, a man prayed repeatedly for a son, and, at last, his wife gave him an heir. The man was overjoyed and cherished the boy. When the lad grew up, the man arranged for his marriage. As the years passed, the man grew old and could no longer work. One day, his son said, 'Father, since you cannot work anymore, you must go away.' He immediately drove his father out of the house. The old man had great difficulty living on the street and surviving on the alms he received from begging. Lamenting, he said, 'He, for whom I had prayed for so long, has driven me from my own home. My refuge has proved to be my bane!'

"Sire," the young man tried again to explain, "just as an elderly man looks to his son for support, the people look to the king for support. Now, Sire, from the king, the guardian of all men, grave danger has arisen. Sire, please recognize the thief, and identify him yourself!"

"Young man!" the king cried. "I do not understand what you are hinting at! If you do not bring me the thief, I will declare that you yourself are guilty!"

"Sire, do you really want the thief to be publicly identified so that he may be punished?"

"Yes, Friend, I do," declared the king.

"Very well, Sire, I will name the thief, but it must be proclaimed in the midst of the assembly."

The king called an assembly of all citizens.

When the people had gathered, the king sat on his throne, and the young man stood in front of him, visible to all the crowd. "Let everyone listen carefully!" the young man called out. "The world is upside down! Water is ablaze! The king has asked me to identify the thieves who stole the precious jewels from his treasury! All of you may well complain of your king and his advisor! From now on, you must see to your own protection! Your refuge has proved to be your bane!"

The people immediately understood the young man's meaning. From all sides, cries went up: "The king and his advisor took the jewels! They themselves threw them into the tank! The king tried to blame someone else! How dare he pretend to search for a thief! The king is a liar! He is a cheat! This king is wicked! He is not worthy to be king any longer! We ought to kill this evil king and his dishonest advisor" Incensed, the people grabbed sticks, stones, and whatever weapons they could find, rushed forward, and beat the king and his advisor to death. Then they anointed the young man and placed him on the throne.

Having concluded his story, the Buddha taught the Dhamma, and both the layman and his son attained the first path. Then the Buddha identified the birth: "At that time, Mahā-Kassapa was the father, and I was the youth skilled in tracing footprints."

169
The Razor-Wheel
Catudvāra Jātaka

It was while staying at Jetavana that the Buddha told this story about an intractable bhikkhu.

"Long ago," the Buddha said to the bhikkhu, "when you were disobedient and ignored the counsel of the wise, you were rewarded with a razor-wheel." Then the Buddha told this story of the past.

Long, long ago, in the days of Kassapa Buddha, a merchant family in Bārānasi had a fortune of at least eighty crores. Both the man and his wife were devout followers of the Teacher and had attained the first path, but their son Mittavindaka was wicked, defiant, and an unbeliever.

When the merchant died, his wife took over most of the business, but Mittavindaka forced her to stop all her charitable donations.

Mittavindaka's misconduct and his lack of generosity were a constant worry to his mother. On a full-moon day, she called him and said, "Son, it is difficult to be born a human being. Since we have gained this privilege, it behooves us to live virtuously and to give alms. Please observe the Uposatha day," she pleaded, "and listen to the Buddha's teaching."

"No thanks, Mother!" Mittavindaka scoffed. "No almsgiving for me! And I have no use for your virtue, either! I'll live as I please and take the consequences! I don't want to hear any more sermonizing!"

"My son," she persisted, "if you observe the Uposatha today, go to the monastery, and listen to the bhikkhus, when you come home tomorrow morning, I will give you one thousand coins."

At the thought of so much money for himself, Mittavindaka could not refuse. He went to the monastery, but, instead of listening to Dhamma, he found a comfortable spot and slept the entire time. Early the next morning, he awoke, washed his face, and returned home.

Fully expecting her son to return, bringing with him the bhikkhu who had preached the sermon, Mittavindaka's mother cheerfully prepared gruel, rice and various curries to offer the bhikkhu for lunch. She arranged a proper seat and awaited their arrival.

When she saw her son coming home alone, she asked why he hadn't brought the bhikkhu with him.

"Why would I have brought the bhikkhu home!" he retorted.

"Well then, you can eat the gruel I prepared for the bhikkhu."

"Where's my money?" he asked brusquely.

"Eat something first." she said, mildly, "Then I'll give you the money."

"No. You promised me one thousand coins when I came home. I'm back. Give it to me. I won't eat anything until I get my money!"

At least, Mittavindaka had gone to the monastery. His mother consoled herself with that thought as she fetched him a purse with one thousand coins. He put the purse in a safe place, drank his mother's gruel, and went out. Being both shrewd and ruthless, Mittavindaka, in no great time, converted his thousand coins into two million.

With that fortune in hand, he decided to trade on the high seas and outfitted a ship. One day, he announced "Mother, I am going to do business with this ship."

"My dear Mittavindaka," his mother cried, "you are my only child! We have plenty of money! We don't need any more! Going to sea is dangerous! Please don't go!"

"Don't try to stop me!" he shouted. "I have made up my mind, and you can not change it!"

"But, my darling son, I must stop you! I don't want to lose you!" she cried, grabbing hold of his hand.

Mittavindaka roughly pushed his mother's hand away. Then, as his anger flared up, he knocked her to the floor and walked out the door without even looking back to see how she was. He went straight to the ship and set sail that very day.

On the seventh day at sea, the wind failed, and the ship sat motionless as if anchored onto the bottom. Lots were cast, and, three times, it fell to Mittavindaka. The husky sailors mutinied, turned on him, and shouted, "You are the cause of our misfortune! If you remain on board, we will all perish!" They forced him into a dinghy and pushed it away from the ship. Immediately, the wind began to blow, the sails filled, and the ship sped away with amazing speed.

Mittavindaka's little boat floated for some time on the waves, and finally washed up on an island. He went exploring and discovered a crystal palace inhabited by four lovely women. Mittavindaka stayed with them for seven days enjoying their favors. At the end of that week, they informed him that they were really vimāna-petas, beings who alternated between seven days of divine bliss and seven days of hellish suffering. They implored him to wait in the palace for only seven days until they could return and entertain him again. Mittavindaka had no patience for waiting, so he set out once more in his little boat.

Soon, he arrived at another island. There, in a palace of silver, for seven days, he enjoyed the favors of eight other vimāna-petas. When they left to undergo their mandatory punishment, Mittavindaka again set out and arrived at an island with a mansion of jewels, where, for another seven days, he was entertained by sixteen other vimāna-petas. Then he dallied for seven days with thirty-two vimāna-petas in a magnificent golden hall.

After he left that island, his little boat arrived at what appeared to be a majestic city, surrounded by a wall with four great gates. Believing this to be the capital of some foreign kingdom, Mittavindaka resolved to enter it and to become king. Actually, this was the great and terrible Ussada Hell with its four gates, but Mittavindaka was blind to that.

As he passed though one of the imposing gates, he saw a man being tormented by a razor-wheel spinning on his head, grinding his skull and slashing his scalp to ribbons. This spinning blade appeared to Mittavindaka to be a beautiful lotus blossom. The chains and fetters the miserable creature wore appeared to be rich garments. Mittavindaka mistook the blood dripping from his head wounds for red sandalwood powder. His groans of pain seemed to be the sweetest of songs.

Approaching the being without the least bit of fear or caution, Mittavindaka called out cheerfully, "My good man, you've been enjoying that lotus flower long enough. Let me have it!"

"My Lord," the suffering creature gasped, "this is no lotus! It is a razor-wheel!"

"Come on!" Mittavindaka retorted, "you're just saying that because you don't want to give it up!"

In a flash, that miserable wretch saw that his torment was at an end. "The force of my evil deeds must be exhausted," he thought. "No doubt, this fellow, like me, struck his mother. Very well, let me give him this razor-wheel." Bowing his bloody head toward the newcomer, he shouted, "Here you are! Take your lotus!"

Instantly, the razor-wheel flew from his head and landed directly on Mittavindaka. Shocked and terrified by the excruciating pain, Mittavindaka screamed, "Take back your wheel! Take it back! It's killing me! I don't want it now!" The other being, however, had already vanished.

As this was taking place, Sakka happened to be making a tour of Ussada hell with his great retinue, and arrived at that spot at exactly that moment. Recognizing him, Mittavindaka cried out, "Sire, this razor-wheel is crushing my head just as a pestle grinds mustard seed! What sin have I committed to suffer this punishment?"

"You had wealth aplenty," Sakka replied calmly but firmly, "but when asked for help, you didn't listen. Your parents tried to lead you to the Path, but you mocked their wisdom. Being greedy, you stopped all generosity in your parents' name. When your own mother begged you to stay, you rebuffed her. She foresaw the danger you were in, but you left her all alone. When she appealed to you, you struck her. With the vimāna-petas—four, eight, sixteen, and thirty-two—you gave in to lust, but you couldn't wait even seven days for them to return. Because of your greed, you have to bear this wheel. Because of your lustful desire, you have to bear this wheel. Because you would not share your wealth, because you would not approach the Path, and because you would not honor your own mother, you have to bear this wheel! Consider the results of your deeds so that the wheel never comes to you again!"

"Sire," Mittavindaka cried meekly, "you seem to know everything that I have done. Even the smallest detail is not hidden from you. Please tell me how long I must suffer this razor-wheel on my head? Can I measure it in years or in thousands of years? How long will this suffering go on?"

"This razor-wheel will roll on and on, grinding and tearing, until the force of your misdeeds has been fully exhausted. No savior will appear to relieve you. Farewell."

Sakka returned to Tāvatimsa, but Mittavindaka fell into unspeakable misery.

Having concluded his story, the Buddha identified the birth: "At that time, you, disobedient bhikkhu, were Mittavindaka, and I was Sakka."

170
Black
Kanha Jātaka

It was while staying at Nigrodhārāma near Kapilavatthu that the Buddha told this story about a smile.

One evening, as the Buddha was walking in Nigrodhārāma with a group of bhikkhus, he gave a smile.

"What is the reason that the Blessed One smiled?" Venerable Ānanda wondered. "Tathāgatas do not smile without cause. I will ask him!" After paying obeisance, Venerable Ānanda inquired about it.

"Long ago, Ānanda," the Buddha replied, "a sage named Kanha lived right here in this spot. He delighted in meditation, and the power of his virtue caused Sakka's throne to become hot." At Venerable Ānanda's request, the Buddha told this story of the past.

Long, long ago, when Brahmadatta was reigning in Bārānasi, there was a wealthy but childless brahmin couple, who desperately wanted a child. The husband undertook vows of virtue and prayed for a son, and, in a short while, his wife conceived the Bodhisatta. When their son was born, his skin was dark, so they named him Kanha (Black). When he was sixteen, his parents sent him to Takkasilā, where he studied all the liberal arts. After finishing his education, Kanha returned to Bārānasi and, in time, inherited all his parents' property.

One day, as he sitting on a luxurious couch and inspecting some of the pieces from his treasure house, he found a gold plate that had been inscribed by his forefathers. Each one had made a notation of how much wealth he had added to the family treasury. As Kanha read it, he sighed, "Ah, those who earned this wealth are gone, but the wealth is still here. Not one of them could take it with him. No one can tie his wealth in a bundle and carry it to the next world."

As he sat there, pondering the gold plate, he thought, "Since wealth is connected with the five fears,[1] one should give away one's wealth in alms. Since this body is subject to disease, one should honor the virtuous. Since life is transient, one should strive for spiritual insight."

Aloud he declared, "What need do I have for all this property? Let me distribute everything in alms and seek perfection!" After getting permission from the king, he spent the next week offering alms to all who asked. After seven days of continuous giving, however, he could perceive no decrease in his wealth. "There seems to be no end to this!" he declared. "What am I waiting for? I will take up the ascetic life at once!" He threw open the doors of his mansion and instructed his servants to allow anyone to take whatever he wanted and to regard it as freely given. Then, regarding all his wealth as both dirty and dangerous, he left the city. All who knew him mourned the departure of this great and generous man.

In the Himavat, Kanha found a pleasant place to stay at the foot of a gourd tree. Not even making a shelter for himself, he stayed in the open air. Eating only once a day and at one sitting, he never cooked anything and restricted himself to what his own tree provided. When the tree flowered, he ate the flowers; when there was fruit, he ate fruit; when there were only leaves, he ate leaves; when there was nothing else, he ate only bark. He stayed perfectly contented in that place for a long time and attained jhānic concentration.

As Kanha continued to take pleasure in his austere life, Sakka's throne grew hot.

Sakka's first thought was to wonder who was attempting to dislodge him from his position. Surveying the world, he saw Kanha and knew that the ascetic had become a sage of dreaded austerity, with great psychic power. "I must go and hear his teaching!" Sakka declared. "Then I will reward him as he justly deserves!"

---

1 Pañca vera, the fivefold guilty dread, which are the fears connected with breaking the five precepts.

The king of devas immediately descended from Tāvatimsa and stood directly behind the ascetic. To see whether Kanha would succumb to anger, Sakka began by ridiculing him. "Who is that swarthy man residing in this black spot. Black, too, is the food he eats. Such blackness is repulsive!"

Kanha surmised that the speaker was Sakka and that this was a test. He replied mildly, "Even though the skin is black, the heart may be pure. It is black deeds which make a man truly black!" Then Kanha gave a discourse to Sakka in which he praised virtue and explained the evil deeds which make one "black." He spoke eloquently, as if he were making the moon rise in the sky.

Sakka was delighted and declared, "Venerable Sir, your lesson was most articulate and nobly spoken! For the fine words which I have heard, I grant you a boon. Choose whatever you wish!"

Kanha thought, "Sakka must have come here thinking that I was trying to oust him from his position in heaven. Let me reassure him that that is not my intent. I will choose only boons which advance my life as an ascetic." Aloud he said, "Your Majesty, you have asked me to choose a boon. I ask to be free from anger, hatred, greed, and lust. To be delivered from these would be for me a blessing."

"Wise Kanha," Sakka replied, "please explain in detail the significance of these boons and why you have chosen them. What harm do you see in anger, in hatred, in greed, and in lust?"

"Your Majesty," Kanha began, "anger, which grows mighty from the seed of impatience, is full of bitterness. I want no part of anger!

"Whenever one feels even the smallest hatred, we see it quickly grow. First just a look, a word, a shove, a fist, a stick, and then one draws a sword! From hatred, anger grows! I want no part of hatred!

"Greed drives men to fraud and deceit, cruel crimes for filthy gain! I want no part of greed!

"Lust is a fetter which leads to acrimony and causes one to sin. I want no part of lust!"

Sakka was deeply moved by Kanha's wise response and offered him another boon.

The sage replied instantly, "In that I am dwelling alone here in the forest, may I be free from sickness and disease which would interrupt my meditation."

Sakka was pleased that Kanha had again selected a boon to aid his ascetic life and declared, "One more boon I grant you!"

"If, indeed, you grant me one more boon, I ask that no creature ever suffer harm on account of me!"

Sakka gladly granted Kanha these six boons, all of which enhanced his life of renunciation. As an additional reward for his wisdom and eloquence, the king of the devas made the sage's tree produce fruit perennially. Sakka placed his palms together in respect and bowed to the ascetic. Then he returned to Tāvatimsa. Kanha, never breaking his concentration, continued his meditation and his ascetic practice. When he passed away, he was reborn in the Brahma heavens.

Having concluded his story, the Buddha identified the birth: "At that time, Anuruddha was Sakka, and I was Kanha."

171
Sharing Merit
Sankha Jātaka

It was while staying at Jetavana that the Buddha told this story about offering the requisites.

In Sāvatthī, a layman, pleased after hearing the Buddha's discourse, invited
him and five hundred bhikkhus to lunch the next day. The Buddha and the
bhikkhus sat in a spacious pavilion which the layman had set up in front of
his house. He served them, made rich offerings, and invited them for the next
day, as well. He continued offering lunch for seven days. On the seventh day,
he presented the Buddha and each bhikkhu a full set of eight requisites. He
also offered the Buddha a pair of shoes worth one thousand coins. He offered
each of the two chief disciples shoes worth five hundred coins. To each of
the other bhikkhus he offered shoes worth one hundred coins. After all the
offerings were made, he sat down near the Buddha to hear the Dhamma.

"Layman," the Buddha said, "your gift is most munificent. Be joyful. You
have given all the requisites to this assembly of bhikkhus. How can this not
prove to be a refuge to you? Long ago, when there was no Buddha in the
world, even one who gave only a pair of shoes and an umbrella to a Pacceka
Buddha found refuge in the great sea because of his gift." At the layman's
request, the Buddha told this story of the past.

Long, long ago, the city of Bārānasi was called Molinī. While Brahma-datta was reigning there, the Bodhisatta was a rich man named Sankha, who delighted in giving. Sankha built alms-halls in six places, one at each of the four city gates, one in the middle of the city, and one near his own door. Every day, he gave away six hundred thousand coins worth of alms to innumerable wayfarers and beggars.

One day, he thought, "At the rate I am giving alms, my wealth will soon be exhausted, and I will have nothing more to give. While I still have some capital, I should sail a trading ship to Suvannabhūmi and replenish my fortune."

Sankha had a ship built, loaded it with goods, and bid farewell to his wife and child. "Until I return, continue to distribute alms generously!" he urged them.

He picked up his umbrella, put on his shoes, and headed toward the port.

At that moment, a Pacceka Buddha, meditating on Mount Gandhamadana, noticed Sankha. "There is a great man who is going to undertake a journey to obtain wealth," the Pacceka Buddha thought. "Will there be any obstacles at sea to hinder him?" he wondered. "Ah, yes! There certainly will!" he foresaw. "If he sees me, however, he will offer me shoes and an umbrella, and, as a result of that gift, he will be saved. Let me help him!" The Pacceka Buddha immediately passed through the air, and alighted not far from Sankha. Under the blazing sun, he walked barefoot over the hot sand and approached the merchant.

As soon as Sankha saw the Pacceka Buddha, he thought, "Here is a rare chance to gain merit. Let me sow a wholesome seed today!"

With a light heart, he hurried to meet the Pacceka Buddha. "Sir," he said, "be so kind as to come into the shade of this tree." He washed the Pacceka Buddha's feet, took off his own shoes, wiped them clean, and put them on the other's feet. Then he offered him his umbrella, as well. After accepting the gifts, the Pacceka Buddha rose into the air and returned to Mount Gandhamadana.

Glad at heart, Sankha continued to the harbor, boarded his ship, and set sail. On the seventh day, the ship sprang a leak, and the sailors could not bail out water fast enough to save her. All on the ship, in fear for their lives, made a great clamor as they called out in prayer, each to his own deity. Sankha chose a man as his companion, and the two of them ate as much sugar and ghee as they could manage. Then they covered themselves with oil and climbed up the mast.

Sankha pointed and cried, "In that direction lies our city!" The two men jumped in that direction, as far away from the ship as they could, knowing that there were sharks and turtles circling the sinking craft.

Although everyone else on the ship perished, Sankha and his attendant survived and continued swimming. On the seventh day of their escape, Sankha realized that it was the full moon, and, even as he swam, he resolved to observe the Uposatha day. He rinsed out his mouth with salt water.

In that sea, there was a deity named Manimekhalā, who had responsibility for patrolling the waters and rescuing any virtuous people who became shipwrecked in that area. If she found anyone who observed Uposatha, lived virtuously, and cared for their parents, she was duty-bound to save them. For the past week she had been negligent, so, when she finally saw Sankha, she became quite upset. "Oh dear," she cried, "the good Sankha has been swimming for seven days! If he were to die, I would be to blame!" She quickly filled a golden plate with divine food and hurried to his aid.

"For seven long days, sir, you have had no food. Eat this!" she said as she offered him the golden plate.

Sankha looked at her, and calmly replied, "No, thank you. I am observing the fast."

His servant, swimming behind, heard what his master said but couldn't see the deva. He thought Sankha was babbling from sheer exhaustion and tried to comfort him. "Sir!" he called out, "why are you gibbering? There is no one here but me. Are you afraid or confused?"

"My good fellow, I am neither afraid nor confused. There is someone else here, though I realize you cannot see her. A beautiful creature is offering me food on a golden plate. I just refused her offer, saying I was contented."

"If you see such a wondrous being," the servant suggested, "you should ask a blessing and inquire whether she is a yakkhinī, a human, or a deva."

"Good thought!" Sankha replied. Then, addressing Manimekhalā, he asked, "You appear kindly, and you offer me food as well. I must ask you whether you are a yakkhinī, a deva, or a woman?"

Manimekhalā replied readily, "I am a powerful deva. I have come here with a heart full of compassion for you in your difficulty. I would like to give you food, drink, and a place to rest. Indeed, I will provide anything you want."

When he heard that, Sankha thought, "Here I am, struggling in the middle of the vast ocean, and a deity offers me anything I want! I wonder why? Have I done anything to deserve this, or is it her own whim?"

To Manimekhalā he said, "Dear Deva, both powerful and beautiful, may I ask why you have come to help me?"

"Two weeks ago, you presented shoes and an umbrella to a Pacceka Buddha, who was walking on the burning sand. I came here today to bring the fruit of those gifts."

"How wonderful!" Sankha marveled. "Here, in the middle of this trackless ocean, my small gift of shoes and an umbrella to that Pacceka Buddha has become a wish-fulfilling gem!"

"Well, Deva," he continued, addressing Manimekhalā, "my only wish is to sail on a sturdy ship with fair winds so that I can reach Molini today."

Manimekhalā instantly created a magnificent bejeweled ship with masts of sapphire, ropes of gold, and sails of silver. The oars and rudder were of pure gold. Manimekhalā filled the vessel with the seven precious things. She lifted Sankha from the water and placed him on the deck. Sankha quickly shouted, "May my servant share in the merit I have gained from my gifts!"

The servant shouted, "Sādhu! Sādhu! Sādhu!" [2]

Instantly, the deva picked him up and placed him next to his master. Then she guided the ship to Molini, placed all the wealth in Sankha's house, and returned to her sea abode.

His fortune more than amply restored, Sankha distributed alms with his own hand and lived a virtuous and blessed life. When they passed away, he, his servant, and all the members of his family were reborn in heaven.

Having concluded his story, the Buddha taught the Dhamma, and the layman attained the first path. Then the Buddha identified the birth: "At that time, Uppalavannā was the deva, Ānanda was the servant, and I was Sankha."

---

2 An exclamation meaning "Well done!"

172

Once Arisen
Culla-Bodhi Jātaka

It was while staying at Jetavana that the Buddha told this story about a bhikkhu who was unable to control his anger.

This bhikkhu was very resentful and easily bore grudges. Frequently, without provocation, he flew into a rage. When the Buddha heard about this, he sent for the bhikkhu and asked whether it was true.

"Yes, Venerable Sir," he confessed.

"Bhikkhu," the Buddha told him, "anger must be restrained. An ill-tempered person harms himself in this world and in the next. Why, having entered my Sangha to achieve liberation, do you continue to show anger? Long ago, a wise man perfectly restrained his anger." Then he told this story of the past.

Long, long ago, when Brahmadatta was reigning in Bārānasi, the Bodhisatta descended from heaven and was born to a tremendously rich couple who had vast properties in a town in the kingdom of Kāsi. The boy was as handsome as a deva, and they named him Bodhi. When he was old enough, they sent him to Takkasilā to study all the arts and sciences. After he returned, his parents arranged his marriage to a young woman of the same caste. It so happened that the young woman had also been reborn from the Brahma heavens, and she had a divine beauty. Neither of them was interested in marriage, but, to satisfy their parents, they agreed. Both of them were pure and without lust, and they lived together in innocence.

When his parents died, Bodhi performed the funeral rites, called his wife, and said, "Lady, take this fortune of eighty crores, and live here happily."

"Good Sir," she replied, "this is not my money. It is your family's wealth."

"I have no need of wealth. I intend to become an ascetic in the Himavat."

"Is the ascetic life exclusively for men?" she asked.

"No," he answered, "women may also become ascetics."

"I have no desire for the phlegm you have spat out of your mouth. I care no more for wealth than you do, so I, too, will become an ascetic."

Together, they gave away all the family wealth as alms and left for the Himavat. Finding a pleasant spot in the forest, they built a hermitage and began living on roots, fruit, and berries.

After living there contentedly for ten years, at the beginning of that rainy season, the two ascetics left to get salt and vinegar and to find a place to stay. They arrived in Bārānasi and established themselves in the royal park.

One day, not long after that, the king said to the park keeper, "Today we will enjoy ourselves in the royal gardens, so get everything in order." When all was ready, the king, with a great retinue, proceeded to the park. The king saw the two ascetics sitting in meditation on a stone slab and instantly developed an infatuation for the woman. In fact, he trembled with desire for her. He felt it necessary, however, to ask the ascetic beside her what she was to him.

"Your Majesty," Bodhi answered, "she is nothing to me. Now, she merely shares my ascetic life, but, when I lived in the world, she was my wife."

"He says that she is nothing to him," the king thought, "but that, in his worldly life, she was his wife. I wonder what he would do if I exercised my royal prerogative and seized her." Aloud, he said, "Sir, if I take this beautiful lady away from you, what will you do?"

"Once arisen," Bodhi replied calmly, "it would never leave me, my whole life long. Just as a rainstorm slakes the dust, quench it while it is still small!"

The king understood but could not restrain himself. "Whether you give her to me or not, I will take her!" he cried. He ordered his servants to seize the female ascetic and to take her to the palace. Bodhi heard her cries and looked once but then looked no more.

No longer interested in staying in the gardens, the king quickly returned to the palace and sent for the woman. He received her with great honor, but she rebuffed him and spoke of the worthlessness of worldly honor. The only value she treasured, she said, was the life of solitude. Unable to gain her consent to be queen, the king ordered that she be lodged in a separate room.

Alone in his chamber, the king tried to assess the situation. "This woman says she is not interested in the honor and glory I can give her," he thought. "That fellow she was with said that he would not let his anger arise but would crush it. He barely looked at his attractive wife as my servants led her away. Some of these ascetics can be quite cunning, though. He's probably scheming how to get revenge! I had better go and see what he's up to."

Agitated and unable to sit still, the king hurried back to the garden, where he found the ascetic stitching up a tear in his cloak. As the king approached him, Bodhi did not look up but silently went on with his sewing.

"What a fraud!" the king thought. "This ascetic is so angry that he won't even speak to me!" Aloud he said, "A while ago, you boasted that you would not get angry, but now anyone can see that you are furious as you just sit there and sew!"

"Once arisen, it never would have left me," Bodhi repeated calmly, "but as a rainstorm slakes the dust, I quenched it while it was still small."

"What have you quenched while it was small?" the king asked. "Maybe it is not anger you're talking about, after all."

"Your Majesty," Bodhi replied, "anger brings wretchedness and even ruin. As it began to arise within me, by cherishing kindly feelings, I quenched it. Without anger a man sees clearly, but, blinded by anger, he forges ahead foolishly. Anger makes our enemies rejoice because it brings us woe and disaster. If stirred, the fires of anger will rise higher and higher, and those angry fires consume their own fuel, leaving only ashes. The man who can calm his anger, thus depriving it of fuel, will find that his happiness and honor increase like a waxing moon. I felt anger arising, but I restrained it perfectly."

This discourse from the ascetic so pleased the king that he ordered his servants to bring the female ascetic back to the park. Begging their pardon for the grievous wrong he had committed, the king invited both of them to stay in the royal park for as long as they wished and promised to support them as was proper. Then he took his leave and returned to the palace.

The ascetics remained in the park, practicing their meditation, until the woman died. After her death, Bodhi returned to the Himavat and continued cultivating the higher stages of concentration. When he died, he was reborn in the Brahma heavens.

Having concluded his story, the Buddha taught the Dhamma, and the bhikkhu who could not control his anger attained the third path. Then the Buddha identified the birth: "At that time, Rāhula's mother was the female ascetic, Ānanda was King Brahmadatta, and I was the ascetic Bodhi."

173
Repudiation
Nigrodha Jātaka

It was while staying at Veluvana that the Buddha told this story about Devadatta.

One day, some bhikkhus mentioned to Devadatta that the Buddha had been very helpful to him. They reminded Devadatta that the Buddha had ordained him, taught him Dhamma, and instructed him in meditation.

Offended by their remarks, Devadatta held up a blade of grass and said, "I can see no good that the ascetic Gotama has ever done me, not even this much!"

Later, in the Hall of Truth, the bhikkhus were talking about this. When the Buddha heard what they were discussing, he said, "Bhikkhus, this is not the first time that Devadatta has been treacherous and ungrateful to friends." Then he told this story of the past.

Long, long ago, when a great monarch named Magadha was reigning in Rājagaha, a wealthy merchant had arranged for his son to wed the daughter of a trader from the countryside. After the couple had been married for some time, the man's family began abusing the wife because she hadn't produced an heir. They were always gossiping about her, and, even within her hearing, they said things like "With a barren wife in our son's household, how can the family prosper?" and "Without a son, how can the family line continue?"

Distressed by all the talk, the wife had an idea. She questioned a dear old nurse she was sure she could trust about the signs and indications of pregnancy. Following the nurse's description and with her complicity, the wife concealed her menses, affected all sorts of cravings, beat her hands and feet, so they appeared swollen, wrapped her belly with bandages, blackened her nipples, and permitted only her old nurse to be present at her toilet. In this way, she pretended to be pregnant and deceived everyone.

Her husband was naturally delighted at the prospect of an heir and showered her with lavish attention. His family, also, began treating her with respect. After maintaining the pretense for nine months, she declared that she wished to return home and to deliver her child in her parents' house as was the custom.

With a large number of attendants, she mounted a carriage and left Rājagaha. Traveling in front of her entourage was a caravan. Each day, at about breakfast time, she reached the spot where the caravan had spent the night. One night, a poor woman in the caravan gave birth under a great banyan tree. Realizing that she would not survive if she left the caravan and that the baby would not survive the rigors of travel with the caravan, she covered her newborn son with a cloth and left him at the foot of the tree. She trusted that someone would find him. The deva of that tree watched over the baby and tenderly cared for him because this was no ordinary child but was, in fact, the Bodhisatta.

When the wife's entourage arrived at the place the next morning, the wife went with her nurse to the shelter of the banyan tree for her toilet. She immediately saw the newly born baby, the color of gold, lying there.

Realizing that this was the answer to her prayer, she called out to the nurse that their object was accomplished. Together, they hurriedly unwrapped the bandages from her belly, and, when the wife was composed, she had the nurse announce that she had just given birth to a son.

Her attendants erected a tent for her to rest in, and a messenger was sent back to Rājagaha with the news. Her husband's parents replied that, since the baby had been born, there was no need for her to continue on to her father's house. The entourage turned around and returned by the same route to Rājagaha.

The family welcomed the baby, and, because he had been born under a banyan tree, they named him Nigrodha. On the same day that Nigrodha had been born, the daughter-in-law of another merchant in Rājagaha gave birth to a son under the branches of a tree, so he was named Sākha; and the wife of a tailor working for that family gave birth to a son in the shop, surrounded by remnants and bits of cloth, so he was named Pottika.

Hearing of the birth of these other two boys, the great merchant sent for them and insisted that the three boys grow up together. When they were old enough, all three were sent to Takkasilā for their education. The sons of the merchants each had one thousand coins to give their teacher for a fee, but Nigrodha himself tutored Pottika.

When their studies were finished, the boys took leave of their teacher and wandered here and there to see something of the world and to learn the customs of other folk. Eventually, they reached the gate of Bārānasi during a festival. Seven days before, the king had died without a successor, and a proclamation, accompanied by the beating of a drum, was being made throughout the city that on the next day a chariot carrying the five symbols of royalty would be driven around to find the new king.

The three friends lay down to sleep under a tree outside the city. At dawn, Pottika awoke and overheard some roosters talking in the branches.

The rooster at the very top had let fall a dropping on the back of one below.

"What just fell on me?" asked the dirtied rooster.

"Don't lose your temper. I didn't mean to do it."

"Oh, so you think my body is a good place for your droppings! Obviously, you don't know my importance!"

"Look! I said it was an accident! And what is your importance, anyway?"

"If someone eats me today, he will get one thousand coins this very day. Isn't that something to be proud of?"

"Pooh! Proud of a little thing like that? The man who eats my fat will become king this morning. The man who eats my white meat will be commander-in-chief, and the man who eats the meat next to my bones will be treasurer!"

Pottika thought, "One thousand coins is a mere trifle. Best to be king!"

Silently he climbed the tree, seized the cock at the top, wrung its neck, kindled a fire, and cooked it under the tree. He gave the fat to Nigrodha and the white meat to Sākha, and he himself ate the meat next to the bones.

When they had finished eating, Pottika said, "Nigrodha, Sir, you will be king today. Sākha, sir, you will be commander-in-chief. I will be treasurer!"

They asked him how he knew this, and he told them what he had overheard.

The three young men went into the city to visit a brahmin and received rice-porridge with ghee and sugar. They left the city again and walked to the royal park.

In the park, Nigrodha lay down on a great slab of stone, and his two companions lay down on the ground beside him. At that time, the royal advisors were following the royal chariot around the city, and the horses headed toward the royal park. "Someone of great merit must be there," thought the chief advisor.

As he entered the park, he saw Nigrodha lying on the stone slab. Lifting the cloth covering Nigrodha's feet, the advisor saw the auspicious marks and realized that they predicted a splendid future. "Why, this young man is destined to be not only the king of Kāsi, but the ruler of the entire Jambudīpa!" he exclaimed. He ordered the musicians to begin beating the gongs and clanging the cymbals to announce to everyone that the king had been found.

The noise awakened Nigrodha, and he removed the cloth from his face. Seeing the huge crowd assembled around him, he turned and lay still for a moment before sitting erect with his legs crossed. The royal chaplain fell to one knee and declared, "Sire, the kingdom is yours!"

"So be it," replied Nigrodha deliberately.

The advisors led him to the chariot, seated him on a heap of precious jewels, presented him with the royal paraphernalia, and formally sprinkled him with water.

King Nigrodha immediately appointed Sākha his commander-in-chief, and the three friends entered the city in great pomp.

King Nigrodha ruled righteously, and his subjects loved him.

One day, King Nigrodha remembered his parents and decided to call them to Bārāṇasi. He summoned Sākha and asked him to take a large retinue to Rājagaha and to bring them back.

"That is not my business!" Sākha replied curtly.

King Nigrodha asked Pottika to go, and he readily agreed. When he arrived in Rājagaha, however, Nigrodha's parents told him that they were comfortable and wealthy enough in Rājagaha, and they declined to leave. Pottika visited Sākha's parents and asked them to move to Bārāṇasi, but they also refused. Finally, he went to see his own parents and asked them, but they replied, "Son, we earn enough from tailoring here in Rājagaha. We have no need of Bārāṇasi."

Disappointed at having failed in his mission, Pottika returned to Bārāṇasi. Before reporting to the king, he thought it would be a good idea to take a rest and to refresh himself, so he stopped at Sākha's house.

"Tell the commander-in-chief that his comrade Pottika is here," he said to the door-keeper. The man did so, but Sākha, having conceived a grudge against Pottika for giving the kingship to Nigrodha instead of to him, shouted, "Comrade indeed! Who is his comrade? That vulgar, lowborn son of a tailor! Throw him out!" Guards seized Pottika, beat him, and kicked him. Then, taking him by the neck, they threw him down the stairs.

"Even though it was through me that Sākha gained his position of commander-in-chief, he treats me like this!" Pottika thought as he lay at the foot of the stairs. "He is thoroughly rude and ungrateful! At least, Nigrodha is a good, wise, and agreeable man. I will go to him now."

Bruised and battered, Pottika picked himself up and went to the palace. He sent a message to the king that Pottika, his comrade, had returned and was waiting to see him. The king asked Pottika to come in immediately, stood as he approached, stepped down from the dais, and embraced his friend warmly. He called his servants and ordered that Pottika be bathed and shaved and that his injuries be looked after. He presented his friend with a handsome set of clothes and invited him to eat at the royal table. As they talked, King Nigrodha asked about Pottika's parents, as well as about his own. He expressed disappointment that none of them had chosen to move to Bārānasi, but he was gratified to learn that they were all well and contented in Rājagaha.

In the meantime, Sākha realized that he had better hurry to the palace. "Pottika is angry and is bound to slander me to the king." he thought. "If I am there, maybe he will feel too intimidated to say anything against me."

Sākha arrived at the palace and stood by the king, but Pottika was undaunted. "Sire," he said, "when I first got back to Bārānasi, I went to Sākha's house, hoping to rest there before coming to you. Sākha refused to see me. He called me a lowborn son of a tailor and did not even recognize me as his comrade. He went so far as to set his men on me. They beat me and threw me down the stairs. Can you believe it? We've been together since we were babies!"

"I have never heard of such ingratitude as Sākha has shown!" cried the king in outrage. "The three of us have always lived together! We've been comrades all our lives, and our shares of this kingdom are entirely from you! A good deed done to a virtuous man returns double, but a good deed done to an evil man is wasted indeed!"

King Nigrodha turned to Sākha, who had stood silent during this exchange. "Well, Sākha," he asked, "do you recognize Pottika as your comrade?"

Sākha would not answer, and the king shouted, "Seize this worthless traitor who refuses to recognize our friend. Get him out of my sight, and kill him!"

"No, Your Majesty!" Pottika cried. "Show mercy! Life, once taken, cannot be brought back. Forgive the fool, and let him live. I wish him no harm."

Moved by Pottika's plea, the king forgave Sākha. Then he offered the post of commander-in-chief to Pottika, who refused it but accepted the position of treasurer.

Pottika prospered in his new post and was blessed with a large family. He was often heard to exclaim that even death with King Nigrodha would be better than living with Sākha.

Having concluded his story, the Buddha identified the birth: "At that time, Devadatta was Sākha, Ānanda was Pottika, and I was Nigrodha."

174
Longevity
Mahā-Dhammapāla Jātaka

It was while staying at Nigrodhārāma near Kapilavatthu that the Buddha told this story about long life.

When the Buddha visited Kapilavatthu for the first time after his Enlightenment, his father, King Suddhodana, invited him and his bhikkhus for lunch at the palace. At this time, the king told the Buddha, "Venerable Sir, when you were practicing extreme austerities, a deva came to me, stood in the air, and told me, 'Your son, Prince Siddhattha, has died of starvation.'"

"Did you believe him, Sire?" the Buddha asked.

"No, Venerable Sir, I refused to believe him and said, 'My son will not die before he has become a Buddha.'"

The Buddha said, "Sire, you did the same thing long ago. Even when a famous teacher showed you some bones, you refused to believe that your son had died young." At his father's request, the Buddha told this story of the past.

Long, long ago, when Brahmadatta was reigning in Bārānasi, a brahmin, Mahā-Dhammapāla, lived with his family in a village called Dhammapāla. Mahā-Dhammapāla was so named because he scrupulously practiced the ten virtues. Everyone in his household, even the servants, also practiced these virtues and, along with him, observed the Uposatha days.

The Bodhisatta was born into this family and was named Culla-Dhammapāla after his father. When he was old enough, his father gave him one thousand coins and sent him to Takkasilā to study all the arts and sciences with an outstanding teacher. Culla-Dhammapāla was soon recognized as first among the teacher's five hundred students.

One day, the teacher's eldest son died unexpectedly. The teacher, surrounded by relatives and students, cried aloud as he performed the funeral rites in the charnel ground. Everyone, except Culla-Dhammapāla, wept and lamented. Afterwards, the students were discussing the death, and one said, "Alas! Such a fine boy, so bright and well-behaved!" Another said, "How tragic for one so young to be cut down and to be parted from his parents!" Culla-Dhammapāla observed, "Yes, he was young, as you say. Why did he die? It is not right for a child to die so young!"

"Culla-Dhammapāla," the others said, surprised and disconcerted by his question, "don't you understand that all living beings must die?"

"Of course, I know that," Culla-Dhammapāla replied, "but people do not die young. They die after they get old."

"But all component things are transitory and impermanent," the other students persisted.

"Yes, everything is transitory and impermanent," Culla-Dhammapāla agreed, "but people do not die when they are young. It is only after they have grown old that they become subject to death."

"Friend, how can you say that?" the other students asked. "Is that the way it is in your family?"

"Yes," Culla-Dhammapāla replied. "In my family, that is the tradition."

When the other students reported this to their teacher, he called Culla-Dhammapāla and asked him directly, "Is it true, Culla-Dhammapāla, that nobody ever dies young in your family?"

"Yes, sir, that is true." replied Culla-Dhammapāla.

The teacher was amazed to hear this and decided to talk to Culla-Dhammapāla's father about it. "If this is true," he thought, "it must be because of the way they live. I must learn what it is and follow their example. I wonder what their rules of virtue are."

After the memorial services for his son were completed, the teacher called Culla-Dhammapāla, his best student, and announced that he was going on a trip. The teacher put him in charge of the school during his absence and asked him to teach all the lessons until he returned, but he didn't mention where he was going.

The teacher secretly gathered some bones of a wild goat, thoroughly cleaned them, sprinkled them with scented oil, and packed them carefully in a cloth. Then he left for Kāsi.

When he reached Dhammapāla Village, he asked for Mahā-Dhammapāla's house. At the gate, he was met by a servant who took his umbrella and bag.

"Please tell Mahā-Dhammapāla that his son's teacher is here from Takkasilā to speak with him," the teacher said.

Mahā-Dhammapāla quickly went to the door and invited the teacher in, seated him on a chair, and performed a host's duty by washing his feet and serving him some refreshments.

When the brahmin had completed all the formalities, the teacher solemnly announced, "Brahmin, while your son, Culla-Dhammapāla, was mastering all his subjects, I quickly recognized that he was my brightest student, and I appointed him as my assistant. Suddenly, by an unfortunate turn of circumstances, he had an accident and lost his life. Sir, all component things are transitory. Please do not grieve for him!"

Mahā-Dhammapāla clapped his hands and laughed loudly. "Why do you laugh, sir?" the teacher asked in a grave voice. "It was not my son who died!" Mahā-Dhammapāla answered with conviction. "It must have been someone else!"

"No, Brahmin. I assure you, your son is dead." the teacher replied firmly. "Look! Here are his bones!" He carefully unwrapped the bones and showed them to the brahmin. "These are your son's bones. I have respectfully brought them to you."

"Those are in no way my son's bones!" Mahā-Dhammapāla declared. "They are perhaps the bones of a goat or a dog. My son is not dead. In our family, going back seven generations, no one has ever died in his youth. You are not telling the truth!"

At that moment, everyone in the house clapped their hands and laughed aloud at the absurd idea that Culla-Dhammapāla, while still a young man, could have died.

The teacher was delighted at this wonderful affirmation of Culla-Dhammapāla's claim. He immediately assured Mahā-Dhammapāla that his son was, indeed, alive and well, and he explained the true purpose for his visit.

"Sir," he continued, "there must be a good reason that no one in your family dies before reaching a ripe old age. What is this reason? Is there some holy practice which you all follow to be assured of such longevity?"

"We observe righteousness at all times and in all things," Mahā-Dhammapāla explained. "Recognizing that all life is precious, we refrain from killing even the smallest living being. This is one reason why no one in our family dies while young.

"We do not envy others their happiness nor covet their possessions. This is another reason why no one in our family dies while young.

"Knowing that a liar will commit any kind of sin, never, not even in jest, do we tell a lie. This is another reason why no one in our family dies while young.

"We avoid bad companions and always associate with the wise. We do not do anything which the wise condemn. This is another reason why no one in our family dies while young.

"We give everyone a chance to speak and listen to him, but, repudiating the ideas of the ignorant, we adhere to the views of the wise. Trying not to associate with fools, we seek friendship with the wise. This is another reason why no one in our family dies while young.

"As we prepare to give alms, we feel joy. While giving alms, we are joyful. After giving alms, we never feel regret. This is another reason why no one in our family dies while young.

"We give to Pacceka Buddhas, to wanderers, to brahmins, to vagrants, to beggars, and to all who are in need. To the hungry we give food, and to the thirsty we give drink. This is another reason why no one in our family dies while young.

"We are faithful to our spouses and never stray outside our marriage vows. This is another reason why no one in our family dies while young.

"We never even think of taking anything, no matter how valuable or how insignificant, which belongs to another. This is another reason why no one in our family dies while young.

"We do not drink alcohol or use drugs which cloud the mind. This is another reason why no one in our family dies while young.

"The children who are taught by their parents to observe these ten virtues are inclined to learning, to righteousness, and to discipline. Everyone in this household, including the servants, practices these ten virtues for the sake of a good rebirth so as not to go to hell. Righteousness protects the righteous as a sturdy umbrella keeps one dry during the monsoon rain. This is why I am sure that my son still lives. Righteousness preserves Culla-Dhammapāla, safe and happy."

"This journey of mine has been a good one!" exclaimed the teacher. "It has indeed been fruitful! I am overjoyed to have learned the ten virtues which protect your family, and, henceforth, I, too, will practice them."

Mahā-Dhammapāla inscribed the ten virtues on a palm leaf for the teacher to take with him. The teacher stayed in the village for a few days before returning to Takkasilā. On his return, he resumed teaching all his students, including Culla-Dhammapāla. When the boy was proficient in all arts and crafts, the teacher sent him home with many followers.

Having concluded his story, the Buddha taught the Dhamma to his father, and the king attained the third path. Then the Buddha identified the birth: "At that time, King Suddhodana was Mahā-Dhammapāla, Sāriputta was the teacher, my followers were the retinue, and I was Culla-Dhammapāla."

175

A Mess of Cow's Fodder
Bilārikosiya Jātaka

It was while staying at Jetavana that the Buddha told this story about a bhikkhu who was devoted to generosity.

This bhikkhu was so charitable that he never ate without sharing his alms, nor did he take even a sip of water unless he was able to share the water with another.

One day, in the Hall of Truth, the other bhikkhus were talking about his excellent qualities. When the Buddha heard what they were discussing, he sent for that bhikkhu and asked whether he was truly so devoted to generosity.

He answered that it was true.

"Long ago," the Buddha said, "this man was faithless and stingy. He wouldn't part with so much as a drop of oil on the tip of a blade of grass. After I humbled him and taught him about the benefits of generosity, he was completely reformed, and that lesson has remained with him even into this life." At the bhikkhus' request, the Buddha told this story of the past.

Long, long ago, when Brahmadatta was reigning in Bārānasi, the Bodhisatta was born into an extremely wealthy family. At his father's death, he inherited all the family properties and business.

One day, as he was reviewing his possessions and accounts, he reflected, "All of this wealth belongs to me, but where are those who accumulated it? It behooves me to distribute my wealth by giving alms." He built an alms-hall in front of his house and gave generously every day. He practiced generosity for the rest of his life and charged his son to continue this practice. When he died, he was reborn as Sakka in Tāvatimsa. The son gave alms as his father had done, and similarly gave his son the responsibility of continuing that tradition of generosity. When he died, he was reborn as Canda, the deva of the moon. His son was reborn as Suriya, the deva of the sun; his son was reborn as Mātali, Sakka's charioteer; and his son was reborn as Pañcasikha, one of the Gandhabbas. His son, the sixth generation, a man named Bilārikosiya, however, was hardhearted, cold, and stingy. He pulled down the alms-hall and thrashed anyone who dared to ask him for even a sip of water. During his whole life, he never gave anyone so much as a drop of oil on the tip of a blade of grass.

One day, Sakka was surveying the world and wondered whether or not the custom of generosity that he had established had continued. He immediately realized that his son had continued to give and had been born as Canda, that his son had been born as Suriya, that his son had been born as Mātali, and that his son had been born as Pañcasikha. Then he saw that Bilārikosiya, the sixth in line, had broken the tradition.

Sakka decided to humiliate this selfish descendent and to teach him the benefits of generosity. He summoned Canda, Suriya, Mātali, and Pañcasikha. "Sirs," he began, "the sixth in our line, a man named Bilārikosiya, has violated our family tradition of generosity. He has torn down the family alms-hall, he drives all beggars away with blows, and he begrudges even a trifle to anyone. Let us teach him a lesson he'll never forget! We must disguise ourselves as brahmins and go to Bārānasi." They all agreed and descended to earth.

When they arrived at the ancestral mansion, Bilārikosiya was at home, having returned from the palace, where he had gone that morning to wait upon the king. Asking his companions to wait and then to follow him, one after another, Sakka stepped through the doorway.

As soon as he saw Bilārikosiya, Sakka shouted, "Sir! Give me something to eat!"

"There is nothing for you to eat here!" Bilārikosiya replied gruffly. "Go somewhere else!"

"Sir!" Sakka retorted, "when a brahmin asks for food, he should not be refused!"

"In my house, there is neither cooked food nor food to be cooked. Go away!"

"Great Sir," Sakka said, "Let me give you a piece of ancient wisdom."

"I don't want your ancient wisdom!" Bilārikosiya protested, "Go away, and do not darken my door again!"

Ignoring him, Sakka continued, "Just to avoid giving, you say that you have nothing, but anyone can see that your storerooms are full. It is a great sin to compound one's stinginess with a lie. The virtuous man lives to give because he is both kind and wise."

Sakka's words pricked the miser's conscience a little, and he relented slightly. "All right," he said, "you might as well come in. You will get something or other."

As soon as Sakka had gone inside, Canda went to the door and asked for food.

"There's no food for you! Go away!" Bilārikosiya shouted.

"But, sir," Canda insisted, "there is already one brahmin inside, so I suppose there must be something for me, too."

"There is no free meal for a brahmin!" shouted the miser. "Be off!"

"If, fearing hunger, a man becomes stingy," Canda declared, "his greed will be repaid with dire hunger in this world and in the next. By overcoming greed and giving freely, one protects himself both now and in the future."

"All right," Bilārikosiya relented, "you might as well come in. You will get something or other."

As soon as Canda had gone inside, Suriya went to the door and asked for food.

"There's no food for you! Go away!" Bilārikosiya shouted.

"But, sir," Suriya insisted, "there are already two brahmins inside, so I suppose there is something for me, too."

"Be off!" Bilārikosiya replied.

"It's hard for wicked men to imitate the good and to give as they generously give," Suriya declared. "When, at last, men pass away, the wicked fall into hell and the good rise up to heaven."

"All right," Bilārikosiya relented, "you might as well come in. You will get something or other."

As soon as Suriya had gone inside, Mātali went to the door and asked for food.

"There's no food for you! Go away!" Bilārikosiya shouted.

"But, sir," Mātali insisted, "there are already three brahmins inside, so I suppose there is something for me, too."

"Be off!" Bilārikosiya replied.

"Though having little, some never fail to give," Mātali declared. "Though having plenty, some never give at all. The small gift from the poor is worth one hundred thousand coins from the rich."

"All right," Bilārikosiya relented, "you might as well come in. You will get something or other."

As soon as Mātali had gone inside, Pañcasikha went to the door and asked for food.

"There's no food for you! Go away!" Bilārikosiya shouted.

"But, sir," Pañcasikha insisted, "there are already four brahmins inside, so I suppose there is something for me, too."

"Be off!" Bilārikosiya replied.

"One thousand coins from a millionaire," Pañcasikha declared, "is nothing compared to the small gift from one who lives on scraps if he is virtuous."

"What do you mean, sir?" Bilārikosiya asked, "Are you saying that a poor man's miserable offering is worth more than a rich man's gift of one thousand coins?"

"Someone who lives an evil life," Pañcasikha replied, "has already discounted the value of what he gives. If he kills or steals, nothing he gives can compare with what has been rightfully obtained and is given with a pure heart."

"All right," Bilārikosiya relented, "you might as well come in. You will get something or other."

The miser beckoned to one of his servants and ordered her to give each of the five brahmins a measure of rice in the husk.

"We never touch rice in the husk," the mendicants told her.

"Master," she said, "they say that they never touch rice in the husk!"

"Well, give them husked rice," Bilārikosiya ordered.

"We accept nothing uncooked," they told her.

"Master," she said, "they say that they accept nothing uncooked!"

"Well, then, cook some cow's fodder, and give it to them!" Bilārikosiya ordered.

She quickly prepared a pot of cow's fodder, and put some in each bowl. Each one put a little of the fodder in his mouth and let it stick in his throat. Rolling their eyes back in their heads, all five of them swooned and collapsed as if they were dead.

Terribly shaken, the servant hurriedly told Bilārikosiya, "Master, those brahmins have choked to death on the cow's fodder!"

"Oh, no!" Bilārikosiya cried. "People will criticize me and call me a villain for giving fodder to those delicate brahmins and killing them!"

"Quick!" he ordered. "Cook a pot of the finest rice! Clean out their bowls, and fill them with the rice! Quick, before anyone comes!"

As soon as the maid had done this, Bilārikosiya went to the door and called out to passers-by, "Look! I gave these brahmins the most fragrant rice from my own table, but they were greedy and gobbled it in big mouthfuls so quickly that they choked. Now they are all dead. I call you to witness that I am innocent in this case!"

As the crowd peered curiously through the door at the brahmins lying on the floor, the five of them suddenly jumped up, spat out the fodder, and declared loudly, "Look at the craftiness of this stingy merchant! He says that he gave us his own food, but, actually, he gave us a mess of cow's fodder. Only when he thought we were dead, did he have this rice prepared!"

"Blind, greedy fool!" the people shouted at Bilārikosiya. "We are not surprised that you gave these brahmins coarse cow's food! For many years, we have seen what you are like! You have broken your family's long tradition of generosity! You destroyed the alms-hall, and you abuse mendicants every day! After you die, will you carry your money in a sack around your neck?"

"Do you know who began building the wealth of this house?" Sakka asked the crowd in a ringing voice.

"We have heard," someone replied, "of the great Bārānasi merchant, who lived here long ago."

"He built the alms-halls," another continued, "and began a tradition of magnanimous generosity."

"Do you know what has become of him?" Sakka inquired further.

"No, we don't." they answered together.

"I was that merchant!" Sakka proclaimed. "Because of my great generosity I was born as Sakka." Indicating his companions one by one, he continued, "My son, who maintained the tradition, was born as Canda. His son was born as Suriya, his son was born as Mātali, his son was born as Pañcasikha, and his son is this cheapskate!

"Our rebirth proves that generosity is very powerful, indeed. Therefore, wise men ought to give generously and to live virtuously!"

To prove who they were, the five devas assumed their divine forms and rose into the air. As they stood in mid-air in all their glory, Sakka continued, "We came here from our heavenly realms to reform this mean-spirited miser, Bilārikosiya, the sixth generation of our family, a traitor to our tradition. Knowing that, because of his stinginess, he would be reborn in hell, we came out of pity for him!"

"Lords, from this moment onward, I will follow the family custom!" Bilārikosiya declared as he paid his respects to his heavenly forebears. "I promise to practice generosity and to distribute alms. Henceforth, I will never eat a single bite without first sharing what I have with others. I will never take a sip of water without sharing. I promise to become kind-hearted and charitable!"

Sakka was extremely pleased with this declaration and established Bilārikosiya in the five precepts. Then the five devas returned to their respective heavens. As long as he lived, Bilārikosiya distributed generous alms to mendicants every day. When he passed away, he, too, was reborn in Tāvatimsa.

Having concluded his story, the Buddha added, "Thus, Bhikkhus, you see that, in the past, this bhikkhu was exceedingly stingy, but I humbled him and taught him the power of generosity. Once he reformed, that habit of generosity has continued from life to life." Then the Buddha identified the birth: "At that time, this generous bhikkhu was Bilārikosiya, Sāriputta was Canda, Moggallāna was Suriya, Mahā-Kassapa was Mātali, Ānanda was Pañcasikha, and I was Sakka."

176
Filial Devotion
Mātuposaka Jātaka

It was while staying at Jetavana that the Buddha told this story about a bhikkhu who looked after his mother.

When other bhikkhus learned that a certain bhikkhu was supporting laypeople, they criticized him and complained to the Buddha about it. The Buddha, however, praised him, saying, "Do not reproach this bhikkhu. Long ago, when separated from his mother, a wise being pined and starved himself." At the bhikkhus' request, the Buddha told this story of the past.

Long, long ago, when Brahmadatta was reigning in Bārānasi, the Bodhisatta was born as a white elephant in the Himavat. When he matured, he became the leader of a great herd of eighty thousand elephants, but, by that time, his mother had become old and blind. Once, he led his herd to forage for food, and they were gone for several days. Every day, after all the elephants were satisfied, he assigned a different young elephant to deliver some of the sweet wild fruit they had found to his mother. Those he sent, however, were always selfish and negligent, and they ate the fruit themselves. When he returned to see his mother, he learned that she had not received any food while he had been gone. He immediately resolved to leave the herd and to take care of her himself. One night, without telling any of the other elephants, he led his mother away and headed for Mount Candorana. When they arrived there, he found a secluded cave near a large lake and made her comfortable.

One day, near that lake, a hunter from Bārānasi got hopelessly lost in the jungle. Exhausted from wandering and afraid that he would never find his way out, he started wailing loudly and bemoaning his fate.

Hearing the sound, the white elephant thought, "There is a man in trouble nearby. It will not do for him to come to grief while I am here, able to save him!" He moved carefully in the direction of the noise. As soon as the hunter saw the elephant, however, he fled in fear. "Sir!" the elephant called out. "Don't be afraid. Tell me why you are upset."

"My Lord," the man replied, surprised to be greeted in such a friendly manner by a fully-grown tusker, "I am lost in this jungle. I have been wandering without food for seven days."

"Don't worry, sir," the elephant said comfortingly. "I will take you to safety." He knelt so that the hunter could easily climb onto his back, and carried him out of the jungle. He showed the hunter the overgrown path that led to the highway to the capital. Then he returned to his mother.

Even while retreating in panic from the great elephant, the greedy hunter had noticed that this was not an ordinary creature. The man had never seen an elephant of such a pure white hue, and he had promised himself that, if he survived, he would inform the king of the existence of this magnificent beast. As he was being carried out of the jungle, he was able to take note of all the landmarks he passed. After he was dropped off, he made his way to Bārānasi as fast as possible.

It so happened that the state elephant, which the king had ridden in every procession and battle of his reign, had just died of old age. When the hunter finally reached Bārānasi, he heard the royal proclamation, accompanied by a drum, that anyone knowing of an elephant suitable for this position should report to the king's men immediately.

Sure that his fortune was made, the hunter hurried to the palace. Requesting an audience, he told the king that, in the distant jungle, near a great lake, he had seen a splendid white elephant, without flaw or blemish. He offered to show the way to the royal mahouts.

A large party set out at once. Following the landmarks he had noted, the hunter led the king's men directly to the spot where he been rescued. The white elephant was feeding at the edge of the lake, and, as soon as he saw the hunter, he realized that he had been betrayed.

"Although I am strong enough to subdue one thousand elephants, and, although I could destroy an entire army if sufficiently enraged, I must not permit anger to arise," he vowed. "If I give way to wrath, my virtue will be impaired. Today, I will not get angry, even if these men stab me with spears." Standing perfectly still, he lowered his great head.

The chief mahout immediately recognized the rarity and the excellence of this pure white elephant. Stepping respectfully into the lotus-covered water, he extended his hand and said, "Come, my son!" Gently grasping the beast by the trunk, he led him out of the lake. The elephant offered no resistance and allowed himself to be led in this way all the way to Bārānasi. The journey took a full week.

When the white elephant didn't return, his mother surmised that he had been caught by the king's men. "All these trees and flowers will continue growing," she sighed, "but my son will be far away from me." Then she proudly declared, "He must be carrying some great king on procession or into battle. Surely, my dear son will comport himself nobly and receive great honor."

The mahout immediately sent a message to inform the king that the great beast had been captured and that he was perfectly suited for the king. In preparation for their arrival, King Brahmadatta had the city decorated like Tāvatimsa. At the city gate, the mahout and the elephant were greeted with music and garlands. Then they were escorted in a procession to the royal stables, where a special stall had been arranged for the magnificent white elephant.

As soon as he heard that the elephant had arrived, King Brahmadatta went to the stables with all sorts of succulent fruit and tender grasses. He offered these delicacies to the white elephant, but the animal would not touch any of the food. "Please eat, noble elephant!" the mahout urged. "You must keep up your strength in order to serve your king!" The king himself also urged the elephant to eat, but the animal replied, "Poor and blind, she waits for me near Mount Candorana. Without me, she is helpless!"

"Noble animal," the king asked, "who is poor and blind? Who waits for you near Mount Candorana?"

"It is my mother!" the elephant replied. "She is blind and helpless. Without me, her only son, to care for her, she must be hungry and forlorn! At this moment, she is probably striking her foot against the root of a tree, searching for me!"

When he heard this, King Brahmadatta was filled with compassion. He ordered the mahout to free the white elephant and to allow him to return to care for his mother. Before leaving Bārānasi, the elephant spoke eloquently to the king about virtue. As he departed, crowds of people showered him with flowers.

When he reached the lake, he found his mother, weak from hunger and sick with sorrow. To refresh her, he drew cool water from the lake with his trunk and gently sprinkled her with it. Without moving, she reproached the sky king for raining unseasonably while her dear son was away from her.

"Get up, Mother!" the white elephant said softly. "Why are you lying there when I have come back to you? Out of pity, the king released me and sent me safely home to you!"

"Long live that king!" his mother cried joyfully. "For returning my dutiful son to me, long may he reign in great prosperity!"

King Brahmadatta did not forget the white elephant. Not far from the lake, he established a town and charged the inhabitants to look after the white elephant and his blind mother. When, at last, she died, the white elephant went to a hermitage named Karandaka where five hundred ascetics resided. Because the white elephant was there, the king generously supported the ascetics.

In Bārāṇasi, the king had a likeness of the white elephant carved in stone, and he paid great respect to it with garlands and incense. Once a year, people from all over Jambudīpa gathered around the statue to celebrate the Elephant Festival in honor of the noble white elephant who refused to eat until reunited with his mother.

Having concluded his story, the Buddha taught the Dhamma, and the bhikkhu who supported his mother was established in the first path. Then the Buddha identified the birth: "At that time, Ānanda was the king, Queen Mahā-Māyā was the blind mother elephant, and I was the noble white elephant."

177

A Debt Remembered
Junha Jātaka

It was while staying at Jetavana that the Buddha told this story about the boons granted to Venerable Ānanda.

During the first twenty years after his Enlightenment, the Buddha had various attendants, including Venerable Nāgasamala, Venerable Nāgita, Venerable Upavana, Venerable Sunakkhatta, Venerable Cunda, Venerable Nanda, Venerable Sagata, and Venerable Meghiya.

One day, the Buddha announced to the bhikkhus that he would like to have a permanent attendant. "I have gotten old," he said. "Sometimes, when I say, 'Let's go this way,' my attendants insist on going another way. Some attendants are careless and drop my bowl and robe on the ground. I want you to choose one bhikkhu to be a permanent attendant."

There was quite a commotion since many, beginning with Venerable Sāriputta, called out, "I will serve you, Venerable Sir! Allow me to serve you!"

The Buddha refused all of them saying, "I have heard your offers, but no!"

Then the bhikkhus urged Venerable Ānanda, "Friend, ask for the post of attendant."

Venerable Ānanda replied, "If the Blessed One will grant me eight boons, four positive and four negative, I will be his attendant. I ask that the Blessed

One never give me a robe which he has received; that he never give me any choice food which he has received; that he not arrange a special residence for me; that he not take me with him when he is invited; that I be allowed to accept invitations on his behalf; that I be allowed to introduce visitors who arrive from afar; that I be allowed to approach the Blessed One whenever doubt arises; and that, whenever the Blessed One gives a discourse in my absence, he repeat that discourse to me as soon as I return. If the Blessed One will grant me these eight boons, then I will attend him." The Buddha granted those eight boons to him, and Venerable Ānanda attended the Buddha for the next twenty-five years.

Among all the bhikkhus, Venerable Ānanda was foremost in five qualities. He was also accomplished in seven ways. Rightly renowned among the Buddha's great disciples, Venerable Ānanda shone like the moon in the sky.

One day, in the Hall of Truth, bhikkhus were talking about Venerable Ānanda. When the Buddha heard what they were discussing, he said, "This is not the first time, Bhikkhus, that I granted a boon to Ānanda." Then the Buddha told this story of the past.

Long, long ago, when Brahmadatta was reigning in Bārānasi, the Bodhisatta was born as his son. He was named Prince Junha, and, when he was old enough, he went to study in Takkasilā.

One night, as he was returning home in the dark from his teacher's house, he bumped into a brahmin. When the man fell to the ground, his almsbowl broke, and he gave a sharp cry. Extremely apologetic for his carelessness, Prince Junha immediately turned around and helped the man to his feet. "Look at this, my son!" the brahmin complained. "You have broken my almsbowl! Now you should give me, at least, the price of a meal!"

"I am sorry!" the prince repeated. "At this time, I cannot give you the price of a meal, but I am Prince Junha, son of King Brahmadatta of Kāsi. After I have inherited the kingdom, you may come to me and ask for the money." Both the prince and the brahmin continued on their separate ways.

Prince Junha completed his education, took leave of his teacher, and returned to Bārānasi. King Brahmadatta was pleased to see how much his son had learned. "Before my death, I have been blessed to see my son!" he rejoiced. "Now he has been well educated, and he will become king!" King Brahmadatta raised the white umbrella over his son and declared him to be King Junha. The prince graciously accepted the throne and began ruling righteously.

As soon as the brahmin in distant Takkasilā heard about the ascension of the new king, he set out for Bārānasi. When he arrived, he found the city beautifully decorated and saw the king riding his elephant in a procession.

The brahmin stood on a slightly elevated spot, stretched out his hand, and cried, "Victory to the king!"

King Junha passed by without noticing him.

"Your Majesty!" the brahmin shouted, realizing that he had been over-looked. "Hear what I have to say! I have come a long way, and I have a good reason to speak with you today!"

King Junha turned his elephant and replied, "Sir, I have heard you, and I have returned. Please tell me what brought you here? What reason do have to speak with me?"

"Sire," the brahmin answered boldly, "I ask that you grant me five villages, one hundred servants, seven hundred cows, gold, and two wives of suitable station for me!"

"Do you have a special power, a charm, or a spell that I should fear?" the king asked. "Are there yakkhas ready to do your work? Or do you, perhaps, have a claim for having served me in the past?"

"No, Sire," replied the brahmin, "I have no special power, no charm, nor spell that you should fear. There are no yakkhas ready to do my work, nor have I ever worked for you. We have, however, met before."

"I can't recall ever having seen your face," the king told him. "Please tell me when and where we met."

"Some years ago, Sire, in fair Takkasilā," the brahmin explained, "on a pitch dark night, you and I collided. I was knocked to the ground, and my bowl was broken. You helped me to my feet, and we had a brief but friendly chat. That was the only time we met."

"Ah, yes!" replied the king. "Now I remember it well! Brahmin, whenever a wise man meets a good man, he should not let that acquaintance fall away. Nor should he forget a promise he has made. Only a fool is ungrateful, and only a fool forgets. Even a trifle done by a wise man should be remembered. Long ago, I promised you recompense. Therefore, today, I grant the boons you ask: five choice villages, one hundred servants, seven hundred head of cattle, gold, and two wives suitable to your station."

"Sire, it is good when the good agree!" the brahmin declared. "I came believing in your virtue, and I have not been disappointed! May you continue to rule in righteousness!"

The king gave great honor to the brahmin who had believed that he would, indeed, keep his word, spoken long before.

Having concluded his story, the Buddha said, "You see, Bhikkhus, that this is not the first time that I have satisfied Ānanda with boons." Then the Buddha identified the birth: "At that time, Ānanda was the brahmin, and I was Junha."

178
Despising No One
Samvara Jātaka

It was while staying at Jetavana that the Buddha told this story about a bhikkhu who had given up striving.[1]

A young man, who came from a good family in Sāvatthī, had become a bhikkhu after hearing the Buddha teach. He had accomplished all the tasks set by his teachers and preceptors and had memorized the Pātimokkha. After five years of study he requested meditation instruction and chose a remote village near the border of Kosala where he could retire to the forest for intensive practice. There he built a hut of leaves. When the villagers saw him, they were so pleased with his demeanor that they offered to supply all his needs.

During the three months of the rainy season, he zealously endeavored to perfect his concentration, but, at the end of that time, he felt that his efforts had been in vain. Concluding that he had no penchant for meditation, he resigned himself to failure. He decided to give up and return to Jetavana where he could, at least, see the beautiful face of the Buddha and hear his sweet words.

---

1   The occasion for this story is the same as that for Tale 65.

His teachers and friends were surprised to see him back at the monastery. When he informed them that he had given up meditating, they scolded him and took him directly to the Buddha.

Seeing them coming, the Buddha asked the bhikkhus why they were bringing him, obviously against his will.

His friends answered, "This bhikkhu has ceased striving."

"Is this true?" the Lord asked the young bhikkhu.

"Yes, Venerable Sir, it is true," answered the bhikkhu.

"Why, Bhikkhu," the Buddha asked him, "have you quit trying? In my Sāsana, no success is possible for a slothful man. Only strenuous effort can lead one to Nibbāna. Long ago, you were strong and easy to teach. Because of that nature, even though you were the youngest of the one hundred sons of the king of Bāranasi, by following the advice of a wise man, you obtained the white umbrella." Then the Buddha told this story of the past.

Long, long ago, when Brahmadatta was reigning in Bāranasi, he had one hundred sons. To each of his sons, the king assigned a separate teacher, with orders to instruct the prince in everything he needed to know. The youngest son was named Samvara. The courtier who taught him was the Bodhisatta himself. Wise and learned, this teacher was like a father to Prince Samvara.

As each of the princes completed his education, his teacher took him to the king, who bestowed upon the young man a province which he could govern on his own.

As Prince Samvara was finishing his studies, he asked his teacher, "Sir, if my father sends me to a province, what am I to do?"

"My son," his teacher replied, "when a province is offered to you, you should refuse it. Say to the king, 'My Lord, I am the youngest of all. If I go, there will be no one near you. Let me remain here at your feet.'"

Not long afterwards, Prince Samvara was, indeed, taken before the king. As he stood respectfully at one side, the king asked him, "Well, my son, have you finished your studies?"

"Yes, Father," replied the prince.

"Choose a province," ordered the king.

"My Lord," Prince Samvara answered, "if I go, there will be emptiness at your feet. Let me remain here near you and nowhere else!"

The king was pleased to hear this and consented. Again Prince Samvara asked his wise teacher, "What else should I to do?"

"Ask the king," said he, "for an old park."

The king consented also to this request.

By giving away the fruits and flowers from the park, Prince Samvara made friends with the powerful people of the city.

Again he asked for advice.

"My boy," answered his teacher, "ask the king for permission to distribute food and money in the city."

Prince Samvara distributed food and money throughout the capital, without the slightest neglect of any person.

Once more he asked his teacher for advice and, receiving permission from the king, he distributed food and wages within the palace itself to all the servants, the cavalry, and the army. He took care of ambassadors and messengers from foreign countries, arranging their lodging and their entertainment. He determined the taxes for all merchants doing business in the city. Everything that had to be arranged, he took upon himself. Prince Samvara was very careful to carry out all these duties with painstaking fairness.

By following the advice of his wise teacher, Prince Samvara made friends with everybody in the royal household, in the capital, and throughout the kingdom. Everyone he met was won over by his kindness, and he was beloved by all.

In due time, the king lay on his deathbed. "When you have passed away, Sire," the ministers asked him, "to whom shall we give the white umbrella?"

"Friends," answered the king, "all my sons have a right to the white umbrella. Please give it to him who pleases you the most."

Seven days after the king's death, after the funeral ceremonies had been properly performed, the ministers gathered to discuss the succession. "Our king ordered us to give the umbrella to the one who pleases us the most. Certainly, Prince Samvara is the dearest to our hearts," they agreed. They voted unanimously to raise the white umbrella of kingship over the young prince.

When the other ninety-nine princes learned that their father was dead and that Samvara had been declared king, they were very angry. "Samvara is the youngest of us all," they protested. "The umbrella does not belong to him! It rightfully belongs to the eldest among us!"

They sent a letter to Samvara, ordering him to either resign the umbrella or fight. As soon as they had dispatched the letter, the brothers marched and surrounded the city with their armies.

The king asked his teacher what he ought to do.

"Your Majesty," he answered, "you must not fight with your brothers. Divide the treasure that belonged to your father into one hundred portions. Send your brothers their ninety-nine fair shares with this message, 'Please accept this share of your father's treasure for I will not fight with you.'" Samvara did as his teacher advised.

Prince Uposatha, the eldest, summoned the other princes. "Brothers," he announced, "there is no way for us to overcome the king. We tried to treat him like an enemy, but he refuses to fight. Instead, he has sent us his wealth. Since we cannot all be king at the same time, I suggest that we raise the white umbrella over him and let him alone be king. Let us meet with him, hand over the royal treasure, and return to our own provinces."

All ninety-nine princes agreed to end their siege of the capital. Laying down their arms, the brothers entered the capital on foot, each followed by his army. King Samvara, seated on a magnificent throne under the white umbrella, welcomed them as they mounted the steps of the palace. Showing all due respect to him as the king, the elder brothers seated themselves humbly.

"My dear brother," Prince Uposatha addressed the king, "our father must have understood your nature very well. He honored us by bestowing a province upon each one, but he gave nothing to you. Was it while our father was alive or after he died that our kinsmen gave the white umbrella to you? Why is it, Samvara, that you sit above us all? Why shouldn't we unite to take the throne from you?"

"My brother," answered King Samvara, "all in the army are loyal to me because I have always paid them fairly for their service. Nobles and teachers all have received presents from my hand. Since I always try to manage business matters wisely, merchants and tradesmen prosper, and they thank me for it. I always give honor where it is due and, in all humility, respect wise men. I am without envy, and, in every case, I try to do what is right. I have nothing but good intentions. I listen to wise counsel and despise no one."

Prince Uposatha was deeply impressed with this account of his youngest brother's character. He realized that Samvara was not boasting but was speaking the plain truth. "Samvara," he said, "the white umbrella is rightfully yours. Continue to sit above us and to rule wisely in righteousness. We will defend you and protect the kingdom from all foes."

King Samvara honored and feasted all his brothers, who remained with him for a month and a half. At the end of that time, they said to him, "Your Majesty, we must return to our homes and make sure that all is peaceful in our provinces. All happiness to your rule!"

Throughout his reign, King Samvara continued to follow the wise counsel of his teacher. At the end of his days, he went to swell the hosts of heaven.

Having concluded his story, the Buddha added, "Long ago, Bhikkhu, you carefully followed instruction. Why do you now not maintain your efforts?" Then the Buddha taught the Dhamma, and that bhikkhu attained the first path. Finally, the Buddha identified the birth, "At that time, this bhikkhu was the great king, Samvara; Sāriputta was Prince Uposatha; the senior bhikkhus were the other brothers; the rest of my followers were their courtiers; and I was the teacher who advised the king."

179
Protecting Relatives
Bhaddasāla Jātaka

It was while staying at Jetavana that the Buddha told this story about help-ing one's relatives.[2]

King Pasenadi was distressed that bhikkhus, after they had received alms from his kitchen, did not stay to eat at the palace. When he asked the Bud-dha about this, the Buddha answered that the bhikkhus prefer to eat where they are served with friendship.

"With whom do the bhikkhus find friendship?" the king asked. "With their relatives or with the Sākyan families," the Buddha answered.

King Pasenadi conjectured that, if he married a Sākyan woman, the bhik-khus would feel that they were related by ties of marriage and would, thus, feel more friendly toward him. To this end, he sent a message to Kapilavat-thu: "Please give me one of your daughters in marriage for I wish to become connected to your family."

When the proud Sākyan princes received this message, they called a meeting. "The king of Kosala has authority over our land," one prince said,

---

2   The first part of the occasion for this story is the same as that for Tale 136, where it is told in detail.

"and, if we refuse his request for a daughter in marriage, he will be angry. On the other hand, it would be a violation of our tradition to give one of our daughters to a non-Sākyan. What should we do?"

Mahānāma spoke up and said, "I have a daughter, Vāsabha-Khattiyā, who is sixteen years old. She is very beautiful, and all her signs are auspicious. From my side, she is of noble birth, but her mother, Nāgamundā, is a slave. We can send her, as a Sākyan girl, nobly born, to the king of Kosala."

The Sākyan elders agreed. They summoned the messengers and told them that they were ready to give a daughter of their clan to the king of Kosala. They added that the messengers might take her with them at once.

"These Sākyans are desperately proud," the messengers said to each other, "especially in matters of birth. They might try to give us a girl who is not a true Sākyan. We must make sure that the girl they are offering us is really of noble birth." To the Sākyan elders they said, "We will take her, but only if we can see that she is allowed to eat with you."

After the messengers had gone to the lodgings arranged for them, the Sākyans met to resolve this new complication.

Mahānāma said, "Don't worry. I have a way to get around it. At my mealtime bring Vāsabha-Khattiyā in to join me, dressed up in all her finery. Then, just as I have taken one mouthful, produce a letter, and say, 'My Lord, you have just received this letter from a neighboring king. It seems to be urgent. Be pleased to hear his message at once."

They agreed to the plan. As Mahānāma was taking his meal, Vāsabha-Khattiyā was beautifully dressed and made up.

"Bring my daughter," Mahānāma said, "and let her take food with me."

"In a moment," they replied. "Just as soon as she is properly dressed." After a short delay, she was brought in.

Expecting to take food with her father, she dipped her hand into the same dish. Mahānāma had taken one mouthful and put it in his mouth, but, just as he stretched out his hand for another, they brought him a letter, saying, "My Lord, a neighboring king has sent an urgent letter to you. Be pleased to hear his message at once."

"Go on with your meal, my dear," Mahānāma told his daughter. Holding his right hand in the dish, with his left he took the letter and looked at it. As he examined the message the maiden went on eating. When she had finished, he used a finger bowl and rinsed out his mouth. The Kosalan messengers had been watching carefully, but they had not perceived the ruse. They thought that Mahānāma had eaten from the same dish, so they were convinced that Vāsabha-Khattiyā was his legitimate daughter.

Mahānāma sent Vāsabha-Khattiyā away in great pomp, and the messengers took her to Sāvatthī. They told the king that they had seen Mahānāma and his daughter eating together and assured the king that she was a purebred Sākyan lady. King Pasenadi was delighted. He ordered that the whole city be decorated, placed her upon a great heap of treasure, and, by sprinkling her with lustral water, made her his chief queen.

Vāsabha-Khattiyā was dearly beloved by the king, and it was not long before she conceived. She delivered a healthy son, and the king sent a message to his grandmother: "A son has been born to Vāsabha-Khattiyā, daughter of the Sākyan king. What should we call him?"

When the king's grandmother heard the question, she declared, "Even before Vāsabha-Khattiyā had a son, she was more than all the world to the king. Now she will be the king's darling (vallabha)."

The courtier returned to the king, but, being slightly deaf, he had misheard and reported, "Your grandmother said that the new prince should be called Vidūdabha." The king assumed that this was an old family name, so he named his son Vidūdabha.

The prince grew up in the palace. One day, when he was seven, he said to his mother, "Mother, all the other princes receive presents from their mother's family. Their grandparents are always sending them all kinds of toys, like elephants, horses, and carts. I have never gotten anything from your parents. I wonder why. Are you an orphan?"

"My dear boy, she replied, "your grandparents on my side are Sākyan kings, but they live a long way off, and that is why they send you nothing."

When he was sixteen, he said, "Mother, I want to see your father's family."

"My dear boy," she replied again, "what would you do when you got there?" Even though she put him off, he begged and pestered her again and again. At last, she relented and said, "Well, go then."

Getting his father's consent, Vidūdabha went to Kapilavatthu with a number of attendants.

Vāsabha-Khattiyā sent a letter ahead of her son, saying, "I am living here happily. Do not let anyone tell my son anything of the secret."

As soon as the Sākyans heard that Vidūdabha was visiting, they declared, "It is impossible to receive him with respect." They sent all their young princes into the countryside.

When Vidūdabha arrived in Kapilavatthu, the Sākyans assembled in the royal rest-house and introduced him to the elders, beginning with, "This is your mother's father" and "This is your mother's brother." Vidūdabha walked from one to the other, saluting each one. He bowed until his back ached, but not one of them returned his greeting. "Why is it that none of you greet me?" he asked.

"My dear boy," one of the elders replied, "all of the younger princes are away in the country." Vidūdabha accepted this explanation and enjoyed the grand entertainment the Sākyans offered him.

After staying a few days, he and his retinue left for home. As soon as they had gone, a slave woman began washing, with milk, the seat which Vidūdabha had used. "Here's the seat where sat the son of Vāsabha-Khattiyā, the slave girl!" she muttered insultingly as she worked.

One of the prince's retainers had forgotten his spear and was just fetching it when he overheard the slave abuse Prince Vidūdabha. He asked what she meant and was informed that Vāsabha-Khattiyā was born of a slave to Mahānāma the Sākyan. After the story was repeated to the soldiers, a great uproar arose, with everyone shouting: "Vāsabha-Khattiyā is a slave woman's daughter!"

When Vidūdabha heard it, he thought coldly, "Let them pour milk over the seat where I sat to clean it! When I become king, I will wash the place with their hearts' blood!"

As soon as the party arrived in Sāvatthī, the courtiers, of course, reported everything to the king. King Pasenadi was furious with the Sākyans for giving him a slave's daughter to marry. He immediately stripped Vāsabha-Khattiyā and Vidūdabha of their royal honors and gave them the allowance he gave to his slaves.

A few days later, the Buddha went to the palace. King Pasenadi paid his respects, sat to one side, and said, "Sir, I have been told that your clansmen gave me a slave's daughter to wed. I am so offended by this Sākyan effrontery that I have cut off the allowances of both mother and son and now grant them only what slaves get."

"Sire," the Buddha replied, "the Sākyans did wrong. If they gave anyone, they should have given a girl of their own blood. But, Your Majesty, I also say this: Vāsabha-Khattiyā is a king's daughter, and, in the house of a noble king, she was sprinkled with lustral water. Vidūdabha, too, was begotten by a noble king. According to wise men of old, the mother's lineage is not important. The lineage of the father is the measure."[3]

When the king heard this, he was pleased, and, saying to himself, "The father's birth is the measure of the person," he restored both mother and son to their previous positions of honor. At that time, the king's commander-in-chief was a Mallan named Bandhula. His wife, Mallikā, was barren, and he told her to return to her family in Kusinārā.

---

3   It was at that point that the Buddha told Tale 7.

"I will go back to my parents' home," Mallikā agreed, "after I have paid my respects to the Buddha." She went to Jetavana, paid her respects to the Buddha, and informed him that she was leaving Sāvatthī.

"Where are you going?" he asked.

"My husband has ordered me to return to my home," she replied.

"Why?" the Buddha asked.

"I am barren, Sir. I have no son."

"If that is all," the Buddha said, "there is no reason for you to leave. Return to your husband."

Mallikā was overjoyed to hear this. She bowed to the Buddha and returned home. When Bandhula asked why she had come back, she answered, "Husband, the Buddha sent me back."

"All right," Bandhula said, allowing her to stay, "the Buddha must have had a good reason for saying that."

Soon after that, Mallikā conceived. In her pregnancy, she had a strong craving and told her husband.

"What is it that you want?" he asked.

"Husband, I want to bathe in and drink the water from the tank in Vesāli where the Licchavis draw lustral water for the sprinkling of their kings."

Bandhula promised to try to satisfy her craving. Seizing his powerful bow, he put his wife in his chariot, left Sāvatthī, and drove to Vesāli.

Near the Vesāli city gate lived a Licchavi named Mahāli, who had been educated by the same teacher as Bandhula. Although Mahāli was blind, he was a wise advisor to the Licchavis. When Mahāli heard the chariot as it crossed the threshold of the gate, he said, "That is the sound of the chariot of Bandhula Malla. Today, there is great danger for the Licchavis!"

The tank in Vesāli was protected by a strong guard, and it was covered with an iron net with a mesh so fine that not even a small bird could get through. Bandhula dismounted from his chariot and put the guards to flight with his skillful swordsmanship. Then he easily burst through the iron net. He led his wife into the tank, bathed her, and gave her water to drink. After bathing himself, he put Mallikā back in the chariot and drove back out of the town by the way he had come.

Meanwhile, the guards had rushed to inform the Licchavi princes, who were furious at this affront to their sovereignty. Five hundred of them harnessed and mounted five hundred war chariots and raced off to capture Bandhula Malla.

As they passed the gate, they stopped to inform Mahāli, and he warned them, "Do not go! He will slay you all."

"Say what you will," they replied. "We are going!"

"Then listen to me! When you come to a place where a wheel has sunk up to the hub, turn back. If you don't turn back then, turn back when you hear the sound of a thunderbolt. If you don't turn back then, turn back when you see a hole in the head of your chariot. Go no further!"

The Licchavi princes left Vesāli in pursuit of Bandhula's chariot.

Mallikā looked back and said, "Husband, there are chariots in sight. They are chasing us."

Bandhula replied, "Tell me when they appear as one chariot."

Mallikā continued watching, and, when all five hundred chariots were lined up and appeared as one, she said, "My Lord, I see them as if there were only one chariot."

"Take the reins," Bandhula ordered, handing her the reins. As he stood to string his great bow, the wheel of his chariot sank into the earth up the hub.

The Licchavis saw the place where the chariot wheel had sunk up the hub, but they did not turn back.

After Bandhula had strung his bow, he tested the string by twanging it, creating a sound like a thunderbolt. The Licchavis heard it, but they did not turn back.

Standing erect in his chariot, Bandhula shot an arrow which pierced the head of each chariot and the body of each Licchavi prince, right where his girdle was fastened. Behind the last chariot, the arrow buried itself in the earth.

Not realizing that they were wounded, the Licchavi princes continued their pursuit. As they came close to Bandhula's chariot, they shouted, "Stop! Hey you! Stop!"

Bandhula stopped his chariot and shouted, "You are all dead men! I cannot fight with the dead."

"What do you mean 'dead'?" they asked.

"Loosen the waistband of the first man," ordered Bandhula. They loosened his girdle, and, the instant it was loosened, he fell down dead.

"All of you are in the same condition," Bandhula told them. "Go home! Set your affairs in order! Give instructions to your wives and families! Then remove your armor!"

They did as he told them. After making arrangements, at the instant each untied his girdle, he died.

Bandhula conveyed Mallikā back to Sāvatthī, and she gave birth to twin boys. After that, she had twin sons fifteen more times, and all of them became accomplished warriors and mighty heroes. Each of her sons had one thousand men under him. When they went with their father to wait upon the king, they filled the courtyard of the palace to overflowing.

One day, some men, who had been falsely charged and had lost their case in court, appealed to Bandhula for justice, claiming that the judges were corrupt and had been bribed to decide against them. Bandhula went to the court, reopened the case, and decided it honestly, giving each man what was rightly his. Many people in the court applauded his fairness.

The king asked what was happening, and, when he heard, he was very pleased. He discharged the corrupt judges and put Bandhula in charge of the court. From that time onward, Bandhula decided cases evenhandedly.

The former judges, deprived of the revenue from their bribes, greatly resented Bandhula. They began slandering him to the king, accusing him of seeking to take the throne for himself. The king listened to these rumors and accusations and grew suspicious. "What can I do?" the king reflected. "If Bandhula is killed here, I will be blamed."

After paying some men to create a disturbance on the border, the king summoned Bandhula. "The borders are ablaze with brigands and rebels. Go there with your sons!" he ordered the commander-in-chief. "Capture the troublemakers, punish them, and restore peace to the region!"

As soon as the hired bandits heard that Bandhula and his thirty-two sons were on their way to the border, they fled. Bandhula quickly restored order and headed back to Sāvatthī. The king had sent other men with instructions to kill Bandhula and all his sons. Not far from the capital, these men ambushed Bandhula. They killed the commander-in-chief and all his sons, decapitated them, and carried all the heads back to the king.

That day, Mallikā had invited the two chief disciples along with five hundred other bhikkhus. Early in the morning, she received a letter informing her that her husband and sons had been killed and beheaded. She read the letter, but, without mentioning the news to anyone, she tucked the letter in her dress and went to offer lunch to the bhikkhus. After the rice had been served, a servant dropped and broke a pot of ghee right in front of the bhikkhus.

"Pots are made to be broken," Venerable Sāriputta said. "Dear lady, do not trouble about it."

Mallikā produced the letter from the fold of her dress and declared, "I have here a letter informing me that my husband and his thirty-two sons have been beheaded. If I do not trouble about that, am I likely to trouble about a dish that is broken?"

At this, Venerable Sāriputta recited the Salla Sutta,[4] which begins "Life is unpredictable and uncertain." After his discourse, all the bhikkhus returned to Jetavana.

---

4   Sutta Nipāta, Mahāvagga 8.

Mallikā summoned her thirty-two daughters-in-law and announced, "Your husbands, though innocent, have reaped the fruit of their former deeds. Do not grieve," she advised them, "nor commit a wrong even worse than the king's by becoming angry."

King Pasenadi's spies heard Mallikā's speech and carried word to the king that she and her daughters-in-law were not angry. When the king heard this, he was deeply distressed and went to Mallikā's house, where he begged forgiveness from her and her son's wives. He offered Mallikā a royal boon, and she graciously accepted.

After arranging the funeral feast, she bathed and went to see the king. "Sire," she said, "you have granted me a boon. The only thing I ask is that you permit my thirty-two daughters-in-law and me to go back to our own homes." The king gave his consent.

Mallikā sent each of her son's wives back to her home, and she herself returned to the home of her family in Kusinārā.

The king gave the post of commander-in-chief to Dīghakārāyana, the son of Bandhula's sister, but this young man felt no loyalty to the king. He was often heard muttering, "The king murdered my uncle."

After the murder of the innocent Bandhula, King Pasenadi was consumed by remorse. He had no peace of mind and felt no joy in being king.

At that time, the Buddha was staying in a park in Ulumpa, a small Sākyan town. King Pasenadi went there, set up camp not far from the park, and went with a few attendants to pay his respects to the Master. When they reached the park, the king handed the five symbols of royalty to Dīghakārāyana and asked the attendants to wait while he went alone into the Buddha's presence.[5]

As soon as the king had gone inside the park, Dīghakārāyana went back to the camp. Leaving only one horse and a female servant for Pasenadi, the commander-in-chief returned with the army to Sāvatthī, where he presented the symbols of royalty to Vidūdabha, thereby declaring him king.

After a pleasant conversation with the Buddha, the king left the park and discovered that he had been abandoned. The servant explained what Dīghakārāyana had done, and the king set out for Rājagaha to ask his nephew, King Ajātasattu, for assistance in capturing Vidūdabha. It was late, however, when he reached the city, and the gates were closed. Exhausted by exposure to wind and sun, he lay down in a shelter and died.

At the first light of morning, the servant began to wail, "My Lord, the king of Kosala is beyond help!" Her cry was heard, and King Ajātasattu was informed. He performed the obsequies for his uncle with great magnificence.

5   This part of the occasion for this story is also described in the Dhammacetiya Sutta (Majjhima Nikāya, 89).

King Vidūdabha, now firmly established on the throne, remembered his grudge against the Sākyans. Resolving to carry out his vow by destroying them one and all, he set out with a large army.

At that time, the Buddha was staying at Jetavana. Surveying the world, he foresaw the destruction threatening his relatives and determined to help them. That afternoon, he went to a spot on the Kosalan border near Kapilavatthu and sat down beneath a small tree which stood near a huge banyan tree. When King Vidūdabha saw the Buddha, he approached and greeted him politely. "Why, Venerable Sir," King Vidūdabha asked, "are you sitting under so thin a tree in all this heat? Please sit beneath this shady banyan, and be cooler."

"Do not worry about that, Sire," the Buddha replied. "The shade of my kindred keeps me cool."

"The Buddha must have come here to protect his clansmen," King Vidūdabha thought. He again paid his respects to the Master and returned to Sāvatthī. The Buddha also returned to Jetavana.

A second and a third time, King Vidūdabha recalled his grudge against the Sākyans. Each time, he set out with his army, and each time, seeing the Buddha seated in the same place, he again returned.

The fourth time that King Vidūdabha remembered his humiliation at the hands of the Sākyans, the Buddha realized that he could no longer protect his kinsmen from the ripening of their previous evildoing, when they had destroyed many innocent lives by throwing poison into a river. Knowing that their past deeds were going to bear fruit, the Buddha did not go to meet King Vidūdabha this time.

Determined to have his revenge, King Vidūdabha attacked Kapilavatthu and slew all the Sākyans, including the babies at their mothers' breasts. Before leaving the city, he took some of their blood and washed the bench where he had once sat. Satisfied that he had fulfilled his vow, he began his return journey.[6]

On the day after the Buddha had stopped King Vidūdabha for the third time, some bhikkhus in the Hall of Truth, were talking about the incident. "Friends," one of them said, "the Buddha's virtue is so great that, just by showing himself, he was able to turn the king back and to save his kinsmen from death. He is a good friend to his clan!"

---

6   That night, King Vidūdabha pitched his camp on the dry bed of the Aciravatī River. Some of his men lay on the banks, and others lay on the river bed. After they had lain down, ants appeared on the ground, disturbing some of each group, and those disturbed changed places. During the night, there was a flash flood, and all those who were sleeping on the river bed, including King Vidūdabha, having committed wicked deeds in previous lives, were washed away and carried out to sea. (Dhammapada Commentary to Verse, 47, Burlingame, Volume 2, p. 45).

When the Buddha heard what they were discussing, he said, "Not now only, Bhikkhus, does the Tathāgata act for the benefit of his kinsmen. He did the same long ago." Then he told this story of the past.

Long, long ago, when Brahmadatta was reigning in Bārānasi, he thought, "All over Jambudīpa, kings live in palaces supported by many columns. What if I were to build a palace supported by only one column? That would truly be a marvel, and it would make me the greatest king of all!" He summoned his architects and builders and told them that he wanted them to create a magnificent palace supported entirely on one column.

"Very good," they replied. They went into the forest in search of a tree which was straight, tall, and strong enough to be the single column of such a palace. They were able to find several suitable trees, but the road was too rough and too steep to transport them. The engineers asked the king what to do.

"You must bring one of those trees to Bārānasi immediately!" the king answered.

"Sire," the engineers protested, "that cannot be done!"

"All right," retorted the king, "look for a suitable tree in my park."

The engineers went to the royal park and found a stately sal tree, which was perfect in every way. This majestic tree, however, was revered by people everywhere. Even the royal family paid their respects to the deity that resided there. The engineers were afraid to fell the tree without consulting again with the king. When the king heard that they had found a suitable tree, he replied without hesitation, "Good! Go and cut it down!"

"So be it, Your Majesty!" they said. Respectfully approaching the tree, the engineers offered garlands of fragrant flowers, incense, and oil lamps. When they had finished their worship, they announced, "Seven days from now, we will cut down this tree. This is the king's command. May the deva who dwells in this great tree not blame us! We ask that he please go elsewhere to live."

Bhaddasāla, the deva who resided in that tree, heard this and thought, "These men are determined to cut down this tree and to destroy my home. My life lasts only as long as my dwelling place. All the young sal trees around this tree are the homes of my relatives. If this great tree is cut, they will also be destroyed. My own demise does not touch me nearly as much as the destruction of my kinfolk. It behooves me to protect their lives."

At midnight, Bhaddasāla went to the king's chamber and stood weeping beside the king's bed. The deva's heavenly splendor filled the entire chamber with a bright radiance. When the king saw the deva, he was terrified.

"Who are you, and why are you crying so piteously?" the king asked.

"My name is Bhaddasāla. Throughout your kingdom, Sire, I am renowned as the most auspicious tree. For one thousand years I have stood in the royal park, and many have honored and worshiped me. Countless towns, palaces, and houses, have been built, but I have never been harmed or molested."

"I want to build a glorious palace," the king replied. "You are so mighty and strong that your single column will support it. It will be a great honor for you!"

"Sire, since you are determined to cut me down, please grant me a favor," Bhaddasāla pleaded. "Please cut off my limbs first. Cut the top branches first, then the middle, and, finally, the lower part of me. If you do that, death will not be so hard for me to bear."

The king was puzzled. "How can it be preferable to be cut in that way?" he asked. "Majestic deva, I do not understand why you wish to be cut up piecemeal!"

"My reason is a noble one," Bhaddasāla explained. "All around me, growing well in my shelter, my relatives are prospering. If I am cut first near the root, they will all be crushed by one huge fall, and that will cause them great suffering."

The king was greatly pleased when he heard this. "This is indeed a noble deva, who does not want his relatives to lose their dwelling-places when he loses his!" he exclaimed. "Noble, indeed, is he who acts for his relatives' welfare and happiness."

"Woodland king!" he continued. "I applaud your noble intention. You want to protect your kindred, so let me relieve your fears. I am touched by your tender concern for your family members. It does you great credit, and I honor it. I will be the better for letting you stand unharmed."

Bhaddasāla expressed his gratitude and established the king in generosity and virtue.

The king listened attentively to the great deva's admonitions and lived accordingly, giving gifts and performing other good deeds. When he died, he was reborn in heaven.

Having concluded his story, the Buddha said, "Thus it is, Bhikkhus, that the Tathāgata has often acted for the good of his relatives." Then he identified the birth: "At that time, Ānanda was the king, my followers were the devas residing in the young saplings of the sal tree, and I was Bhaddasāla, the deva of the great sal tree."

180

The Physician
Kāma Jātaka

It was while staying at Jetavana that the Buddha told this story about a brahmin.

One day, a brahmin who lived in Sāvatthī went to the bank of the Aciravatī River and began clearing a piece of land for cultivation.

After gathering alms in the city, the Buddha, knowing full well what was to come, walked out of his way in order to talk with the man. When he saw the brahmin cutting trees, he asked, "What are you doing, Brahmin?"

"Gotama," replied the man, "I am clearing this spot to make a field."

"Very good!" the Buddha said. "Go on with your work."

After that, the Buddha regularly walked that way to speak with the brahmin. They discussed the man's progress as he was removing the felled trunks, as he clearing away the brush and weeds, as he was plowing, and as he was building up the embankments around his field to hold the water.

On the day of sowing, the brahmin declared, "Today, Gotama, I have my own plowing festival. When my grain is ripe, I will give alms in plenty to the Order, with you at their head."

The Buddha accepted his offer with silence and went on his way. Later, the Buddha saw the man standing beside the field and asked, "What are you doing today, Brahmin?"

"Watching my crop, Gotama!"

"Very good," the Buddha said and walked on.

"How often Gotama the ascetic comes this way!" the brahmin thought. "No doubt, he wants food. Well, when the time comes, I will give him plenty!" From these many little talks and this long association, there arose in the brahmin a great confidence in the Buddha.

The field of grain ripened, and the man prepared to harvest his crop on a particular day. The night before that, in the upper reaches of the Aciravatī River, there was a sudden and severe downpour, which created a flash flood. The river rose so fast and so high that the brahmin's entire crop was washed away. When the water subsided, not a single stalk of grain was left standing. When the brahmin saw his empty field, he was so overcome with sorrow that he could barely stand. Somehow, he made it home and, devastated and depressed, lay down on his bed.

Realizing that the brahmin was overwhelmed with sorrow, the Buddha thought, "I will be his support."

The next day, after gathering alms in Sāvatthī, the Buddha sent the bhikkhus back to the monastery and went with an attendant bhikkhu to the brahmin's house.

When the man heard that the Buddha was coming, he took heart. "My friend must have come for some kindly talk."

After accepting the proffered seat, the Buddha asked, "Why are you dejected, Brahmin? What has occurred to upset you?"

"Oh, Gotama!" the man answered. "From the time that I cleared the trees on the land near the river, you know what I've been doing. I planted the seeds, promising you alms when my crop ripened. Now a flood has carried off everything. There is nothing whatsoever left from all my work! More than one hundred wagonloads of grain were swept away! That is why I am grieving."

"But will your grieving bring back what has been lost?" the Buddha asked.

"No, Gotama, it will not."

"If it will not, why grieve?" the Buddha asked him. "When you have wealth or grain, you have it, but, when it is gone, it is gone. All conditioned things are subject to destruction. Do not brood over your grain!"

To comfort him further, the Buddha taught the Kāma Sutta,[1] regarding the abandoning of sensual desires and attachments, at the conclusion of which, the brahmin's grief disappeared, and he attained the first path.

---

1   Sutta Nipāta, Atthakavagga, 1.

Having eased the brahmin's mind and relieved his suffering, the Buddha stood up and returned to the monastery.

Soon, the whole town knew what the Buddha had done. In the Hall of Truth, bhikkhus were talking about this. One of them said, "Friends, it is remarkable how the Buddha made friends with the brahmin, became close to him, consoled his grief by teaching him the Dhamma, and established him on the path!"

When the Buddha heard what they were discussing, he said, "This is not the first time, Bhikkhus, that I have cured this man's grief. I did the same long ago." Then he told this story of the past.

Long, long ago, when Brahmadatta was reigning in Bārānasi, he had two sons. He appointed the elder crown prince and the younger commander-in-chief. When the king died, the courtiers prepared for the crown prince to assume the throne, but he protested that he cared nothing about being king. He insisted that his younger brother inherit the kingdom in his stead. The ministers and advisors tried to dissuade him, but he was adamant, and the younger brother was crowned king. The elder brother, furthermore, refused to stay in the capital in any official capacity whatsoever. He left Bārānasi and went to the frontier, where he stayed with a rich merchant and worked with his hands. When the merchant learned that his laborer was a king's son, however, he would not allow him to work anymore. The merchant insisted that the young man be waited upon properly as a prince. Thus, without undue exertion on his part, the prince came to live comfortably in that remote area.

After some time, officers of the king traveled along the border to carry out a census and to assess taxes. In each town and village, they conducted a survey of the fields, households, and businesses. When they reached the village, where the prince was staying, the merchant appealed to the prince. "Lord," he said, "we have been happily supporting you. Please send a letter to your younger brother, the king, and ask that our taxes be waived."

The prince readily agreed. "Your Majesty," he wrote, "I am living with this merchant's family. I beg you to waive their taxes for my sake." As soon as the king received the letter, he granted the request.

The other villagers immediately appealed to the prince, offering to pay him directly if he got their taxes waived, as well. He sent another letter, and the king waived the taxes for the entire village.

Soon, people all along the border had been relieved of taxes and were making payments to the prince. He was treated with great deference and honor and became extremely wealthy. In direct proportion to his importance, influence, and property, his greediness increased.

When he asked for control of the district, his brother readily granted it. When he demanded control of the entire border region, his brother granted that, too. Even when he claimed the title of crown prince, his brother offered no objection. Finally, he wanted to govern the entire kingdom and set out for the capital with a huge army. Taking a position outside the capital, he sent a letter demanding that his younger brother either give him the kingdom or fight to keep it.

When the king read this message, he thought, "This fool refused the kingdom, the title of crown prince, and everything else. Now he wants to take it all by force of arms. If I were to slay him in battle, it would be a great dishonor for me. I do not want to be king!"

He immediately sent his brother a message, "I have no wish to fight. You may have the kingdom without any conditions."

The elder brother accepted the offer and demoted his younger brother to crown prince. Even as king, however, his greed did not stop. In his avarice, he began eyeing the riches of neighboring realms.

As Sakka was surveying the world to see who was keeping the precepts and who was not, who was looking after his parents and who was not, who was giving alms and who was not, and who was living virtuously and who was not, he perceived that the king of Bārānasi was being consumed by greed.

"That fool!" Sakka thought. "Why can't he be satisfied with being king of Kāsi! I must teach him a lesson before it is too late."

Disguising himself as a young brahmin, Sakka went to the palace and sent word that he wished to have an audience with the king. Since he appeared to be a bright young man, he was promptly admitted. He wished victory to the king, and the king asked why he had come.

"Sire," he replied, "I have a proposal to offer to you, but I would appreciate privacy."

Sakka's power was so strong that everyone immediately withdrew. As soon as the two of them were alone, Sakka announced, "Your Majesty! I know three cities, beautiful, prosperous, full of energetic citizens, and strong in troops, horses, and elephants. With my own knowledge and power, I will manage to deliver these three cities to you, but you must not delay. You must proceed at once!"

The king, insatiably greedy for more land, more revenue, more arms, more power, and more of everything, immediately gave his consent. "Good, Your Majesty!" Sakka replied. The king of the devas was able to muddle the king's mind so that he did not ask for any further information, and Sakka disappeared.

The king immediately called in his courtiers and shouted, "That youth promised to manage the capture of three cities! We must begin right away. Send a drum around the city! Announce the campaign! Mobilize the army! Make no delay! I am about to take three cities!"

"Very good, Sire! What was the youth's name?" the chief advisor asked.

"I don't know," the king replied. "I didn't ask him."

"Did you offer him hospitality?" the chief advisor asked. "No, I didn't," replied the king.

"Where is he staying?" the chief advisor asked.

"I don't know!" replied the king. "I forgot to ask! Go! Look for him! He must be found!"

Officers searched everywhere for the young man, but they found no sign of him. They reported back to the king that they could not find him and that no one in the whole city had even seen him. When the king heard this, he felt that a black cloud was hanging over him. He became gloomy and morose.

"My lordship over three great cities is lost," he moaned repeatedly. "I have lost incomparable glory. That young man must have been angry with me. I should have given him some money for expenses or, at least, offered him a place to stay!"

Greed gripped the king's mind and body, and he developed a fever. His digestive system broke down, and his bowels produced a bloody flux. He ate, but the food came out undigested and coated with blood and mucous. The royal physicians were mystified. Specialists were called, but they, too, were helpless to cure him. His strength dissipated, and he was completely exhausted. The royal illness was discussed everywhere, and it was rumored that, if a treatment were not found, the king would soon die.

At that time, the Bodhisatta, after mastering all branches of learning in Takkasilā, had just returned to his parents' home in Bārānasi. When he heard about the king, he went directly to the palace. He announced that he could cure the mysterious disease and asked to see the king.

The king grumbled that, since renowned doctors had failed, there was no point in wasting time and energy consulting a young lad. "Pay his expenses, and send him away," he ordered an attendant.

"I want no fee for my treatment," the young graduate declared. "If I succeed in healing the king of his ailment, he can pay me the price of the remedy I apply."

Mildly curious, the king relented and asked the youth to enter.

The young man paid his respects to the king and said, "Fear nothing, Sire! I will cure you in no time, but, first, please tell me the origin of your disorder."

The king's anger flared up, and he shouted, "What is that to you? Make up your medicine, and leave me alone!"

"Sire, we physicians work according to a method. First, we must learn from what the illness arises. Then we can prepare a suitable remedy for it."

Reassured by his tone of voice, the king relented. "Well, my son," he said, "it's like this." Beginning with the young man who had offered him dominion over three great cities, the king explained all that had happened. "Thus, my son, my illness was caused by greed. Cure it if you can!"

"All right, Sire," said the youth. "Can you capture those three cities by grieving?"

"Of course not, my son," replied the king.

"Since that is so, Sire, and, since you know it to be so, why do you grieve? Everything, animate and inanimate, will change and break up. Everyone must pass away and must leave everything behind. Ultimately, we have nothing, not even our own bodies.

"Sire, even if you managed to rule over four cities, you could not eat four plates of food, recline on four couches, or wear four sets of robes at the same time. It is better not to be the slave of desire. Desire has no natural limit, and, when it increases, it grinds one down with weariness and allows no escape from the four lower realms.

"If a man who desires something has his desire fulfilled, he is, of course, glad for a while, but desires for more crowd in on him just as oppressive thirst worsens during the hottest season.

"For an undiscerning man, the more he has, the more he wants, and the more his craving grows. For the greedy man, all the rice, the fields, the cattle, the slaves, the gold, the silver, the jewels, the horses, and the women in the world will not suffice. He will never be satisfied. The wise man, however, knows this and maintains a righteous course.

"Sire, a covetous king, who has subdued the whole wide world right up to the ocean, will not be satisfied but will begin craving for what lies beyond the ocean!

"Brooding on desires breeds discontent and suffering. One who turns from desires finds the true cure. Satisfied by wisdom, he is contented.

"It is best to be a man of wisdom. Such a man is never a slave of desire. He cannot be burned by the fire of lust.

"Crush your desires, before they destroy you. The man who wants little, who is not greedy, and who does not try to win everything is like the sea, which is impervious to the fire.

"Consider each desire that is abandoned as a happiness truly won. The man who wants complete happiness must abandon all lust and craving."

As the youth was speaking these wise words to the king, he focused his attention on the king's umbrella, and, through the purity of its whiteness, attained jhānic concentration.

At the same time, the king recovered completely. With a lightness of mind, he stood up and said, "When all the physicians and specialists in the kingdom could not cure me, a youth has restored me and made me whole with the medicine of his wisdom!"

"You gave me eight pieces of wisdom, each worth one thousand coins. I want to pay you this sum for your sweet and healing speech."

The youth replied, "For one hundred, one thousand, one million, nay, one million times one million coins, I care nothing, Your Majesty! As I spoke those last words to you about wisely abandoning lust and craving, desire died in my heart!"

This pleased the king even more, and he exclaimed, "This youth is both wise and good beyond all expectation! He has shown me that desire is, in actual truth, the mother of misery and the cause of my suffering!"

"Your Majesty!" said the youth, "Be judicious, and walk in righteousness!"

Having admonished the king, he rose into the air and flew to the Himavat, where he began living as an ascetic. For the rest of his life, he cultivated the Four Brahma Vihāras, and, when he passed away, he was reborn in the Brahma heavens.

Having concluded his story, the Buddha identified the birth: "At that time, this brahmin was the king, and I was the wise young man."

181

The Great Black Hound
Mahā-Kanha Jātaka

It was while staying at Jetavana that the Buddha told this story about living for the benefit of the world.

One day, in the Hall of Truth, some bhikkhus were talking about the great efforts the Buddha had made for the welfare of the world. "The Buddha has given up his own comfort and lives for the good of others. He often takes his robe and bowl and goes on a journey for the sake of just one person," one bhikkhu said. One by one, the bhikkhus enumerated some of the great feats the Buddha had accomplished to this end.

"He set in motion the Wheel of the Law when he taught the five ascetics,[1] and, by teaching the Anattalakkhana Sutta, he led them all to arahatship."

---

1 During his quest for Enlightenment, Gotama had been joined by five ascetics. In Uru-velā, shortly before beginning meditation under the Bodhi tree, he accepted a meal from a young woman named Sujātā. When the five ascetics saw this, they assumed that, by breaking his fast, he was giving up his quest, and they abandoned him. After Enlightenment, the Buddha walked to Isipatana, near Bārānasi, where they had gone, and taught his first sermon, the (continued) Dhammacakkappavattana Sutta, the Discourse Setting the Wheel of Dhamma in Motion (Samyutta Nikāya, Mahāvagga, Sacca Samyutta, 56, 11).

"He went to Uruvelā, where he performed three thousand five hundred miracles and ordained one thousand ascetics with matted hair. Then, when he delivered the Adittapariyaya Sutta (Fire Sermon)[2], at Gayāsīsa, he led them all to arahatship."

"He walked three gavutas to meet Mahā-Kassapa and to give him higher ordination."

"He traveled two hundred yojanas to meet Mahā-Kappina and to establish him in arahatship."

"He walked thirty yojanas to convert that cruel murderer, Angulimāla, and to give him ordination."

"At another time he walked thirty yojanas, to teach Ālavaka, to establish him in the first path, and to save the life of the prince."

"He spent three months in Tāvatimsa to teach eight hundred million devas."

"He went to the Brahma heavens to cure Baka-Brahmā of his false views and taught innumerable devas there."

"Every year, he travels from kingdom to kingdom, giving the refuges and precepts to all who ask."

"Neglecting neither nāgas nor garulas, he teaches all who are capable of understanding virtue."

When the Buddha heard what they were discussing, he said, "It is no wonder, Bhikkhus, that I, who now have perfect wisdom, do so much for the benefit of the world. Long ago, also, before I attained enlightenment, I made great efforts for the benefit of the world." Then he told this story of the past.

Long, long ago, a king named Usinara was reigning in Bārānasi. A long time had passed after Kassapa Buddha had declared the Four Noble Truths, liberating multitudes from bondage, but the Teaching had been forgotten, and the religion had fallen into decay. Bhikkhus were indulging in the twenty-one wrong means of livelihood. Bhikkhus had abandoned celibacy and were fathering children with bhikkhunīs. Laypeople had also forsaken their religious duties. Everyone was pursuing the ten courses of unwholesome action, and, when they died, they were being reborn in the realms of suffering.

Sakka noticed that no new deities were being born in the various heavens. As soon as he had surveyed the world, he realized what was happening. "What can I do about this?" he mused. "How can I restore the religion so that it will last another one thousand years? Ah, I have it!" he declared. "I must scare mankind. Then I can remind them of the Teaching."

Sakka summoned his charioteer, Mātali, and transformed him into Mahā-Kanha, a gigantic black hound with four formidable fangs as big as plantains.

---

2   Samyutta Nikāya, Salāyatana Vagga, Salāyatana Samyutta, 35, 28.

Around the fierce-looking beast's neck was a five-chain collar, to which Sakka attached a long, stout leash. Sakka himself took the guise of a powerful forester wearing yellow garments and a red garland. He also put a red garland on Mahā-Kanha. Sakka was carrying a mighty bow, fitted with a coral-colored bowstring, and, with his fingers, he was twirling a diamond-tipped arrow. Firmly grasping Mahā-Kanha's leash, Sakka descended from Tāvatimsa to a place about a yojana away from Bārānasi.

"The world is doomed to destruction!" he called out three times in a sonorous voice, frightening all who heard, as he and Mahā-Kanha walked toward the city. Though restrained by the leash, Mahā-Kanha terrified everyone they passed as he snarled and snapped. People rushed to the palace for safety. The king immediately ordered the city gates closed. When Sakka and Mahā-Kanha arrived at the gate, Sakka repeated his cry, and they leaped over the wall, eighteen hatthas high. As the pair proceeded to the palace, Sakka still shouting, "The world is doomed to destruction!" and Mahā-Kanha still growling fiercely, townspeople ran into their houses and bolted their doors. When they reached the palace, the courtyard was filled with people, and the great doors were tightly shut. The king was watching from the terrace with the ladies of the palace. Mahā-Kanha jumped up, put his front paws on the window sill, and gave a great howl. The sound of that howl resounded throughout the universe, from hell to the highest heaven.[3] Everyone was petrified with fear and rendered speechless.

Finally, the king gathered up his courage. He looked down at the street and shouted, "Forester! Why did your hound howl?"

"He is hungry," Sakka answered,

"All right," said the king. "He will be fed." He ordered servants to send out not only his own breakfast, but all the food from his entire household. The hound made one mouthful of it and howled again.

"Forester! Why does your hound continue to howl?" asked the king.

"He is still hungry," Sakka replied.

The king ordered that the day's ration of fodder and grain for all the royal horses and elephants be given to the hound. Mahā-Kanha finished that also in one gulp and howled again.

"Forester! Why does your hound continue to howl?" asked the king.

"He is still hungry!" Sakka replied.

The king ordered that all the food—rice, curries, meat, bread, fruit, and sweets—that had been prepared that day throughout the city be given to the

---

3 Four great sounds that were heard throughout Jambudīpa were made by Mahā-Kanha, Ālavaka (q.v. in Glossary of Personal Names in Volume III), Kusa (Tale 206), and Punnaka (Tale 215).

hound. Townspeople quickly ran to their houses and returned with all the food they could find. It was dumped in a gigantic pile in the courtyard. The ravenous hound devoured every bit of the food and howled again.

"This is no dog!" the king thought. "He must be a yakkha. I wonder where he is from and why he has come." His voice quaking with fear, the king called down, "Forester, your hound is mighty, fierce, and as black as night! His pure white fangs are razor-sharp. Around his neck is a heavy chain collar. Tell me, why is he here with you?"

"Mahā-Kanha has not come here to hunt game, Your Majesty," Sakka replied. "His job is to punish men when I turn him loose!"

"What do you mean, Forester?" the king asked, stricken with terror. "Will the hound devour all of us or only your enemies?"

"Only my enemies, Your Majesty."

"Well then, who are your enemies?" asked the king.

"Those, Sire, who love unrighteousness and live wickedly."

"Describe them to us," said the king apprehensively.

"When men who call themselves bhikkhus," Sakka began, "forgetting how to wear their robes and why they carry a bowl, seek their livelihood by proscribed means, I will release Mahā-Kanha.

"When bhikkhunīs behave loosely in the world and follow their own pleasure, I will release Mahā-Kanha.

"When ascetics become moneylenders and charge usurious rates, I will release Mahā-Kanha.

"When teachers, who have preserved the wisdom of the ancients, use their knowledge simply for trickery, I will release Mahā-Kanha.

"When children neglect their aged parents, I will release Mahā-Kanha.

"When children call their aged parents fools and show them no respect, I will release Mahā-Kanha.

"When men commit adultery and seduce young defenseless girls, I will release Mahā-Kanha.

"When men arm themselves and commit robbery and murder wantonly, I will release Mahā-Kanha.

"When men, with evil in their hearts, tell lies to deceive and cheat their friends and neighbors, I will release Mahā-Kanha.

"These, Your Majesty, are my enemies! It is these wicked sinners whom Mahā-Kanha will devour!" As he allowed a little slack on the leash, the great hound sprang forward and barked ferociously. Everyone in the palace recoiled in terror.

Suddenly, Sakka and Mātali assumed their heavenly forms. Blazing with beauty and glory, they stood in the splendid chariot, suspended in mid-air above the palace. "Your Majesty, I am Sakka!" Sakka proclaimed. "Seeing that the world was about to be destroyed, I came here to warn you. Mankind has forsaken the paths of virtue taught by Kassapa Buddha! Everywhere, men are following evil ways. As they die, because of their evil deeds, they are being reborn in the realms of suffering. Heaven is almost empty! Do not allow yourselves to fall into hell! Be vigilant!"

As Sakka continued his exhortation, he repeated the teaching of Kassapa Buddha, established the multitude in the five precepts, and encouraged them to practice righteousness and generosity. Satisfied that he had accomplished his mission, Sakka returned with Mātali in the chariot to Tāvatimsa. The people paid heed to his lesson, and the religion continued for one thousand more years.

Having concluded his story, the Buddha identified the birth: "At that time, Ānanda was Mātali, and I was Sakka."

182
The Hook
Mahā-Paduma Jātaka

It was while staying at Jetavana that the Buddha told this story about Ciñcā-Mānavikā.

After the Buddha's Enlightenment, his teaching quickly became popular, and many people followed him. Soon, his teaching had spread far and wide, and he and his Sangha of bhikkhus were receiving great honor and liberal donations. The teachers of other sects became like fireflies after sunrise. Their honor and gifts dwindled away, and they loudly complained, "Is the ascetic Gotama the only Buddha? We are also Buddhas! Do you think that the gift given to him is the only one to bring great fruit? What is given to us also has great fruit for you! Give to us, too! Please do not neglect us!"

Despite their protests, their share of donations did not increase. They met in secret to discuss their plight. "If things continue like this, we're going to be ruined!" they declared to each other. "How can we discredit Gotama so that people stop respecting him and giving to him so generously?"

One of them suggested, "Let's get Ciñcā-Mānavikā to create a scandal. That will work!" Ciñcā-Mānavikā was a female ascetic in Sāvatthī. She was attractive, fair, and graceful.

When Ciñcā-Mānavikā next visited the ascetics' monastery, she greeted them, but they ignored her completely. Upset by their silence, she asked, "What fault have I committed? I spoke to you three times!" No one paid any attention to her. Again, she asked, "What have I done? Why don't you speak to me."

Finally acknowledging her presence, one of them asked her condescendingly, "Sister, haven't you noticed that the ascetic Gotama has created a great problem for us? He is depriving us of the honor and generosity that we used to receive."

"No, sirs," she replied. "I was not aware of that. What can I do about it?"

"If you are truly our friend and wish us well," he said, "you will manage to discredit Gotama, ruin his reputation, and put an end to the gifts he receives."

"I see," Ciñcā-Mānavikā replied slowly. "All right. That's an easy matter. Leave everything to me, sirs." Without saying another word, she left.

Using all her feminine wiles, Ciñcā-Mānavikā began devoting herself whole-heartedly to the task she had undertaken. Every evening, as devotees were leaving Jetavana after listening to the Buddha, Ciñcā-Mānavikā, in a strikingly bright robe and with garlands of flowers in her hand, casually strode toward the monastery. She smiled at the people as they passed her going the other way. If anyone asked her where she was going, she sharply replied, "What business is it of yours where I go to spend the night?"

Surreptitiously, she went to the monastery of her friends, the rival ascetics, which was near Jetavana. In the early morning, when the Buddha's lay devotees were going to Jetavana to pay their respects, she walked slowly back to the city, again smiling and giving the impression that she had spent the night at Jetavana.

If anyone asked where she had stayed, she replied, "Where I sleep is no business of yours!"

Ciñcā-Mānavikā continued this ruse for six weeks. Then she began answering, "I spent the night at Jetavana with Gotama the ascetic in his cell." Those whose faith in the Buddha was not strong wondered whether this could be true.

After several more months, she wound bandages around her belly to give the appearance of pregnancy. If someone asked, she declared that she was with child by Gotama. Some fools even believed her.

Finally, after eight months, she tied a wooden disk to her belly and covered it with her loose red robe. Then she beat herself all over with an ox's jawbone, to produce swelling and discoloration. Pretending to be weary with advanced pregnancy, she went to Jetavana, while the Buddha was teaching to a large assembly. She pushed her way through the crowd, stood directly in front of the Buddha, and shouted, "Oh great ascetic, Gotama! You preach to multitudes! Sweet is your voice, and soft are the lips that cover your teeth! You have gotten me pregnant, and the time for my delivery is near! Why haven't you provided me with a chamber for the childbirth? Why haven't you given me any medicine or assigned me a proper midwife? If you can't do what should be done yourself, why don't you ask one of your lay supporters to do it for you? I'm sure that the king or Anāthapindika or Visākhā would be glad to help you! You know how to take your pleasure, but you don't know how to care for that which will soon be born!" That shameless woman reviled the Tathāgata as one might try to dirty the face of the moon with a handful of filth.

The Buddha stopped his discourse and in a clear, firm, and ringing voice said, "Sister, whether what you say is true or false, only you and I know!"

"That is true, Gotama," she retorted. "This happened through something that only you and I can know."

At that moment, Sakka's throne became hot, and the king of the devas perceived that the cause was Ciñcā-Mānavikā's false accusation.

Sakka immediately summoned four devas and transformed them into four mice. All together, they descended to Jetavana. The mice scampered inside Ciñcā-Mānavikā's robe and gnawed through the cords securing the disk on her belly. Sakka caused a puff of wind to lift her robe, revealing her lie for all to see. Suddenly, the wooden disk fell on her feet and severed her toes.

"A witch is accusing the Supreme Buddha!" shouted a devotee. Outraged, some people spat on Ciñcā-Mānavikā as they drove her away. As soon as she stepped outside Jetavana, the great earth opened into a wide abyss, and flames of Avīci Hell rose from the depths. Ciñcā-Mānavikā was enveloped in the flames and fell into that lowest of hells. The reputation of the rival ascetics was destroyed, and they no longer received any gifts or support, while the honor of the Buddha and the alms he received grew even more abundant.

The day after the incident, bhikkhus were talking about what had happened. When the Buddha heard what they were discussing, he said, "Not only this time, Bhikkhus, has this woman falsely accused me and suffered dire destruction. It was the same long ago." Then he told this story of the past.

Long, long ago, when Brahmadatta was reigning in Bārānasi, the Bodhisatta was born as the son of his chief queen. Because his face was as clear and beautiful as a lotus flower, they named him Prince Paduma. When he was old enough, he was educated in all the arts and sciences.

When the prince's mother died, the king took another queen and appointed his son the crown prince. Shortly afterward, the king had to go with his army to quell an uprising on the border. He told the queen to stay in the palace until he returned.

"My Lord, I will not stay here," she replied. "I will go with you."

"The battlefield is a dangerous place," he insisted. "It is no place for a queen. It is much better that you wait here in safety. You need not worry about me. I will soon return. In my absence, Prince Paduma will be in charge. I will tell him to make sure that you are well taken care of. Farewell, my dear!"

The king ably defeated the rebels and restored peace to the kingdom. He led the army back to Bārānasi and pitched camp outside the city walls. As soon as Prince Paduma learned of his father's return, he ordered that the city be decorated to welcome the king and to celebrate his victory. The queen watched the prince moving around the palace as he was giving orders to the courtiers. She was struck by how handsome he was and soon became enamored of him.

Prince Paduma completed his task and, as he was taking leave of the queen, asked, "Can I do anything for you, Mother?"

"Do you call me 'Mother'?" she asked as she rose up and took his hands. "Lie on my couch."

"Why?" he asked, quickly withdrawing his hands.

"Just until the king comes," she said sweetly. "Let us enjoy the pleasures of love!"

"Mother!" he cried, horrified by her proposal. "In that my father, your husband, is still living, you are my mother! What you are suggesting is completely against all moral law! How could I do such an evil thing with you?"

Again and again, she tried to seduce the prince to lie down with her, but he stood firm, unresponsive to her charms. "Do you refuse me?" she asked.

"I most certainly do refuse you, Madam!"

"Then I will speak to the king and have you beheaded!" she snarled.

"Do as you wish," answered the prince in disgust. With a perfunctory bow, he left.

Suddenly, the queen realized that if Prince Paduma told the king what she had done, she was a dead woman! "I must see him first!" she cried in a panicked voice.

Although the servants announced that her meal was ready, she left her food untouched and hurried to her chamber. She put on a soiled robe, scratched herself with her nails, and ordered her attendants to tell the king that she was ill.

After the king had completed his victory procession around the city, he entered the palace. Surprised not to find the queen waiting for him on the throne, he asked where she was.

"She is ill," the attendants told him.

He rushed to her chamber and inquired what was wrong. She lay on her bed with her back to the king and pretended not to have heard anything.

He asked three times, and, finally, she replied, sobbing, "My Lord, why do you ask? Please be silent! Other married women must suffer even as I do!"

"Who has annoyed you?" the king asked angrily. "Tell me quickly, and I will have him beheaded."

"Who did you leave in charge when you went away?" she asked as she wiped her eyes.

"Prince Paduma."

"He came into my room and made advances. I said, 'My son, do not behave in that way! I am your mother!' Say what I would, he cried, 'There is no king here but me! I will take you to my palace and enjoy your love!'" The queen began sobbing again, and continued, "He seized me by the hair, but I would not yield to his advances. He beat me and left."

The king believed her completely and did not bother to investigate the matter at all. "Guards!" he shouted, as furious as a serpent. Several guards came running, and he ordered them, "Go to Prince Paduma's palace. Bind him, and bring him to me!"

The guards hurried to the prince's palace, arrested the prince, tied his hands tightly behind his back, and beat him. They put a garland of kanavera flowers around his neck and marched him toward the king's palace. Even in the street, they continued beating him cruelly.

The prince knew that this was the queen's doing, but, instead of resisting, as he was led away, he simply cried out, "Mark my words! I am not one who has committed an offence against the king! I am innocent."

The entire city was agitated by the news. "Have you heard?" people cried. "The king is going to execute Prince Paduma at the bidding of a woman!"

Townspeople flocked to the prince as the procession passed and fell at his feet. "You do not deserve this, my Lord!" they shouted. "It is unjust, good prince!"

At last, they arrived at the palace, and the guards hauled the prince before the king. At the sight of him, the king's anger flared up even more. Unable to restrain what was in his heart, he cried, "This fellow is no king, but he has certainly tried to play the king! He may be my son, but I will not tolerate his insult to the queen! Take him away! Kill him! Throw him over the thieves' cliff!"

"Father," the prince said calmly, "I have committed no crime. Do not kill me on the false testimony of a woman."

The king seemed not to hear.

The women of the palace sent up a great cry of lamentation, "Dear Paduma, noble prince, you do not deserve this fate!"

The generals, the courtiers, and all the important citizens of Bārānasi appealed to the king. "Sire!" one pleaded. "The prince is a good and virtuous man. He respects the traditions of the kingdom; he is your heir! Do not slay him at a woman's word, without a hearing!"

"It is a king's duty to act prudently." said another. "A king should never punish an offence without sifting through the evidence and hearing the defendant's testimony."

"A king who punishes a fault before investigating is like a blind man who blindly eats what's on his plate—flies, bones, and all."

"The ruler who punishes the innocent and lets the guilty go free does not deserve to rule at all!"

"Sire, it is never wise to decide in anger. A king who is too gentle is contemptible, but also unworthy is one who is too harsh. You must be aware of who you are and keep to the middle path."

"Your Majesty, do not execute your son for the sake of a woman. It is not seemly."

None of this wise counsel touched the king to make him change his mind. He rejected his advisors' arguments, and he refused to listen to a single word from the prince himself.

"Though the whole world stands against my queen," declared the king, "I side with her against you all! Leave me alone! Take him away! Follow my orders! Throw him over the thieves' cliff!" he repeated.

The women again cried out in lamentation. As the executioner and the guards led the prince away, the entire populace followed along, wailing and loudly protesting this injustice.

"Do not try to prevent the execution of this fellow!" the king warned the people. "Executioner!" he shouted. "Make sure that this criminal is thrown head over heels and that he is killed by the fall!"

When they arrived at the top of the cliff, the deva who resided there comforted the prince. "Fear not, Paduma!" he whispered in the prince's ear. The executioner seized the prince and threw him headfirst over the precipice, but the deva, by the power of his kindliness, caught the prince and pressed him to his heart. The prince felt a divine thrill as he was transported to the abode of the nāgas.

The nāga king welcomed the prince and gave him half of his kingdom and wealth.

Prince Paduma stayed with the nāgas for a year. Then he announced that he wanted to return to the realm of men. Disappointed to lose such a noble friend and companion, the nāga king asked why the prince wished to leave.

"I want to go to the Himavat," the prince replied, "and to become an ascetic."

The nāga king had no objection to this noble goal and immediately gave his consent. In fact, he gladly conveyed the prince to the Himavat and provided him with the requisites of an ascetic.

Living simply in a forest hermitage, Prince Paduma embraced the ascetic life and diligently cultivated meditation. One day, a forester from Bāranasi who had stopped to pay his respects to the ascetic, stared at his face and asked. "Sir, aren't you the great Prince Paduma?"

"Yes, I am," he replied.

The forester stayed there for a few days. As soon as he returned to Bāranasi, he went to the palace. "Your Majesty," he said to the king, "your son is alive and has embraced the religious life. He is living in a hut of leaves in the Himavat. I stayed with him just before coming here."

"Have you really seen him with your own eyes?" asked the king.

"Yes, Sire," the forester assured him.

The king assembled a great host and set out for the place the forester had described. On the outskirts of the forest, he pitched his camp. With a few of his courtiers, the king went forward and found his son sitting at the door of his hut of leaves. He paid respects and sat down. The courtiers also saluted him and sat on one side.

Paduma invited the king to share his wild fruits.

"My son, I had you thrown down a deep precipice. How can it be that you are still alive?" asked the king.

"Father," Paduma replied, "as I fell, the deva who resides on that hill protected me and transported me to the nāga realm."

After a few minutes of pleasant conversation, the king asked, "My son, what are these woods to you? Come back to Bāranasi with me," he pleaded. "With my blessing you shall reign!"

"Father," Paduma replied evenly, "I had swallowed a hook, but now I have extracted it. I am happy."

"What hook?" asked the king. "What are you talking about?"

"The hook I refer to is lust for sensual pleasures and the craving for power. By renouncing these, I have pulled out that hook. I have, thus, found happiness and peace. I have no desire to become king. The power and glory of kingship mean nothing to me now. Keep your crown, but I urge you to observe the ten duties of a king. Forsake evil, and rule righteously."

The king listened attentively to his son's teaching and departed reluctantly. On the way back to the capital, he asked his courtiers, "On whose account did I create a breach with a son so virtuous?"

"Your Majesty," they replied, "it was on account of the queen."

Realizing that the queen had, indeed, falsely accused his son, the king ordered her to be seized and to be thrown headfirst over the thieves' cliff.

Having concluded his story, the Buddha added, "Thus, Bhikkhus, you see that, once before, this woman maligned me and brought about her own dire destruction." Then he identified the birth: "At that time, Ciñcā-Mānavikā was the queen, Devadatta was King Brahmadatta, Sāriputta was the deva of the hill, Ānanda was the nāga king, and I was Paduma, the prince who became an ascetic."

183

Mangoes Out of Season
Amba Jātaka

It was while staying at Jetavana that the Buddha told this story about Devadatta.

Devadatta declared, "Gotama the ascetic is not my teacher! I myself will be the Buddha!" Thus, he created a schism in the Order and began ordaining bhikkhus and bhikkhunīs on his own. Five hundred newly ordained bhikkhus followed Devadatta to Gayāsīsa, but, after a time, the two chief disciples, Venerable Sāriputta and Venerable Moggallāna, went there, preached to the five hundred, and persuaded them to return to the Buddha. When Devadatta learned what had happened, hot blood gushed from his mouth, and, for nine months afterwards, he was bed-ridden and grievously ill. As Devadatta's end approached, he wanted to see the Buddha once more, even though the Buddha had declared that that was impossible in this life. Determined to try, however, Devadatta had himself carried on a litter. When he reached Jetavana, he stopped the litter beside the pond outside the monastery to bathe himself. Just as his foot touched the ground, the earth opened wide, and Devadatta fell into Avīci Hell.[1]

---

1   After suffering for one hundred thousand eons in Avīci, Devadatta will be reborn as a

One day, bhikkhus in the Hall of Truth were talking about what had happened. When the Buddha heard what they were discussing, he said, "Not now only, Bhikkhus, but, long ago, too, Devadatta denied his teacher and met dire destruction." Then he told this story of the past.

Long, long ago, when Brahmadatta was reigning in Bārānasi, the Bodhisatta was born as a candāla in a village far from the capital. He knew a charm which caused mango trees to bear fruit out of season. With this remarkable charm, he and his family had all the mangoes they could eat, and he earned a good living as a fruit vendor. In every season, he was able to sell ripe mangoes, which were as golden and as sweet as the fruit of the devas.

At that time, the family of the king's chief advisor was stricken by a virulent fever, and they all died except for one son. The young brahmin, orphaned by this disaster, went to Takkasilā where he studied all the arts and sciences of the day. When his education was complete, he bade farewell to his teacher and began to travel about the country. In his wanderings, he arrived in the candāla village where the fruit vendor lived.

The brahmin boy happened to see the candāla selling ripe mangoes and was surprised because it was not at all the season for such fruit. "Without doubt," he thought, "this fruit vendor has a charm for ripening fruit out of season. Such a charm is beyond price! I must get him to teach it to me." Concealing himself, he secretly kept an eye on the fruit vendor. He followed him, learned where he lived, and kept watching to see how he got his fruit.

Early the next morning, the fruit vendor took his carrying pole, walked deep into the forest, and stopped about seven paces from a large a mango tree. As he stood there, reciting a charm, he threw a handful of water on the tree. Instantly, the dried leaves fell, new leaves sprouted, blossoms opened and fell, and fruit appeared. Within a few seconds, the tiny mangoes swelled and ripened into the largest, most succulent fruit the young brahmin had ever seen. After eating one or two of the mangoes, the fruit vendor filled his baskets, hung them on his pole, and carried them to the village to sell.

The brahmin lad hurried back to the fruit vendor's house. When the man's wife came to the door, the brahmin, feigning ignorance, asked, "Where is the teacher?"

"He's gone to the forest." she answered.

---

man and will become a Pacceka Buddha named Atthissara. The Dhammapada Commentary to Verse 17 (Burlingame, Volume 1, p. 240) relates that, at the moment of being swallowed by the earth, Devadatta declared that he had no refuge other than the Buddha. Devadatta was one of five who were swallowed by the earth in the Buddha's time. The other four were Suppabuddha, Yasodharā's and Devadatta's father; Ciñcā-Mānavikā (Tale 182); Nanda, a brahmin youth who raped Venerable Uppalavannā; and the yakkha Nandaka.

The young brahmin thanked her and said that he would wait for her husband to return. While he stood there, he thought, "I will manage to get the charm by becoming this candāla's servant!" As soon as he saw the fruit vendor coming, he solicitously relieved him of his carrying pole and heavy baskets and took them into the house.

The fruit vendor scrutinized the young brahmin carefully and said softly to his wife, "Lady, this youth has come to learn my charm, but, even if he gets it, since he is not a virtuous man, no charm will stay with him." The young brahmin stayed on and did whatever needed doing around the house. He chopped wood, pounded rice, carried water, and even did some of the cooking. When a son was born, the brahmin took over much of the housework and cared for the baby.

One day, the fruit vendor's wife said, "Husband, this lad, well-born though he is, for the sake of the charm, is doing a lot of menial tasks for us. Why don't you let him have the charm, whether or not he is able to keep it?"

Her husband agreed, and, the next day, he took the brahmin youth with him to the forest. After teaching him the charm, the fruit vendor said, "My boy, this is indeed a priceless charm, and it will bring you great prosperity and honor, but I must warn you that there is a very important condition. If the king or one of his ministers asks you who your teacher was, you must not conceal my identity. If you are ashamed to say that you learned this charm from an outcaste and lie by saying that your teacher was a great brahmin, you will lose the charm."

"Why would I hide your name?" asked the lad. Then he declared, "If anyone asks me, I will certainly say that I learned it from you, right here in this village!"

Saluting his teacher, the young brahmin left the village and made his way to Bārānasi. Skillfully using the charm, he sold basketfuls of mangoes and became quite well-to-do.

One day, the royal gardener presented the king a mango which he had bought from the young brahmin. As soon as the king tasted it, he exclaimed, "My good man, this is the most delicious mango I have ever eaten! Pray tell me where you found it! This is not even the season for mangoes!"

"Sire," the gardener replied, "there is a young man who sells mangoes in Bārānasi all the year round. I got it from him."

"Tell him," said, the king, "that from now on he is to bring mangoes directly to me!" The brahmin began delivering mangoes everyday to the palace, and, in time, he became a servant of the king. In his new position, he prospered greatly, and, little by little, he gained the king's confidence, as well.

One day, while the king was eating one of the brahmin's mangoes, he said, "Tell me where you get these mangoes, so sweet, so fragrant, and so beautiful even out of season. Does a nāga or a garula or a deva give them to you, or do you have some magical power of your own?"

"No one gives them to me, Sire," answered the brahmin. "I have a priceless charm with which I can produce these excellent mangoes in any season."

"You don't say!" exclaimed the king. "Will you show me this charm one of these days?"

"By all means, Your Majesty. I would be delighted to," replied the brahmin.

The next day, the king went with the brahmin to the royal park and said, "Please show me the charm."

The brahmin approached a barren mango tree and stopped precisely seven paces away. As he recited the charm, he threw a handful of water on the tree. Instantly, the dried leaves fell, new leaves sprouted, blossoms opened and fell, and fruit appeared. Within a few seconds, the tiny mangoes swelled and ripened into beautiful fruit. The king's courtiers applauded enthusiastically. After the king had eaten some of the succulent fruit just off the tree, he gave the brahmin a great reward.

Out of curiosity, the king asked, "Young man, who taught you this marvelous charm?"

The brahmin had never been asked this before, and he was caught off guard by the king's question. He remembered his teacher's warning but immediately reasoned to himself: "I have thoroughly memorized this charm. I know that I will never forget it. I am not going to degrade myself by admitting that I learned it from a candāla. That would be shameful!" Standing proudly before the king, he said, "Your Majesty, I learned this charm while I was studying in Takkasilā. It was taught to me by a world-renowned teacher, a most respected brahmin!"

"I am impressed!" replied the king. "You must have been a very good student!" Then the king and the brahmin returned to the palace.

A few days later, the king again had a craving for mangoes. He took the brahmin to the royal park, sat on a stone bench, and told the brahmin to produce some of his delicious fruit. The youth approached the barren mango tree and stopped seven paces away. He opened his mouth, but nothing came out. Try as he might to remember the charm, he could not recall a single word. He stood there frozen. He realized that he had indeed lost it, and he did not know what to do.

The king watched him and wondered what was wrong. "Young man, why is no fruit appearing on the tree?" he asked.

"Sire, the hour and moment are not suitable," he lied. "In order for the charm to work, the planets must be in conjunction. As soon as the conditions are auspicious, I will produce your mangoes."

"That's strange!" the king thought. "Young man!" he said aloud. "You never mentioned anything about planets and conjunctions before. You said you could produce mangoes in any season. What does this mean?"

"Oh, no!" the brahmin thought frantically. "I cannot deceive this king! I must tell the truth, even if it means that he punishes me!" Falling on his knees, he cried, "Your Majesty! I did not learn this charm from a famous brahmin in Takkasilā! I learned it from a candāla in a small village on the border of Kāsi. I was so ashamed to admit that my teacher was an outcaste that I lied. When he taught me the charm, he warned me that, if I denied him and concealed his identity, I would lose the charm, but I did not believe him. He knew that I would be ashamed of him, and he warned me, but I lied anyway, and now I have completely forgotten the charm! I'm sorry! I shouldn't have lied!"

"You fool!" shouted the king. "You stupid fool! You had a priceless treasure, and you threw it away! With something as valuable as that charm, what difference could birth make? If you find a massive honeycomb, what difference whether it is on a neem tree, on a castor tree, or on a palas tree? The honey is sweet, and the tree that has it is the best. Likewise with khattiya, brahmin, vessa, sudda, and candāla. Whoever teaches right, that man is the best!" The king ordered his men to seize the foolish young brahmin. "Go back to your teacher," the king shouted, "and beg his forgiveness. If you can relearn the charm, you may return. If not, leave my kingdom, and never come back!"

"What can I do?" the young brahmin cried, finding himself stripped of his position and his pride. "Now there is no refuge for me except my teacher." He decided to return to the village, to beg his teacher's forgiveness, and to learn the charm again.

The fruit vendor saw the brahmin from a distance and said to his wife, "See, my dear. Here comes that scoundrel again. I'm sure he has lost the charm I gave him."

The brahmin greeted the fruit vendor, who simply asked, "Sir, why have you returned?"

"Oh, my dear teacher!" the brahmin cried. "Sometimes a man thinks he is on level ground, but he falls into a pit. A person may step on what seems to be a stick but finds that it is a venomous black snake. A blind man can easily stumble into the fire! I am ruined! I lied! I denied you! The spell is gone! I am utterly ruined! Please, wise teacher! Kind teacher! I beg you to forgive me and to teach me the charm once more!"

"Young man," the teacher replied, "give a timely warning to the blind man, and he'll steer clear of the pit, but look at you! I very clearly told you not to lie, yet here you are again, begging me for what I already gave you. After I taught it to you, I explained the condition. You never would have forgotten it if you had acted wisely. You had a good living, foolish man, but you threw it away because you were too proud to tell the truth. To such a fool as you, ungrateful and unrestrained, why would I ever again give that mighty spell? Get out of here!"

As the dejected young brahmin walked away from the village, he cried to himself, "What is life to me now?" Without hope for his future, he wandered deep into the forest and died there, alone.

Having concluded his story, the Buddha repeated, "Not now only, Bhikkhus, but in former days, too, Devadatta denied his teacher and met dire destruction." Then he identified the birth: "At that time, Devadatta was the ungrateful young brahmin, Ānanda was the king, and I was the candāla teacher."

184
Revenge Backfires
Phandana Jātaka

It was while staying on the bank of the Rohini River that the Buddha told this story about a quarrel.

The Sākyans and Koliyans had gathered there and were ready to go to war over water to irrigate their crops.[1] The Buddha told this story of the past.

Long, long ago, when Brahmadatta was reigning in Bārānasi, there was a great black lion living in the forest at the edge of the Himavat. One day, this lion lay down beneath a massive phandana tree.[2] As he was lying there, waiting for prey, a strong wind dislodged a dead branch from the tree. When the branch fell, it hit the lion with a sharp, painful blow on the shoulder. Thinking that he was being attacked, the lion leaped up and ran a few steps.

---

1 The Rohinī was a small river which formed the border between the Sākyan and Koliyan kingdoms. There was a dam constructed across the river, which enabled people on both sides to use the Rohinī's water to irrigate their crops. At one time, there was a drought, which caused conflict between the two peoples over the water. With war imminent, the Buddha appeared between the two armies and convinced the leaders of the folly of wholesale slaughter over water. Grateful for the Buddha's restoring peace, both groups sent young men to him to be ordained as bhikkhus.

2 Palāsa or flame of the forest (Butea monosperma).

He turned back, but, not seeing anything, he thought, "That wasn't a tiger or another lion. It must be that the deva of this great phandana tree resents my lying here. I don't see any other explanation."

He strode back to the tree and angrily raked the trunk with his sharp claws. "I don't eat a single leaf or break any of your branches!" he roared. "You tolerate other animals! Why can't you put up with me? What have I ever done to you? Just wait! I'll destroy you down to the roots! You'll be no more than a pile of wood chips!" The furious lion wondered where he should begin searching for a woodcutter to carry out his threat.

That morning, a wheelwright from a nearby village of carpenters went in search of wood for his trade. Leaving his wagon at the edge of the forest, he took his ax and his hatchet and began searching on foot for suitable trees. He saw the fierce lion scratching the tree and ran to hide. When the lion turned away from the tree, he noticed the wheelwright and thought, "A forester! This is my chance!" He approached the man, but, without getting too close, he called out, "Sir! With that sharp axe, tell me, what kind of tree are you looking for?"

The man was completely taken aback by hearing a lion speak, but he decided that, if the lion was going to be friendly, he should be friendly, too. Perhaps the lion could even help him find the right tree. "Your Majesty!" he answered, "I earn my living by making wheels. I am looking for wood that is suitable for making strong wagon wheels. You roam the forest, so I'm sure that you know it well. Can you tell me what tree would be the best for my purpose?"

"This is indeed my lucky day!" thought the lion. "Here is exactly the man I was looking for!" Aloud he said, "You don't want wood from a sal tree or an acacia tree. The wood you want comes from a tree called phandana. That wood is sturdy but pliable. It is by far the best wood for wheels!"

"This is indeed my lucky day!" thought the wheelwright. "What does that phandana tree look like?" he asked the lion. "What kind of leaves does it have? Is its trunk shiny or rough? Can you describe it to me?"

"My good man," the lion replied, "I don't need to describe the phandana tree to you. It is right here! This is the tree I'm talking about. Its branches bend but never break. This phandana tree I'm standing under will give you excellent wood for your wheels—hub, spokes, and rim."

Satisfied that he had accomplished his aim, the lion moved away, and the wheelwright prepared to fell the tree. When the deva of the tree saw the axe, he thought, "I never dropped anything on that lion. He has no reason to hate me or to seek revenge, but now he is destroying my home! Before that happens, I must find a way to destroy him, as well!"

Disguising himself as a forester, the tree-deity approached the wheelwright and said, "Hello, my good man! That's a fine tree you've found! What are you going to do with it after you've cut it down?"

"I plan to make some wagon wheels."

"Really? How did you learn that this is the best wood for wheels?"

"A black lion just told me."

"I see. That lion gave you good advice. You can certainly make fine wheels out of this wood. Let me tell you something else. To make your wheels even stronger, and to keep them from wearing down around the outer edge, you should place a strip, about four inches wide, of the flayed hide of a black lion. That skin will protect your wheel like iron. If you do that, I guarantee that you will have the best wheels in Jambudīpa!"

"That's very interesting!" replied the wheelwright. "How can I get the hide of a black lion?"

"What a silly question!" laughed the deva. "Didn't you just tell me that a black lion told you about this wood? The tree isn't going to run away. The lion can't be far off. Go and find him, and tell him you need his help to cut down the tree. Bring him here, and ask him to show you where to cut. He won't suspect anything. When he sticks out his jaw to point to the place where you should cut, hit him with your axe, and kill him!"

"This day is doubly lucky for me!" The wheelwright exclaimed. He did exactly as the deva suggested. After he had killed the lion, he skinned the beast and ate the tenderest meat. Then he cut down the tree and carted away the wood.

Having concluded his story, the Buddha added, "In this way, the phandana tree destroyed the lion, and the lion destroyed the tree. Each managed the death of the other. In the same way, among men, when a feud arises, both sides court destruction! It is better to live in harmony, to be of one mind, and to avoid the useless kind of conflict which the lion and the tree engaged in. Learn to live in peace with all men. Wise men praise righteousness, and those who practice it will surely attain peace."

The two kings took heed of the Buddha's discourse, reconciled their differences, and called off the battle. Then the Buddha identified the birth: "At that time, I was another deva who lived in that forest and saw everything that happened."

185

Even Faster Than That
Javanahamsa Jātaka

It was while staying at Jetavana that the Buddha told this story about the Dhanuggaha Sutta.

"Suppose, Bhikkhus," the Buddha said, "four skilled archers, standing together and facing the four points of the compass, each shot an arrow from where he stood. Suppose, also, that a man were to run out and to catch those arrows before they could touch the ground. That man could be said to be the epitome of swiftness. Well, Bhikkhus, even swifter than that man are the sun and the moon. Even swifter than the sun and the moon are the devas who run ahead of them. Even swifter than the devas is the decay of the elements of life. Because the decay of the elements of life is the swiftest of all things, you should train yourselves: 'We will live heedfully.'"[3]

Two days later, the bhikkhus were talking about this sermon in the Hall of Truth. "Friends, the Buddha's vivid illustration explaining the weakness, the unreliability, and the impermanence of the elements of life was enough to strike terror in the heart of anyone, believer and unbeliever alike!"

---

3 This is a brief paraphrasing of the Dhanuggaha Sutta (Samyutta Nikāya, Nidāna Vagga, Opamma Samyutta, 20, 6).

When the Buddha heard what they were discussing, he said, "It is no wonder, Bhikkhus, that my teaching impressed upon you how impermanent the elements of life are. Long ago, even as a mere animal, I demonstrated that same impermanence, and my teaching alarmed the king of Kāsi and his entire court." Then he told this story of the past.

Long, long ago, when Brahmadatta was reigning in Bārānasi, the Bodhisatta was born as a beautiful golden goose, who became the leader of a flock of ninety thousand geese. One day, having led his flock to eat wild rice growing in a pool in the plains of Jambudīpa, he returned with them in a leisurely flight over the city of Bārānasi to their home on Cittakūta.

King Brahmadatta saw the flock of geese and remarked to his courtiers, "That majestic goose, leading the others, must be a king like me!" He developed a fondness for the great bird and resolved to meet him. Collecting garlands and perfumes, he went with many musicians to look for the king of the geese.

Surprised to find himself honored in this way, the goose king asked the other geese, "When a human king comes to pay this sort of respect to me, what does he really want?"

"He wants to make friends with you, My Lord," they answered.

"All right," the goose king declared, "I will become friends with this king of Kāsi!"

Some time later, the king of the geese gathered water from Lake Anotatta on one wing and fragrant sandalwood powder on the other and flew to Bārānasi. Finding King Brahmadatta sitting in the royal park with his courtiers, he sprinkled the king as a mark of respect and friendship. Then he flew with his flock back to Cittakūta. From that time on, the king always kept watch for the great goose, thinking: "Perhaps, my comrade will come today."

One day, two of the youngest birds in the flock had the idea of challenging the sun in a race. Being well brought up, they asked permission from their king, who told them, "Lads, the sun is incredibly swift. It is unimaginable for you to try to beat him. In fact, you very well might die in the attempt. Do not try to do such a foolish thing!" The two young birds asked the king's permission a second and a third time, but each time he refused.

Being young and headstrong, however, the two birds decided, in spite of the king's warning, to go ahead with their race without his permission. One morning, before dawn, they perched on the peak of Yugandhāra and waited for the sun to appear.

The king noticed their absence and guessed what they were going to do. "If I don't go," he thought, "those two will die in the attempt. I must save their lives."

He flew immediately to Yugandhāra and sat beside them. As soon as the sun peeped above the horizon, the young geese took off and flew along ahead of the sun. The king also took off and flew along beside them.

After several hours, the younger bird grew lightheaded and felt a burning pain in the joints of his wings. "Sire," he gasped, making a sign to the king, "I can't go on!"

"Don't be afraid," said the king. "I will save you!" He helped the young bird onto his back and carried him all the way to Cittakūta to rejoin the rest of the flock.

The king immediately returned to fly beside the other bird. Just before noon, that young bird also faltered. Feeling the same lightheadedness and the same pain in the joints of his wings, he made a sign to the king and gasped, "Sire, I can't go on!" The king rescued him in the same way and carried him back to Cittakūta.

Having saved the lives of the two young birds and confident that he was himself the fastest of all birds, the goose king declared, "Let me test my speed against that of the sun!" It was exactly noon, and the sun was directly overhead, when he alighted on Mount Yugandhāra. With one great beat of his wings, he arose and overtook the sun. Flying first in front and then behind, he realized, "It is mere child's play for me to fly with the sun. It is better that I fly to Bārānasi and have a talk about righteousness and truth with my friend, King Brahmadatta."

Turning sharply, he traversed the entire world from end to end. Then he flew over all of Jambudīpa and, in an instant, arrived in Bārānasi. The great goose was flying so high that he encompassed the entire city in his shadow. When he saw the palace, he slowed his flight, descended, and landed directly outside the window where King Brahmadatta stood.

"My comrade has come!" cried Brahmadatta with delight. Preparing a golden seat for the goose king to perch on, he said, "Welcome, my friend. Please come in, and consider yourself at home!"

The goose king settled on the golden seat, and Brahmadatta anointed him with refined fragrant oils. He offered the great bird sweet rice and sugared water in golden dishes and asked, "My friend, you have come alone? From where have you just come? What have you done recently? Please tell me all there is to tell!"

When King Brahmadatta heard about the race with the sun, he begged, "Friend, please show me your own swiftness!"

"Your Majesty," the goose king replied, "that swiftness cannot be seen!"

"Then show me what you can," King Brahmadatta pleaded. "All right, Sire. I can show you something," the goose king agreed. "Summon your best archers."

King Brahmadatta sent for his finest archers, and the goose king selected the four who could shoot the fastest. The two kings, the archers, and all the courtiers went into the courtyard below. In the center of the courtyard, the goose king had a tall stone column erected. He asked for a bell to be tied around his neck and then he perched on the top of the column. He asked the archers to take their places with their backs to the column, each facing one of the cardinal directions. "Now, Your Majesty, have these four men shoot their arrows at the same moment. I will fly from here, catch all four arrows before they touch the ground, and bring them back to lay them at the archers' feet. You will be able to tell that I am flying by the tinkling of this bell, but you will not see me at all."

The archers shot their arrows, and the great goose disappeared. Everyone could hear the bell, but no one could see even a trace of the bird. Almost instantly, he had returned with all four arrows and laid them at the men's feet. Then he resumed his perch on the stone column.

"Did you see my speed, Sire?" asked the goose king.

King Brahmadatta admitted that he had seen nothing. "You must understand," the great bird added, "that that speed was neither my fastest, nor even my normal velocity. It was actually one of the slowest speeds that I am able to fly. That is but an indication of how swift I am."

Astounded, King Brahmadatta asked, "Well, Friend, is there anything swifter than you?"

"Yes, my friend, there is," replied the goose king. "One hundred, one thousand, nay, even one hundred thousand times faster than I can fly at my fastest is the decay of the elements of life. These elements of life pass away at an unimaginably rapid rate! Every moment, they are vanishing!"

Hearing this, King Brahmadatta was completely shaken and gripped by the fear of death. He turned pale and suddenly fainted. His attendants promptly sprinkled water on his face to revive him.

After the king had regained his composure, the great goose continued speaking gently. "Sire," he said, "do not fear. This is natural. It is a process which is constantly going on. Do not be afraid, but, nonetheless, recollect death. Walk in righteousness, give alms, and do good. Be mindful."

"My Lord," King Brahmadatta cried, "how can I live without a wise teacher like you? Do not return to Cittakūta. Stay here, and be my teacher! Dear friend, let me keep you near!"

The king of the geese replied, "Your Majesty, if I were to accept this honor from you, it might one day happen that you become inebriated and say to your men, 'Cook that royal bird for my dinner!'"

"No! Never!" protested the king, "I swear that I will never touch strong drink again. I promise never to love anything more than you, my teacher and my friend!"

"It is easy to understand the cry of a jackal or of a bird," the goose cautioned, "but the word of a man is never sure.

"A man may say, 'This is my friend, my companion, my kin,' but then, one day, affection disappears, and hatred takes its place.

"The one you hold in your heart, wherever he may be, is near to you, but the one whom you dislike, even though he lives with you, is far away.

"One who cares for you, though he is across the sea, is close, but an enemy, though he lives in your house, is distant.

"One who overstays his welcome may find that his friend has become his foe. Rather than risk your friendship, Sire, I prefer to take my leave," the goose king said evenly.

"Even though I beg you to stay, I know that you will not listen," replied King Brahmadatta. "I wish you would reconsider, but I can see you are adamant. Before you go, please grant me one favor. My dear teacher, please come back, and visit me here!"

"If I live, and if you live, Sire," the goose replied, "perhaps I will come again. If death does not interfere, perhaps we will meet again. Be mindful!"

With that ringing admonition, the great goose flew back to Cittakūta.

Having concluded his story, the Buddha identified the birth: "At that time, Ānanda was King Brahmadatta, Moggallāna was the younger bird, Sāriputta was the elder, my followers were the geese of the flock, and I was the wise and swift goose king."

186
A Tawny-Skinned Brahmin
Takkāriya Jātaka

It was while staying at Jetavana that the Buddha told this story about Venerable Kokālika.[4]

Long, long ago, when Brahmadatta was reigning in Bārānasi, the Bodhisatta was named Takkāriya and was a student of the king's advisor, a tawny-skinned brahmin who had lost all his teeth. The advisor's wife was committing adultery with another brahmin who looked remarkably like her husband. The advisor had tried time and again to stop his wife, but without success. He didn't want to kill the man outright, but he was constantly trying to devise some scheme to get rid of his rival.

One day, he went to the king and said, "Sire, your capital is the greatest city in all of Jambudīpa, and you are the most powerful king. It is, therefore, not right, Your Majesty, that the southern gate of the city remain so poorly constructed and so ill-omened."

"Well, Advisor," replied the king, "what is to be done about that?"

"You must bring good luck by setting it right."

"How is that to be done?"

---

4   The occasion for this story is the same as that for Tale 88, where it is told in detail.

"First, we have to tear down the old gate. Then we have to gather new and unblemished timbers. Then, during an auspicious conjunction of the stars, we must perform a sacrifice to the guardian deities of the city. After that, we can begin to erect the new gate."

"By all means, do it," ordered the king. "I leave it entirely in your hands."

The advisor immediately had the old gate demolished and ordered the carpenters to prepare new timbers. When this had been done, he informed the king, "Your Majesty, tomorrow there will be an auspicious conjunction. Before the day is over, we must carry out the sacrifice and lay the foundation for the new gate."

"Excellent!" replied the king. "Now, what do you need for the ceremony?"

"Your Majesty, a great gate is guarded by powerful devas. These devas require a great sacrifice. In this case, we must find a tawny-skinned, toothless brahmin, of pure blood on both sides. His blood must be offered in a solemn ceremony, and his body must be laid below the great foundation stone. When the magnificent gate rises above it, this will guarantee good fortune for you and for your city."

"Excellent!" repeated the king. "I order you, my trusted advisor, to find such a brahmin and to have the gate built over his body."

The advisor was delighted. "Tomorrow," he gloated triumphantly, "I will see the end of my rival!"

He was so excited that, when he got home, he could not keep quiet about his plot. "You foul hag!" he berated his wife. "You have cuckolded me long enough! Tomorrow, your lover will die at my hands. I've seen to that!"

"What do you mean?" his wife cried. "How can you kill an innocent man?"

"Well, my dear," the brahmin explained very matter-of-factly, "the king is building a new southern gate. He needs a victim for a sacrifice. He has commanded me to find a tawny-skinned brahmin, whose body will be crushed beneath the foundation stone. Your lover is a wonderful specimen of a tawny-skinned brahmin, and I have chosen him for the sacrifice."

She immediately sent her paramour a message: "Tomorrow, the king will slay a tawny-skinned brahmin as a sacrifice! You must flee immediately." The man did as he was advised, but, before he left, he told his friends of the plot, and every other tawny-skinned brahmin also departed hurriedly from the city.

The next morning, the advisor gleefully gave the king explicit directions to his rival's house. "There," he said, "you will find a toothless tawny-skinned brahmin. As soon as you arrest him and deliver him to the southern gate, the sacrifice can proceed."

The king sent soldiers to the house, but, of course, the brahmin was not there. When they returned to the king empty-handed, he ordered, "Search the city! Bring me a toothless tawny-skinned brahmin! Anyone will do!" The soldiers searched the entire city, but they could find no one to fit the description.

"You are wasting time!" shouted the king angrily. "My gate must be erected! We have to conduct the sacrifice today! Find me a toothless tawny-skinned brahmin!"

"Your Majesty," the soldiers replied, "except for your advisor there is no such man in the city!"

"My advisor," retorted the king, "cannot be sacrificed!"

"But, Your Majesty," one soldier continued, "your advisor explained very emphatically that there will not be another auspicious conjunction of the stars until the end of the year. We dare not wait that long to construct the gate. A city without a gate is an open invitation to our enemies. There is no question. We must sacrifice your advisor. He fits the requirements exactly. Surely, we can find another brahmin to perform the sacrifice and to become your new advisor."

"But," the king protested feebly, "where can we find another brahmin as wise as he?"

"What about his disciple, Sire? Make young Takkāriya your advisor, and have him perform the ceremony,"

The king immediately sent for Takkāriya, greeted him cordially, and announced that he was being promoted to Chief Advisor. His first duty, the king informed him, was to perform the sacrifice at the southern gate. Then the king ordered soldiers to arrest the former advisor and convey him to the construction site, where Takkāriya also went, accompanied by a great crowd. Takkāriya directed that a pit be dug exactly where the foundation stone was to be laid and that an awning be placed over it. Then he led his teacher into the pit.

When they reached the bottom of the pit, the old brahmin wept and moaned, "What a fool I was! My plan came so close to succeeding perfectly, but I couldn't keep quiet. I stupidly told that wicked woman of a wife what I was going to do. I have killed myself with my own words! Just as a frog in the jungle calls the snake which devours him, I have brought myself into this pit."

"Yes, Master," Takkāriya agreed, "you made this pit your own grave. The man who speaks at the wrong time brings ruin upon himself, but you are certainly not alone in this. Let me tell you a story.

"Once, here in Bārānasi, there was a courtesan named Kali, who could earn one thousand coins in a single day. Unfortunately, Kali had a brother named

Tundila, who, being a drunkard and a gambler, wasted all the money she gave him. Kali tired of this and ordered her maids to throw her brother out empty-handed if he came back. Sure enough, one day, Tundila was playing cards, and he lost everything, including his clothes. Wearing only a dirty loincloth, he went to his sister's house, but the maids refused to let him in.

"One of Kali's patrons, the son of a rich merchant, happened to see Tundila and asked him why he was crying.

"'I lost at cards and came to ask my sister for help, and her maids threw me out.' the brother explained.

"'Well,' the patron said, 'let me speak to your sister!'

"The young man entered the house and gently scolded Kali: 'Your brother is outside in only a rag. Why don't you give him something to wear?'

"'I will give nothing.' Kali answered. 'If you are so fond of him, you can give him something yourself.'

"It was the custom in that establishment that each patron was provided with an exquisite robe to wear during his stay. As soon as the rich young man had donned his robe, he gave his own clothes to Tundila, who put them on and hurried to the tavern. The next morning, when the maids took the robe, the young man, of course, had nothing to put on. Nevertheless, the women shouted, 'Be off, young man!' and sent him away naked.

"People laughed at him, and he was ashamed, but he had to admit that it was his own fault. He should have kept his mouth shut and not interfered in what was not his business.

"At another time," Takkāriya continued, "two careless shepherds let their flocks mingle in a pasture near Bārānasi, and two of the rams began to fight. A fork-tail bird saw them getting ready to charge and thought, 'These two will crack their heads and kill themselves. I must stop them.' 'Uncles, don't fight!' he cried, but the rams paid no attention. The bird mounted first on the back of one ram and then on the head of the other. He continued urging them to stop, but they ignored him. Finally, crying, 'Fight, then, but kill me first!' he placed himself between the two rams, who continued butting each other as hard as they could. The bird was crushed as completely as if he had been smashed in a mortar by a pestle. Like you, Teacher, no one else was to blame—he did it to himself.

"At another time, some villagers sent a man up a tree to gather fruit. When they saw a dangerous black snake slithering up the tree, they warned the man, and he became terrified. Four men grabbed the corners of a cloth and, standing at the foot of the tree, shouted, 'Young man, jump!' He did what they told him to do, but they could not support his weight. The four fell forward and cracked their heads together, and all of them died on the spot. You could say, Master, that, like you, those men killed themselves for no reason at all.

"At yet another time, some thieves stole a nanny goat and planned to roast her in the jungle. To keep her quiet, they muffled her and tied her up in a bamboo grove. As they were about to kill her, they found that they did not have a knife. They suddenly realized that, even if they killed the goat, they wouldn't be able to cut up her meat without a knife, so they let her go. 'This must be due to some merit of hers!' they shouted as the goat bounded away.

"Thinking that she was safe, the goat began playing in a nearby bamboo grove. As she was kicking up her heels, she knocked over a basket a crafts-man had left there while he was gathering bamboo. When the basket fell over, out dropped a knife which he had been using. The thieves, hearing the metallic sound, ran to see what it was and discovered the knife. One of the thieves quickly grabbed the knife and dispatched the unsuspecting goat so that all of them could enjoy the meat. That nanny goat, like you, was killed by her own folly.

"On the other hand," Takkāriya continued, "those who are moderate of speech and mindfully watch their words often escape death!

"A hunter once managed to capture a kinnara couple which he presented to the king. The king had never seen such creatures before and asked the hunter what they were.

"'Sire, they are kinnaras, and they can sing sweetly and dance delightfully!'

"The king rewarded the hunter generously and sent him on his way. Then he turned to the kinnaras and commanded them to sing and dance.

"'Our music and dance are full of meaning,' the kinnaras thought. 'If we do not convey that message, singing and dancing will be useless. If these humans do not understand, they will abuse us. Those who speak too much, speak falsely!' For fear of uttering a false note, the kinnaras neither sang nor danced. The king begged them again and again, but they remained still.

"Finally, the king grew angry and shouted, 'These creatures are neither devas nor heavenly musicians! They are nothing more than stupid beasts palmed off by a lying and greedy hunter! Kill them both and cook them. Serve me one for tonight's supper and the other for breakfast tomorrow morning.'

"When she heard this, the kinnarī thought, 'The king is angry and planning to kill us. Now is the time to speak.' Aloud she said, 'One hundred thousand melodies badly sung are not worth one good song. For fear of singing poorly, we have been silent.'

"'Excellent!' cried the king. 'That creature is well-spoken. Let her go,' he ordered his servant, but take the other one and kill him. I'll have him for breakfast.'

"'If I hold my tongue now, the king will kill me,' the kinnara thought. 'I must speak now, too.' Aloud he said, "Cattle depend on the weather, and men depend on the cattle. Your Majesty, I depend on you, and my wife depends on me. Afraid of committing a fault, we have been silent. Sire, different beings have different ways. What wins praise from one, may bring only blame from another. Many men have many minds. Because everything is relative, it is difficult to know what is right to do!'

"'Excellent!' the king shouted again. 'This wise kinnara also speaks the truth. It was fear of making a mistake that kept this couple quiet. Now, out of fear for their lives, they speak, and wisely, too. I will also reward his speech. Let him go!'

"The king called the hunter back and ordered him to release the kinnaras in the same place where he had caught them."

"Thus, you can see, Master, how carefully the kinnaras watched their words. By speaking only at the right time and by speaking well, they were set free, but you, by speaking at the wrong time and by speaking excessively and ill, have come to great misery."

The old brahmin could respond only with more weeping. "Fear not, Master," Takkāriya comforted him. "I will save your life."

"I am doomed!" the brahmin wailed. "How can you possibly save me?"

Climbing out of the pit, he announced to the king and to the multitude, "The proper conjunction of the planets has not yet taken place. We must wait another day." In the middle of the night, he carried a dead goat to the tent and said to his master, "Go where you will, and live!"

The next day, Takkāriya performed the sacrifice with the body of the goat, and no one was the wiser. The gate was erected, and the city remained safe.

Having concluded his story, the Buddha added, "Thus, you see, Bhikkhus, that this is not the first time that Kokālika has been destroyed by his own words." Then he identified the birth: "At that time, Kokālika was the tawny-skinned advisor, and I was the wise Takkāriya."

187
The Treacherous Bankrupt
Ruru-Miga Jātaka

It was while staying at Veluvana that the Buddha told this story about Devadatta.

Whenever anyone remarked how helpful the Buddha had been by ordaining him and teaching him, Devadatta invariably retorted, "Not so! I ordained myself! On my own I learned the Dhamma!" If anyone reminded him that it was because of the Buddha that he received gifts, alms, support, and honor, Devadatta replied, "It is by myself that I gain gifts and honor! Gotama has never done me any good, not even so much as a blade of grass is worth!"

One day, in the Hall of Truth, bhikkhus were talking about Devadatta's lack of appreciation and his ingratitude. When the Buddha heard what they were discussing, he said, "This is not the first time, Bhikkhus, that Devadatta has been ungrateful. Long ago, I even saved his life, but he did not appreciate it." Then the Buddha told this story of the past.

Long, long ago, when Brahmadatta was reigning in Bārānasi, a great merchant with a fortune of eighty crores, had a son named Mahā-Dhanaka. Believing that the boy would find studying tiresome, the merchant neither provided for his education nor taught him anything about business. Mahā-

Dhanaka grew up idle and ignorant. He spent all of his time eating, drinking, gambling, singing, and dancing. When he came of age, his parents arranged a marriage for him with a girl from a suitable family.

After his parents died, Mahā-Dhanaka surrounded himself with drunkards and gamblers. In a very short time, he had squandered the entire family fortune. In order to continue his profligate life style, he borrowed money, but, seeing as he had no income, he could not repay his debts.

He tried to borrow more money, but was refused. His creditors began pressing him to repay what he owed. Unable even to leave his house without being dunned for money, he thought, "What is my life to me? If I cannot live as I'm accustomed to, it's better to die!" He called all the money lenders, merchants, and shopkeepers who were hounding him and announced, "There is family treasure buried on the bank of the Gangā. Bring all your bills and invoices, and come with me. If you will help me dig up the treasure, I will repay everything I owe you."

All together, they went to Gangā. When they reached the bank of the river, Mahā-Dhanaka pretended to study the landscape and to pace in several directions. He told the others to begin digging here and there. While they were all occupied with this work, he ran and threw himself into water, and the swift current carried him away. At first, he was glad to be rid of his creditors, but he was soon gripped by the fear of death and began crying out pitifully.

At that time, the Bodhisatta had been born as a handsome deer. His hide was like burnished gold, and his hooves were black and shiny. He had spiraled silver horns and eyes like polished gems. He had left his herd to stay alone in a pleasant grove of mango and sal trees near a bend in the river.

Around midnight, the golden stag heard a cry of distress. "That sounds like a man in the river!" he thought. "While I am alive, I won't let him die!"

Leaping up, he ran as fast as he could to the river. As soon as he could make out Mahā-Dhanaka struggling to stay afloat, he called out, "Hello! You there! Have no fear! I will save you!" The golden stag jumped into the water and swam toward the man. Though completely exhausted, Mahā-Dhanaka managed to clamber onto the deer's back, and the compassionate stag carried him back to his resting place in the grove. Mahā-Dhanaka slept soundly, and, when he awoke, the golden deer offered him wild fruit he had collected from the forest. When the man had recovered from his ordeal, the deer said, "Now, sir, I will lead you out of this forest and set you on the road to Bārānasi. Go in peace! I ask you, however, not to tell anyone that you have seen a golden deer. Please do not reveal my location to the king or to anyone else. Please do not let anyone know that I am staying here."

Mahā-Dhanaka promised the golden stag that he would protect the secret and followed his deliverer out of the forest.

In Bārānasi, King Brahmadatta's queen-consort, Queen Khemā, had a vivid dream in which a great golden deer preached the law. When she awoke, she was still enthralled. "If there were no such a creature," she thought, "I would not have seen him in my dream. I will ask the king about this!"

She sought out the king and described her dream. When she had finished, she declared, "Dear husband, I must hear the discourse of that golden deer. If I don't, I will die of regret!"

"My dear, if such a creature exists in the realm of men, you will have it," he assured her.

The king sent for his royal advisors and asked, "Is there such a thing as a golden deer?"

"Yes, Sire," they replied. "The golden deer certainly exists, though we have never seen one."

The king issued a proclamation and had it inscribed on a golden plate: "Anyone who provides information leading to the capture of a golden deer will receive as a reward this purse containing one thousand coins and this elephant!" He gave the golden plate to a courtier who mounted a royal elephant with the purse at his feet in the howdah. The courtier rode around the city reading the inscription at every corner.

It was at this moment that Mahā-Dhanaka returned to Bārānasi. As soon as he heard the proclamation, he ran after the elephant and called to the courtier, "I have seen a golden deer! Take me to the king!"

The courtier dismounted from his elephant and took Mahā-Dhanaka to the palace.

"Is it true," the king asked him, "that you have seen a golden deer?"

"Yes, Your Majesty, it is true," replied Mahā-Dhanaka. "Now give me the reward you promised."

The king was rather taken aback by Mahā-Dhanaka's greediness, but, for his queen's sake, he was pleased with the news of the golden deer.

"Tell me," he said. "Where is this remarkable deer to be found?"

Mahā-Dhanaka described the path leading to the forest and the mango and sal grove at the bend in the Gangā.

"Can you lead us to that place?" asked the king.

"Yes, I can," replied Mahā-Dhanaka.

The king immediately ordered that preparations be made and soon set out with a large entourage.

When they were within sight of the grove, Mahā-Dhanaka pointed and said, "There, Your Majesty! The golden deer lives in that grove of mango and sal trees."

The king ordered his soldiers to surround the grove and not to let the deer escape. With their weapons at the ready, the men formed a circle around the grove. When they were all in place, they began shouting, beating the bushes, and closing in.

The golden deer heard their shouts and realized that he was in danger. "That sounds like a great army," he thought. "I must be careful." After standing up slowly, he looked around and saw the king. "Where the king stands is where I must go to be safe," he thought, and he began running in that direction.

When the king saw the golden stag, he thought, "That magnificent deer must be very strong! If he charges me, I will frighten him with an arrow. If he tries to run away, I will hit him with my arrow to weaken him, but I must take him alive." As the king stood facing the golden deer, he strung his bow.

The deer continued running toward him, so the king fitted an arrow and pulled back the string. When the deer saw this, he called out urgently, "Your Majesty! Please hold fast! Do not let your arrow fly!"

The king was enthralled by the golden stag's melodious voice. He lowered his bow and let it fall to the ground. Then he stood still, as if transfixed. The golden deer approached the king more slowly, continuing to speak. "Please tell me, Sire, who it was that brought you here. Who told you that you would find a golden deer living in this grove?"

When the king's soldiers heard the beautiful voice of the golden deer, they, too, dropped their weapons and drew near to listen as he spoke to the king.

With his voice as sweet as honey and as soft as the tinkling of a bell, the deer repeated his questions, "Sire, who brought you here? Who told you that I was living in this grove?" Just then, Mahā-Dhanaka approached to find out what was happening.

The king pointed him out and said, "That is the man who told me that you were here."

The golden deer looked directly at Mahā-Dhanaka and cried, "I would have done better to have saved a log from drowning than to have saved you!"

"What do you mean?" the king asked. "What is going on? What is wrong here? Who are you blaming? A man? A beast? A log?"

"Sire, I am blaming this man!" replied the golden deer. "He was being carried away by the swift current, but I rescued him from drowning. When I showed him the way out of the forest, he solemnly promised never to tell anyone that he had seen me nor to reveal my place of refuge. Now, even though I saved his life, I am in mortal danger because of his treachery. If you have anything to do with this wicked man, you will surely regret it!"

"You scoundrel!" the king shouted furiously at Mahā-Dhanaka. "How could you reward such kindness with rank betrayal? You deserve to die!" Picking up his bow and aiming an arrow directly at the traitor, the king cried, "I'll let fly this arrow and pierce your cruel heart! After showing such ingratitude, you don't deserve to live!"

"Please, Your Majesty!" the golden deer spoke again, intervening with a voice as sweet as the most fragrant blossoms. "Of course, this wicked man should be ashamed of his contemptible deed, but killing is never right. Please do not harm him. Let the wretch go free. Give him, Sire, everything you promised, for, after all, he did what he told you he would do. As for me, I freely offer you my services. I will do whatever you desire."

"Noble animal!" the king exclaimed. "You are not only magnificent to behold, but your conduct is exemplary and worthy of a boon! How remarkable that you return good for evil in this way! Men!" he ordered his soldiers. "Release this ingrate! Give him his reward, and let him get out of my sight!"

The golden deer again spoke to the king. "Sire," he said, "it is easy to understand the cry of a jackal or of a bird, but the word of a man is never sure. A man may say, 'This is my friend, my companion, my kin,' but then, one day, affection disappears, and hatred takes its place."

"Oh, king of the deer! Do not imagine that I am like that! I will not withhold the boon I have offered you, not even if it costs me my kingdom. You will always be my friend! I guarantee that I will keep my word. Please trust me!"

The king asked the golden deer to choose a boon, and the deer replied, "Your Majesty, I would ask that all creatures within your kingdom be free from danger."

"Granted!" exclaimed the king. "Now let us return together to Bārānasi!"

The king invited the golden stag to deliver a discourse not only to Queen Khemā but to the entire court. When the deer agreed, the king declared a festival and ordered that the city be decorated. Standing on a beautiful dais especially erected for him, the great stag spoke in his rich golden voice. He admonished everyone to practice generosity and to act virtuously at all times. To the king, he taught the ten duties of a king. When the festival ended, the golden deer returned to the forest and rejoined his herd.

The king sent a courtier, accompanied by a drummer, around the city to read his proclamation: "I, Brahmadatta, king of Kāsi, hereby grant protection to all living creatures within the borders of my kingdom! From this day on, no one is to harm any beast or any bird!"

Herds of deer began roaming the countryside, devouring crops, but no one dared chase them away. Finally, driven to desperation, a contingent of farmers complained to the king that they could not harvest what they had planted because of the depredations of the deer. They appealed for relief.

The king listened sympathetically, but he declared, "To the noble golden deer, I granted the boon of safety, peace, and life for all creatures. I gave my word, and I cannot go back on that. No matter what the people wish, even if my kingdom should cease to exist, I cannot break that sacred promise!"

News of the king's decision spread far and wide. The people realized that there was nothing more they could say. When the golden deer learned that the farmers were suffering, he assembled all the deer. "From now on," he declared, "you must not devour the crops of men!" Then he sent a message to the court, requesting that every farmer in the kingdom mark his fields so that the deer would know not to graze there. When this was done, farmers and deer once more lived in harmony. Even to this day, when deer see a field so marked, they do not touch the crops.

Having concluded his story, the Buddha identified the birth: "At that time, Devadatta was Mahā-Dhanaka, Ānanda was King Brahmadatta, and I was the golden deer."

188

From a Few Words
Sarabha-Miga Jātaka

It was while staying at Jetavana that the Buddha told this story about the wisdom of Venerable Sāriputta.

In the seventh year after the Buddha's Enlightenment, a rich man of Rā-jagaha placed an expensive sandalwood almsbowl on the top of a high pole and issued a challenge to ascetics to get it down. Encouraged by Venerable Moggallāna, Venerable Pindola used his supernatural power to rise into the air and to retrieve the bowl.

Many people were impressed, and the followers of other ascetics chided their teachers, "Why didn't you use your supernatural powers and get the bowl?"

Those ascetics scoffed and belittled the feat. "Such a thing means nothing to us. Why should we display our true abilities for the sake of a small wooden bowl? The greedy Sākyan bhikkhus were just showing off!"

The Buddha rebuked Venerable Pindola for using his powers in perform-ing a tawdry magic trick for such an unworthy end. The bowl was forfeited to the Sangha to be ground into sandalwood powder, and bhikkhus were thereafter forbidden to display any supernatural powers they might possess.

When the ascetics from other sects heard about this, they thought, "Since Gotama has prohibited the use of supernatural powers, he will not perform any miracles himself." They began to speak differently about such feats. "Actually," they said to their followers, "our supernatural powers are much greater than those of Gotama's disciples. If we wanted to, we could very easily outdo any of them. We could even outdo Gotama himself! In fact, we challenge him! If he performs even one miracle, we will perform one twice as difficult, twice as amazing!"

When bhikkhus reported this to the Buddha, he calmly replied, "I will accept their challenge."

When King Bimbisāra heard about this, he asked the Buddha, "Will you perform a miracle, Venerable Sir?"

"Yes, Sire, I will."

"Wasn't a prohibition placed on the display of supernatural powers?" the king asked.

"The prohibition was given to my disciples. No such rules limit what a Buddha may or may not do. Although others are forbidden to pick flowers and fruit in your royal park, Sire, certainly that rule does not apply to you!"

"Where do you intend to perform your miracle, Venerable Sir?"

"In Sāvatthī, under a Ganda mango tree."

"What must I do?" asked the king.

"Nothing is needed, Sire."

The next morning, while the Buddha and the bhikkhus were walking for alms, people asked the bhikkhus what the Buddha was going to do. "Under a Ganda mango tree, near the city gate of Sāvatthī," the bhikkhus replied, "the Blessed One will perform a twofold miracle which will confound the ascetics of other sects."

People began talking excitedly, "This miracle is going to be fantastic! I mustn't miss it! Let's go to Sāvatthī!" Many locked their doors and followed the Buddha out of the city. Rival ascetics and their disciples also joined the throng. They declared to any who would listen that they, too, would perform a miracle in the same place.

In Sāvatthī, King Pasenadi asked the Buddha, "Is it true, Venerable Sir, that you are going to perform a miracle here?"

"Yes, it is true," the Buddha replied. "When?"

"One week from today, on the full-moon day of Āsālha."

"Shall I prepare a pavilion for you, Venerable Sir?"

"That will not be necessary. In the place where I will perform my miracle, Sakka will prepare a jeweled pavilion twelve yojanas in diameter. You need do nothing on that account."

"Shall I announce the event, Venerable Sir?"

"Proclaim it widely if you wish, Sire."

Every day for seven days, the king sent his royal crier throughout the city on a richly caparisoned elephant to announce, "On the full-moon day of Āsālha, under a Ganda mango tree near the gate of Sāvatthī, the Buddha will perform a twofold miracle, which will utterly confound all rival ascetics!"

No one knew what a Ganda mango tree was, but, in order to prevent any miracle, the rival ascetics ordered their followers to cut down every mango tree of any kind in and around the city of Sāvatthī.[1]

When the proclamation was made on the last day, Sakka used his power to extend its range so it could be heard far beyond Sāvatthī. He also shortened the distance so that everyone who wanted to attend would be able to reach the city gate in time to see the event.

On the morning of the day appointed, the royal gardener was taking an exceptionally large, ripe, and flawless golden mango to the palace for the king's breakfast. When he saw the Buddha on his almsrounds at the city gate, he thought, "This fruit is worthy of the Blessed One!" He offered it to the Buddha, who immediately sat down and ate it. When he finished, he handed the seed to Venerable Ānanda and said, "Give this seed to the gardener. Let him plant it at this spot. Because his name is Ganda, the tree that grows here will be known as the Ganda mango tree." As soon as Ganda had smoothed the earth over the seed, a red shoot burst through the soil. As a crowd watched, the shoot grew into a magnificent tree with a straight and sturdy trunk and thick branches full of dark green leaves. When it reached one hundred hatthas in height, tiny flowers bloomed on every branch, and bees swarmed around the tree. The flowers quickly became small green fruit, which swelled into golden mangoes. A slight breeze arose, and the newly ripened fruit began falling to the ground. Bhikkhus picked up some of the luscious mangoes and carried them back to the monastery.

That evening, Sakka summoned Vissakamma and ordered him to create the magnificent jeweled pavilion. A vast crowd filled the pavilion, which was, as the Buddha had told the king it would be, twelve yojanas long. Myriads of devas who had come to witness the miracle hovered in the air above the pavilion.

As the full moon rose, the Buddha appeared and stood beneath the branches of the tree. Suddenly, water gushed from the upper part of his body, and flames shot out from the lower part. Then he reversed the order. Next, flames shot out from his right side, and water gushed from the left. Then he

---

1 One version of this story says that they paid the owners of the trees. Another says that they cut down the trees without permission, which infuriated many people.

reversed that order, as well. The fire and water never mingled.[2] Every pore of his body emitted rays of six colors creating a resplendence beyond words. That marvelous light reached up to the Brahma heavens and down to the hells. As the Buddha preached to the devas and the people, he walked up and down a jeweled walkway which he had created in the air. The Buddha also multiplied himself innumerable times in the branches of the tree such that each listener was able to see and to hear according to his own particular disposition and level of understanding. All those who had not had faith in the Buddha before this became his followers, while those who had already had faith became more zealous in their practice of the Noble Eightfold Path and in their desire for Nibbāna.

Every Buddha performs this twin miracle, and it is the tradition that, after performing it, he goes to Tāvatimsa. Thus, did the Buddha disappear from Sāvatthī and, in only three steps, reach Tāvatimsa, where he spent the rains retreat, preaching the Abhidhamma to devas, including his mother, who had descended from Tusita in order to hear the Teaching.

Just before the end of the rains retreat, Venerable Moggallāna went to Tāvatimsa to confer with the Buddha about the ceremony marking the end.

"Where is Sāriputta spending the rains retreat?" the Buddha asked.

"Venerable Sir, after witnessing the great twin miracle, he went to Sankassa and has remained there."

"Moggallāna, in one week's time, I will descend from this heaven to Sankassa, near the city gate. Let those who wish to behold the Tathāgata descending gather there."

Venerable Moggallāna informed the people of Sāvatthī and, at the appointed time, transported a multitude to Sankassa, thirty yojanas away, in an instant.

When the Buddha informed Sakka that it was time for him to return to the realm of men, the king of the devas ordered Vissakamma to build a staircase. Vissakamma created a triple staircase. The center stairs were bejeweled, with silver and gold stairs on either side. The top rested on the peak of Sineru in Tāvatimsa, and the foot was positioned beside the gate of Sankassa. The Buddha descended the center stairs. On one side, Sakka was carrying the Buddha's robe and bowl, and, on the other, Brahmā was holding an umbrella. Many other devas paid their respects with divine garlands and heavenly perfumes. When the Buddha reached the bottom step, Venerable Sāriputta greeted him at the head of the great assembly.

---

2 Although the fire and water appeared to be simultaneous, they were actually alternating. This is called yamaka-pātihāriya, which can be done only by a Buddha since no one else has perfected his power of concentration to the point of being able to alternate so quickly between water and fire kasinas.

The Buddha thought, "Moggallāna has amply demonstrated his supernatural power. Upāli has been recognized as thoroughly versed in the Vinaya, but Sāriputta's wisdom, which is second only to mine, has not yet been adequately shown. Let me allow him to demonstrate the brilliance of his wisdom!"

First, the Buddha asked a question which even ordinary people could answer. Then he asked a question which could be answered only by those who had attained at least the first path. Successively, he asked questions requiring the attainment of the second, third, and fourth paths. After asking a question which Venerable Moggallāna could answer, the Buddha asked a question which only Venerable Sāriputta could understand, and that great disciple answered it with ease.

The entire assembly marveled at the depth of Venerable Sāriputta's understanding. Thence forth, everyone recognized the excellence of the wisdom of the Captain of the Teaching.

Next, the Buddha asked Venerable Sāriputta another question, which required the understanding of a Buddha: "Some are on the way, and some have reached the goal. What are the manners and the conversation of each?"

Venerable Sāriputta immediately understood that the Blessed One was asking him to describe the proper deportment of bhikkhus as they progress toward arahatship, but he was not sure on what the Buddha wanted him to base his answer—the five aggregates, the four elements, or the organs and objects of sense. The Buddha realized Venerable Sāriputta's hesitation and knew that with only one hint, Venerable Sāriputta would be able to expound the answer. "Sāriputta," he said, "consider 'this being'!" Venerable Sāriputta immediately understood that he was to base his answer on the aggregates, and he completely and perfectly formulated the answer to the Buddha's question.

Finally, Venerable Sāriputta posed a question, which opened the way for the Buddha to teach the Dhamma with great eloquence to the assembly,[3] which extended for twelve yojanas and comprised thirty crores of beings, including both devas and men, and all, without exception, were satisfied with his teaching.

When his discourse was finished, the Buddha left Sankassa and proceeded to Sāvatthī. The next day, the bhikkhus were talking about Venerable Sāriputta's wisdom and how skillfully he had explained in full what the Buddha had asked in brief. When the Buddha heard what they were discussing, he said, "This is not the first time, Bhikkhus, that Sāriputta has answered at length a question briefly put. He did the same before." Then he told this story of the past.

---

3 Sāriputta Sutta (Sutta Nipāta, Atthakavagga, 16).

Long, long ago, when Brahmadatta was reigning in Bārānasi, the Bodhisatta was a handsome stag in the forest.

King Brahmadatta was extremely fond of hunting. He was a very good hunter, and he judged other men on their skill in hunting.

One day, he went with a large party to the forest and told his courtiers, "Anyone who lets a deer get past him will be punished!"

The men realized that the deer had to go toward the king, so they placed him at the head of the path. They surrounded a great thicket and began beating the ground. The mighty stag leaped from the thicket and tried to flee. He darted here and there, looking for an escape route, but, on three sides, archers were standing at the ready. The deer ran toward the king, who was standing a little apart as his men had planned. When the king saw the powerful stag with blazing eyes rushing toward him, he was so dazzled he could hardly see. He shot his arrow, but the stag was quicker, and the arrow missed its mark. The stag burst free, found a clear path, and bounded away like a cloud before the wind.

The courtiers began to make sport of the king, laughing and joking about the deer that got away. This made the king furious. "I'll show you!" he shouted. "I'll catch that stag if it's the last thing I do!" Grabbing his sword, he tore off on foot after the deer. He ran for three yojanas without losing sight of the stag. When the animal plunged back into the deep forest, the king was following closely behind. Right in the middle of the path was a deep pit, formed when the roots of an ancient tree that had fallen rotted away. The pit was full of water. Even before it saw the pit, the great deer sensed water and swerved to avoid it. The king was oblivious to the danger and fell in.

Realizing that he was no longer being pursued, the great deer stopped and turned back. He cautiously approached the pit and saw the king, struggling to keep his head above the water. Although he knew that the king had tried to slay him, the stag felt no malice toward him, but only compassion. "I will not allow this king to die in this wild spot," he resolved. "I will deliver him from this great peril!" Aloud he shouted, "Don't be afraid, Sire! I will rescue you from the pit!"

Working as earnestly as he would for his own son, the great deer managed to free the king from what otherwise would have been his muddy unmarked grave. When, at last, the king was safely out of the watery pit, the deer rested briefly. Then, placing the king on his back, he transported him back to within hailing distance of his hunting party. Before returning him to the courtiers, the stag admonished the king to rule righteously and established him in the five precepts.

The king was so pleased with the teaching that he did not want to part from his rescuer. "King of the deer," he begged, "please come to Bārānasi with me! You may rule my kingdom!"

"Sire," the stag replied, "I am an animal! I have no use for a kingdom! If you have any affection for me, keep the precepts I have taught you, and instruct your subjects to keep them as well. Do good deeds, and be generous. Rule wisely and with righteousness." Bidding farewell, the stag returned to the forest.

Even after the king had returned to the city, the recollection of the noble qualities of the great stag who had saved his life filled his eyes with tears. He immediately mounted his royal elephant and, surrounded by a division of his army, led a procession around the city. To the accompaniment of a drum, a crier read out his proclamation: "From this day on, all the inhabitants of Bārānasi are to observe the five precepts!" He did not tell anyone, however, of the great kindness that had been done to him by the stag.

At daybreak the next morning, after a good night's sleep on his gorgeous couch, the king again remembered the stag's noble qualities and sat up cross-legged. With a joyful heart, he began singing:

> "Never give up hope, my good man! Be wise, and keep up your courage! I, indeed, have reached my goal!

> "Never give up hope, my good man! Be wise, and keep your spirits up, no matter how pressed! I fought the waves and reached the shore!

> "Strive on, my good man! Be wise, and keep up your courage! I, indeed, have reached my goal!

> "Strive on, my good man! Be wise, and keep your spirits up, no matter how pressed! I fought the waves and reached the shore!

> "One who is wise, though overwhelmed with pain, never gives up hope that bliss will come again.

> "Men have many feelings of both joy and woe, but, unaware and heedless, they march on straight to death!

> "The unexpected happens, while what one expects does not; just wishing does not make one happy."

Just as the king had begun singing, his chief advisor had arrived at the door and was about to go in. Not wishing to disturb the king, however, he had hesitated, unannounced, and stood at the door listening so that he heard all that the king sang. As soon as the king finished, he tapped lightly. "Who is there?" asked the king.

"It is I, Sire," replied the advisor.

"Come in, Teacher," the king called.

"Long live the king!" the advisor said, as he entered. "I am very pleased that your hunting trip yesterday was so rewarding. I'm very sorry that you missed the deer and that the others mocked you so mercilessly. You must have been very tired after chasing the stag for such a long way. Perhaps that is why you fell into the pit. How marvelous that the magnificent stag, feeling compassion, rescued you from drowning! That was very kind and courageous of the animal! It is wonderful that he was completely free from thoughts of anger and vengeance! It is also wonderful that you, in recollecting his magnanimity, would sing such beautiful words of praise!"

"Teacher!" exclaimed the king. "You may have heard about my missing the deer from some of the courtiers, but I have told no one about my falling into the pit and my encounter with the stag. How did you know? Were you there yesterday? Have you met a witness that I did not see?"

"No, Sire, I was not there," the advisor assured him. "Nor have I heard about your hunting trip from anyone else. I happened to overhear your song just now, and I understood clearly everything that happened. From your own sweet words, I understood exactly what you were describing. Thus, can a wise man discern the full meaning of what he hears in brief."

The king was delighted at his advisor's mental acuity and rewarded him handsomely.

Encouraged by the teaching of the deer, King Brahmadatta devoted himself to almsgiving and to good deeds. Following his exhortation and example, the citizens of Bārānasi also practiced morality and generosity, and many were reborn in heaven. Sakka noticed the sudden increase in arrivals in Tāvatimsa and understood the cause. He decided to test the king.

One day, the king and the chief advisor went to the royal park for target practice. As the king was about to shoot, Sakka caused the magnificent stag to appear between the king and the target. Recognizing the king of the deer, the king froze and could not release his arrow.

Sakka caused the advisor to say, "Sire, your arrow has been certain death to many powerful foes! Why do you hesitate now? Certainly, venison is proper meat for warriors like you. Prove your skill and kill that deer!"

"Of course, a stag is a suitable target for a warrior's bow," replied the king, "but I am grateful to this animal, and I dare not think of killing it."

"Actually, Your Majesty," the advisor continued, speaking for Sakka, "if you kill it, thereby fulfilling your obligation as a warrior, you will become king of the devas. On the other hand, if you hesitate from mere sentimentality, you doom yourself to hell and to judgment by King Yama."

"So be it!" the king declared. "Even to escape from King Yama's wrath, I will not harm this deer. When I was helpless, without hope, and drowning in that pit, it was this very stag who saved my life! How could I kill my benefactor, who showed me such mercy and forgiveness?"

After hearing those brave words, Sakka revealed himself and stood poised in the air. "Long live the righteous King Brahmadatta!" he proclaimed. "This ruse, including the words your advisor spoke, constituted a test, and you have nobly proved your gratitude and virtue. May you continue to rule your kingdom with wisdom and righteousness. Continue to guide your subjects along the path of generosity, and your kingdom will be at peace. Live blamelessly, and you will be reborn in heaven!" The stag vanished, and Sakka himself returned, with great glory, to Tāvatimsa.

Having concluded his story, the Buddha identified the birth: "At that time, Ānanda was King Brahmadatta, Sāriputta was the chief advisor, and I was the noble stag."

Glossary of Terms

Abhidhamma: Abstract Teaching; the collection of texts in which the underlying doctrinal principles presented in the Suttas are reworked and reorganized into a systematic framework that can be applied to an investigation into the nature of mind and matter. The Abhidhamma Pitaka is the third division of the Tipitaka.

aggregate: See five aggregates.

Ājīvika: a sect of naked ascetics; followers of Makkhali Gosāla.

anumodana: a Dhamma teaching given by the Sangha following an offering, meant to encourage the donor, to rejoice in the donation, to dedicate the merit made, and to invite others to share in it.

arahat: a fully-enlightened one, who, having freed his mind of all defilements, has attained Nibbāna and is not subject to further rebirth.

Asadisadāna: the unmatched offering which occurs only once for each Buddha.

Āsālha: the eighth month of the Indian lunar calendar; the beginning of the rains retreat.

asseveration of truth (saccakiriya): a statement of truth, the force of which is used to obtain a desired result.

asura: a class of pugnacious, but cowardly and perpetually angry, beings, roughly equivalent to Titans. Sakka evicted the deva-asuras from Tāvatimsa while they were drunk. They continue to maintain a heavenly existence in a place outside, but equal to, Tāvatimsa. There are, quite distinct from this, beings called asura-kāya, sometimes referred to as peta-asuras and niraya-asuras. These beings lead a miserable life in the third woeful realm. Their suffering is very similar to that of the peta and niraya realms.

bael a Bengal quince; a woodapple.

bhikkhu: a fully ordained monk in the Buddha's order; a man who has left the household life to seek the end of suffering. He lives a life of discipline in accordance with the Vinaya.

bhikkhunī: a fully ordained nun in the Buddha's order; a woman who has left the household life to seek the end of suffering. She lives a life of discipline in accordance with the Vinaya.

Bodhi tree: the tree under which a Supreme Buddha attains Enlightenment. Within the Sāsana of that Buddha, saplings from that tree, wherever they are planted, are respected. For Gotama Buddha, the Bodhi tree was the pipal tree (Ficus religiosa).

Bodhisatta: one striving for Buddhahood; "a Buddha-to-be." The term is used to describe someone from the time he makes his aspiration and receives confirmation from a living Buddha until his full Enlightenment.

Brahmā: a deva in the non-sensual heavens of form or formlessness which are called the Brahma heavens.

Brahma heavens (Brahma-loka): the highest heavens, where beings enjoy blissful existence. Birth in these realms is achieved by practicing concentration meditation, particularly on the Four Brahma Vihāras to the point of attaining jhāna.

Brahma Vihāra: See Four Brahma Vihāras.

brahmin (brāhmana): a member of the highest caste in Indian society, respected as such and qualified to perform rituals and sacrifices. Rejecting the caste system, the Buddha used the term to refer to one who was worthy of respect, not because of birth, but because he had reached the goal and had become an arahat.

Buddha: one who attains full Enlightenment on his own. A Supreme Buddha is one who, having discovered for himself the liberating path of Dhamma, after its having been forgotten by the world for a tremendously long period of time, teaches others so that they, too, may attain Enlightenment. There have been and will continue to be innumerable Supreme Buddhas. The Bodhisatta made his aspiration to become a Buddha at the time of Buddha Dīpankara. From that time until he became the Buddha Gotama, there were twenty-four Supreme Buddhas, the last being Kassapa Buddha. The next Buddha will be Mettaya Buddha.

catumadhu: literally, four sweet things. This mixture of ghee, oil, honey, and jaggery is allowable as medicine for members of the Sangha in the afternoon.

candāla: an outcaste; an untouchable; someone born outside (below) the four castes.

caste: the system of social class in traditional India. The four main castes, said to have been created by Brahmā, are: brāhmana, brahmin, teacher, priest; khattiya, warrior, king, ruler; vessa, businessman, artisan, farmer; sudda, worker, servant to the others

cetiya: a stupa; a pagoda; a monument, originally a mound, enshrining the relic of an enlightened one or commemorating a great event. The term can also be used for a funerary mound, particularly in pre-Buddhist times.

craving (tanhā): the longing for sense pleasures, for existence, and for non-existence; the origin of suffering. Craving is the second of the Four Noble Truths.

crore: ten million.

defilement (kilesa): any of ten unwholesome, mind-defiling qualities. These are: 1. greed (lobha); 2. hatred; (dosa); 3. delusion (moha); 4. conceit (māna); 5. speculative views (ditthi); 6. skeptical doubt (vicikicchā); 7. mental torpor (thīna); 8. restlessness (uddhacca); and 9. shamelessness (ahirika); 10. lack of moral dread (anotappa). The first three are considered the root defilements from which all the others arise.

determination (adhitthāna): the resolute will-power which forces all obstructions out of one's path, such that, no matter what may come in the form of grief or disaster, one's eyes never turn from the goal. Determination is the eighth of the Ten Perfections.

deva: a heavenly being; a deity. This can be a resident of one of the heavens or a guardian or spirit of a tree, a hill, a doorway, or some other entity.

Dhamma: the Buddha's Teaching. Dhamma-vinaya is the Buddha's own term for the religion he founded.

dhutanga: the ascetic practices allowed by Buddha to be voluntarily undertaken. They are: 1. wearing only rag robes; 2. having only one set of robes; 3. eating only almsfood; 4. not skipping any house on almsrounds; 5. eating only one meal a day; 6. eating only from the bowl; 7. refusing any further food; 8. staying in the forest; 9. staying under a tree;

10. staying in the open (without a roof or a tree for shelter); 11. staying in a charnel ground; 12. accepting whatever accommodation is offered; and 13. never lying down.

Discipline: See Vinaya.

eight precepts: See precepts.

energy (viriya): the mental vigor or strength of character, which is the persevering effort to avoid or to overcome evil and unwholesome things and to develop and to maintain wholesome things. Energy is the fifth of the Ten Perfections.

Enlightenment (bodhi): the state of complete understanding, the supreme awakening from the stupor caused by the mental defilements, and the perfect comprehension of the Four Noble Truths; Nibbāna.

eon (kappa): a world-cycle; a world-age; the period between the formation and the destruction of the world.

equanimity (upekkhā): maintaining an even balance in times of happiness and adversity in the face of praise or blame; discerning rightly, viewing justly, and looking impartially, with neither attachment nor detachment, with neither favor nor disfavor; not to be mistaken for indifference or callousness. Equanimity is the tenth of the Ten Perfections and the fourth of the Four Brahma Vihāras.

first path: See four stages of Enlightenment.

five aggregates (pañca khandha): the five aspects or factors of clinging; the physical and mental components of the personality and of sensory experience, which make up individual existence: 1. form (rūpa), 2. feeling (vedanā), 3. perception (saññā;), 4. mental formations (sankhāra), and 5. consciousness (viññāna).

five extraordinary powers: the powers attainable by perfecting mental concentration. They are: 1. magical power (iddhi-vidha); 2. divine ear (dibba-sota); 3. penetration of the mind of others (ceto-pariya-ñāna);); 4. divine eye (dibba-cakkhu); and 5. remembrance of former existences (pubbenivāsānussati).

five precepts: See precepts.

five symbols of royalty: sword, umbrella, crown, slippers, and fan.

Four Brahma Vihāras: also called the Four Divine Abidings; the four sublime abodes that are attained through the development of meditation on: 1. loving-kindness (mettā), 2. compassion (karunā), 3. sympathetic joy (mudita), and 4. equanimity (upekkhā).

four elements (dhātu): the four physical properties which are the ultimate constituents of all matters. They are: 1. earth, solidity (pathavi); 2. water, cohesiveness (āpo); 3. heat, fire (tejo); and 4. air, wind (vayo). All four are present in every material object, though in varying degrees of strength. Sometimes, the Buddha spoke of five or six elements, in which case, space (ākāsa) or space and consciousness (viññāna) are included.

Four Foundations of Mindfulness (satipatthāna): the bases for maintaining moment-by-moment mindfulness and developing mindfulness through meditation. They are: 1. contemplation on the body; 2. contemplation on feelings; 3. contemplation on the mind; and 4. contemplation on mental objects.

Four Great Kings (cātummahārājikā): the four powerful devas who reign over the lowest plane of heaven and serve as guardians of the four quarters. They are: Vessavana of the north, Dhatarattha of the east, Virūlhaka of the south, and Virūpakkha of the west. Their retinues consist of, respectively, yakkhas, gandhabbas, kumbhandas, and nāgas. Life in this realm lasts ninety thousand years, and beings are reborn here because of various acts of faith, prompted by rather unrefined motives. Their realm is located mid-way up Mount Sineru.

Four Noble Truths (cattāri ariya saccāni): 1. All forms of existence are subject to suffering. 2. The origin of suffering is craving. 3. The extinction of suffering, Nibbāna, is possible by eliminating craving. 4. The Noble Eightfold Path is the way to bring about the extinction of suffering.

four stages of Enlightenment: the four levels of progress on the path to Nibbāna. They are: 1. stream-enterer (sotāpanna), one who has attained the first path and who will undergo no more than seven rebirths, none of which will be lower than a human being; 2. once-returner (sakādagāmi), one who has attained the second path and will be reborn only once more in the human world and will attain Nibbāna in that life; 3. non-returner (anāgāmi), one who has attained the third path and will attain Nibbāna without being reborn in any sensuous realm; 4. fully-enlightened one (arahat), one who has attained the fourth path, Nibbāna, and will not be reborn again.

fourth path: See four stages of Enlightenment.

gandhabba: the lowest form of deva, inhabiting the realm of the Four Great Kings. The Buddha described gandhabbas as dwelling in the fragrance (ganda) of plants and flowers.

Gang of Six (chabbaggiya): the six bhikkhus frequently mentioned as being guilty of various Vinaya offences. These bhikkhus—Assaji, Punabbasu, Panduka, Lohitaka, Mettiya, and Bhummaja—were notorious for causing trouble.

Gaṅgā: the modern Ganges River.

garula (Sanskrit, garuda): an enormous supernatural bird; the implacable foe of the nāgas.

gavuta: one-fourth of a yojana.

generosity (dāna): a virtue which confers upon the giver the double blessing of inhibiting the immoral thoughts of selfishness and of developing the pure thoughts of selflessness. Generosity is the first of the Ten Perfections and the first of the ten duties of a king. Dāna often refers to giving alms to ascetics and members of the Sangha or to the alms thus given.

good deeds (kusala kamma): the wholesome, skillful, and meritorious actions which are bound to result eventually in happiness and a favorable outcome, whereas bad deeds (akusala kamma) lead to unhappiness and unfavorable results.

Great Renunciation (abhinikkhamana): Prince Siddhattha's act of leaving home in search of Enlightenment.

hattha: a hand; a measurement, similar to a cubit; namely, the distance from the elbow to the end of the middle finger.

Himavat: the region of the Himalaya Mountains. It is said to be three hundred thousand yojanas across with eighty-four thousand peaks, the highest being five hundred yojanas tall. The region includes seven great lakes—Anotatta, Kannamunda, Rathakāra, Chaddanta, Kuṇāla,

Mandākinī, and Sīhappapātaka. Its forests have always been the refuge for ascetics. The region includes a mountain called Mahāpapāta where Pacceka Buddhas traditionally pass into final Nibbāna. The Himavat is inhabited by many supernatural creatures, and female nāgas go there to give birth.

impermanence (anicca): the doctrine that anything that has arisen will pass away. All conditioned things are in a constant state of flux and are of the nature to decay. Impermanence is the first of the Three Characteristics.

insight (vipassanā): the intuitive understanding of the reality of existence.

Jain: a sect of naked ascetics, followers of Nigantha Nātaputta.

jambu: a rose apple; a pink and green fruit. See Jambudīpa.

Jambudīpa: Land of the Rose Apple; the traditional name for the Indian subcontinent.

jhāna: mental absorption; a state of strong concentration in which the mind becomes fully immersed and absorbed in the chosen object of attention. There are eight jhānas (atthasamāpattiyo): four fine-material (rūpa jhāna) and four immaterial (arūpa jhāna).

kadamba: a tree with bright orange or yellow flowers, thought to reunite separated lovers.

kanavera: Indian oleander, a shrub with foul-smelling red flowers. A garland of these flowers (vajjhāmāla) was hung around the neck of a criminal on his way to execution.

kasina: an external device used to develop meditative concentration. There are ten kasinas in all: the elements—earth, water, fire, and air; the colors—blue, red, yellow, and white; and space and consciousness.

kathina: the ceremony marking the end of the rains retreat, when laypeople gather to express gratitude to the Sangha and to make a special offering of gifts, particularly new robes. Traditionally, the Sangha of a monastery receives an offering of cloth from laypeople and gives it to one of its members, who then dyes, cuts, and sews it into a robe before dawn of the following day.

Kattikā: in the Indian lunar calendar, the last month of the rainy season. It also refers to the constellation of Pleiades and to a traditional festival.

khattiya: See caste.

kinnara (female, kinnarī): a creature, half-bird and half-human, which lives in the Himavat.

kumbhanda: a low form of deva inhabiting the realm of the Four Great Kings. The name refers to a gourd or a pot (kumbha). They are so called, perhaps, because their bellies are like pots.

kuti: a bhikkhu's residence.

loving-kindness (mettā): a great regard, much deeper than goodwill, friendliness, or kindness, for all beings in all realms. It is the universal love through which one neither fears nor instills fear in any other being. Loving-kindness is the ninth of the Ten Perfections and the first of the Four Brahma Vihāras.

lower realms (apāya): woeful realms; states of deprivation; the four lowest planes of existence into which a being is reborn because of past unwholesome actions. They are: hell, the peta realm, the asura realm, and the animal realm. Of course, none of these states is permanent.

meditation (bhāvanā): mind training; mind development. There are two distinct types of meditation: tranquility (samatha) and insight (vipassanā). Tranquility meditation, which was practiced even before the Buddha's time, involves focusing the mind on an external object. Through this concentration, one can attain extraordinary powers and the jhānas. There are forty subjects suitable for tranquility meditation. Insight meditation requires concentration, but the goal is to develop purity of mind and insight into the Three Characteristics, which leads to Nibbāna. Meditation is the second section of the Noble Eightfold Path.

merit (puñña): the quality which purifies and cleanses the mind as the result of wholesome action. Accumulated merit can be shared with other beings, whenever that intention is expressed. There are ten meritorious actions:

1. generosity; 2. morality; 3. meditation; 4. reverence; 5. helping others; 6. sharing one's merit with others; 7. rejoicing in the merit of others; 8. teaching the Dhamma; 9. listening to the Dhamma; and 10. correcting one's views.

mindfulness (sati): self-collectedness; bare attention; the clear and single-minded awareness of what is actually happening in us and to us at the successive moments of perception.

morality (sīla): restraint through the precepts. For a layman, this means keeping the five or eight precepts. For an ascetic, there are additional rules, and, for a bhikkhu or a bhikkhunī, there are many more. Morality also includes all wholesome action of body, speech, and mind. Morality is the second of the Ten Perfections, the second of the ten duties of a king, and the first section of the Noble Eightfold Path.

nāga: a great supernatural serpent, capable of assuming the form of a human or a deva. The traditional enemy of the nāga is the garula. Sometimes a nāga swallows stones, hoping that, in that way, it will be too heavy to be carried away by a garula.

neem: a tree common in South Asia, considered beneficial for its medicinal properties. All parts of the tree are extremely bitter. Neem twigs are commonly used to make toothsticks for cleaning the teeth.

Nibbāna: Enlightenment; arahatship; the fourth path; liberation; the freeing of the mind from defilements (kilesas); the end of the round of rebirth (samsāra). The term refers to the extinguishing of a fire, so it also connotes stilling, cooling, and peace.

Nikāya: division, group. A group of texts within the Sutta Pitaka, the Collection of Discourses, of the Tipitaka.

Noble Eightfold Path (ariya magga): the Fourth Noble Truth. The factors are: 1. Right View; 2. Right Intention; 3. Right Speech; 4. Right Action; 5. Right Livelihood; 6. Right Effort; 7. Right Mindfulness; and 8. Right Concentration; This Path can be divided into three sections: Morality, 3–5; Meditation, 6–8; and Wisdom, 1–2.

non-self (anattā): the doctrine that neither within nor outside of the bodily and mental phenomena of existence can be found anything that, in the ultimate sense, can be regarded as a self-existing, real ego-entity, soul, or self. Non-self is the third of the Three Characteristics.

Pacceka Buddha: a fully enlightened Buddha who has attained perfect insight, but neither creates a Sangha nor establishes a Sāsana. Offerings to a Pacceka Buddha are of great efficacy. A Pacceka Buddha can also grant boons and make predictions.

panic: a type of millet which was made into a gruel. It was also used as a medicine.

Parinibbāna: a synonym for Nibbāna, though often used to refer to the passing away of a fully-enlightened one, particularly of a Supreme Buddha or a Pacceka Buddha.

path and fruit (magga-phala): the attainment (path) of one of the four stages of Enlightenment and the result (fruit) thereof.

patience (khanti): forbearance which includes enduring any suffering inflicted upon oneself by others. Patience is the sixth of the Ten Perfections and the ninth of the ten duties of a king.

Pātimokkha: the code of discipline for bhikkhus and bhikkhunīs, which is recited at every full and new moon.

Perfection (pāramī): See Ten Perfections.

peta: a hungry ghost; a miserable being born in the peta realm, one of the four lower realms. Petas are often depicted with huge bellies and tiny mouths which do not allow them to eat enough to ease their hunger. They are completely dependent for food and clothes on merit shared with them.

Plowing Festival: a festival in ancient India in which the king used a ceremonial plow to mark the beginning of the plowing season. Once, when Prince Siddhattha was a boy, he sat under a jambu tree during this festival and, for the first time, practiced meditation. The shadow of the tree continued to provide shade all day. Seeing this, King Suddhodana paid obeisance to his son.

precepts (sīla): virtue; morality; the training rules voluntarily undertaken to restrain one from doing unwholesome actions.

(a) five precepts (pañcasīla): 1. to abstain from killing, 2. to abstain from stealing, 3. to abstain from sexual misconduct; 4. to abstain from lying; and 5. to abstain from taking alcohol and drugs which cloud the mind. These are considered by Buddhists to be the minimum code of morality for a human being.

(b) eight precepts (atthasīla): the five precepts, except that the third becomes "to abstain from all sexual activity," plus 6. to abstain from eating after noon; 7. to abstain from indulging in music, singing, and dancing and from adorning the body; and 8. to abstain from using a large or high bed or chair. These are usually undertaken by laypeople on Uposatha days.

rains retreat (vassa): the period from July to October, corresponding roughly to the monsoon rainy season, when every bhikkhu and bhikkhunī is required to stay in a single place, without traveling, unless there is an urgent reason to do so.

rebirth (punabbhava): renewed existence in samsāra; the arising of a new group of the five aggregates after death. The consciousness arising in the new person is neither identical to nor different from the old consciousness, but is part of a causal continuum with it. Rebirth, which is conditioned by intentional action (kamma), may take place on any plane. [See The Thirty-one Planes of Existence]

renunciation (nekkhamma): giving up certain luxuries and worldly pleasures. Ultimately, renunciation, which implies freedom from sensual lust, is withdrawal from worldly life and pleasures by adopting the ascetic life to practice meditation and to make spiritual attainments. Renunciation is the third of the Ten Perfections.

requisites: (a) eight requisites (attha parikkharāni): the things which a member of the Sangha should have. They are: three robes, an almsbowl, a razor, a needle, a belt, and a water strainer.

(b) four requisites (cattāro paccaya): the things a member of the Sangha needs to sustain himself or herself. They are: robes, food, a dwelling place, and medicine.

Sakka's throne: the marble seat of the king of the devas, located in Sudhammā Hall. It grows hot and begins to shake for two different reasons. The first is the occurrence of a great injustice which requires Sakka's intervention. The second is that someone is performing an extremely meritorious act, which indicates, perhaps, that that person is striving to be reborn as Sakka in Tāvatimsa, in which case Sakka would be on the verge of losing his office.

sāmanera: a novice monk (sāmanerī, a novice nun), who keeps ten precepts, which are the eight precepts, with the seventh split into two, plus (10) to abstain from accepting gold and silver (money). A sāmanera or a sāmanerī is a candidate for higher ordination as a bhikkhu or a bhikkhunī.

samsāra: the round of existence through rebirth.

Sangha: the Buddha's order of bhikkhus and bhikkhunīs.

sāsana: dispensation; the legacy of a Supreme Buddha; the Buddhist religion. [See Dhamma]

second path: See four stages of Enlightenment.

seven precious things: gold, silver, pearls, gems, lapis lazuli, diamonds, and coral.

silk-cotton tree: a very large tree related to the kapok tree.

sudda: See caste.

suffering (dukkha): the doctrine that all phenomena and all experience are inherently unsatisfactory and lead to mental anguish. Suffering is the first of the Four Noble Truths and the second of the Three Characteristics.

Sutta: Discourse; a sermon attributed to the Buddha or to one of his closest disciples. The Sutta Pitaka, the Discourse Collection, is the second division of the Tipitaka. It is divided into five Nikāyas. The first four Nikāyas contain most of the actual discourses, or suttas. The Jātakas are included in the last Nikāya, Khuddaka Nikāya, or Minor Texts.

sympathetic joy (muditā): taking delight in the happiness or good fortune of others. Sympathetic joy is the third of the Four Brahma Vihāras.

tank: a man-made reservoir, usually rectangular, often with stone steps leading to the water for bathers.

Tathāgata: literally, "Thus Come One," an epithet which the Buddha used to describe himself.

Tāvatimsa: the Heaven of the Thirty-Three; the realm of Sakka, king of the devas.

ten courses of unwholesome action (dasa-akusala-kamma-patha): 1. killing any being; 2. stealing; 3. committing adultery; 4. lying; 5. slandering; 6. using harsh speech; 7. engaging in frivolous gossip; 8. being covetous; 9. having ill-will; and having wrong view. Abstaining from these constitutes the ten courses of wholesome action (dasa-kusala-kamma-patha).

ten duties of a king: the ten qualities a king must have to be considered a righteous ruler. They are: 1. generosity (dāna); 2. morality (sīla); 3. sacrifice (pariccāga), willingness to sacrifice everything—comfort, fame, even his life—for the people; 4. honesty (ajjava), integrity—neither fearing some nor favoring others and never taking recourse in any crooked or doubtful means to achieve one's ends; 5. kindness (maddava), gentleness which tempers firmness, so that a ruler is neither harsh nor cruel; 6. austerity of habits (tapa), self-control, shunning indulgence in sensual pleasures, and keeping the five senses under control; 7. freedom from ill-will (akkodha), bearing no grudge against anyone and acting with forbearance and love; 8. harmlessness (avihimsa), non-violence and a commitment to peace; 9. patience (khanti); and 10. non-opposition or uprightness (avirodha), ruling in harmony with the people, not opposing their will, and cultivating the spirit of amity among the people. (A different list is given in the text of Tale 210.)

Ten Perfections (dasa pāramī): the ten qualities of character which must be developed completely for one to attain Buddhahood, but of which the partial development is meritorious for any being. They are: 1. generosity (dāna); 2. morality (sīla); 3. renunciation (nekkhamma); 4. wisdom (paññā); 5. energy (viriya); 6. patience (khanti); 7. truthfulness (sacca); 8. determination (adhitthāna); 9. loving-kindness (mettā); and 10. equanimity (upekkhā). Each of these is given a separate entry in this glossary.

third path: See four stages of Enlightenment.

thirty-two parts of the body: one of the meditation subjects taught by the Buddha. They are: 1. hair of the head (kesa); 2. hair of the body (loma); 3. nails (nakha); 4. teeth (danta); 5. skin (taco); 6. flesh (mamsa); 7. sinew (nahāru); 8. bone (atthi); 9. marrow (atthimiñja); 10. kidneys (vakka); 11. heart (hadaya); 12. liver (yakana); 13. membrane (kilomaka); 14. spleen (pihaka); 15. lungs; (papphāsa); 16. intestines (anta); 17. mesentery (antaguna); 18. stomach (udariya); 19. feces (karīsa); 20. brain (matthalunga); 21. bile (pitta); 22. phlegm (semha); 23. pus (pubba); 24. blood (lohita); 25. sweat (seda); 26. lymph (meda); 27. tears (assu); 28 serum (vasa); 29. saliva (khela); 30. nasal mucous (singhānika); 31. synovial fluid (lasika); and 32. urine (mutta).

Three Characteristics (ti-lakkhana): the three basic facts of existence which are inherent in all conditioned phenomena. They are: 1. impermanence (anicca); 2. suffering (dukkha); and 3. non-self (anattā).

tinduka: an Indian persimmon.

Tipitaka: (literally, "Three Baskets"), the Buddhist canon; the collection of primary texts which form the doctrinal foundation of Buddhism. The three divisions are: 1. Vinaya Pitaka, Book of Discipline; 2. Sutta Pitaka, Book of Discourses; 3. Abhidhamma Pitaka, Book of Abstract Teaching. After the Buddha's Parinibbāna, the Teaching was arranged as the Tipitaka at the First Buddhist Council, a gathering of five hundred arahats. All the texts were memorized and, for about five hundred years, were transmitted and preserved orally. They were first written down in Sri Lanka about 100 B.C.E. when, due to hardship and famine, the number of bhikkhus declined to the point that it was feared that the Teaching would be lost.

toothstick: See neem.

Triple Gem (ti-ratana): the Teacher (Buddha), the Teaching (Dhamma), and the Order (Sangha).

truthfulness (sacca): keeping one's word and fulfilling a promise at any cost. It is said that a Bodhisatta may, at times, violate the other precepts but that he never tells a lie nor forsakes truthfulness. Truthfulness is the seventh of the Ten Perfections.

twenty-one wrong means of livelihood (ekavisati anesana): prac-tices which bhikkhus are forbidden to perform. They are: 1. medical practice; 2. acting as a messenger; 3. doing things at the behest of laymen; 4. lancing boils; 5. giving oil for medical application; 6. giving emetics; 7. giving purgatives; 8. preparing oil for nose-treatment; 9. preparing oil for medicine; 10. presenting bamboos; 11. presenting leaves; 12. present-ing flowers; 13. presenting fruits; 14. presenting soap-clay; 15. presenting toothsticks; 16. presenting water for washing the face; 17. presenting clay-powder; 18. using flattering speech; 19. speaking half-truths; 20. fondling children; and 21. running errands.

Uposatha: a day reserved for religious observance, corresponding to the phases of the moon (one, two, or four). In Buddhist practice, on Uposatha days, lay people gather to listen to the Dhamma and to observe eight precepts. On the new-moon and full-moon Uposatha days, bhik-khus assemble to recite the Patimokkha rules.

Veramba wind: a strong wind which blows at a great height.

vessa: See caste.

Verocanamani: the octagonal gem which Sakka gave to King Kusa (Tale 206). It is mentioned twice in Tale 216.

Vinaya: Discipline; texts concerning the rules of conduct governing the Sangha. The Vinaya Pitaka, the Collection of Discipline, is the first division of the Tipitaka. The Vinaya Pitaka also includes the story behind the origin of each rule. The rules are summarized in the Pātimokkha. There are 227 rules for bhikkhus and 311 for bhikkhunīs. Dhamma-vinaya is the Buddha's own term for the religion he founded.

water of donation (dakkhinodaka): water which the donor pours over the right hand of the recipient when a gift is made, indicating that the gift is freely given and dedicating the merit gained.

wisdom (paññā): right understanding of the real nature of the world; seeing things as they really are; ultimately, insight into the Three Char-acteristics. Wisdom is the fourth of the Ten Perfections and the third section of the Noble Eightfold Path.

yakkha (female, yakkhinī): a demon; an ogre; a superhuman being, often hostile to man. Some yakkhas resemble devas, but others resemble petas. They have strange characteristics; for example, they have red eyes, they cannot wink, and they cast no shadow. Sometimes, they are said to be repelled by palm leaves and iron. Their king is Vessavana, one of the Four Great Kings.

yojana: the distance a team of oxen can travel in one day; about twelve miles.

Glossary of Personal Names

This glossary includes those who were contemporaries of the Buddha. It does not include the innumerable characters who appear in the stories of the past. The two exceptions are Kassapa Buddha and Vipassi Buddha. (The numbers in parentheses at the end of each entry indicate the tales in this anthology in which the individual appears.)

Ajātasattu: the son of Bimbisāra, king of Magadha. Prince Ajātasattu became a generous supporter of Devadatta, who encouraged Ajātasattu to kill his father and to usurp the throne. Ajātasattu also aided Devadatta in his attempts to kill the Buddha. After Devadatta's death, King Ajātasattu repented and became a devoted follower of the Buddha, but his parricide prevented him from making any attainments. After a long rule, Ajātasattu was killed by his own son, Udāya, who had been born on the day that Bimbisāra died. According to the commentaries, Ajātasattu was reborn in hell, where he will suffer for 60,000 years, eventually becoming a Pacceka Buddha. (56, 62, 94, 130, 132, 179, 193, 212)

Ajita Kesakambala: one of the six teachers who were contemporaries of the Buddha. He taught materialism, stating that all is annihilated at death. (62)

Ālavaka: a yakkha in Ālavi, thirty yojanas from Sāvatthī. Vessavana, king of the yakkhas, had given him permission to eat anyone who stepped into the shade of the huge banyan tree near his mansion. The king of Ālavi, while hunting, did so, but avoided death by promising to send one victim daily. For twelve years, he sent prisoners, and later children. Finally, the only offering available was the king's own son. With compassion for the prince, the king, and the yakkha, the Buddha went there, but Ālavaka was away. When the gatekeeper went to inform Ālavaka, the Buddha entered the mansion and began teaching the yakkha's wives. Ālavaka returned and tried to kill the Buddha, first by frightening him and then by exhausting him. After going out from and reentering Ālavaka's house three times, the Buddha refused to leave again. Ālavaka then asked the Buddha a series of questions which had been handed down to him from Kassapa Buddha. The Buddha easily answered all of them. Ālavaka was delighted. He understood everything the Buddha said and attained the first path. The next morning, the king's men arrived and gave the prince to the yakkha. Ashamed of his former practices, Ālavaka handed the child to the Buddha. The king gave the reformed yakkha a special house, and the people gave regular vegetarian offerings. His conversion is one of the Eight Great Victories of the Buddha referred to in the Jayamangala Gāthā. (181, 216)

Ambattha: a brahmin, proud of his lineage and his learning, and the follower of another teacher. When the Buddha taught the Ambattha Sutta (Dīgha Nikāya, 3), Ambattha's teacher and other students were converted, but not Ambattha himself. According to the commentary, the Buddha knew that Ambattha would not benefit and, therefore, wasted no time on him. (216)

Ānanda: an eminent bhikkhu; the last personal attendant of the Buddha [See Tale 177]; "Treasurer of the Teaching." He was a Sākyan prince and a first cousin of the Buddha. Soon after ordaining, Venerable Ānanda attained the first path, but it was only after the Buddha's Parinibbāna, just in time to attend the First Buddhist Council, that Venerable Ānanda attained arahatship. Most suttas begin "Thus have I heard" because, at that council, Venerable Ānanda recited each discourse as he had heard it from the Buddha.

Venerable Ānanda was foremost among the bhikkhus in 1. having heard many of the Buddha's discourses; 2. having a good memory; 3. having mastery over the sequential structure of the teachings; 4. being steadfast in study; and 5. being the Buddha's attendant.

Venerable Ānanda was accomplished in seven ways: 1. in the doctrine; 2. in knowledge; 3. in knowledge of causes; 4. in investigation; 5. in having an eidetic memory with penetrative comprehension; 6. in applied attention; and 7. in the potentiality of Buddhahood. (5, 6, 8, 10, 14, 15, 16, 17, 20, 30, 32, 33, 34, 36, 40, 42, 55, 60, 61, 63, 65, 66, 67, 68, 73, 75, 77, 80, 82, 88, 91, 94, 95, 96, 98, 99, 104, 105, 106, 109, 112, 113, 116, 119, 121, 126, 130, 136, 144, 145, 147, 148, 150, 152, 153, 154, 155, 156, 157, 158, 160, 162, 163, 165, 170, 171, 172, 173, 175, 176, 177, 179, 181, 182, 183, 185, 187, 188, 189, 190, 196, 197, 198, 199, 203, 206, 207, 208, 210, 211, 213, 214, 215, 216)

Anāthapindika: a wealthy merchant, the great patron of the Buddha who built Jetavana Monastery near Sāvatthī. He appears in the occasions for many of the stories and attained the first path, but he is not mentioned in the identifications. (1, 10, 21, 22, 36, 98, 105, 108, 134, 136, 161, 182,)

Angulimāla: a bhikkhu. He was a serial murderer who was converted by the Buddha and became an arahat. [See Tale 207] His conversion is one of the Eight Great Victories of the Buddha referred to in the Jayamangala Gāthā. (29, 147, 181, 207, 216)

Anuruddha: an eminent bhikkhu; a Sākyan prince and first cousin of the Buddha. He was foremost among bhikkhus endowed with the divine eye. [See Tale 8] (8, 81, 95, 102, 167, 170, 190, 191, 197, 207, 210, 211, 215, 217)

Asita: a brahmin ascetic. A few days after Prince Siddhattha was born, Asita went to the palace. Instead of paying respect, the baby turned and touched the ascetic's head with his feet, signifying that he was the nobler. Asita smiled and then wept. He smiled because he knew that Prince Siddhattha would become a Buddha. He wept because he was too old to live to become his disciple. (217)

Baka-Brahmā: a deva in the Brahma heavens. Correcting his wrong view is one of the Eight Great Victories of the Buddha referred to in the Jayamangala Gāthā. [See Tale 151] (136, 151, 181, 216)

Bandhula: a son of a chieftain of Malla, who became commander-in-chief of King Pasenadi of Kosala. His wife's name was Mallikā [See Tale 179] (179)

Bhaddaji: a bhikkhu. He was the son of a wealthy merchant of Bhaddiya, a city in Anga. The Buddha went there to teach him. After hearing the Buddha's discourse, Bhaddaji attained arahatship. When the Buddha explained to Bhaddaji's father that, on that day, Bhaddaji had either to ordain or to pass away, the merchant let his son ordain. (This is related in the occasion to Jātaka 264, which is not included in this collection) This is one of the few instances in which a layman became an arahat. [See Suddhodana] (214)

Bhaddakaccānā: See Yasodharā.

Bhaddā-Kāpilānī: an eminent bhikkhunī. She was the daughter of a brahmin in Sāgala, a city in Madda. She was married, but the marriage was never consummated. (This took place very much as in Tales 129 and 206.) Her husband was named Pippali-mānava. They left the home-life together. He ordained as Venerable Mahā-Kassapa, and she lived as an ascetic until the bhikkhunī order was established. Soon after ordaining as a bhikkhunī, she attained arahatship. She was foremost among bhikkhunīs who could recall former lives. (210)

Bhaddiya: an eminent bhikkhu. He was a Sākyan prince. He was foremost among the bhikkhus of aristocratic birth. [See Tale 8] (8)

Bimbisāra: the king of Magadha and a strong supporter of the Buddha. He attained the first path. He was killed by his son Ajātasattu. (62, 132, 188, 193, 212, 214)

Channa: a bhikkhu. He was born on the same day as Prince Siddhattha and became his charioteer. He accompanied the prince at the time of the Great Renunciation, but returned to Kapilavatthu. Refused permission to leave the household life, he did not ordain until the Buddha returned to Kapilavatthu. Because of his closeness to the Buddha, he became conceited and could neither overcome his pride nor fulfill his monk's duties. He was chastised and punished for his obstinacy several times, the last instance being just before the Buddha's Parinibbāna. When Venerable Ānanda informed him of the Buddha's declaration that he was to be shunned by the Sangha, he was completely tamed and attained arahatship, at which point the penalty automatically expired. (142, 198, 217)

Ciñcā-Mānavikā: a female ascetic in Sāvatthī. At the instigation of rival ascetics, she accused the Buddha of making her pregnant. Exposing her lie is one of the Eight Great Victories of the Buddha referred to in the Jayamangala Gāthā. [See Tale 182] (80, 182, 217)

Citta: a merchant in Macchikāsanda, a town in Kāsi. When Venerable Mahānāma visited Macchikāsanda, Citta built a monastery in his garden, Ambātakārāma, which he presented to the Sangha. While listening to Venerable Mahānāma teach the Dhamma there, Citta attained the third path. He was foremost among laymen in teaching the Dhamma. (190)

Culla-Nandikā: nothing further seems to be known. (216)

Dabba: an eminent bhikkhu. He was the son of a Mallan family in Anupiya. He was born while his dead mother was being cremated on the funeral pyre. He heard the Buddha teach when he was seven years old and asked to be ordained. Attaining arahatship at the age of seven, he had extraordinary powers. He assumed the post of meals' designator and was very good at it. He was foremost among bhikkhus in assigning lodgings. [See Tale 5] (5)

Devadatta: one of the Buddha's cousins. He became a bhikkhu along with the other Sākyan princes. [See Tale 8] He was a rival of the Buddha, and tried to kill him several times. He also created a schism in the Sangha. Finally, he was swallowed by the earth and fell into hell. The origin of the implacable enmity which Devadatta felt toward the Bodhisatta and the Buddha is related in Tale 3. (1, 3, 8, 9, 10, 13, 18, 28, 32, 44, 51, 54, 56, 57, 62, 68, 71, 81, 85, 90, 91, 93, 94, 95, 115, 118, 128, 130, 135, 140, 141, 153, 164, 173, 182, 183, 187, 193, 198, 199, 201, 204, 212, 213, 214, 216, 217)

Dhammadinnā: an eminent bhikkhunī. She was the wife of Visākha of Rājagaha. When Visākha heard the Buddha teach, he attained the third path. On returning home, he gave his consent for his wife to ordain. She became a bhikkhunī, stayed in a nunnery near Rājagaha, and soon attained arahatship. Later, she returned to Rājagaha to revere the Buddha and taught the Dhamma to her former husband. She was foremost among bhikkhunīs in teaching the Dhamma. (217)

Dhanuggaha-tissa: a bhikkhu. He was an officer in King Pasenadi's army. No more is known of him. [See Tale 193] (193)

Ditthamangalikā: no one with this name can be identified at the time of the Buddha. (195, 216)

Gotama: the clan name of Prince Siddhattha. After leaving home, the Bodhisatta was called Gotama the Ascetic during the six years before his Enlightenment. Even after his Enlightenment, he was called Gotama the Ascetic by followers of other teachers. The Buddha is called Gotama Buddha to distinguish him from other Buddhas.

Jīvaka: the physician to King Bimbisāra and to the Buddha. He became a prominent lay follower of the Buddha and built a monastery for the Buddha in his mango grove in Rājagaha. After the death of King Bimbisāra, Jīvaka continued serving King Ajātasattu. (4, 62, 199)

Kāludāyi: an eminent bhikkhu. He was the son of a Sākyan minister. He was born on the same day as Prince Siddhattha and grew up with him. After King Suddhodana learned of his son's Enlightenment, he sent ministers to invite him to Kapilavatthu. The first nine times, the messengers ordained, became arahats, and forgot the king's request. Finally, the king ordered Kāludāyi to make the invitation, but allowed him to join the Sangha beforehand. Kāludāyi became a bhikkhu and attained arahatship, but, at the proper time, he informed the Buddha of his father's request. Kāludāyi was foremost among bhikkhus at reconciling families. (190)

Kassapa Buddha: the twenty-fourth Buddha and the third Buddha of the present eon. (23, 79, 95, 169, 181, 207, 217)

Khemā: an eminent bhikkhunī; one of the two chief female disciples of the Buddha. As the chief consort of King Bimbisāra, she was so proud of her golden skin and her beauty that she would not visit the Buddha. Finally, the king persuaded her to go to Veluvana. The Buddha conjured up the image of a woman as beautiful as a deva, who stood facing him. As Khemā gazed at this woman, whose extraordinary beauty far exceeded her own, the woman passed from youth to extreme old age and died. This so dismayed Khemā that, when the Buddha preached to her on the vanity of lust, she attained arahatship. With the consent of Bimbisāra, she entered the Sangha. She was foremost among bhikkhunīs in insight. (138, 209, 217)

Khujjuttarā: a slave woman belonging to Queen Sāmāvatī, who was one of the wives of King Udena. When Khujjuttarā heard the Buddha teach, she attained the first path and, subsequently, taught the queen. She was foremost among laywomen for her extensive knowledge. It is her record of the Buddha's teaching that forms the Itivuttaka, part of the Khuddaka Nikāya. (138, 190, 206)

Kisāgotamī: an eminent bhikkhunī. She came from a poor family in Sāvatthī but married into a rich family. She was disdainfully treated until she bore a son. When the boy died, just as he became old enough to run about, Kisāgotamī was so distraught with grief that she carried his body here and there, seeking medicine to revive him. People laughed at her, but one wise man directed her to the Buddha. The Buddha asked her to bring him a handful of mustard seed from a house where no one had ever died. In the course of her search, she grasped the truth, laid the child's body in the charnel ground, and requested admission to the Sangha. She attained the first path, and, soon after, became an arahat. She was foremost among bhikkhunīs in wearing coarse robes. (217)

Kokālika: a bhikkhu. The commentaries differ on his identification. In some sources there are two bhikkhus with this name, so they are called Culla-Kokālika and Mahā-Kokālika. In other sources, all references are to the same person.

Culla-Kokālika was one of the chief supporters of Devadatta and a great friend of the bhikkhunī Thulla-Nandā, who also supported Devadatta. Once, Culla-Kokālika complained that he had never been allowed to recite the Dhamma. When the monks gave him the chance, he put on brightly colored robes and went to the assembly. He tried to speak, but perspiration poured from his body, and he babbled incoherently. His confusion proved that his learning was a sham. (57; though Kokālika is not mentioned, the same incident is related in 9, 44, 68, and 183)

Mahā-Kokālika quarreled with Venerable Moggallāna and Venerable Sāriputta and, as a result, fell into hell. [See Tale 88] (88, 101, 131, 186)

Kosala-Devī: the sister of King Pasenadi, a wife of King Bimbisāra, and the mother of King Ajātasattu. (132, 193)

Kumāra-Kassapa: an eminent bhikkhu. He became a sāmanera at the age of seven. He was foremost among bhikkhus in eloquence. [See Tale 10] (10)

Kundalī: a bhikkhunī with the name Bhaddā-Kundalakesā. She was the daughter of a wealthy merchant in Rājagaha. One day, she saw a young man being led to his execution and fell in love with him. Her father bribed a guard and had the man released to her. From that point on, her life parallels Tale 161. (His name was also Sattuka.) After pushing Sattuka over the cliff, Kundalī joined the order of Ajivikas (a group of naked ascetics). At her ordination, all her hair was pulled out with a comb. It grew back curly (kundali), hence her name. She left the Ājīvikas and wandered from city to city, seeking debates, in the manner described in Tale 111. In Sāvatthī, Venerable Sāriputta challenged her and converted her in the same way as in that tale. Venerable Sāriputta sent her to the Buddha, who taught her a discourse, and she attained arahatship. She was foremost among bhikkhunīs in swift intuition. (216)

Kutadanta: a learned brahmin of Magadha. The Buddha arrived in his village while Kūtadanta was making preparations for a great sacrifice, and, wishing this sacrifice to be successful, Kūtadanta consulted the Buddha. The Buddha taught the Kūtadanta Sutta (Dīgha Nikāya 5) to him, and he attained the first path. The conversion of Kūtadanta is considered one of the great spiritual victories of the Buddha. (216)

Lakuntaka: an eminent bhikkhu. He was born in a wealthy family in Sāvatthī. Though extremely short (lakuntaka = dwarf), he was very handsome and had a beautiful voice. Taking the body as the object of meditation, he achieved insight and attained arahatship. He was foremost among bhikkhus in having a sweet voice. (84)

Laludāyi: a bhikkhu, notorious for saying the wrong thing at the wrong time and place and for arguing with learned bhikkhus. He is cited as an example of a person who did no good either to himself or to others. (5, 47, 87)

Losaka Tissa: a bhikkhu who attained arahatship, but failed to receive enough to eat. [See Tale 23] (23)

Madhuvasettha: a brahmin of Sāketā in Kosala. His son, Mahānāga, became a bhikkhu and attained arahatship. (190)

Mahā-Brahmā: a great deva. This refers not only to a particular being, as indicated in Tale 195, but, perhaps, to any resident of the highest Brahma heavens. (195)

Mahā-Kappina: an eminent bhikkhu, He was the king of Kukkutavata, a large kingdom northwest of Takkasilā. Every morning, he sent men to question travelers about news of distant lands. One day, when traders from Sāvatthī were asked for news, they replied, "Sire, we cannot tell you with unwashed mouths." After rinsing their mouths and clasping their hands, they reported the appearance of the Buddha. Mahā-Kappina rewarded the traders, renounced the world, and went to find the Buddha. With an asseveration of truth, he and his companions crossed three rivers without getting the horses' hooves wet. The Buddha perceived them with his divine eye and met them on the bank of the Candabhāgā River, where he taught them the Dhamma, and they all became arahats. Venerable Mahā-Kappina was foremost among bhikkhus in teaching other bhikkhus. (181)

Mahā-Kassapa: an eminent bhikkhu. He was born a brahmin named Pippali in the village of Mahātittha in Magadha. He didn't want to marry, but was finally wed to a like-minded woman, Bhaddā-Kāpilānī. (This took place very much as in Tales 129 and 206.) Never consummating their marriage, they slept separated by a chain of flowers and left the home-life together, When they came to a crossroads, they agreed that it was not proper to stay together and went in opposite directions. The earth trembled at their virtue. The Buddha felt the earthquake, understood its meaning, and traveled three gavutas to meet Pippali. Seated under a tree, Pippali listened to the Dhamma and was ordained as Mahā-Kassapa, On their way to Rājagaha, the Buddha wanted to sit, so Venerable Mahā-Kassapa folded his outer robe as a seat. The Buddha felt the robe and praised its softness. Venerable Mahā-Kassapa offered it to him. "And what would you wear?" asked the Buddha. Venerable Mahā-Kassapa requested the Buddha's rag robe, saying that he would prize it above the whole world. Venerable Mahā-Kassapa was foremost among bhikkhus in upholding minute observances of form. After the Buddha's Parinibbāna, Venerable Mahā-Kassapa called together five hundred arahats for the First Buddhist Council in Rājagaha. (102, 124, 126, 168, 175, 181, 190, 191, 207, 210, 212)

Mahā-Kosala: the king of Kosala and father of King Pasenadi. (132, 193)

Mahā-Māyā: the mother of Prince Siddhattha and the wife of King Suddhodana. As the mother of a Bodhisatta in his last life, she died seven days after the baby was born. She was reborn in Tusita heaven. After the Twin Miracle, she descended to Tāvatimsa to listen to the Buddha teach the Abhidhamma. [See Tale 188] (7, 20, 65, 83, 102, 163, 176, 188, 202, 206, 207, 209, 212, 217)

Mahā-Pajāpati-Gotamī: the first bhikkhunī. She was Mahā-Māyā's sister and was also married to King Suddhodana. After Mahā-Māyā's death, Mahā-Pajāpati-Gotamī nursed and cared for Prince Siddhattha. After having attained the first path, she requested ordination, but the Buddha refused twice. Finally, after Venerable Ānanda interceded, the Buddha agreed and ordained her as the first bhikkhunī, and she soon attained arahatship. She was foremost among bhikkhunīs in seniority and experience. (91, 141)

Mahānāma: a Sākyan king. He was the elder brother of Anuruddha and a great patron of the Buddha and the Sangha. He sent Vasabbha-Khattiyā, his daughter by a slave woman, to King Pasenadi. [See Tale

179] The Buddha declared that Mahānāma was foremost among laymen in giving choice alms to the bhikkhus. (7, 72, 179)

Makkhali Gosala: one of the six teachers who were contemporaries of the Buddha. He taught fatalism, stating that man is powerless in the face of predestination. (62)

Mallikā (1): the chief queen of King Pasenadi. She was the daughter of a garland maker in Kosala (mala = garland). At age sixteen, on the day she offered a portion of sour gruel to the Buddha, King Pasenadi made her his chief queen. She was always devoted to the Buddha, and, in her knowledge of the Dhamma, she was wiser than the king. She was one of the Buddha's outstanding female lay disciples. (33, 114, 119, 160, 197, 200)

Mallikā (2): the wife of Bandhula, who was King Pasenadi's commander-in-chief. [See Tale 179] (179)

Mantidatta: a bhikkhu. He was an officer in King Pasenadi's army. No more is known of him. [See Tale 193] (193)

Māra: a deva. Residing in the highest heaven of the sensuous worlds, he is the lord of the world of passion. He attacked the Bodhisatta with a great army hoping to prevent his Enlightenment under the Bodhi tree. Māra's elephant is named Girimekhala. The Buddha's victory over Māra is one of the Eight Great Victories of the Buddha referred to in the Jayamangala Gāthā. (22, 71, 204)

Mātali: Sakka's charioteer. (16, 95, 175, 181, 211)

Moggallāna: an eminent bhikkhu; one of the two chief disciples of the Buddha. He was born as Kolita in a village near Rājagaha on the same day as Sāriputta. The two were childhood friends and ordained together. Venerable Moggallāna was foremost among bhikkhus in extraordinary powers. [See Sāriputta] (9, 21, 32, 34, 57, 63, 64, 68, 85, 88, 101, 121, 128, 142, 149, 175, 185, 188, 189, 190, 191, 209, 212, 213, 214, 215)

Nālāgiri: an elephant from the royal stables of Rājagaha. In an attempt to kill the Buddha, Devadatta instructed the mahouts to give Nālāgiri extra alcohol and to release him on the street while the Buddha was going on his almsrounds. As Nālāgiri was charging, Venerable Ānanda stepped in front to protect the Buddha. Using his extraordinary power, the Buddha forced Venerable Ānanda aside and extended loving-kindness toward the elephant. Tamed by that loving-kindness, Nālāgiri knelt at the Buddha's feet, and the Buddha taught him the Dhamma. If Nālāgiri had not been an animal, he would have attained the first path. The townspeople were so impressed that they threw their ornaments and jewels on the elephant, completely covering him. From then on, he was called Dhanapāla (Treasurer). The Buddha's taming of Nālāgiri is one of the Eight Great Victories of the Buddha referred to in the Jayamangala Gāthā. (91, 130, 141, 198)

Nanda: an eminent bhikkhu. Being the son of King Suddhodana and Mahā-Pajapati-Gotamī, he was the Buddha's half-brother. When the Buddha returned to Kapilavatthu, he gave his bowl to Nanda to carry. Although Nanda was to marry that day, the Buddha asked him to ordain, and he could not refuse. Nanda ordained and became an arahat. He was foremost among bhikkhus in self-control. [See Tale 76] (76, 90, 102)

Nigantha Nātaputta: one of the six teachers who were contemporaries of the Buddha; now known as Mahāvīra, the founder of Jainism. He taught a doctrine of extreme restraint in order to avoid suffering, which is the result of wrong action. (62, 133)

Pakudha Kaccāyana: one of the six teachers who were contemporaries of the Buddha. He taught eternalism, stating that matter, pleasure, pain, and the soul are eternal and do not interact. (62)

Pārileyya: an elephant. Once, when two groups of bhikkhus refused to settle their quarrel, the Buddha went to stay alone in the forest near Kosambi. While he was there, Pārileyya and a monkey carefully looked after him. This incident is mentioned in Tale 143. It was on this occasion that the Buddha also told Tale 155. (190)

Pasenadi: the king of Kosala. Quite early in the Buddha's ministry, King Pasenadi became his follower. His devotion to the Buddha lasted until the king's death. (7, 10, 23, 28, 33, 40, 63, 82, 83, 98, 104, 114, 119, 132, 158, 160, 162, 179, 193, 197, 200, 205, 207)

Patācārā (1): a bhikkhunī. She had three sisters and a brother, Saccaka. Their parents were both wandering debaters, who had been encouraged by the Licchavi princes to marry and to settle in Vesāli. Patacara and her sisters became wandering debaters, too, but they were defeated by

Venerable Sāriputta. They became bhikkhunīs, and Venerable Patācārā attained arahatship. [See Tale 111] (111)

Patācārā (2): an eminent bhikkhunī. She was the daughter of a rich merchant of Sāvatthī and eloped with a servant. When her first baby was due, she wanted to return to her parents' house. She and her husband set out, but, after she delivered on the way there, they went back home. The second time she became pregnant, she again went into labor on the road. When a storm arose, her husband went to get branches to make a shelter and was killed by a snake. After Patācārā found his body, she continued to Sāvatthī with her two sons. She was weak after childbirth, but she had to cross the flooded Aciravatī River. Carrying her newborn baby across, she laid him down and started back for her elder son. In midstream, she saw a hawk swoop down and snatch the baby. She shouted to scare the bird away, but her shouts were misunderstood by the toddler, who thought she was calling him and ran toward her. Before she could reach him, he fell into the water and was swept away. Devastated by her triple loss, she reached Sāvatthī, only to learn that her parents and brother had also been killed when their house collapsed in the storm. Seeing their funeral pyre, she went mad and began raving with grief and wandering naked though the city. (Patācārā means "garment walker.") Eventually, she reached Jetavana, where, restored to presence of mind by the Buddha's Teaching, she attained the first path. She was ordained and attained arahatship. She was foremost among bhikkhunīs in knowledge of the Vinaya. (217)

Pilinda Vaccha: an eminent bhikkhu who was well-known for his extraordinary powers. He was a brahmin with some magical abilities, but when the Buddha appeared, he lost his powers. Hearing that the Buddha knew a greater magic, he became a bhikkhu in order to learn it. The Buddha gave him some meditation subjects, and he attained arahatship. King Bimbisāra built a monastery for him and provided a village with five hundred attendants to support it. It was in this village that the incident related in Tale 152 took place. He was foremost among bhikkhus in being dear and delightful to the devas. (152)

Pilotika: a Paribbājaka, a religious wanderer. He often served the Buddha and the Sangha. His conversation with Jānussoni, another Brahmin who was an eminent follower of the Buddha, was expanded upon by the Buddha to form the Culla-hatthipadopama Sutta: The Shorter Elephant

Footprint Simile (Majjhima Nikāya, 27). In the third century B.C.E., when Emperor Ashoka's son, Venerable Mahinda, arrived in Sri Lanka, it was this sutta which he first taught to King Devānampiyatissa. (216)

Pindola: an eminent bhikkhu. He was the son of the chaplain of King Udena of Kosambi and became a successful teacher in Rājagaha. Seeing the gifts bestowed on the Buddha's disciples, he became a bhikkhu, but continued to be greedy. By following the Buddha's advice, he conquered his greed and became an arahat. Then, with a lion's roar (a bold and thunderous declaration of his power), he announced his readiness to answer the questions of any doubting bhikkhus. He was foremost among the bhkkhus in making a lion's roar. (188, 195)

Potthapāda: a Paribbājaka, a religious wanderer, who was converted by the Buddha. (216)

Punna: an eminent bhikkhu. He was born in Kapilavatthu and was ordained by his uncle, Venerable Kondañña, one of the first five bhikkhus. He became an arahat and was close to Venerable Sāriputta. It was after hearing a discourse by Venerable Punna that Venerable Ānanda attained the first path. He was foremost among bhikkhus in teaching the Dhamma. (102, 190)

Purāna Kassapa: one of the six teachers who were contemporaries of the Buddha. He taught amoralism, which denies both reward for good deeds and punishment for bad.

Rāhu: an asura chieftain. He is jealous of the devas of the sun and the moon and stands in their path with his mouth wide open. Eclipses are said to occur when those orbs fall into his mouth. (152, 165, 207, 216)

Rāhula: an eminent bhikkhu. He was the son of Prince Siddhattha and was born on the day that the Bodhisatta left the household life. When the Buddha visited Kapilavatthu, Rāhula's mother sent the boy to the Buddha to ask for his inheritance, and the Buddha asked Venerable Sāriputta to ordain him. When his grandfather, King Suddhodana, heard of this, he objected, and the Buddha declared that no young man should be ordained without the consent of his parents. Venerable Rāhula became an arahat and was foremost among bhikkhus in being eager for training. (83, 109, 123, 129, 134, 138, 154, 156, 163, 172, 189, 209, 212, 215, 217)

Rāhula's mother: See Yasodharā.

Sabhiya: a bhikkhu. As a Paribbājaka, a religious wanderer, he was famous as a dialectician. From a list he had received from his mother, he devised twenty questions which he put before ascetics and brahmins, but none could answer them. He visited the Buddha in Veluvana, and, at the end of the discussion, he entered the Sangha and attained arahatship. (216)

Saccaka: a Nigantha of Vesāli. His clan name was Aggivessana. He was teacher of the Licchavis and the brother of Patācārā. After the Buddha defeated him in a debate, he became a follower. His conversion is one of the Eight Great Victories of the Buddha referred to in the Jayamangala Gāthā. (111, 216)

Sakka: the king of the devas. His realm is Tāvatimsa. Rather than belonging exclusively to a particular being, Sakka refers to the office of king which is held by different beings in succession. [See Sakka's throne in Glossary of Terms] (16, 22, 34, 60, 76, 78, 81, 84, 90, 95, 100, 102, 108, 110, 111, 114, 134, 138, 146, 156, 159, 167, 169, 170, 173, 175, 180, 181, 182, 188, 190, 193, 197, 201, 203, 204, 206, 207, 208, 209, 210, 211, 212, 213, 214, 215, 216, 217)

Sañjaya Belatthiputta: one of the six teachers who were contemporaries of the Buddha. He taught an evasive doctrine, denying both existence and non-existence. (62)

Sāriputta: an eminent bhikkhu; one of the two chief disciples of the Buddha; "Captain of the Teaching." He was born in a village near Rājagaha. His name was Upatissa, and he had a childhood friend named Kolita. One day, Upatissa met Venerable Assaji, one of the first five bhikkhus, heard him recite two lines of a verse, and attained the first path. He hurried to Kolita and, repeating the lines he had heard, established his friend in the first path. Together, they invited their former teacher, Sañjaya Belatthiputta, to visit the Buddha, but Sañjaya refused to go. Upatissa and Kolita (Moggallāna) ordained together. Venerable Moggallāna attained arahatship in seven days, but it took Venerable Sāriputta two weeks longer. He was foremost among the bhikkhus in wisdom. Venerable Sāriputta's wisdom was second only to the Buddha's. (6, 9, 21, 23, 32, 33, 57, 63, 64, 65, 68, 76, 79, 85, 86, 88, 90, 91, 98, 101, 102, 109, 110, 111, 113, 118, 119, 120, 121, 128, 136, 139, 142, 145, 146, 149, 150, 157,

160, 174, 175, 177, 178, 179, 182, 185, 188, 189, 190, 191, 194, 198, 201, 207, 208, 209, 212, 213, 214, 215, 216, 217)

Sātāgira: a yakkha. He was present at the birth of Prince Siddhattha and at the First Sermon of the Buddha. At the latter, he was distracted because he was searching for his friend Hemavata. Later that day, when he met Hemavata in Rājagaha, Hemavata suggested that they hurry to the Himavat because the region was covered with flowers. Sātāgira explained that the reason for the flowers was the appearance of the Buddha and enumerated the Buddha's qualities. Together, they went to Isipatana to hear the Buddha. Their conversation in Rājagaha was overheard by a laywoman named Kāli-Kuraragharikā, and, through it, she attained the first path. Sātāgira and Hemavata also happened to be in Ālavi when the Buddha converted Ālavaka. Unable to pass over the yakkha's mansion and perceiving the reason, they went inside and congratulated the Buddha on his victory. Kāli-Kuraragharikā was foremost among laywomen who achieved insight from hearsay. (190)

Siddhattha: the personal name of Gotama Buddha. He was born in Kapilavatthu, the capital of Sākya, as the son of King Suddhodana and Queen Mahā-Māyā. At twenty-nine, on the day that his son Rāhula was born, despite King Suddhodana's precautions, Prince Siddhattha saw the Four Sights—an old man, a sick man, a corpse, and an ascetic—which prompted him to leave home and to become an ascetic.

Suddhodana: the Sākyan king and the father of Prince Siddhattha. Mahā-Māyā was his chief queen, and, after she died, her sister Mahā-Pajāpatī-Gotamī took that position. King Suddhodana tried to prevent his son from leaving the world by shielding him from unpleasantness and surrounding him with luxury. Later, King Suddhodana invited the Buddha to Kapilavatthu. [See Kāludāyi] When the Buddha walked for alms in Kapilavatthu, King Suddhodana reproached him for begging, but the Buddha replied that going on almsrounds was the custom of all Buddhas. Hearing that, King Suddhodana attained the first path. Much later, on hearing the Buddha teach to him again, he attained arahatship just before he died. This is one of the few instances in which a layman became an arahat. In such a case, the person must, on that day, either ordain or pass away. [See Bhaddaji] (7, 20, 83, 143, 174, 202, 206, 207, 208, 209, 216, 217)

Sunakkhatta: a Licchavi prince of Vesāli. He became a bhikkhu but disrobed to follow other teachers. He publicly defamed the Buddha, complaining that the Buddha had neither performed any miracles nor shown him the beginning of things. The Buddha scolded him, enumerating his own extraordinary powers and saying that he had not promised to explain the beginning of things. The Buddha pointed out that he taught only suffering and the end of suffering. (214)

Thulla-Nandā: a troublesome bhikkhunī who was close to Devadatta. Although she was an eloquent speaker, she was also greedy and was accused of misappropriating gifts given to other bhikkhunīs. She enjoyed men's company and went out unattended. She was jealous of other bhikkhunīs and frequently quarreled with them. Her misdeeds led to the establishment of quite a few of the Vinaya rules. (52)

Upāli: an eminent bhikkhu. He was the barber of the Sākyan princes and ordained with them. [See Tale 8] He attained arahatship and was foremost among bhikkhus in Vinaya. (8, 188)

Uppalavannā: an eminent bhikkhunī; one of the two chief female disciples of the Buddha. She was extremely beautiful and had been sought by kings and commoners from all of Jambudīpa, but her father suggested that she ordain, and she readily agreed. One day, while she was sweeping the Ordination Hall in Jetavana, she concentrated on the flame of a lamp as a fire-kasina, attained jhāna, and became an arahat. She was foremost among bhikkhunīs in extraordinary powers. (102, 111, 138, 154, 171, 190, 198, 208, 209, 210, 212, 213, 216, 217)

Uruvela-Kassapa: a bhikkhu. He was an ascetic in Uruvela and had five hundred disciples. His brothers, also named Kassapa, were also ascetics and had three hundred and two hundred disciples, respectively. The Buddha spent an entire rainy season with them, performing many miracles and trying to convert them. Even after the Buddha had overcome two powerful nāgas, the Kassapas were unconvinced, and Uruvela-Kassapa still believed himself to be an arahat and the Buddha's superior. Finally, the Buddha was able to convert him, and the three brothers, with their one thousand followers, were ordained. A little later, the Buddha taught the Fire Sermon (Ādittapariyāya Sutta), and they all attained arahatship. Uruvela-Kassapa was foremost among bhikkhus in having a large following. (214)

Vessavana: one of the Four Great Kings. His kingdom is in the north, and he is king of the yakkhas. (6, 147, 168, 202, 215)

Vidūdabha: the son of King Pasenadi and Vāsabha-Khattiyā. [See Tale 179] (7, 179)

Vipassi Buddha: nineteenth of the twenty-four Buddhas. (217)

Visākhā: the chief laywoman disciple of the Buddha. When she was seven years old, she heard the Buddha teach in Anga and attained the first path. Later, her family moved to Sāketā in Kosala. She moved to Sāvatthī when she married into a family that followed the Niganthas. After she converted her father-in-law, Migāra, she became known as "Migāra's mother" (Migāramātā). In Sāvatthī, she built Migāramā-tupāsāda, a monastery in the Eastern Park (Pubbārāma), and gave it to the Buddha. She was foremost among laywomen who ministered to the Sangha. (10, 98, 182, 203, 217)

Vissakamma: a deva. He is Sakka's chief architect and builder. (188, 202, 208, 210, 217)

Yama: the king of hell. (93, 188, 206, 210, 214)

Yasodharā: the wife of Prince Siddhattha and the mother of his son, Rāhula. She was also called Rāhula's mother (Rāhulamātā), and Bim-bādevī. After Prince Siddhattha left home, she showed her loyalty by abandoning luxury, wearing yellow robes, and taking only one meal a day. After the bhikkhunī order was established, she ordained as Venerable Bhaddakaccānā and attained arahatship. (83, 102, 109, 129, 134, 154, 156, 163, 172, 201, 206, 212, 215, 216, 217)

The Thirty-One Planes of Existence

The Immaterial World (*Arūpa-loka*)

Level	Realm	Inhabitants	Cause of rebirth there
28–31	*Arūpa*	Devas of the formless realms. Mind only; no body	Four immaterial jhānas

The Fine-Material World (*Rūpa-loka*)

Level	Realm	Inhabitants	Cause of rebirth there
23-27	*Suddhāvāsa*	Devas of the Pure Abodes. Beings who have attained the path of non-returning are reborn and attain arahatship here. Brahmā Sahampati resides here.	Fourth jhāna
22	*Asaññasattā*	Non-percipient Devas. Body only; no mind	
21	*Vehapphala*	Devas of Great Reward	
20	*Subhakinha*	Devas of Refulgent Glory	Third jhāna
19	*Appamānasu-bha*	Devas of Limitless Glory	
18	*Parittasubha*	Devas of Limited Glory	
17	*Abhassara*	Devas of Brilliant Radiance	Second jhāna
16	*Appamānābha*	Devas of Limitless Radiance	
15	*Parittābha*	Devas of Limited Radiance	
14	*Mahā-Brahmā*	Great Brahmā. Often refers to the first resident of this heaven, but all beings here and above can be called Mahā-Brahmā	First jhāna
13	*Brahmā-purohita*	Brahmā's Ministers	
12	*Brahmā-parisajja*	Members of Brahmā's Retinue	

(Left margin, vertical: Brahma Heavens (Brahma-loka))

		The Sensuous World (*Kāma-loka*)		
	Level	Realm	Inhabitants	Cause of rebirth there
Happy Realms (*Sugati*)	11	*Paranimmita-vasavattī*	Devas who wield control over the creations of others. Abode of Māra	Ten courses of wholesome action, generosity, morality, and wisdom
	10	*Nimmānarati*	Devas who delight in creation	
	9	*Tusita*	Contented Devas. Bodhisattas are reborn here prior to their final human birth	
	8	*Yāmā*	Comfortable Devas. Devas who live in the air, at ease, free of all difficulties	
	7	*Tāvatimsa*	The Thirty-three Devas. Abode of Sakka. Large numbers of attendant nymphs also live here	
	6	*Catumahārājika*	The Four Great Kings, who guard the four qauarters. Yakkhas, gandhabbas, kumbhandas, nāgas, and deva-asuras also live here. This realm and all the above are divine heaven realms, *deva-loka*.	
	5	*Manussa*	Humans	
Woeful Realms (*Apāya*)	4	*Asura*	Asura-kāya	Ten courses of unwholesome actions
	3	*Peta*	Petas (Hungry ghosts)	Lack of virtue, holding to wrong views
	2	*Tiracchāna*	Animals	Behaving like an animal
	1	*Niraya*	(The hells, of which there are eight, *Roruva* is the fourth highest. *Avīci* is the lowest and worst. *Ussada* is the collective name for lesser hells that surround each of the great hells.)	Killing one's parents, killing an arahat, injuring the Buddha, creating a schism in the Sangha

Map of Jambudīpa

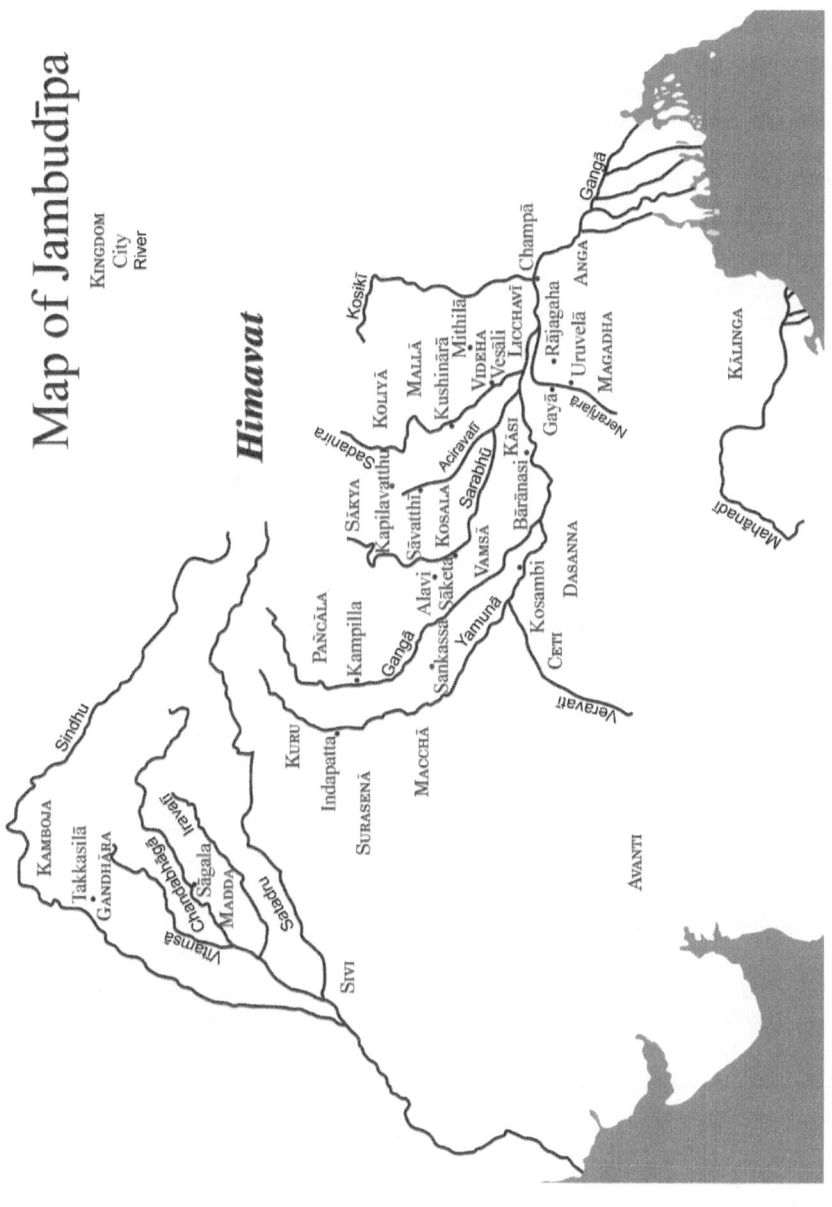

Table of Correspondence
Jātaka Numbers from the Pāli

JTB = Jātaka Tales of the Buddha (This Anthology)
PTS = The Jātaka or Stories of the Buddha's Former Births, Pāli Text Society
Book = Nipāta, Division of the Pāli in which the Jātaka is included

JTB	PTS	Book	JTB	PTS	Book	JTB	PTS	Book
1	1	I	36	83	I	71	168	II
2	2	I	37	87	I	72	177	II
3	3	I	38	89	I	73	178	II
4	4	I	39	91	I	74	179	II
5	5	I	40	92	I	75	181	II
6	6	I	41	96	I	76	182	II
7	7	I	42	107	I	77	183	II
8	10	I	43	109	I	78	186	II
9	11	I	44	113	I	79	190	II
10	12	I	45	115	I	80	193	II
11	14	I	46	118	I	81	194	II
12	18	I	47	123	I	82	195	II
13	20	I	48	124	I	83	201	II
14	22	I	49	125	I	84	202	II
15	28	I	50	128	I	85	206	II
16	31	I	51	131	I	86	207	II
17	32	I	52	136	I	87	211	II
18	33	I	53	137	I	88	215	II
19	34	I	54	139	I	89	218	II
20	35	I	55	140	I	90	220	II
21	37	I	56	141	I	91	222	II
22	40	I	57	143	I	92	234	II
23	41	I	58	144	I	93	240	II
24	43	I	59	146	I	94	241	II
25	46	I	60	148	I	95	243	II
26	48	I	61	149	I	96	251	III
27	50	I	62	150	I	97	252	III
28	51	I	63	151	II	98	254	III
29	55	I	64	153	II	99	257	III
30	63	I	65	156	II	100	267	III
31	67	I	66	157	II	101	272	III
32	73	I	67	159	II	102	276	III
33	77	I	68	160	II	103	278	III
34	78	I	69	161	II	104	282	III
35	80	I	70	166	II	105	284	III

JTB	PTS	Book	JTB	PTS	Book	JTB	PTS	Book
106	286	III	144	379	VI	182	472	XII
107	288	III	145	385	VI	183	474	XIII
108	291	III	146	386	VI	184	475	XIII
109	292	III	147	398	VII	185	476	XIII
110	300	III	148	400	VII	186	481	XIII
111	301	IV	149	401	VII	187	482	XIII
112	302	IV	150	402	VII	188	483	XIII
113	305	IV	151	405	VII	189	486	XIV
114	306	IV	152	406	VII	190	488	XIV
115	308	IV	153	407	VII	191	490	XIV
116	309	IV	154	408	VII	192	491	XIV
117	312	IV	155	409	VII	193	492	XIV
118	313	IV	156	411	VII	194	493	XIV
119	314	IV	157	412	VII	195	497	XV
120	315	IV	158	413	VII	196	498	XV
121	316	IV	159	417	VIII	197	499	XV
122	318	IV	160	418	VIII	198	501	XV
123	319	IV	161	419	VIII	199	503	XV
124	321	IV	162	420	VIII	200	504	XV
125	322	IV	163	421	VIII	201	506	XV
126	323	IV	164	422	VIII	202	510	XV
127	324	IV	165	425	VIII	203	512	XVI
128	326	IV	166	427	IX	204	514	XVI
129	328	IV	167	429	IX	205	520	XVI
130	329	IV	168	432	IX	206	531	XX
131	331	IV	169	439	X	207	537	XXI
132	338	IV	170	440	X	208	538	XXII
133	339	IV	171	442	X	209	539	XXII
134	340	IV	172	443	X	210	540	XXII
135	342	IV	173	445	X	211	541	XXII
136	346	IV	174	447	X	212	542	XXII
137	352	V	175	450	X	213	543	XXII
138	354	V	176	455	XI	214	544	XXII
139	356	V	177	456	XI	215	545	XXII
140	357	V	178	462	XI	216	546	XXII
141	358	V	179	465	XI	217	547	XXII
142	359	V	180	467	XII			
143	371	V	181	469	XII			

Bibliography

Burlingame, E.W., translator, Buddhist Legends, London, The Pali Text Society, 1921, reprinted in 1990 and 1995; a complete translation of Dhammapada Commentary. About sixty of the stories are shared with the Jātakas.

Chandavimala, Ven. Rerukane, Analysis of Perfections, translated by A. G. S. Kariyawasam, Kandy, Sri Lanka, Buddhist Publication Society, 2003; a succinct treatment of the Ten Perfections and how they can be developed.

Cowell, E. B., editor, The Jātaka or Stories of the Buddha's Former Births, London, The Pali Text Society, 18951907, reprinted in 1990; a complete translation of the Jātaka Commentary, including all 547 stories.

Harischandra, D.V.J., Psychiatric Aspects of Jātaka Stories, Galle, Sri Lanka, Upuli Offset, 1998.

Karunaratne, David, translator, Ummagga Jataka (The Story of the Tunnel), Colombo, Sri Lanka, M.D. Gunasena & Co. Ltd., 1962.

Malalasekera, G. P., Dictionary of Pāli Proper Names, London, The Pali Text Society, 1938, reprinted 1960 and 1974.

Na-Rangsi, Dr. Sunthorn, The Four Planes of Existence in Theravada Buddhism, Kandy, Sri Lanka, Buddhist Publication Society, 2006.

Recommendations for Further Reading

Bhikkhu Bodhi, Editor, In the Buddha's Words, An Anthology of Discourses from the Pali Canon, Somerville, Massachusetts, U.S.A., Wisdom Publications, 2005; a collection of suttas selected to serve as an introduction to the Buddha's Teaching.

Dhammapāla, Ācariya, A Treatise on the Pāramīs, A Discourse from the Majjhima Nikāya, translated from the Pali by Bhikkhu Bodhi, Wheel No. 409/411, Kandy, Sri Lanka, Buddhist Publication Society (BPS), 1996; a lucid translation of a sixth-century discussion of the Ten Perfections, drawing from both Theravada and Mahāyana texts.

Dhammika, Ven. S., Middle Land, Middle Way: A Pilgrim's Guide to the Buddha's India, Kandy, Sri Lanka, BPS, 2008; A description of the sites important to the life of the Buddha.

Gunaratana, Ven. Henepola, Mindfulness in Plain English, Somerville, Massachusetts, U.S.A. Wisdom Publications, 1992; a practical and straightforward guide to vipassanā meditation and its benefits for everyone.

Kawasaki, Ken and Visākhā, Strive on with Diligence, The Buddha and His Teaching, Kandy, Sri Lanka, Buddhist Relief Mission, 2002; www.brelief.org; a multi-media presentation in DVD and VCD format, presenting the life of the Buddha and basic Dhamma through art and scenes from around the world.

Nyanaponika Thera and Hellmuth Hecker, Great Disciples of the Buddha, Their Lives, Their Works, Their Legacy, edited by Bhikkhu Bodhi, Kandy, Sri Lanka, BPS and Somerville, Massachusetts, U.S.A., Wisdom Publications, 2003; biographies of many of the Buddha's disciples who appear in the Jātakas.

Piyadassi Thera, The Buddha's Ancient Path, Kandy, Sri Lanka, BPS, 1974; a clear explanation of the Buddha's Teaching.

U Pandita, Sayadaw, In This Very Life, Liberation Teachings of the Buddha, Kandy, Sri Lanka, BPS, 2007; a guide to vipassanā meditation and an analysis of the workings of the mind.

ABOUT PARIYATTI

Pariyatti is dedicated to providing affordable access to authentic teachings of the Buddha about the Dhamma theory (*pariyatti*) and practice (*paṭipatti*) of Vipassana meditation. A 501(c)(3) non-profit charitable organization since 2002, Pariyatti is sustained by contributions from individuals who appreciate and want to share the incalculable value of the Dhamma teachings. We invite you to visit www.pariyatti.org to learn about our programs, services, and ways to support publishing and other undertakings.

Pariyatti Publishing Imprints

Vipassana Research Publications (focus on Vipassana as taught by S.N. Goenka in the tradition of Sayagyi U Ba Khin)

BPS Pariyatti Editions (selected titles from the Buddhist Publication Society, co-published by Pariyatti in the Americas)

Pariyatti Digital Editions (audio and video titles, including discourses)

Pariyatti Press (classic titles returned to print and inspirational writing by contemporary authors)

Pariyatti enriches the world by

- disseminating the words of the Buddha,
- providing sustenance for the seeker's journey,
- illuminating the meditator's path.